"A hilarious and irreverent exposé of one of our most venerated institutions from the privileged perspective of an insider. In the tradition of the best satirists, Rao hides nuggets of wisdom and truth in the pages of her laugh-out-loud scenes."
—Rishi Reddi, author of *Karma and Other Stories*

"As Lauren Weisberger did for fashion assistants, Rao sheds light on the exacting and often outlandish environment of not-much-talked-about legal clerkships."
—Phawker.com

"Rao's wit shines in her debut. . . . Here is the legal system exposed and skewered for what it is: haplessly human."
—*Publishers Weekly*

"Saira Rao demonstrates her razor-sharp wit and fabulous eye for the absurd in her debut novel, offering up a quirkily adorable protagonist and a vivid cast of supporting characters. The plot of *Chambermaid* will keep readers furiously turning the pages, and the delicious *bon mots* peppered throughout will guarantee that they giggle the whole way through."
—Martha Kimes, author of *Ivy Briefs*

"We thoroughly enjoyed *Chambermaid*."
—AboveTheLaw.com

"Simply a great read."
—Sarah Estes Graham, *The University of Virginia Magazine*

"*Chambermaid* delivers post-law school ennui without the frayed nerves and student-loan debts endured by lawyers. Better yet, it makes us root for them. You get an insider's peek into their world, and then are allowed to return to your own grind."
—Raymond Cummings, *East Bay Express*

"A smart, in-depth look behind the courtroom walls, revealing the lack of honor toiling for an Honorable judge, showing the devil *really* wears a black robe. Luckily for Rao's determined, funny heroine, justice is ultimately served."
—Jill Kargman, coauthor of *The Right Address* and author of *Momzillas*

"Hysterical! I highly recommend it."
—LegalAntics.com

CHAMBERMAID

CHAMBERMAID

A Novel

Saira Rao

Grove Press
New York

This novel is entirely a work of fiction. The names, characters, and
incidents portrayed in it are the work of the author's imagination.
Any resemblance to actual persons, living or dead, events, or localities
is entirely coincidental.

Published simultaneously in Canada
Printed in the United States of America

FIRST PAPERBACK EDITION

Library of Congress Cataloging-in-Publication Data

Rao, Saira.
      Chambermaid : a novel / Saira Rao.
         p.   cm.
      ISBN-10: 0-8021-4372-5
      ISBN-13: 978-0-8021-4372-3
      1. Law clerks—Fiction.   2. Lawyers—Fiction.   I. Title.
   PS3618.A69 C47
   813' 6—dc22   2006053521

Grove Press
an imprint of Grove/Atlantic, Inc.
841 Broadway
New York, NY 10003

Distributed by Publishers Group West

www.groveatlantic.com

www.sairarao.com

08 09 10 11 12   10 9 8 7 6 5 4 3 2 1

for my mother
Sybil Greenie Rao

Simply put, clerking is one of the most stimulating legal jobs available. Clerks are on the inside of the judicial process. They are privy to the law before it becomes law. They read the parties' briefs, hear their arguments, and, in turn, enhance their own substantive and procedural legal background immeasurably. Whether someone is planning for a career in litigation or transactional law, a judicial clerkship is an incomparable entree into the legal profession.

—"What Is a Judicial Clerkship," Duke Law School Web site

CHAMBERMAID

Chapter One

Breathe in. Now out.

I was twenty-eight years old with no criminal history and a Juris Doctor. I paid my bills on time, always remembered birthdays, and sometimes even washed my trash before recycling it. At best, I had the logistics of life down pat. At worst, one could argue I was marginally lame. In light of this, you can understand why I was a bit distraught that breathing had become a problem.

Then there were the hot flashes. Could I be menopausal? I hovered over my keyboard. Just one quick Google search on menopause. My hands began to twitch. Who could blame them? I was committing a cardinal sin. Twitch twitch twitch. Breathe in. Now out. Jumping Jack Flash. Who was I kidding? I definitely needed hormones, before the facial hair made a cameo. Nobody liked a lady with a 'stache.

"Where's the McMillan file? You know she's looking for it!" Janet said in an angry, stifled whisper. I shrugged my shoulders, unwilling to commit two fouls at once—talking and using the Internet. Janet tensed up like a constipated poodle. In spite of her daily invective, I still felt a wee bit bad for Janet. The lady had been railroaded more times than Amtrak's busy northeast corridor. Twenty years in this institu-

tion had turned what I assumed was originally a good-natured suburbanite (Janet then) into angry roadkill (Janet now). After all, it had only
been a month for me and already the hair and hot flashes had com-
menced. Based on the precedent standing before my very eyes, I knew
my future was bleak.

Great! My "early menopause" search had elicited 26,715 hits. I definitely
had it. Breathe, hot flash, twitch. I couldn't believe I had just been pitying
angry Janet when I'd morphed into a full-fledged freak show. I glanced
back at Matthew to see if he was still breathing. I was beginning to worry
that Matthew was going to simply die one day, crouched over, staring at
his computer, and we wouldn't even know it until *she* yelled for him. If he
wasn't in the torture chamber in under two seconds, only then would we
know of his untimely demise. Maybe I'd Google "sitting up dead." Surely,
that was worse than the Pause.

Just as my twitchy tendons were reaching for the keyboard again, Evan
the judicial evangelist came sauntering by my desk, pausing so briefly I almost didn't have to look up at him. Almost.

"Have you finished *Robinson* yet?" This was stated more as an accusation
than a question. Accusation verified by his ever so polite pivot and turn. With
his impossibly straight back facing me, Evan whispered: "Well, *I'm* handing in *Welbert* and with any luck will get something *challenging*."

I truly didn't know how Harvard Law School managed to do it, but
somehow that place picked the world's most vapid, chainsaw-to-spinal-cord
annoying people to fill its esteemed corridors. Grades, LSAT scores, whatever. The true test was being able to irritate your grandmother into committing murder in a minute flat.

Alas! I heard a stir from behind. Could it be Matthew? I turned and
indeed he had managed to sit up and was stretching in my direction. I furrowed my brow. He rolled his eyes. Translation. Me: "What?" Matthew:
"Evan is a total moron." Communication complete. Over the past few
weeks, we had managed to master the universal language of judgment
without actually speaking.

DING! "Thirteenth floor, going down!" It was the judge's elevator, our only warning of her impending arrival.

"SHEEEEERAAAA!!! SHAYYYLLLLA!!!"

Not this again. The decibels I'd grown accustomed to. But my name was SHEILA. Not Sheera. Not Shayla. Not Sheba (though I secretly liked it when she called me Sheba).

"GET IN HERE NOW! ARE YOU DEAF?!!"

I wish.

I dashed into the torture chamber, skidding to a stop before the Honorable Helga Friedman. She was clearly pissed. Vertical eyebrows. Penciled in. Squinty eyes. Lips curled. Dancing bouffant. She was about to pounce. So was her bright red lipstick, which was curiously everywhere but on her lips.

"Yes, Judge."

"I read your memo in *W.A. versus Trenton*. Do they not teach you English in Pakistan?"

Not the Pakistan thing again. I was Indian. Not that I was one of those Indians who hated Pakistan. It's just that I wasn't Pakistani. Just like I wasn't Croatian.

"Your Hon—Your hon—"

"I surmise not. All I can say is that it doesn't take a Supreme Court justice to interpret basic state statutes—and you failed to do even that!"

"I, um, Your Hon—"

"NO! NO! NO!"

The dreaded hat trick of noes. It wasn't a good sign.

"I AM A FEDERAL JUDGE!"

Indeed, among other things.

"Can you even comprehend what I'm saying here? *Can you?*"

Eyes got even smaller. Bouffant started break-dancing. Little hand reached for big Supreme Court casebook. Slow mo. Hand lifted book.

"I just, um, thought—"

WHACK!

She'd nailed me, yet again. This time smack in the face.

"NOW, GET OUT! GET OUT!" She pounded her small fist on the desk.

I stumbled back to my cubicle, a trickle of blood running down my cheek. Could you catch hemophilia? Bleeding to death sounded sort of nice, cozy even.

Parking it in my tattered swivel chair, I stared longingly across the Delaware River at Camden, New Jersey. Just six months ago, I had been a well-liked editor on the *Columbia Law Review*. I had a killer wardrobe, a darling (rent-stabilized) apartment in the West Village and a fabulous group of friends.

Now, I was plotting an escape to New Jersey with dried blood on my face.

I was a federal court of appeals law clerk. Pushing thirty. Postured. Proud. Praying for hemophilia. This was certainly the best experience of my life. Just like everyone at Columbia Law had promised.

09-15, 4:09 AM
Basic Member
😣 **Help!!!!!!!!!!!!!!!!!!!!!!!!!!!!!!!!!!!!!!!**

I know I am about to sound crazy, but it is Wednesday and I have only gotten letters saying they have received my application packet. I am starting to freak out here. I know that a girl in my Sec Reg class got an inteview on the 2d circ. Why isn't anyone calling me?!!😨

12-24, 01:23 PM
amyolive
Basic Member

Why won't these judges CALL???

Hi all. I am waiting to hear from 3 judges who obviously don't know they are about killing me! Don't they understand that this is my LIFE they're talking about????? Why can't they at least let me know if I DIDN'T get it???? It's Christmas for Christsakes! Have they no spirit!!!! Merry Christmas. 😊

The above serve as illustrative examples of the kind of environment that law schools create. A climate in which the law student—the most paranoid, risk-averse overachiever this universe has to offer—is brainwashed from the very first day of school to believe that if he or she doesn't get a judicial clerkship, life will effectively end.

Sure, we'd all heard about the glitz and glamour of a law degree. Three short years, a mere hundred twenty thousand dollars, and voilà! "You can do anything!"

ACLU. State Department. District attorney. President of the United States.

There was just one little glitch. You needed a judicial clerkship. A federal one if at all possible.

Sheila Raj: "How does one get a job at the U.S. attorney's office?"

Torts professor: "Well, that's impossible unless you clerk."

Sheila Raj: "I'd love to teach here someday."

Constitutional Law Professor: Loud sigh followed by "You'll definitely need a *court of appeals* clerkship, if not one on the Supreme Court." Courts of appeals are one rung below the Supreme Court. Typically, to even be considered for a Supreme Court clerkship, one has to have first completed a court of appeals clerkship, and as such, said appellate clerkship is the most prestigious gig one can obtain straight out of law school.

Lesson: Sheila Raj, along with all of her nervous classmates, wouldn't be employable without a clerkship. This was a bit of a problem, considering that getting a perfect score on the LSAT seemed easier. Top-ten law school. Straight As. Two law professors attesting to your legal genius. In a place where As were less common than all-night raves, obtaining a clerkship seemed to be an insurmountable task.

Luckily for me, taking law school exams turned out to be like learning how to ride a bicycle. After a few falls during my first semester torts final, I got back up and probably could have given Lance Armstrong a good run.

As such, the entire Columbia Law School community insisted that I apply to every federal judge in the United States of America and its outlying territories. And why not? According to every professor and former law clerk, working for a judge was "the best job you'll ever have."

A sample page from Columbia Law's clerkship center read: "Judge Sanders is brilliant and a wonderful mentor," "Writing opinions with Judge Nederholm is the most exciting experience I've ever had—professional or otherwise," "You'll learn more in a year from Judge Franklin than during the rest of your entire life."

Based on what everyone said and wrote, a clerkship was better than drugs, sex, and rock and roll combined. It was incredible that all the 1960s hippies didn't turn to the law rather than to acid and Janis Joplin. I had to have it. Not only for my own personal growth but also to land the job of my dreams.

After interning in the Immigrants Rights division of the American Civil Liberties Union the summer after my One L year, I was sold. I was going to fight the good fight. Protect the disenfranchised from the almighty government. Make America what the founders had envisioned. It was clear that I needed a clerkship to land a job there without first having to slave away in the litigation department of a big New York City sweatshop.

Yet even a fiery litigator from such a sweatshop would be hard pressed to crack the case of the clerkship.

United States Federal Judges v. Sheila Raj, Third-Year Law Student

Facts: For weeks, hundreds of thousands of law students packed into Columbia Law's library, sitting for hours on end, cutting, pasting, printing, stuffing, and sealing hundreds of envelopes with a good old-fashioned ass kiss. New York, Miami, Chicago, Washington DC, Philadelphia, St. Louis, Cincinnati, Dallas.

Even the lady at the post office thought Raj was a weirdo ("Girlfriend, if you don't get a job for all this"—pointing to an overloaded cart of applications before turning her head back and forth). Being pitied by a postal worker didn't exactly inspire confidence.

Question presented: Does Raj get a clerkship and live happily ever after, or not and die?

Holding: Nearly two hundred applications in over a dozen cities yielded three whole interviews. The first one—a district court judge in Manhattan. Sure, Judge Cortland wasn't on a court of appeals, but he was in New York. A huge plus. When asked the paradigmatic question, "Do you have anything to add?" Raj responded, "Yes, I'm a hypochondriac." Not the right answer. The second go-round involved Chicago and too much nervous talk about the wind. No dice.

Three's the charm! Sheila Raj landed an offer from the Honorable Helga Friedman, court of appeals judge in Philadelphia, President Gerald Ford appointee, first woman ever to sit on a federal court of appeals and former Penn Law professor. In sum, a Legal Goddess.

I accepted on the spot.

I knew I'd miss my life in New York, but spending one short year in Philadelphia was going to make my career. Heck, it'd probably make my life.

The city of brotherly love beckoned!

"Sheels, it's *adorable!* It's *huge!* Check out the gorgeous floors and ohmyGod—you get *tons* of natural light!" my sister, Puja, squealed as we entered my new apartment on Twelfth Street between Spruce and Pine, smack in the middle of the "gayborhood." Like South Beach and Chelsea, the gay mafia had transformed this neighborhood from filthy to fabulous in a matter of two years. And I was right in the middle of it all. Darling café to the left, independent bookstore straight ahead, French bistro to the right. As for my apartment, it felt like a palace compared to my place in New York. "Eight hundred fifty square feet of pure prewar charm!" That's what the ad said in the *Philadelphia Inquirer* and it was true. The most charming part? Eight hundred fifty bucks a month! For that, you'd be lucky to get bedbugs and a bathroom share in Brooklyn.

"Yeah, Sheila, this is even better than you described. For once I don't think you exaggerated," Sanjay said, playfully squeezing my shoulder. Sanjay and I had been dating for about two years. He was a radiology resident in Reston, Virginia, my hometown. I'd known him since I was about three minutes old, as our parents had been best friends since their medical school days in India. Any semblance of incest had been avoided thanks to the fact that Sanjay was four years older than me and had failed to acknowledge my existence until a few years earlier, when we'd seen each other at Thanksgiving. A girl couldn't have asked for a more dependable or decent man. And shy of landing the lead in a Bollywood film, our mothers couldn't have been happier.

"You know, you guys, I think I may never leave Philly," I said, taking in my palace. "You can actually live like a normal person rather than a starving bag lady."

"Yeah, since you totally starved and were a bag lady in New York. Jesus, you were probably the only graduate student in the city who lived around the corner from Pastis," Puja replied. Sanjay, seemingly bored, retreated to the bathroom.

"Anyway, what I meant was that I think I have the potential to be a *huge* hit in this town. You know—the big fish, small pond scenario. It doesn't hurt that I clearly live in the most fashionable neighborhood and—"

BANG! BANG! BANG!

"Hey, hello?" a man whispered (loudly) at my prewar door.

"My fans have already come to see me!" I sauntered over, smiling.

It's not that I was expecting Elton John with a fruit basket, but Mister Rogers? Before me was a gray-haired man with thin eyebrows and a sprayed-on tan.

"Uh, um, hey, where is he?" Mister Rogers peered inside, eyes darting from side to side. Puja waved, warily.

"That's not a man!" he exclaimed. Puja had long straight hair (which she talked about incessantly), was five foot four, 110 pounds. She was wearing a short skirt and pink flip-flops. It didn't take a detective to figure out that my sister was, in fact, not a man.

"Who are you looking for?" I closed the door a bit so he'd stop eyeballing my 850-square-foot gem. He was starting to freak me out.

"Hey, hey up here! Up here!" a timid male voice beckoned from above. I looked up, along the winding staircase of my new building. Standing two floors up was a twenty-something guy in designer jeans and a tight-fitted black T-shirt with the word "bitch" on it. If he hadn't been emaciated and wearing a three-seasons-ago shirt, he'd be really cute—just the kind of fag I'd have been more than happy to hag.

Mister Rogers muttered a "Sorry" before bounding up the stairs.

"Hey"—cough—"hey you"—cough, cough—"welcome to the building!" the skinny guy yelled to me.

"Thanks."

And with that, we both closed our doors.

Things were slightly off in Mister Rogers's neighborhood.

Chapter Two

⚖

My first day of work! I put on my Monday best and hummed through the beautiful cobblestone streets of Center City, Philadelphia. After skillfully maneuvering myself through what felt more like a village—how quaint!—than a city, I arrived at the courthouse, a large, nondescript brown building at the corner of Market and 6th Streets, a mere twenty-five-minute walk from home. Even better, it was right across from Independence Hall! This was the birthplace of America and I was in the thick of it. I couldn't believe my good fortune.

Inside, I followed the cardboard signs that read, "New Clerks" in uneven black marker. I was careful to smile at all the security guards. There were dozens of them. But of course. This was a really important place where really important business went down. This was tax money being well spent.

The signs directed me through three or four different corridors—all brown and poorly lit—to a windowless room where other nervous Nellies loitered about in suits. Before I could open my mouth to introduce myself to a smallish, balding guy with a big mole on his nose, Martha Stewart's doppelgänger flew through the door, came to a screeching halt, and started grinning like a horny frat guy.

"Welcome, clerks! We are just soooooo happy you're here. Just a few things before you can get crackin'!"

For some reason, I've always felt embarrassed when people drop the *g*s off the end of conjugated verbs. So, I quickly turned my head to avoid eye contact with Ms. Martha. What I found was more troubling—many clerks had already broken off into little cliques. Why had nobody invited me? What was the matter?

Thankfully, we got ushered out before I could totally freak about the lost popularity contest. Unceremoniously shoved out the door, I got pushed against the man with the mole, who had just turned to talk to a tall skinny girl.

"Where did you go to law school?" he asked her without saying hello.

"Northeastern."

Apparently that wasn't the right answer, and with nary a pause, he turned his back to her and walked away. Basically, Northeastern wasn't a top-twenty law school, so the girl wasn't worth his time.

Grades distinguished you in law school, making all of us future law clerks the kings of the hill while we were there. Since we were no longer in law school, grades were now defunct, and a new system of marginalization had emerged—where you went to law school. I had hovered above such pettiness in law school, though, and couldn't be bothered now. This year's focus was becoming Judge Friedman's best friend. On the way to the elevator, I smiled just thinking about it.

"Hey, Sheila, can you join me at the club for a game of squash?" the judge would ask one random Tuesday afternoon.

"Sure thing, Judge. Funny, that reminds me of *Wasp v. Wasp,* 360 F.2d 1, where the second circuit found Wasp I to be liable for Wasp II's eye injuries during a game of squash."

"Bravo, Sheila, bravo!" The judge would clap as the interns kissed my grits.

Or, better yet, the whole gang sitting poolside with cocktails. One of my coclerks would note: "This reminds me of the time the dreadfully pinko liberal ninth circuit found martini-sipping poolside to be tortious activity."

"Ah yes, but you forget there's a circuit split on the issue, thanks to the fourth circuit," I'd insightfully advise.

Round of applause. Sheila takes a bow.

DING! Thirteenth floor, going up. Forget Mr. Smith and Washington, Judge Friedman's Special Friend had come to Philadelphia! It was curious that there were no "Welcome, Sheila" signs, but instead a tiny black plaque with an arrow pointing to "The honorable Hel Friedman." Ring. Buzz. Turn the knob.

Smack! I'd opened the door directly into the judge. Her Honor was standing right before my virgin eyes. About four feet ten inches tall, her crooked feet, polyester pantsuit, sunglasses the size of Fat Albert's behind, and a massive bun atop her tiny head.

"Hello, Judge Friedman." I smiled, extending my hand down. Even at five foot two (and a quarter), I towered over the lady.

She curled her lips upward. It wasn't a smile. Her eyebrows slanted inward. It was a frown.

"Hello. You must be Shayla," she said unenthusiastically. But I couldn't blame her for being indifferent—and mispronouncing my name. Judge Helga Friedman was a busy woman.

"Yes, I'm SHE-LA. It's nice to see you." "Nice" wasn't exactly right, but "It's to see you" seemed totally wrong.

"Well, I cannot ever remember you people. You just come and go. Half the time I don't even know *whom* I've hired." I laughed. She didn't. It wasn't a joke. I'd just packed up my life to come work for this woman and she didn't even know who I was. I could've been an eighty-year-old Korean man and she wouldn't have known the difference.

"Come come, we have LOTS of work to do," she ordered, turning and marching off. I stumbled in her trail, racking my brain for something clever to say.

"Philly is just such a cool town," I blurted. The minute I said it, I realized that I was not at all cool.

"First of all, it's PhilaDELPHIA, and second of all, what is *cool* about it?" She didn't turn to address me. Seeing as I'd been there for all of forty-eight hours, I was slightly stumped, and I had a feeling "cheesesteaks" wouldn't have gone over well with this crowd. But it didn't matter, because the judge didn't seem to want a response and instead just led me through a door into a room that looked vaguely familiar from my interview a year earlier.

Inside was the most desperate-looking duo I'd ever seen. Desperation Sally Struthers–style. Only, it'd take way more than fifty cents a day to save either of them. It seemed like they might cry at any moment, which would have been a little awkward for everyone. The judge pointed to the desperate man without so much as a look in his direction. "That's Roy." Little arm swung around to the desperate female: "And that's Janet. They're my secretaries." Nobody moved except the judge, who sauntered over to a box in front of Janet's desk and started flipping through what appeared to be mail.

Taking it all in, I barely noticed that neither Janet nor Roy had bothered to return my hello. To the left of the box was a heap of multicolored booklets and to the right, stacks of humongous white books. It didn't seem like this office would go paperless anytime in the next, say, three to four centuries. The paper trail went in all directions. I looked east, west, north, and finally south, where I spotted an unsightly wall-to-wall red carpet.

Visually trapped, I considered closing my eyes but ruled against it, quite certain that sleepwalking on day one wouldn't have been well received. Then again, judging from Roy and Janet, sleep-sitting didn't seem to be much of a problem.

"That's for you," the judge barked, motioning toward one pile of paper. "It's your first case." And with that, she dragged her leg—my initial thoughts were confirmed, her right one was markedly longer than the left—and proceeded into her office.

"Um . . . should I go somewhere?" I asked the air, the paper, the red carpet, and anyone but Roy and Janet, both of whom refused to acknowledge me.

Roy groaned and nodded his head toward an adjacent room. Then he stood . . . and I was mesmerized. Hypnotized. The guy was an icon of something. Of what, I wasn't sure, but it was something. This was truly the rarest of specimens. He was five foot ten. His skin was whiter than his teeth (which weren't even in the category of white). Even better, he had the most wondrous of mullets. The best way to describe it would be "careful." Meticulously groomed. Wisped—but ever so gently with nary a superfluous strand. And perfectly colored. Like a horse's tail. Not brown. Not blond. Not even blondish brown. The color and care almost made the mullet so nondescript that you got duped into thinking it wasn't a mullet at all but a cashmere ascot or some such thing. I wanted to pet it.

"You're here," he whispered and pointed to a small, shaky cubicle with carpeting on the sides. When I looked over, I noticed the grand finale: fanny pack perched atop pleated pants! I hadn't seen a fanny pack in at least a decade. I recalled a few here and there during my clichéd backpacking trip through Europe after freshman year in college. But Roy wasn't backpacking. He wasn't a college freshman. And this place certainly wasn't Rome.

I carefully placed my first case on my new desk.

"I just got back from vacation," Roy said in a hush. "I'm a medievalist—Felemid McDowell's the name—and I was at the BIG MEDIEVAL festival in southern Jersey." His eyes went wild. As for me, I concentrated on not gawking.

"I'm a twelfth-century Irish bard. My wife is the daughter of a sixteenth-century Jewish merchant." No gawk.

"We're way more into Markland than the Society for Creative Anachronisms." Maybe slight gawk.

He then pivoted, turned, and skulked back to his room.

I sat down; my head was spinning. Medieval what? Irish beard? Twelfth-century McDonald's? Jewish merchant from *what* century? Creative macramé?

As I turned to grab my case materials, out of the corner of my eye I caught a little person, big bun, even bigger sunglasses, peering over a newspaper. There was the judge staring at me. Oh no!! Though the clerks' room was separated from the judge's office by the secretaries' den, all doors were open. The result: judge facing my cubicle. Staring (or was she glaring?) at me.

I waved. She didn't wave back.

"Pssst. Back here."

I turned and about ten feet behind me was a portly brunette sitting at another cubicle. I got up, the judge watching my every move, and slowly walked toward the brunette.

"You must be Sheila," the woman stated in a manner that was almost accusatory. She didn't even stand to shake my hand. I was beginning to feel like everyone hated me. Or maybe I was being paranoid? Mental note: Find shrink in Philly.

"Yes, and you are Laura, I take it?" I whispered, kneeling so we could see eye to eye.

"Yeah, I got here a little early. You know, to beat the crowds," she said, pointing to her computer screen, already displaying the minutiae of a Westlaw case. "And I'm working on a *really* interesting case involving an unreasonable search," she explained.

What happened to "How are you?"

Without an appropriate response to the Fourth Amendment comment, I simply nodded, smiling.

"So, you went to Columbia. I went to Chicago. I was editor of the *Law Review* and finished Order of the Coif. Did you Coif it?" Order of the Coif is the highest honor bestowed upon graduating law students. It means you're a pocket genius who's managed to get straight As for three years straight.

While I'd done well in law school, I certainly hadn't "Coifed it." I had, however, managed to maintain a social life and regularly visited my parents in northern Virginia, unlike the Coifers I knew, who had maintained a studying life and regularly visited only the library. I had a feeling Laura didn't really want to hear about my friends and family.

"Um, it's nice to meet you," I managed, backing away in the hopes of a stealth escape.

"Well, you're in for such a treat. I can already tell the work here's going to be beyond stimulating. This is a constitutional claim." Her eyes ballooned. "To think, my first case and *I* am going to decide whether this guy gets a second chance or not and it involves"—she lowered her voice and looked around—"an *African American* defendant and a *white* police officer. Just like law school exams!" She smiled with an open mouth, bringing her hands together in a silent clap.

"Laura, that's great, really great for you," I whispered. "I hope I'm half as, er, lucky as you with my case. Speaking of which, I should probably get started." I raced back to my cubicle.

I glanced left—staring judge. A quick turn right—carpeted wall. Even the cubicles were carpeted. The plus side was the utter lack of distractions. I opened my packet of materials, which consisted of red, white, and blue legal briefs. The blue one contained the plaintiff's argument. I dug in. And had a minor stroke. I didn't understand any of it. From what I could tell, it was a complicated labor dispute, and I had never taken labor law.

The first brief alone was sixty pages and there were half a dozen other briefs. How on earth was I going to read the next three briefs, the zillion cases cited, and write a coherent bench memorandum that the judge would not only read but also rely on during oral arguments?

Oral arguments take place in blocks known as "sittings." Sittings are the staple of all courts of appeals. Prior to clerking, sitting was something I did when I wasn't standing or sleeping. While a clerk, sittings are things that ensure you never sleep well. Every active judge on the third circuit had seven sittings per year. Each sitting consisted of a panel of three judges—all randomly assembled by the clerk of the court, the court manager. Judges were given their sitting schedules not months but years in advance. They knew when they were sitting, whom they were sitting with, and where they were sitting—which was almost always one floor up from Judge Friedman's chambers. This was to ensure that there would never, *ever*, be any surprises. In the legal profession, the only thing more loathsome than mediocrity is surprise.

It was the law clerks' job to dissect the cases for their respective judges. In short, we read the legal briefs and case law before churning out mammoth bench memorandums, which were essentially book reports with a suggested solution at the end.

I hadn't written a book report in two decades and summarizing Judy Blume was markedly less daunting than dissecting the so-called "work preservation doctrine," a nearly extinct aspect of labor law. After three solid hours, I'd barely made a dent in the first brief, which seemed like a bit of a misnomer, considering it was close to 120 pages long.

I needed lunch.

"Hey Laura, want to head to the cafeteria with me?"

"No, I brought my lunch. Thanks. Must be nice to have the time to step out. I mean, this case is really tough." She smirked.

"Wow, great. Good for you. I mean, good that you brought your lunch. Not good that the case is tough. OK, well then."

She smirked again. I lost my appetite.

The cafeteria was on the second floor, and as soon as I set foot inside, I wished I hadn't.

Inside was a *Twin Peaks* revival. Yet, even the show's biggest fans wouldn't have wanted to be on this set. To my left was a gaggle of Janet clones, each looking more unhappy than the next. One quick right turn later and yet another group of unapproachable middle-aged women masking their anger with apathy. I headed straight toward the food. My middle school cafeteria was better than this. Before me was a delectable smorgasbord of everything you'd never want: gristly pork chops, bony chicken-fried steak, limp broccoli soaked in a greenish oil, and poached Krab. With a *K*. I felt myself becoming fat and frail just looking at it all.

I forced myself to request the unimaginable. "Hi. I'll take the Krab and some broccoli." A wide-eyed man with a hairnet silently stared at me. "Um, hi, I'd like the Krab and broccoli, please," I said. Stare.

"Could you please show me where that is, ma'am?" he earnestly requested. I wondered if, in addition to a clean record, one needed a staring problem to land a job at the federal courthouse.

"It's right in front of you. You know, that fake Krab stuff," I said, pointing.

"I'm sorry, ma'am, it's just that I can't see. I'm blind."

Was this some sort of joke? From the horrified looks of everyone around me, I surmised not. Great, I was going to hell now.

"Oh my God! I'm so sorry," I squeaked. But it was too late. Judging from the looks I was getting from the others, the damage was done. It didn't help that the man then killed me with kindness.

"Don't worry about it, miss. I'm Ernie." He grinned. I couldn't speak and even if I could, I didn't want to disclose my name. About ten people there wanted to rip my eyes out. So, I simply waited as Ernie scooped up a pork chop and a chicken-fried steak. I handed the cashier a ten. She looked at me. Me at her.

The lady behind me couldn't control herself. "What's wrong with you?!" Her eyes burned. "You have to tell her what you gave her. She's blind." I'd apparently missed the sign alerting the masses to all the blind folks.

"Oh, uh, it's a ten. Um, keep the change. Um, see you later." Did I just say that to the blind lady? She wouldn't be seeing me later. She wouldn't be seeing anything ever. And there I was, rubbing it in. I was a terrible person. I returned to the main dining area, chicken-fried animal in tow.

Secretary gangs engaged in silent turf wars. Clerks in pleats hovered in various corners. I wondered how they'd become so chummy already. This was worse than finding a friend to sit with in middle school. At least then there was chocolate milk.

For a split second, I considered taking my food upstairs and eating it there, but the thought of eating a chicken-fried steak was distressing enough, and I couldn't endure the judge's stare fest on top of it all. Instead, I squeezed into an unassuming nonclerks corner. Peace and quiet. Just me and my deep-fried meat. What was a chicken-fried steak? A bird? A cow? A little of both? Whilst pondering, I heard some disconcerting ramblings.

"Did you hear about Judge Jones? He's, like, six months behind on his opinions," an emboldened pleat loudly whispered from the west. Gasps all around. Everyone was entranced.

From the southeast, a clerk, donning what looked like a fedora, soapboxed to a group of mesmerized fans: "And then Judge Fleck said, 'Well, what do you expect, Scalia penned that one.'" Cackles. Impossible. Even the lunchtime gossip was a snooze fest.

Scalia jokes are the all time worst. I'm not talking about the lawyer joke genre, mind you, a wretched one for sure. Example: What's the difference between a lawyer and a vampire? Punch line: A vampire only sucks blood at night. Scalia jokes constitute more of a jurisprudential subgenre. In the knee-slapping corridors of every law school, one learns how Justice Thomas never speaks and Justice Scalia doesn't believe in considering legislative history when considering the constitutionality of a law. Based on those two truths that are self-evident of nothing in particular, a whole assembly line of law jokes has emerged. There's a reason Jerry Seinfeld never told any of them.

"Sheila?" The fedora had approached my bench, and upon closer inspection, I realized he'd been in my Fed Courts class. "Hey, Sheila. It's Brian. You know, from Columbia." He parked himself right in front of me so I was forced to stare at his puny crotch. Suddenly my bird didn't look so bad. "I didn't know you were clerking here," he continued. And I didn't know that it was possible that Scalia's distaste for congressional activity could still keep you in stitches after all these years.

"Yep. I take it you are, too. Who are you clerking for?" The question rolled off my tongue before I even knew what I was saying.

"Judge Fleck," he said so proudly you'd have thought the pope had just canonized him. He graciously followed up with a pregnant pause to allow me to congratulate him for landing a clerkship with the chief judge, yet another rung in the endless hierarchy. The appellate clerks were better than the district court clerks. Clerking for the chief judge made you clerk king.

Who was I to dethrone Brian? Not to mention, he was wearing an American flag pin on the buttoned-down collar of his grainy shirt. It would have been unpatriotic of me not to salute him.

"Wow, that's great." I barely got out the last word before Brian started giggling like a slumber party princess.

"Yeah, he's sooooo cool. My coclerks and a couple of other clerks I've met around are over there," he said and pointed to his audience, all of whom were watching our conversation in awe. "What about you? Who are *you* clerking for?" This was clearly going to be the year's million-dollar question.

"Friedman. Judge Friedman?" What I muttered sounded more like a question than an answer. A mere week earlier, I had said that name with such pride. I was going to Philadelphia to clerk for Judge Friedman! Now, I could barely say the words as a statement, as if I myself didn't believe them.

"Wow, I hear she's tough," Brian quickly said, before adding, "but really really smart."

Of course. One could never say something even remotely negative about a judge without a qualifying compliment. But I couldn't blame him really. He'd spent three long years in law school, too, where judges are sacrosanct.

"What do you mean by tough?" I asked curiously.

Brian started fidgeting. "Uh, nothing, nothing, like, you know, she's really tough on lawyers, I think." Then he looked behind him, as if the boogeyman were standing there.

"Hey, Brian, I really have to get back," I lied, staring at my full plate of carcass. Silence. "We should definitely get lunch sometime," I blurted. Classic. The paradigmatic panic invitation. To escape one awkward social situation, I'd suggest a longer, planned awkward social situation. I tossed the bird and fled.

The judge was standing in front of Janet's cubicle when I returned.

"Hi, Judge. How are you?" I asked, smiling.

"What does that mean? That is a totally irrational question!" She marched off toward her elevator.

Had I accidentally told her to fuck off or something? Maybe I'd developed Tourette's and nobody had the heart to tell me? Had my mother taught me bad manners? Maybe "How are you" *was* irrational?

Ding! Thirteenth floor, going down.

I reached for the phone to call Puja. I was hoping she could shed a little light on my irrationality.

"What do you think *you're* doing?!"

I swiveled my chair around. There was Janet, standing with her hands on her hips.

"Ah, I was going to call my sister?" Another statement-turned-question in less than ten minutes.

"Well, you cannot use the telephone. I don't know who you think you are, but the only time law clerks and secretaries can use the phone is to answer it for the judge." Full stop. She clenched her hips.

"O-K. What about emergencies? Can we not call nine-one-one, say, for fires or death, or—"

"Only the judge has emergencies." Janet returned to her desk.

"Oh, and Sheila, don't think about using the Internet. She gets *really* mad about that one," Janet hollered from the other room.

Terrific. That left staring as the only option for procrastination. It started to make sense. Staring seemed to be everyone's favorite pastime. The judge had stared at me all morning. Aside from Janet's ten-second lecture, all she and Roy had done since I'd arrived was stare (Janet in a not so nice way, Roy in a brain-dead sort of way).

The place was a training camp for mimes.

I set in for a good long stare at Camden, New Jersey, but was forced to resume working once the judge returned from lunch. In fact, I was knee-deep in laborese when she sauntered through the clerks' room, the bags hanging from her hands and arms signaling her departure for the day. Laura and I turned to face Her Honor. I stopped myself from saying anything that could be perceived as subrational. You know, like "Good night" or "Bye."

The judge's lips turned downward.

"Oh. I forgot to say earlier. There are no vacations. I do not take a vacation, so why should you?! After all, *I'm* the judge and you are my clerks and if I'm not going anywhere, why should you?!"

Laura and I simply nodded. It was perfect. What better thing to hear on your first day of work than it'd be another 364 days until a day off.

"Sheba, you are rilly rilly thin," the judge said.

Huh?

And then the judge glared in Laura's direction.

OH GOD!

Laura was at least thirty pounds overweight. And, the judge had just told her that in so many words. I prayed that Laura's fixation on the Fourth Amendment had precluded her from processing the insult.

DING! Thirteenth floor, going down.

And she was off!

Just as I was about to snatch my purse and run, I felt a tap on my back.

TAP! TAP! TAP!

I swiveled around. It was Laura and she'd managed to pull up a chair right behind me. She must have caught on after all. I was prepared to provide the necessary counseling.

"Hey. Do you notice how homophobic everyone is here?"

Had she meant to say *fat-a-phobic*?

"Do you even *know* what it's like to be a lesbian in this country?" Her mouth went improbably vertical.

I didn't. I also didn't know what it was like being a periodontist. But it didn't matter. Laura didn't seem to want an answer at all.

"Well, it's really *really* hard." She looked pained.

I was suddenly intrigued. A real-life lesbian! And she was my coclerk. I would actually have a lesbian friend! Puja had recently convinced me that lesbians were more fabulous than gay men. She'd just left a big investment bank for a loftier job with a leveraged-buyout shop. It wasn't the insane amounts of money that wooed her but the fashionable lipstick lesbian with an even more fashionable Hamptons home where she regularly entertained the glitterati.

"Everybody is so *cruel,*" Laura blurted, her eyes getting bigger and bigger, mouth larger and wider. Suddenly she looked like a Moonie. I wondered if lesbian Moonies were fabulous. I had a feeling Puja would say no.

"I mean, when I was at Brown, like barely anyone outside the Women's Studies Department would talk to me. And then at Chicago, people would just stare. *Stare at me.*"

"Laura, wow, I'm so sorry that—"

"Well, whatever, have a good night." With that, she ejected herself from my personal space and returned to her cubicle, restoring a silent order.

I walked into my empty apartment that night and collapsed onto the yellow velour couch I'd inherited from my parents years earlier, while a junior at the University of Michigan. It had been a long day.

I closed my eyes and prayed. Puja and I had been raised part Hindu (Dad), part Catholic (Mom), and part Episcopalian (grade school). While incoherent in the formative years, this theological medley proved very useful as an adult. It allowed us to unabashedly beg for favors from the Man Upstairs (Catholic), drink when the prayers were or weren't answered (Episcopalian), and ultimately not give a crap because we'd probably be reincarnated as frogs anyway (Hindu). I was at stage one and started crossing my heart, hoping to die. I needed salvation, or a little help at least.

How would I endure twelve months in such an environment?

A boss whose hobbies included mimery and fat jokes, a patronizing, persecuted lesbian for a coclerk, and a macraméing medievalist as a secretary? It was a bit more than I'd bargained for. Not to mention, I had not one single friend in Philly and felt deathly alone.

I'd asked Sanjay to transfer to the University of Pennsylvania Hospital for the final year of his residency. He'd scoffed at the request, citing a would-be disruption to an "impeccable group synergy." Maybe I should have demanded it nevertheless. A live-in boyfriend, even one who had to be kidnapped, would have been welcome. And James, my friend from Columbia, wasn't starting his clerkship in Camden until the following week.

I was all alone in Pennsylvania.

Are you there, God? It's me, Sheila.

Chapter Three

DING! Thirteenth floor, going down!

"Roy! Roy! I smell smoke! Did you smoke in here!" Her voice was shriller than most fire alarms. I jumped out of my seat. I imagined Roy probably peed in his.

"Um. Uh. Your Honor."

For the love of all that's holy and good, just spit it out, Sir Felemid McDowell. I quietly arose and peered around the corner. Tall, grown medievalist shaking so fiercely his mullet and fanny pack rattled. Little woman with squinty eyes, bun touching fanny pack, shaking fist at said man.

"I don't smoke here," Roy managed to spill.

There. He'd said it. He didn't do it.

"Well, I smell it and it's awful. THERE WILL BE NO MORE SMOKING! Not here. Not there. Not anywhere!"

The judge was banning smoking? In all of Pennsylvania? The country? The world? She couldn't do that. It'd be tough even for Congress or the United States Supreme Court to do that. Surely Roy would point out this logistical snafu. The only person who could make Roy quit smoking was Roy.

"Yes, Judge." Just like that, he was taking it. Maybe the judge was more powerful than I'd initially thought. A little fist-shaking and she could make smokers quit.

The judge whipped around to Janet.

"Bob is not doing well today," she barked. Bob was the judge's husband. The word on the street was that he was a billion years old and had been trying to knock off for years. In addition to being deaf and suffering from dementia, Bob had lived through ten or so heart attacks, and each time, the judge apparently would order the doctors to electrocute him back to life.

"Sorry to hear that, Judge," Janet replied.

"What!? What is *that* supposed to mean? That's so stupid! What are you sorry about? You're sorry!" The miracle worker had miraculously turned empathy into a curse within five seconds flat.

And now she stood in the doorway, staring directly at me. What about my prayers?

"Shaylee!"

"Yes, Judge," I said, forcing myself to face her.

"How are you coming along with that case?"

"Um. Ahh—"

"What's the issue?" she demanded. To be fair, I should have known the issue after two full days.

"Um. Well, it's this union and they're mad because they say that, um—" ZAP!

"I do not have time for this nonsense. You're rilly rilly slow and not at all clear. I have law clerks to quickly—and succinctly—state the issues. I want that bench memo on Monday!"

That gave me three days to figure out how to escape the chamber, change my identity, and find a nice two-bedroom Afghani cave.

As soon as the judge assumed staring position in her office, she picked up the phone. This was a first. For such an important woman, the judge didn't receive many calls. Over the past two days, the phone hadn't rung once. She didn't call anyone either. I was curious. She was probably just calling Philip Morris and RJ Reynolds to let them know she'd just put them out of business. It was the least she could do.

RING! Speakerphone. I'd get to hear the whole thing!

"HU-LLO," a very old, dear-sounding man answered.

"BOB! BOB! BOB!" Heavy breathing from his end. "Go outside! Sit on the patio—that's why I had it built, damn it!" With that, she slammed the phone and started screaming again. "Where's what's-his-name? What's-his-name! What's-his-name!!"

What the heck was going on? What was what's-his-name? I pretended to keep working. At this rate, I'd definitely have the memo finished within three to four years.

"Where. Is. He?" Type. Type. Type. "Shandraaaaaa!!!!" I jumped for the second time that day, and it wasn't even 9 AM.

"Yes, Judge." Maybe I'd been too harsh on Roy. The words "Yes, Judge" were the only ones that produced themselves.

"Where is who's-it?"

Who was who's-it and how was I supposed to know his or her whereabouts? And wasn't it totally clear that I didn't know anything about anything.

"Him. Him!" She pointed out the door, in the direction of Roy.

Case cracked. Roy apparently had multiple personalities. In addition to being a middle-aged, fanny-pack-wearing secretary *and* a twelfth-century tribal poet singer from Ireland, Roy was also "what's-his-name" and "who's-it." How obvious.

"Um. I'm not sure, Judge. He must have just gone to the bath—"

"Yes, Judge!" Who's-it came plowing into her office from who-knows-where. Thank God.

"I know you can't do anything, but xerox this," she snarled, shoving a crumpled piece of paper in his traumatized face.

"Yes, Judge." He bowed like a drunk samurai and stumbled off. Incredible. The woman exposed her tonsils to the East Coast just to get a copy made? Maybe she was nuts? I'd never been around a certifiably crazy person before, so I couldn't be sure. But for two days straight, all she'd done was alternately glare and stare. Today, she was pistol-whipping anyone in her path. It was clear she hated Roy most, which was particularly sad as it seemed like he was lacking in the self-confidence department to begin with.

Before Roy could screw up the xeroxing, it started again.

"JANET!!!!"

"Yes, Judge." Those magic words again. Janet jumped into the torture chamber.

"Have we heard from Judge Adams in *Morgan versus Taylor?*" she asked, lips pursed.

"Um, er, Judge, her secretary just sent me an e-mail saying she needed to talk to you about *Morgan* before signing on." Janet braced herself.

"What! What! Why are you just telling me this *now?*"

"Because I just got the e-mail a minute ago and—"

"Let's not forget something! You work for me! Not for Judge Adams!"

"Yes, Judge."

"That woman is getting way too big for her britches. I'm not taking this from her!!!" Judge Friedman obviously didn't like Judge Adams. Then again, she didn't seem to like anyone, not even her husband. Janet, the messenger, was caught in the crossfire.

"Judge, er, um, do you want me to call Judge Adams's chambers?"

"No! I'll call her myself. This is RIDICULOUS!" The fact that another judge actually read and wanted to comment on an opinion before it became law for thousands of people—that was ridiculous? "Give me her number," the judge demanded.

"Um, OK, I'll go get it." Janet turned toward her desk.

"What? You don't have it here? Forget it. I'll do it myself. Can't you do anything? You, you, you're so stupid you make me want to die. Get out!"

The judge never called Judge Adams. Instead, she sat behind her desk for the rest of the day, muttering to herself about "big britches" and how "this will have to stop." The woman talked to herself all afternoon, which I strangely preferred to her staring. Having her occupied with something enabled me to make headway on the labor case. By the time she picked up her phone, I'd waded through a dozen cases and was about to commence my bench memo.

"Good afternoon, Judge Fleck's chambers," said a timid-sounding voice. It was Brian.

Lucky for me, the judge seemed fond of the speakerphone.

"It's Judge Friedman. Give me Judge Fleck."

"Sure. Um, um, Your Honor." Brian was such a Goody Two-shoes. He was one of those law students who often stayed after class to tell the professor how "interesting" his or her lecture had been. But when faced with a real-life judge, Brian could barely speak.

"Hello, Helga," Judge Fleck said flatly.

"Richard, this is getting ridiculous. I mean, Linda is way too big for her britches. This has to stop!" Why was she calling Judge Fleck to complain about Judge Adams's britches? Granted, I didn't know much about the inner workings of the federal judiciary, but I was quite sure that chief judges were supposed to ensure that their courts ran smoothly, not to derail the process of editing and reviewing opinions and surely not to referee playground politics.

"Helga, I just don't understand why you get so upset with her. What has she done now?" He was definitely annoyed. My ears perked up.

"I sent her a beautiful opinion last week. And she just won't approve it, damn it! She always wants to talk about it. You, as chief, really need to talk to her," she ordered.

Judge Fleck sighed loudly. He clearly wasn't buying any of it. I hadn't known Helga Friedman for long, but I knew enough to know that standing up to her took guts. It was no wonder Brian and his coclerk went around reiterating Supreme Court justice jokes. Even I would laugh at a Scalia joke delivered by a human brave enough to actually sigh at Judge Friedman.

"Helga, I'll talk to her about it," he lied before hanging up.

Before I could glance over, the judge was hovering above me, standing in my cubicle.

"Did you know that I was the first woman ever to have been given the presidential commission?" She smiled, patting her bun.

I wondered if she knew that two long, slightly curly hairs were coming out of her right nostril.

"Ah, yes, Judge, I did know. That's really amazing. Really amaz—"

"Well, I don't have time for this! And you should make time for eating. You're rilly rilly thin."

I should have been thankful. Puja and I had been trying to catch anorexia since we were tots. I'd never been successful. Not that I was fat, I just wasn't rilly rilly thin. It had to stop. How could Laura take much more?

As expected, Laura came tapping. I vowed to be supportive.

"Yes?" I swiveled around, attempting to appear welcoming. It didn't matter how I appeared, however. Laura didn't see me. Just herself. All she had to do was hit "play" from the previous two nights.

"I really think Janet is homophobic. Do you even know how hard it is to work when she just stares at me? *Stares* at me when I walk through their office?" Not this again.

I was sticking to fag haggery. Frankly, homophobia was totally passé, and while Janet wasn't the friendliest kid in class, she certainly hadn't exhibited specific animus toward Laura. As for the staring, Laura had no room to complain. Last count: the judge had stared at me for about eighteen hours, and we had exactly another 2,120 hours to go before the end of the year.

"Yeah, that really sucks, Laura," I said, patting her on the back. It was enough to send her back to her cubicle and allowed me the opportunity to take my sympathy to Janet. Fat was one thing. But Janet had just been told that the mere sight of her made the judge want to off herself.

"Um, Janet, are you OK?" I asked, carefully approaching her cubicle.

She looked up from a book, seething. Did I say something wrong again? Was "Are you OK" in the same irrational category as "How are you?"

"Why don't you just go back to your big office and do whatever it is that YOU people do!" Janet practically spit in my face. It was then that I noticed she was simultaneously reading the Bible and clutching a cross pendant around her neck.

Apparently I'd landed in Psych 101. Cycle of violence: father beats child, child grows up and beats his own children, and so on. Unfortunately, the law clerks were pretty close to the bottom of the chain, as interns didn't start for another week or so. But Roy was definitely at rock bottom, which seemed like a dangerous position. If I were the judge, I wouldn't want to piss off a man who wore armor and carried a sword on the weekends.

Judge Friedman buzzed me in the late afternoon.

"She-la. That Judge Adams can't do anything. She can't do what's-its-name—whatever that case is you're working on. So, stop working on it. We're giving it to another panel."

Very rarely in one's life does the unbelievable occur. Sextuplets. Winning the lottery. Dolly the cloned sheep. And now, Judge Adams's inability to work on the labor case—and my salvation. I wanted to call the producers at Dateline NBC.

Judge Adams was on the panel for Judge Friedman's next sitting, but she had to recuse herself from my case. Her husband was the venerated mayor of Philadelphia, and his last campaign had accepted large sums of money from one of the unions that was a party to the case. This created an obvious conflict of interest for Judge Adams. Anytime a judge was recused from a case, it was bestowed upon a different panel. This, of course, stank for the parties, as it delayed their appeal. But for me, it was liberation from labor law hell.

After appearing to be duly outraged by Judge Adams's "ineptitude," I accepted my next assignment, whose body weight was twice that of my previous case. The initial panic borne from its girth dissipated once I opened the first brief. It was a death penalty case. Though capital punishment jurisprudence proved daunting in its mind-bending complexity, it carried the highest stakes—life or death—and as such, I welcomed the challenge.

I was especially intrigued considering the recent spate of DNA evidence proving that countless innocent people had been executed over the past decade. Outraged by these findings, the governor of Illinois had called for a moratorium on all executions until further review. The governor of Pennsylvania had not taken a similar measure, and the man appealing his death sentence was nearing the end of the line. I pored over the first fifty pages without so much as a desire to procrastinate. This is why I had come to Philadelphia, to be a part of such important work.

It didn't hurt that I actually felt capable of interpreting the law involved. The crux of the case was strictly Sixth Amendment, which provided criminal defendants the right to a public trial, jury, and counsel. Although we had spent much of our first-year constitutional law class dissecting right-to-counsel cases, I'd never encountered as riveting a case as the one I was now reading:

Dell Nelson, a thirty-six-year-old African American male, sits on death row at SCI Greene in Waynesburg, south of Pittsburgh, roughly a nine-hour drive to Philadelphia, where Nelson was born and raised. In 1988, days after Nelson's eighteenth birthday, twenty-year-old Peter Nussbaum, a junior at the University at Pennsylvania, was found shot to death, execution-style, near Arch Homes, the public housing complex where Nelson resided with his grandmother and three young sisters. Dell Nelson was . . .

DING! Thirteenth floor, going down.

I was astounded that (a) I'd been so engrossed in my work that I had failed to notice the judge's departure and (b) that the judge had made said departure without insulting anyone.

I read a few more pages before putting Dell Nelson and Peter Nussbaum away for the night. As I turned off my computer, I remembered that our two fellow coclerks would be starting the next morning.

Judging from the clerks I'd encountered thus far, I trusted that the chances of either of them being friendly were slim to none. At that point, however, I'd settle for colleagues who didn't crack jokes about Supreme Court justices, scoff at non-top-five law school graduates, and accuse others of homophobia. Another week and I'd probably be willing to date a convicted serial killer as long as he didn't want to discuss *Law Review*.

Laura came tapping instantly. She was breathing more heavily than usual with one finger extended. Then bent. Then extended again. On my shoulder. Tap, tap, tap. I took a deep breath and rotated my chair. I wanted a cheeseburger, not a lecture.

"Sheila. I'm quitting."

I was confused. Quitting what? Her nightly sermons?

"What?" I asked, totally at a loss.

She just stood there speechless, not realizing I wasn't accusing but was actually asking a question.

"Laura, I'm asking you a question. *What* are you quitting exactly?" I slowly enunciated.

"This fucking job."

My head was spinning.

"I just can't take it here. That woman is *such* a bitch."

This was serious. She was serious. The whole week, while she bitched about Janet, Roy, anybody, everybody, not once had she mentioned the judge. I had figured Laura was like all the other peons around the courthouse who'd never breathe a bad word about a judge and would take any and all judicial abuse. I was wrong. Again. My arms dropped, along with my jaw, heart, lungs, intestines, and maybe one kidney. Nobody quits clerkships.

NOBODY.

Laura could have told me that she was actually a black man or that she had just bitten off the head of a small horse. She even could have said that she'd just given birth to a child in the bathroom, clipped off the umbilical cord with a stapler, and FedExed the baby to Argentina. All of these things were more plausible than her actual words.

I'm quitting. I just can't take it here.

Sensing I wasn't going to respond in this century, Laura plowed ahead.

"I mean, I've spent my entire life getting comfortable with my weight. With who I am"—she started crying—"and that—that bitch—has destroyed me in one week. And I thought my dad was bad. I mean, I've had diarrhea all week."

I reached for Laura's hand, encouraging her to continue, while shutting out the damaging imagery.

"I mean, you can't say you haven't noticed, Sheila. She practically calls me fat to my face. And this after I've worshipped that woman and her Leffert opinion"—sniff sniff—"I mean, I practically memorized every word of that thing. For someone who's done"—sniff—"so much for women's rights, she's totally destroyed this woman!"

So, Laura had caught on after all. She wasn't stupid. She was Chicago Law's valedictorian, something she managed to remind me of even in her darkest hour.

"I mean, I only graduated at the top of my class! I don't deserve this shit."

And she didn't. But neither would the person who graduated at the bottom of her class. The fact is, nobody's boss should make them feel bad about their weight. I understood. I didn't even try to stop her.

"Laura. You need to do whatever it is that you need to do. What are you going to say?"

As it was, she wasn't going to say anything. Instead, Laura left the judge a hate letter in the box in front of Janet's desk.

Chapter Four

⚖

A clerk should never comment on the judge's views or work habits, or offer a personal appraisal of the judge's opinions. Even when directly asked, the clerk should say only something like, "I enjoy working for the judge and I cannot comment beyond that."

— "Conduct, Protocol, and Ethics," *Law Clerk Handbook*

Friday morning, I took a shower, dried my hair, looked in the mirror, and screamed.

Since I was a child, I'd suffered from trichotillomania, a rare disorder where one compulsively picks at his/her hair. Panic triggered picking. The night before, I'd come home, sat in the dark for hours, and picked a small bald spot on the right side of my head.

But I needn't have worried. That spot would blend right in a few short hours from now when I was tarred and feathered. TGIF!

The twenty-five-minute walk to work did little to sooth my nerves. I headed into the Dunkin' Donuts just across the street from the courthouse in the hopes that coffee would help. It was the same DD I'd patronized five mornings in a row. I approached the counter.

"What you haveeng?"

This was not promising. Every morning, at the same time, I'd come face-to-face with the same boy from Laos. My order hadn't changed once. Large with skim. No mochalatta, carmelita, nolita, frappashita. Also, I was a court of appeals law clerk, practically royalty. My esteemed order should have been committed to memory.

Whoever said reality was perception and vice versa hadn't met the ten-year-old kid numbly staring at me, with a glimmer of sympathy. The Department of Labor would have had a field day at this particular DD. Child labor laws, perhaps not big in Laos, were still fashionable in the United States. The kid should have been in school.

"A large coffee with skim milk and one sugar. Please," I calmly asked, patting my bald spot. Honey attracts more bees than vinegar. I smiled.

"One laahj wit one sugah ant skeem!" the kid yelled to his colleague, who could barely see over the counter. Said colleague wasn't a day older than six and seemed deaf. While my twice-removed aunt probably heard my order in New Delhi, it did not seem to register with anyone at DD. It was possible that everyone there was hard of hearing, considering the blaring Christian rock. The laminated posters of little blond girls with pigtails, plaid skirts, and knee-highs petting unicorns didn't help. It was a moment I'd never quite envisioned for myself.

Adding to the ambience were two kids behind me. Both in Liberty Bell hats and hemmed jeans shorts.

"I'm going to have a Boston crème," Tween 1 announced.

"But you're in Philadelphia . . . NOT Boston!" Tween 2 replied.

The laugh track came from their parents, who were wearing his-and-hers blue T-shirts. His read: "Abigail Adams was here." Hers said: "John Adams was here." The words were embossed on their heaving chests in red, white, and blue. The thought of getting felt up by Abigail and John Adams was more disgusting than imagining your grandparents doing it. *No mas café.*

Outside DD, a particularly kind heroin addict, who didn't stare at my hair, was serving as doorman that day. Maybe she didn't stare because her eyes were rolling to the back of her head. According to the *Philadelphia Chronicle,* Philly was the new Seattle. The heroin here was cheaper and purer than anywhere else in the country. This impressive fact translated into a pack of addicts swarming around the courthouse, begging for money. Some of their best work went down at the Dunkin' Donuts, where throngs of emaciated skeletons would fight over who got to open and close the door for a dime. The blond girl, who couldn't have been older than fifteen, kindly opened the door. I gave her my coffee cash and proceeded on my merry way. Aside from the fact that I could have sworn I spotted her liver, lungs, and pelvic bone through her thin skin, it was a rather pleasant exchange, especially considering how feverish I felt when I turned and spotted the courthouse.

The words "JUSTICE FOR AL" that wrapped around the top of the building didn't help. Considering the corner of junkies and my own dim fate, "Al" was indeed the only one getting any justice.

"Good morning, missy!!" With my myriad ailments, I'd barely noticed Duane, the tight-polyester-panted man who stood in front of the courthouse every morning, smiling and waving uncontrollably.

"Good morning to you, too," I replied, smiling. It was important to pacify Duane. After September 11, the powers that be decided to add him as the first line of defense against terrorism. Everyone in Philly was obsessed with being the next target. The fear was that the Liberty Bell would be taken out. With all the beautiful old churches and museums in Philadelphia, I couldn't figure out why the bell got so many accolades. Replacing that thing with a tree, a memorial, a trash can wouldn't be the worst thing in the world. But I kept that to myself. It would have been grossly unpatriotic to speak of it. And everyone knew what became of grossly unpatriotic brown people—Guantánamo.

In any event, Duane didn't seem like the obvious choice for a top counter-terrorism mission. The guy was so busy checking out every woman's legs that he'd probably let me bring in a nuke, provided I was wearing a skirt.

After getting the twice-over, I courageously proceeded to "security," a process which made the Dunkin' Donuts–Duane one-two punch seem like a day at Canyon Ranch. Reluctantly, I placed my cell phone in a crusty plastic box and then onto the rickety conveyor belt. Cringing through the metal detectors, the chanting predictably began.

"Phone in the bucket. Phone in the bucket. Phone in the bucket!"

What did that mean anyway? Why did they say it repeatedly? Most important, why were a dozen people involved? Not to mention, all the screaming drew presumably unwanted attention to their most unusual uniforms: clip-on bow ties (for women also), pleated pants, which created the illusion of pregnancy (for men also), and some form of facial hair (especially for the women). After everyone in the tristate area was made aware that there was some phone in some bucket somewhere, I flashed my ID card and retrieved my offending phone.

Which brings me to my ID card. Tragic. I just couldn't understand how I—a watered-down version of Indira Gandhi—managed to look like a battered Janet Reno in the picture. I looked like an old white woman with gigantism, a bowl haircut, and yellow teeth. Particularly mysterious for a short, long-haired South Asian. As if that weren't enough, the chanters wouldn't give it a rest.

"She's got the red phone! She's got it!" A female guard looked at me with pity after studying my picture. Being pitied by a woman with a bow tie and mustache had to be the dictionary definition of rock bottom. Thankfully, she lost interest in me the second she had the chance to belittle someone. "No red phone. Check it, kiddo," she growled at the district court clerk behind me. Self-esteem restored. The red phone signaled an individual's right to bring a mobile phone into the courthouse. All judges enjoyed this right. So, too, law clerks to court of appeals judges. All other court staff, including district court law clerks, were required to check their phones with security. Lucky for me, I was an accomplished appellate law clerk, which, according to the government, meant that I was less likely than my district court comrade to blow up the building.

By the time I approached the elevator, I was exhausted and it wasn't even 8 AM. Now it was time for the elevators. While seemingly innocuous, they presented their own set of problems. The courthouse elevators represented everything that was wrong with the current state of American conversation.

My first week of work had thus far provided the following breakdown, and I had a feeling it wasn't an anomaly:

Monday: one overweight black lady; one underweight white guy, bad teeth; one Indian Janet Reno. Bad everything. "Howwasyourweekendtooshort," the lady said to the elevator wall. Guy: "Aren't they always." Reno: Nothing.

Tuesday: similar racial, gender, aesthetic breakdown. "When's the sun gonna come out? We've just had the worst summer!" "I just don't know. Never saw a summer like this one." Reno: Nothing.

Wednesday: See Tuesday + "isitalmosttheweekendyet?" Reno: Nothing.

Thursday: See Wednesday + "It's supposed to rain Saturday morning but then get nice for a few hours Saturday afternoon, and then rain Saturday night and then Sunday is a wash but for maybe one hour in the afternoon. And—it's *almost* Friday!" Reno: Twitched.

I dreaded the elevators as much, if not more, than the guards. The only saving grace was that the judges had separate, but unequal, elevators. As I battled the chanting phoniacs and engaged in meteorological banter about how Wednesday was not Friday and Monday was actually Monday but it was almost Friday on Thursday, the judges parked their luxury cars in a private underground garage and rode a private elevator straight to their respective chambers. This contemporary *Plessy v. Ferguson* regime proved ineffective, as the craziest person in that place was a certain robed rascal who wouldn't hesitate blowing up anybody who failed to give her due respect.

Reluctantly, I hopped the 'vator for the masses along with two girls around the same age as me—clerks, I surmised—and one woman who looked like she'd just swallowed some nails for breakfast—plaintiff's attorney, definitely. It didn't seem like anyone knew anyone else. Maybe I'd be spared. Wrong again. Plaintiff's attorney turned to me—gasp!—"Thank God it's Friday." DING! Thirteenth floor.

And there I was. The early battles of the morning had obfuscated the grander war I'd be facing that day. Laura had quit and the judge didn't know yet.

Entering the clerk's cave, I remembered happily that the new clerks would be there. Medieval Roy had already guided them to their respective cubicles, both of which were in the very back of chambers—farther away from the judge's office and out of her immediate sight. I'd been geographically screwed. I put down my purse and glanced behind at Laura's cubicle. Empty. Chair meticulously tucked under desk. Computer off. Multicolored case carefully closed and neatly stacked. You wouldn't have even known she'd been there but for the one that got away—a plastic Twinkies wrapper. I had to hand it to Laura, the wrapper was a clever and final fuck you.

Maybe Laura had more chutzpah than I'd thought. But I'd spent enough valuable moments thinking about Laura and couldn't spare any more. Laura had made her bed and shoved me and the new clerks into it. We'd be paying for her "sins." Speaking of which, I had to warn—never mind introduce myself to—Matthew and Evan.

I hurried to the back. To my left was a visibly confused guy who was staring at his blank computer screen, unopened case on his desk. Nostalgia. He reminded me of myself five days earlier. Hearing my footsteps, he looked up immediately and stood, revealing the first pair of flat-front pants I'd seen on a guy in the courthouse. His bluish green eyes sparkled a tad when he extended his hand.

"Hey, I'm Matthew. I take it you're either Sheila or Laura?" He smiled, revealing a small dimple in his right cheek and, more important, perfectly sized teeth. My mother had always warned against men with small teeth ("not to be trusted, those men"). As for big teeth, they were unsavory for obvious aesthetic reasons.

"I'm Sheila. And as for Laura, you should know that she quit. But the judge doesn't know yet. And won't know until she reads the letter Laura left for her. So, just beware. And, don't tell Roy or Janet. Let's just see what happens." I turned to my right, toward a guy I assumed was Evan. I was momentarily paralyzed as I'd not expected an African American. I had yet to spot a black law clerk around the courthouse (in fact, out of the three black law students in my class at Columbia, none had received clerkships).

Judge Friedman deserved some respect for hiring not one, but two, minority law clerks. Evan didn't look up. Instead, he sat perfectly straight, arms bent, holding a blue brief close to his horn-rimmed glasses. He had been there for all of three minutes and was not only working but actually seemed engrossed in his case. He must have heard my conversation with Matthew, which had taken place about six feet away from him. Just in case he didn't, I parked myself over his desk. He didn't move, didn't even flinch.

"Hi. I'm Sheila. [Pause.] Nice to meet you. [Pause.] Laura quit. [Long pause.]" Evan barely looked up, evidently unconcerned. No hello. No nice to meet you. No nothing. Eyes remained focused on prized brief. His loss. That legal eagle was about to get shot down and he didn't seem to care.

Three clerks. Three strangers. Same fate.

DING! Thirteenth floor, going down.

"That's her," I whispered to nobody in particular. I rushed back to my cubicle, flung myself into my chair, and started staring. I heard someone breathing heavily behind me. Matthew had crept up behind me, just out of sight of the torture chamber.

"What's going on?" He whispered.

"SHHHHHAAYYYLLLLLAAAA, get in here and bring Mike and Esther!!!!!!"

I jumped, practically knocking Matthew over. "Just don't say anything. She wants us in there." I pointed toward the torture chamber. His concern transformed to obvious fear. I touched Matthew's arm and continued: "It'll be fine. Just don't say anything. Wait here." I ran back to retrieve Evan, who was still sitting and reading like a gnome. I couldn't tell if he had progressed or was staring at the same page from before.

"Evan, she wants to see us," I explained. He looked up sheepishly but wasn't budging. Desperate times called for desperate measures. I leaned over, grabbed his arm, yanked the blue brief from his grasp, and pulled him up.

"Come with me," I insisted, prying him from his chair. Collecting Matthew along the way, we scurried past Medieval Roy and Janet, who had bowed their heads and stopped breathing. No wonder Roy preferred twelfth-century Ireland. A more innocent time and place.

"SHEEEEBBBAA!!!"

We were standing shoulder to shoulder in the torture chamber before she could even finish slaughtering my name for the second time in less than a minute. The judge approached. The intrepid investigator. The glaring began. Up, down, left, right, and then again. This whodunit charade was particularly aggravating because our short Sherlock Holmes was herself holding the smoking gun, which, incidentally, contained a signed confession by the culprit, who was definitely not in the lineup at that moment.

Incredibly, though, today wasn't about Laura. Instead, it was about the three clerks whose only crime was showing up for work on time. With letter in hand, the judge dragged all twenty inches of herself and her lengthier leg toward me and parked it.

"Sheila!" Did she have any other words in her repertoire?

"What do you know about this?!" She shoved the letter, which I could have sworn was actually steaming, in my face.

"Ummm. Ahhh—"

"DO YOU THINK I'M A—" she was searching the letter for Laura's exact words—a HOSTILE BITCH?!"

Wow. Did Laura actually say that? The judge stood staring. Waiting. Oh no, she actually wanted an answer.

Am I a hostile bitch? Yes? Maybe? Was I under oath? Could I lie to a federal judge? To spare my life. Definitely.

"No," I perjured myself softly. But it wasn't a lie technically. "Crazy" seemed more accurate. It didn't matter; my answer wasn't good enough.

The judge stood there, inches away from me, glaring. Tail in air. Bun twitching. It appeared that her bouffant twitched when angry. Left, right, left, right. A true marvel. Thankfully, as I became engrossed in her epileptic hair, she lost interest in me. She turned to Evan.

"Which one of you two is Esther?" Did she not notice that there wasn't another woman in the room? I gave Evan a little nudge. Nothing. He couldn't move. He couldn't speak. I bet Evan had plenty to say in Con Law, Evidence, and Torts. But now, he didn't have the nerve to tell his boss that he wasn't a lady.

"Excuse me, ma'am, I'm Matthew," Matthew said in a way you could tell he'd said a million times before.

"*What* did you call me?" she slowly turned, eyes burning in Matthew's direction.

"Um . . . mm . . . mmmm?"

"I am not a m-a-a-m," she slowly enunciated, so utterly offended it was as if Matthew had just called her a c-u-n-t. "I am a *federal judge*. I do *not* see an *m* anywhere in *judge*. I am Judge. Judge. Judge. It is *that* simple."

Matthew stared, speechless. It was clearly the first time *ma'am* had gotten him into a pickle.

"Are you too stupid to comprehend that?!"—she stepped back before continuing—"Well, it turns out that *you* people have lost a coclerk." Brilliant. Within a minute, she'd made Laura's defection a reflection on us and not her. "I should have expected this. Chicago is barely a top-five school. I did her a favor." She was pacing back and forth in front of us, like a military commander in front of the rank and file. "Not to mention the fact that I normally like the gays. But not this one."

Did an allegedly liberal federal judge just say that out loud?

"I *know* the three of you will never speak of this to anyone. You will have another coclerk by day's end. I have thousands of people who want to work for me," she sneered, seizing bun coming to a rest. Ego restored. "But then again, you all know that. You're here, aren't you?" With that, she smiled, turned, and returned to her desk. We just stood there, like mute morons. "Get out! And shut the door behind you, Esther." Evan practically sprinted out, Matthew not far behind. I followed, gently shutting the door behind me.

The whole episode lasted about three minutes. In that time, Janet and Roy hadn't moved an inch. Were they human? At that moment, I didn't really care. I needed to take a load off and call my parents, my friends, Puja. Never before had I been falsely accused of a crime in a court of martial law. I took a long, deep breath, sat, and reached for the phone before remembering that I wasn't allowed to. Heartbroken, I reluctantly replaced the receiver.

Midday, the judge surreptitiously called Matthew and ordered him to move to Laura's cubicle immediately. That way it was as if he had been there all along. But for that call, I would've thought the judge dead. Her door remained closed all day. Even so, nobody dared speak or move. Nobody went to lunch. Hell, nobody went to the bathroom.

Then at 5:30, the judge emerged, walked into the clerk's cave and announced to nobody in particular: "Kate is starting during the September sitting. She's from the staff attorney's office. She's Jewish." Then, just as quickly, she turned and walked out.

DING! Thirteenth floor, going down.

I took a deep breath but had to wait to exhale. Roy was before me.

"Dude, what's goin' on?" He nervously smiled and ran his chapped hands through his tame mullet. Its serenity somehow made him look at once scared and homicidal.

"Not much, Roy." What else could I say?

"Hey, Roy, how are you?" Matthew asked, having just walked over. The question curiously stumped Roy. He startled cackling like a hyena and swaying back and forth. The effect was a bit troubling.

"Man"—back, forth, cackle—"she's just such a bitch. Today, she told me my xeroxing was bad again," he sniveled, waiting for the pity party to get rocking. He'd have to get jiggy elsewhere.

The judge had just convicted us of crimes committed by another—and in Matthew's case, on his first day—and Roy was complaining to *us* that she criticized *him?* I didn't have anything nice to say so I opted to not say anything at all.

"That sucks," Matthew managed.

That's all it took to whisk Roy back in time.

"Dude, I can't wait until this weekend. It's gonna rock. I'm training for the Battle of Hastings, which is incredible. Hey you ought to come watch! It's in three weeks. And then on Sunday, we're working at the Great Medieval Yard Sale." That one silenced polite Matthew. Thankfully, Roy took a hint, giggled, and walked out. Matthew shot me a questioning look. I nodded, assuring him that, indeed, the whole episode had actually happened.

Moments after Roy blessed us with his disappearing act, Janet appeared. I felt like a hungover priest trapped in the confessional box. I wanted them all to go away.

"Did Laura *really* quit?" Janet was strangely excited.

I nodded. I couldn't believe that she had to ask. Maybe she had actually been dead all day. It didn't matter; Janet had definitely come alive.

"WOW!!! That's a record. Five days!" she said, clapping ecstatically.

"Others have quit?" I was confused. I'd never heard of a law clerk quitting, let alone one of Judge Friedman's. Janet sneered, clearly enjoying her newfound power of information.

"Yeah, what's wrong with you! Usually, every five years or so someone quits. I don't know why you people continue coming here. I just don't feel sorry for you." I wanted to tell Janet that we had something in common, namely that I didn't feel sorry for her, either. I couldn't feel sorry for anyone at the moment. I was too busy drowning in her breaking news.

The judge had driven half a dozen clerks to quit over the years and it had remained a well-kept, dirty little secret. The files in Columbia Law's Clerkship Center were filled with pages of adoring testimony from her former clerks, who had "learned so much" from Judge Friedman, "couldn't have asked for a better experience," and "loved and respected" the judge.

But maybe the judge deserved the respect she bestowed upon herself. I didn't know many people who could snap their fingers and make people disappear, and Judge Friedman did just that. After that day, it was as though Laura "the gay" had never existed at all.

Like a scene from a movie that went straight to video, a poodle licked my leg on the way home. It was ninety-five degrees outside. Hot, sweaty, sad, dog saliva drenching hairy leg. I looked up. Owner looked proud. And looked just like her dog. I dragged myself into my apartment, almost tripping on what I figured was a shoe. It was a mouse. At that point, I felt so beaten down, I didn't even bother cursing. Instead, I just crawled into bed. It was 7 PM on Friday night and I was under the covers, fully dressed. I had clerked for exactly one week. All I wanted to do was stay in bed until Monday morning—or, better yet, until the end of the year—but I couldn't.

Brian had forwarded me an invitation to "Clerks in the Commonwealth: Let's Get (Il)Legal!" It was the first organized clerks' happy hour, and I hadn't even made the first cut. Apparently the cool clerks who whipped up the plans didn't consider me to be one of them. Brian had generously sent it along and I'd agreed to go in thirty seconds flat hoping the faster I RSVP'd yes, the faster I could forget I hadn't really even been invited. So, instead of sleeping for about a hundred hours straight, I had to whoop it up with a pack of law clerks who didn't even want me there.

The only saving grace was that James had moved into an apartment in my building that very day. James was clerking for a district court judge in Camden. He got to take a week off after the bar exam and before the start of his clerkship, so he'd been in East Hampton with some of our law school friends the past few days before heading to Philly.

It was 9:04 PM when James came knocking. Judging from the amount of drool spilling over my pillow, you'd have thought I'd been asleep for weeks. Or that my tongue had been surgically removed. With his tan and new designer jeans, James didn't look like he'd spent the day unpacking. But the guy was still too skinny for his own good. James and I had been seated next to each other in Torts on day one at Columbia. Aside from one drunken indiscretion after our Property final, we'd maintained a strictly platonic relationship, since we both admitted that said indiscretion felt dangerously close to incest.

"Hey there." He smiled, shoving a bottle of pinot noir in my face. I grabbed it and led him into my sparse living room. Thanks to my paltry salary, the only furniture I had was the yellow couch and an old IKEA coffee table, which had too many scratches and a few screws loose. This, of course, further separated me from my friends who'd gone straight to law firms where they were getting paid in six digits, had five weeks of vacation, and free gym memberships. It was tough to recall why I'd secretly considered them the unlucky ones.

"Welcome to Philadelphia!" I tried to sound exactly the opposite of how I looked and felt. He didn't buy it.

"What's up, Sheila? No offense, but you look terrible."

"Um. Well, thank you. And if you must know, my coclerk quit and the judge just about ripped my head off today. Oh, and I didn't tell you this earlier, but I didn't even make the first-round cut for this bar thing tonight. Brian—you remember, from Fed Courts—had to forward me the invite. So, we're your basic party crashers."

"You mean she quit—as in the clerkship? She actually quit the clerkship? I didn't know people did *that*." James's eyes bulged.

"Well apparently they do do that and one in particular already *did* do *that*."

"Oh my God. I mean—"

"James, it's done. I don't really want to talk about it right now. Can you please open that bottle? I'll make myself look unterrible and we can head to this *fantastic* place."

An hour later, the two of us were standing outside of Rouge, Rittenhouse Square's premier hot spot. A thick red velvet rope separated James and me from the legions of law clerks we could see inside.

"Nope, not on the list," the bouncer announced gleefully. This wasn't good. Sure, I'd been turned away from hot New York nightclubs in my

day, but this was a restaurant-cum-bar in Pennsylvania. As we were about
to split, Brian came stumbling out, fedora clinging on for dear life, half
a glass of red wine in one hand, blond coed in the other. The girl couldn't
have been more than twenty-two years old.

"Sheila. James—what's up, man!" Brian high-fived James and lunged
toward me for a hug but instead nicked my left breast. The humiliation
wouldn't stop. "This is Robin." He smiled, revealing fierce merlot-stained
teeth. "She's a junior at Penn." No way. Some sorority girl was going to
bed Brian, with his red teeth and all. Maybe this law clerk thing was an
amazing rap after all. Brian turned to the bouncer: "Dude, they're totally
cool." The bouncer nodded at Brian, and in an instant the red rope had
parted. We'd arrived. Never mind it was on account of Brian, who'd apparently gained ownership of the town in a few short days.

Inside were dozens, hundreds, what felt like thousands of really smart-
looking people smiling, laughing, and patting one another on the back. I
recognized a few from around the courthouse but nobody seemed to have
a clue who I was. How were all of these law clerks already friends?

Brian returned sans coed, who'd presumably come to her senses. He
beelined to me and James.

"Man, who are you clerking for?" he asked James with what's-
the-meaning-of-life-style intensity. James glanced at me, clearly a bit
unnerved.

"Um, I'm clerking for Judge Harris in Camden. How are you liking—?"

"*I* am clerking for Judge Fleck"—big smile, pause for accolades—"and
Harris? Isn't he a *district* court judge?"

Oh no. James's district court status was about to get us ditched. I should
have been happy. Instead, I pathetically tried to keep Brian's attention.

"So, how do you know everyone here?" I pointed around the bar.

"Well, we all went to the Judicial Clerk Institute out at Pepperdine. It
was totally awesome," he bragged. "And frankly, I'm surprised not every
law clerk was required to go. Judge Fleck, for one, paid for each of his law

clerks to attend. And frankly, I don't know how you guys will even do in chambers without the institute. We learned a ton. Now if you'll excuse me. I see someone I summered with at the ACLU." And he was off.

Boring someone like Brian was upsetting to begin with. *Frankly,* the institute was overkill. I couldn't bear to be the law clerk failure, as Brian had insinuated. I had to get in with the instituters. Maybe I'd use my ACLU connection with Brian the next time I got his ear.

"Are you kidding me? I can't believe that he actually became a bigger loser *after* law school," James complained. "And as for that clerk camp, I can't think of anything lamer than summer camp for law clerks." He downed his vodka and got another. I, on the other hand, was stuck on our horrific social status and couldn't shake the camp thing.

"James, I really think we're not a hit here. This is bad. Nobody seems to have any interest in us and they all seem to be friends and maybe the camp was a bad time, but I think we're totally effed for not having gone. Aren't you worried at all?" I beckoned for a little camaraderie.

"I'm only worried that Brian may have scored the only cute girl here. Present company excluded of course. And I was really hoping to get some action my first night in town." He scanned the room. Perspective restored. James wasn't one to get sucked into the legal caste system. For obvious reasons, caste systems were tougher for us Indians to avoid.

The two of us vowed to make some friends. There was a group of about eight clerks who appeared to be more laid-back than the rest. We approached them. I awkwardly squeezed my way in between a redheaded girl who looked my age and a tall, brown-haired guy.

"Hello. My name is Sheila," I said and smiled, attempting an air of sophistication while sipping from my straw. He looked confused. "Oh, right. Right. I clerk for Judge Friedman and went to Columbia," I clarified.

"No j'est pauz blah blah blah franch franch franch."

Turned out they were Parisian college students on a field trip to Philly. While James practiced his French on a seemingly prepubescent girl (and we wondered why the French hated Americans), I plowed ahead, feeling a bit looser from the vodka.

"Hey guys, are you clerks?" I blanketly asked one group, wincing. My pickup line horrified even me. The Frenchies scorned in my direction. Or in James's, since he'd meekly slunk next to me after getting hosed by Le Cindy Brady. A guy in a V-neck T-shirt was kind enough to respond.

"Uh. Yes. We're all law clerks. Why? Are *you?*" he demanded, wrinkling his mouth in perplexity. I was beginning to feel like I had toilet paper coming out of my pants.

"Yes, my name is Sheila. And this is James. We're both clerking." V-neck looked even more confused and gave his posse a knowing look.

"Well, neither of you looks familiar at all." The posse nodded in agreement.

"We didn't go to the Clerk Institute," I ventured.

"Oh. *Yale* really encourages us to go," a girl in the group quickly answered and then they all turned their backs to James and me, returning to what must have been a very important conversation.

We were zero for zero. Right as I was about to give up, I spotted a lone ranger in the corner, nursing a scotch. I dragged James over.

"Hey. We're clerks. Are you?" Jeez.

"Yeah. I am. But don't ask me where I went to law school, because it sucks and then you won't want to talk to me." James and I chuckled.

"Well, it couldn't be worse than not going to this clerk camp thing," James offered, and I nodded in agreement. Our would-be friend smiled.

"Hey. I'm Kevin. I didn't go to clerk camp. I did go to Rutgers."

The 12-step plan for Clerks Coming Clean.

"Hi. I'm Sheila. I didn't go to clerk camp. I did go to Columbia."

"I'm James and ditto as to the rest of what Sheila said." James bought the three of us another round. Kevin was our new best friend. Upon closer inspection, he was also gay, which was my evening's first victory. What kind of self-respecting woman could live in the gayborhood without a gay sidekick? Not to mention, the years had taught me that unless you got fat and/or unfashionable, your gay male friends would stand by you, whereas boyfriends always left you in the lurch.

Kevin had a boyfriend ("but we can see other people"), had gone to Chapel Hill undergrad ("but only because I was in state"), then moved to New York and tried modeling ("but only because I didn't know *what* to do"), before finally heading to Rutgers Law ("but only because they gave me money"). The only thing separating a man with compulsive caveats from one with suicidal tendencies was a healthy ego. And Kevin clearly had one of those, as evidenced by his two-year attempted modeling stint (Kevin did not look like a model).

Kevin lived near James and me. He moved there because it was the gayborhood. I moved there because it was cheap and cute. James moved there because he was lazy and I found him a place. We were a natural trio. So much so that we didn't even broach the subject of our particular judges until two drinks later. As it turned out, Kevin was clerking for Judge Adams.

"Yeah, Adams is pretty cool from what I can tell so far, but holy shit— my coclerk Jana is *terrible.* On our first day, she sauntered over to me and said, and I quote, 'I was on the *Virginia Law Review,* so if you need help— you know—with anything, just ask. You know, I don't know about *Rutgers'*"—Kevin imitated—"I mean, *Virginia,* big fuckin' deal. *You know,* it's not like she went to Stanford. Puh-leez!" I loved it. Even as he complained about the hierarchy, he reinforced it.

"Well, at least Jana didn't quit already. My coclerk just *quit.* She left a hate letter for my judge." Admittedly it was a desperate attempt to one-up Kevin. It worked.

"What?! I didn't know people quit clerkships! Are you for real!" Kevin looked genuinely shocked. But I was beginning to think he always looked that way. "But I have to say, I have heard that Friedman can be pretty bitchy."

Before I could respond, a twiggy brunette, who appeared to have jacked the Banana Republic next door, came over.

"Hey, Kevin. Aren't you going to introduce me to your friend?" she said, coyly smiling at James while smoothing her tweed lapel.

"Hey, Jana," Kevin flatly stated, with a faint sigh of exasperation. "This is James. And this is Sheila. Sheila. James. This is Jana. My coclerk." I smiled, about to speak, but Jana quickly turned her back to me, focusing on her prey.

"So, James, wherever did you come from?"

"Rochester."

"You mean you went to Rochester Law?" She was crestfallen.

"No. I'm from Rochester. You asked me where I was from," James explained matter-of-factly.

"Oh. Well. Where did you go to *law school?*" she implored impatiently.

"Columbia. I went to Columbia Law."

Jana looked like she was about to wet her pants with glee. "Wow. That's great. You know, I went to Virginia"—she smiled widely—"and I was on the *Law Review* there." James nodded. I looked at Kevin, who'd lost his personality.

"That's great. Did you like Virginia?" I cut in, attempting to insert myself. Jana turned, barely, in my direction, obviously annoyed that I was interrupting what she deemed to be a private conversation.

"It was great. It's *Virginia*. What's not to like!" she sneered before returning to James. I returned to Kevin, hoping to resurrect him. We headed back to the bar.

"Wow. You've got quite a year ahead of you with that one!" I said. "Hey, Kevin, want to share a cab back to the hood?"

He nodded. James decided to stay, curiously engrossed in conversation with Jana. Men never ceased to amaze me in terms of what they would endure to get laid. Then again, I couldn't really blame him. I'd probably recite the Bill of Rights to Sanjay if it meant sex in return. It'd been ages since

Sanjay and I had done *it*. With his rotation schedule, we saw each other once a month, if that. And even then, Sanjay was often "too tired."

I was about to get off at my apartment building when Kevin suggested the infamous "final final." You know, the last drink that sounds like a terrific idea at the time and a terrible one the next morning. We parked it at Tryst, a gritty neighborhood joint with cracked maroon pleather booths.

"So, what's your story, Sheila? Where are you from, et cetera?" Kevin asked earnestly.

"Well, I'm from Reston, Virginia. Went to Michigan undergrad. Worked in Miami as a television news producer before heading to New York for law school. That's it. In a nutshell."

The sign of the aging twenty-something was having lived in about five cities, with about three different jobs, and being able to explain it all in about forty-five seconds. Kevin nodded.

"So why did you leave TV? It seems so much more interesting than law."

Severe grass-is-greener syndrome—another sign.

"TV news was much more entertaining than the law for sure. It's just that it felt incredibly shallow. Leading newscasts with 'South Florida: It's Always Bikini Season' somehow left me feeling dirty and depressed. And I felt like it was so reactionary. We were always chasing after something that had already happened. I actually felt pretty powerless . . . but then again, I feel pretty powerless now."

It was as though I hadn't spoken in years, the quickness with which the words came spilling out. And wow, I'd never quite articulated that before. I'd left a coveted job as a news producer in Miami for this. Perhaps the law wasn't quite as reactionary, but hell, I'd take a nuclear reaction at this point if I could trade in the loneliness and insecurity brought on by patronizing pedigree whores. At least the other journalists, including my former bosses, never sat around talking about where they went to college and what honor societies they'd been (or not been) in.

Had I made a colossal, life-destroying mistake? Kevin had just passed out sitting up. Definitely yes, in terms of the final final.

One meatball sub and a particularly sad Celine Dion song later, I was sound asleep on top of the covers, tomato sauce smeared on the pillow.

Chapter Five

Peter Nussbaum had JFK Junior's looks, Einstein's brains, and Mother Teresa's spirit—a chiseled, philanthropic wunderkind. At least that's what the commonwealth of Pennsylvania would have had you believe. The deputy attorney general ("AG") painted such a glorious picture of the guy, you'd think that had he not been gunned down, Peter Nussbaum would probably be a senator, if not the president or the pope, by now. His death was tragic and premature, no doubt. Then again, wasn't death always those things? I, for one, had never heard someone say: "She died not a moment too soon and it was downright joyous."

Maybe it was because Peter was a young, attractive, Ivy League student that his death seemed particularly tragic. Also, because he had been shot at such close range, you could imagine the terror preceding his untimely demise. Nobody deserved that. By the time his body was discovered by a little kid who'd strayed from the housing development's playground, pigeons and rats had already feasted. I had to hand it to the deputy AG—he was a master of the macabre, inserting ghastly, gripping (and legally inconsequential) details wherever possible. It served him well, since twenty pages into the state's brief, I experienced a visceral reaction and yearned to throw the book at the demon who'd done such a thing to poor, defenseless, gorgeous Peter Nussbaum. But the death penalty?

As a philosophical matter, I was firmly against capital punishment. The government should never have the power to take a human being's life. Yet as a law clerk, it was my job to advise Judge Friedman how to decide cases after interpreting the facts within the confines of the law. The Pennsylvania State Legislature had passed a statute allowing for the death penalty and therefore my philosophical views had no place.

That said, it seemed that Dell Nelson, the defendant, had received a bum deal. It was true he was no saint. Dell was a famed drug dealer at Arch Homes, the public housing development where Peter's body was discovered. He was the go-to guy for anything—speed, heroin, crack, cocaine. You name it, he had it. But he wasn't the kind of drug dealer you saw in the movies. According to neighbors, he was the classic nice guy. Soft-spoken, quick to laugh, generous to a fault ("You needed to borrow a couple bucks for some diapers or somethin', Dell was your man"). Apparently, the only thing that agitated Dell was when people messed with his sisters or grandmother ("He punched one motherfucker in the face after he called little Izzie a slut").

A week after Peter's death, Dell Nelson was arrested outside of his apartment, after having returned from a trip to the grocery store. His arrest came amid a media feeding frenzy. It was a victory for the University of Pennsylvania's president, dean, and provost, as well as for the Philadelphia police chief, the mayor, and the governor of Pennsylvania, all of whom had "vow[ed]" to catch the killer.

A jury convicted Dell Nelson of aggravated murder and sentenced him to death. During the trial, it was revealed that Peter Nussbaum had raped Dell's sister Izzie, a fact the district attorney used to establish motive. A clerk at the liquor store around the corner from Arch Homes testified: "When I was lockin' up one night a week before the shootin', I heard Dell say to that boy, 'You touch my sister again, and I'm going to kill you.'" Blatant hearsay, but Dell's lawyer never objected, and consequently the jury considered it to be direct evidence of guilt. It didn't help the defense that

Peter owed Dell a considerable sum of money. Even though Peter's family owned Tartac, the country's most profitable tar company, Peter never seemed to have enough money to subsidize his formidable crack habit.

Dell's murder trial lasted two days, shorter than most misdemeanor trials. Throughout much of it, Tip Evans, Dell's middle-aged public defender, slept. He failed to deliver a closing argument, and during the sentencing phase of the trial, Tip did not present an iota of mitigation evidence. Mitigation evidence is offered in death penalty cases to spare the defendant's life. Peter's rape of Dell's sister, Peter's constant pestering of Dell for drugs, and the fact that Dell had lost his parents at the age of ten (his mother to heroin, his father to jail), forcing him to drop out of school and raise his sisters, would have served as effective mitigation. So, too, the pages and pages of glowing commentary about Dell's character by his neighbors, family, and friends. Tip Evans didn't mention a word of it, effectively leading Dell to the electric chair. It was this inaction that Dell was appealing now. Question presented: Was Dell Nelson deprived of his Sixth Amendment right to counsel when his lawyer, Tip Evans, failed to present mitigating evidence, failed to cross-examine a witness for the prosecution, and waived final argument during sentencing?"

The Pennsylvania Supreme Court affirmed Dell's conviction and sentence. So did the federal district court, finding that Tip Evans's actions (or lack thereof) were not egregious enough to be considered ineffective for constitutional purposes.

Dell, now thirty-six years old, appealed to the third circuit, and that's where I came into the picture. Our panel—Judges Friedman, Adams, and Stevens—had the power to decide that, as a matter of law, Dell Nelson had been denied his constitutional rights. If so decided, he'd be granted a resentencing with his new lawyer. If not, the guy would be dead within a matter of months, maybe a year. The court of appeals was his last real hope, since the Supreme Court rarely heard death penalty cases.

Putting down the state's brief, I felt dizzy. This was real. A real person's life hung in the balance. So, too, justice for a dead man. Until now, it'd never occurred to me just how difficult it was to be a judge. On TV, in the movies, and even in law school, with scant appearances of reality, such decisions seemed easy, obvious almost. That was hardly the case here. With newfound respect, I glanced over at Judge Friedman, who was sitting upright, glaring in my direction.

I smiled. Nothing. I waved. Nothing. I couldn't be bothered; I was actually engrossed in my work. No sooner had I reopened the state's brief then Judge Friedman appeared in my cubicle, sunglasses gliding down her nose, bags in hand.

"You're rilly rilly taking a long time on this case, Sheera." The snickering was a dead giveaway that she wasn't referring to my thoroughness.

"Um, it's a death penalty case, Judge Friedman, and there are about a dozen briefs here, so—"

"I am a federal judge and do not have time for you to reflect on every word of every brief. If you didn't realize it, this is not your only case for our sitting. So, I suggest that you work on your reading skills, something I would have thought a law school graduate would have mastered."

"Um, OK, but—"

"But nothing. I want that bench memo by the end of the week," she demanded before scurrying to the elevator.

I'd barely gotten through the two main briefs and had yet to touch any of the amicus briefs, which were written by outside groups with an interest in the case. Not to mention, I hadn't started the copious legal research a case like this warranted.

"Hey, don't worry about that. You're doing fine, I'm sure of it."

I spun around, shocked to hear Matthew's voice. He was halfway out the door before I could thank him for his kind words. I grabbed three of the briefs, my purse, and headed home.

As I turned the corner, just a block from my apartment, a tall, emaciated Asian man with pockmarks and a greasy combover sauntered over to me. He wore pinstriped denim overalls with no shirt underneath, giving the illusion that his shoulders were a hanger.

"Want anything?" he demanded. Kind of a general question, I thought. "Um . . . not really. Thanks." Nothing. Just stares. What was with all the staring in this town?! Unable to deal with the uncomfortable silence, I plodded forward. "Well, maybe I'd want to move out of Philly and back to New York."

"You know, Philly is the fifth-largest city in the country! Five. Number five!!" Aside from his screaming louder than the security guards, his actual words were curious considering that in the short time I'd been there, and every Tom, Dick, and John Adams had rattled off this most mediocre statistic to me. This guy was the third person to brag about it. *See also:* Pam from membership at the Liberty Gym and unnamed taxi driver from undetermined Eastern European country.

"What does fifth-largest mean anyway and why is everyone obsessed by this fact? I mean, what's the big deal?" No deal for me. He'd lost interest, ditched me on the stoop, and approached a middle-aged man in a silver Mercedes SUV stopped at the red light in front of us. Getting blown off by a homeless man seemed par for the course.

I walked into my apartment, threw my purse on the floor, and nestled into my couch. It was at times like these that I wished I had a TV. The one I had in New York had belonged to my roommate, Jill, and I didn't have enough money to buy one for myself.

Well, you know what they say: If you don't have a television, get yourself a meatball. I grabbed what was left of Sunday night's dinner (take-out foot-long sub).

"What are you looking at?" I sneered at my fridge. It was literally looking at me and I at it, each disgusted by the other. The thing was nasty. In fact, my whole apartment was nasty. I'd just moved in and already my place was a sty. I hadn't cleaned a thing, hadn't bothered to take out the trash. Now I was arguing with my kitchen. I really needed human interaction. Sanjay had been with patients all day and Puja in meetings. Unfortunately, James hadn't gotten home from his first day of work and I didn't know Kevin well enough for a bitch fest.

"What am I going to do?" I said out loud, madly wagging my finger to nobody. "There's no way I'm going to finish this memo on time." I first noticed that I was saying things out loud to myself last Wednesday, when I was in the bathroom at work. "Lilac. My favorite," I'd muttered to the soap dispenser. Had I just say that out loud? I had. For a minute, it scared me. Was I going crazy? Was I already crazy? But I succumbed to the sink, toilet, and trash can after Laura alerted me to her exit strategy. I surmised that Nelson Mandela had done his fair share of talking to objects while in jail, and he went on to become president of South Africa. Perhaps the private monologues weren't a sign of insanity but instead a precursor to world leadership.

The phone rang. "Hi, Mom."

"Sheila. You know what? Your father and I have decided that you really need to have a home telephone. I mean, just imagine if something happened to you and then what would you do? I mean, your cell phone sometimes just rings and rings and we can't call you at work and—"

"MOM!" I reminded her of who she was.

"Oh, yes, anyway, how was your day? You know, I'm getting really worried. You just don't sound like yourself."

"Well, I don't particularly feel like myself. This hasn't exactly turned out to be the dream job I thought it would be. And today, the judge told me that I was slow and a bad reader, which really—"

"That woman will rot in hell. You've always been the smartest reader in your class. And I still can't believe she won't even let you use the phone to call your mother!" Amazing how my mother managed to make the worst part of my job about her.

"Mom, I really don't want to talk about this right now," I lied. The apple didn't fall far from the tree and I desperately wanted to talk about myself. "Anyway, everything will be fine. How are *you*?"

"You" was all it took, and the next thing I knew was that Aunty Priya had screwed over Aunty Sudha (Sanjay's mother) and how everyone at the Hindu center was taking sides. The Reston Aunty Posse never let you down. My mom was in the middle of explaining a particularly fascinating vindication (involving a sari heist) on the part of Aunty Radha (against Aunty Priya for said Sudha screw-over) when James came knocking. I managed to extricate myself from the subcontinental intrigue and let James in. He looked like he'd seen a ghost. Turned out, he'd spent the day with one. Well, an almost one.

"Sheila," he said, and plowed past me into the apartment and onto my couch, "this is awful. This is beyond awful. I don't know what to do. For real." His eyes got big. I'd never seen James so freaked out. Before I could ask any questions, he pulled a beer out of his pocket. Hidden booze wasn't a good sign. He opened the bottle on the edge of my coffee table, took a long swig, and continued. "It's, it's unimaginable. The guy. My judge. [Swig.] He can't walk. He's got some heinous gout or something, and he can't walk but refuses to retire. [Swig.] He gets around on an electric scooter. With a basket. And a horn. [Swig.]" OK, an old robed dude on an electric bike with a basket may have been more bizarre than a short, squat deranged old lady with a dancing bun.

"James. Deep breaths. Was he sick when you interviewed with him? And what about Rebecca?" I asked, optimistically hoping that his coclerk could provide a silver lining.

"Well, funny you ask. She is the worst. Get this. The judge has somebody who drops him off at the building. He then requires one of his clerks to retrieve him at the elevator with the scooter. THIS MEANS THAT I HAVE TO RIDE THE ELECTRIC SCOOTER FROM CHAMBERS TO THE ELEVATOR. Do you even know how embarrassing that is? Do you?!!!" The problem was I didn't, only because I'd never seen, let alone ridden, an electric Huffy. But I could imagine. "Anyway, I assure you it sucks. This morning, I showed up. Looking spiffy in this new Hickey Freeman suit. After introducing myself to the secretary, I was introduced to Rebecca, who said, and I quote, 'Um. Hi. The judge is waiting for you downstairs. There's the scooter. You better go get him.'" I hate when guys mimick girls because it's always the same nasal, bitchy voice and pouted lips. "Anyway, I will cut to the chase. I found myself riding this thing, having to lift the judge from his caretaker's car—the caretaker is another story, for later—and place him into the scooter. There was a snafu. And I dropped him. I dropped the judge right on the ground. In front of the Camden courthouse." (Chug.)

I laughed out loud. I knew it was the wrong thing to do, but my mouth was tired of the open position it had taken since James's arrival. The image of James carrying his judge was one thing, dropping him was another. James got up, grabbed another beer from his pocket, and continued.

This was definitely as weird as Helga Friedman's joint. James had graduated Phi Beta Kappa from Dartmouth and had worked at the Brookings Institute in Washington DC, where he hobnobbed with some of the premiere thinkers of our day before attending Columbia Law School, where he served as an editor on the *Law Review*. All of this, of course, in preparation for the biggest job of his life. It was a good thing he'd studied and worked his little pinstriped ass off for over a decade. Otherwise, he probably wouldn't have been ready to bench-press a federal judge.

"Sheila. Are you registering this? I dropped the judge. I dropped the judge. I thought that I may have killed him. He didn't move for a whole minute, then simply ordered, 'Hey Jim. Jimboy. Pick me up, kiddo. We have a very busy day.' I don't know how I did it, but the next thing I know is he was scooting himself into chambers, with me walking a few steps behind. Rebecca scowled and said, 'I won't be doing that. I'm a girl. You're a boy. You're strong. I'm not. Good luck with that.'"

The trials and tribulations of my day seemed trivial in comparison.

"Shit, Sheila, I'm going to have to start working out. I'm really scared I'm going to drop him everyday. Once may be OK, but I can't drop a federal judge on a New Jersey sidewalk EVERY DAY. Shit. If I knew I was going to have to arm-curl an old person during my clerkship, I would have bagged Con Law Two in favor of the gym. Fuck."

One couldn't argue with that.

Chapter Six

☗

Brian took me up on my offer. He had e-mailed me about lunch no less than five times over the course of several weeks. What lawyers lacked in personality, they made up for in sheer determination.

I tiptoed out of the clerks' cave when the coast was clear (read: when Evan was in the bathroom). Evan had blossomed into a jewel of a jackass, one that I avoided at all costs. I'd learned of this the hard way.

During the second week of work, in an attempt to bond, I suggested a group lunch to Evan and Matthew. I joined them in the cafeteria after a pit stop in the bathroom, arriving moments after war had broken out. Evan was leaning over the counter screaming at Ernie: "It's right there, can't you see it!?"

"I am a *blind* man—BLIND!!!" Ernie yelled, sticking him with a huge plate of deep-fried chicken livers.

A few steps behind Evan, I carefully—and kindly—instructed Ernie to serve me the sweet potatoes and roasted chicken: "Hi, Ernie. How are you? Yes, the chicken, it's to your right. Yes, thank you, Ernie." Matthew followed my lead and walked away with exactly what he'd ordered.

Incredibly, pissing off the entire cafeteria (just as I'd done a week earlier) didn't hinder Evan from staining my ears worse than Aunty Nirmila at my cousin's wedding. This was quite a feat considering Aunty Nirmila had cornered me for two full hours, shoving glossy head shots of Lakshman, her best friend Anjili's single thirty-four-year-old son from Bangalore in front of me. "But he's engineeeeeeeer, Sheila. Baby, please, you'll make us all soooo happy if you come meet him. You're not getting any younger." I'd just celebrated my sweet sixteenth. And Lakshman couldn't have gotten any grosser. Glossy after glossy revealed a short, squat man grinning like a dog in heat and the only thing he might have engineered was the patch of curly hair spilling out of his pimply ear. The one of Lakshman with tight white jeans on top of a miniature pony was the final straw. Evan's lecture was worse.

The moment we squeezed our way in between a pack of secretaries, Evan ditched his shame over openly ridiculing a blind man and dug right into the livers—then into Matthew and me.

"So, you guys *did* go to Pepperdine's Judicial Clerkship Institute, right? I mean, I don't remember either of you, but I figure you had to have."

"I don't know what you're talking about," Matthew stated, nonplussed. From my end, I tried to move the conversation away from the horror camp.

"So, how did you like living in Boston?" I said, eking out a feeble attempt at conversation change.

"You guys!!! I cannot believe you didn't go. It was only the most amazing, *critical,* experience for an incoming clerk," Evan gasped, definitely not making me feel better.

"I've just never heard of it. What is it?" Matthew implored. Evan sighed indignantly.

"Well, like a dozen judges—all federal of course—mostly appeals judges from the ninth circuit come and tell you basically how to be an *amazing* clerk. You really should have gone. I can't believe Columbia didn't tell you about it. And Yale—what do they even teach you there? Harvard *insists* that its clerks—and most Harvard grads get the clerkship of their choice— go to the institute." He smiled smugly, lending the air of having rested his case. It turned out to be his opening statement.

"Well, I guess we're screwed," Matthew said, refusing to look up from his chicken wings.

"Well, you aren't *necessarily* screwed, but you're definitely going to have trouble," Evan diagnosed. "I mean, Professor Chemerinsky—*the* Chemerinsky—even taught a course called Troubleshooting—When Westlaw and Lexis Just Aren't Cutting It!"

"Chemerinsky isn't all that," Matthew replied. "Maybe I'd have gone if Professor Sunstein were there. Noah Feldman, perhaps. But Chemerinsky? No thanks."

What? I'd have gone if Owen Wilson were there. Luke Wilson perhaps.

Undeterred, Evan proceeded to recite the CliffsNotes version of the institute. It was in between the Rationale Rodeo and Stare Decisis Swamp that I started feeling faint.

Forty-five minutes later, Matthew was barely sitting up, staring numbly as if roofies had been involved. I wish I'd been roofied. That way I would have been able to black out this entire experience. Instead, I fell into a spiral, freshly convinced I'd fail at the clerkship. What was the best experience for everyone else would be the worst for me.

From that day forward, I vowed never to break bread with Evan again. My resolve weakened a little, though, when I heard a muffled voice from around the corner while awaiting the elevator. Could it be Evan? Or worse—the judge? Sitting on the floor, in the dark, was Matthew whispering into his cell phone.

"Oh, sorry, I didn't mean to interrupt," I said, backing away. Since our famed bonding lunch, Matthew and I had barely spoken a word to each other. This was due to apathy rather than dislike—he seemed to have exactly zero things to say.

"No, no you didn't interrupt. I was just squeezing in a call to my girlfriend," he said, standing and following me to the elevator. "I was going to grab something to eat. Um, want to join me?"

"Actually, I'm meeting some other clerks for lunch," I replied. We both stepped into the elevator. "You're more than welcome to come with us."

"Thanks, that'd be nice," he said, nodding his head, smiling.

The elevator opened into the courthouse lobby. Standing before our eyes were Brian and a grim gaggle of geeks. Ten of them. Matthew and I made a dozen neat. Never mind my name or how I was doing, each one of them instantly wanted to know: "Who do you clerk for?" At the speed of light, I'd been asked that very question by all ten of them. So fast, in fact, that I was unable to answer before being asked again. Dizzy Gillespie.

Brian had made a reservation at the Continental, a Stephen Starr restaurant everyone in Philly raved about. In less than a decade, Mr. Starr had evolved into a local icon, with Ben Franklin his only real rival.

Even the duck buses, filled with harems of duck-shaped whistle-blowing children and their parents, would pull up in front of Starr's restaurants. Then a twenty-something with a crew cut and Tommy Hilfiger jeans would retrieve a megaphone (shaped like a duck bill) and scream: "This here is a Ste-VEN Starr restaurant." Everyone on the bus would scan their map and blow their whistles in proud recognition. The Continental was Stephen Starr's gem. A Pan-Asian restaurant with specialty martinis (how novel!).

Within moments of having been seated, it became apparent that Evan wasn't a statistical anomaly. Complex calculus wasn't required to compute that Evan times ten was markedly worse than times one. Just about everyone there had attended Clerk Camp, where Evan was a B-list celebrity.

"Why didn't you bring Evan?" Anne from Stanford Law wanted to know.

"I forgot Evan was clerking in Philadelphia. Awesome!" Jeff from Georgetown yelped gleefully like he'd just discovered King Tut's tomb.

"That's so cool—Evan's your coclerk! He's so funny!" NYU Nathan raised his hand for a high five. Had he accidentally dropped the word *looking* after *funny,* or had he meant to imply that Evan had a sense of humor? Either way, it was nothing short of distressing that Evan was my entree into this bizarro world. Even more distressing, when the conversation turned away from Evan, it took a plunge.

"Can you *believe* they granted cert? I think *Bowers* may be overturned!" Georgetown Jeff excitedly pulled out a printed sheet of all the cases the Supreme Court had decided to hear that term. Judging from the looks of unencumbered excitement, I knew it wasn't a joke.

"Frankly, I can just *imagine* what that would do to habeas!" Brian tipped his fedora for effect. Everyone was mesmerized. Was anyone going to point out the obvious—namely, that Brian was full of bull? While I was the first to believe that *Bowers v. Hardwick,* the notorious Supreme Court case upholding sodomy laws, should be overturned, I was unaware of anyone wasting away in prison on sodomy charges. After all, the writ of habeas corpus allowed courts to release prisoners who were being held in violation of the U.S. Constitution. Prisons were filled with drug dealers, not fashion-forward queens.

"Actually, I doubt it'd do anything to habeas," I blurted out, hoping that pragmatism was still worth something. From the looks of utter disgust all around, you would have thought I'd said I ate shit sandwiches for breakfast, which incidentally didn't seem so bad compared to the Continental's signature "Oriental Ginger Noodle Salad."

"Clearly, you don't have a handle on habeas," Brian sneered.

"The Great Writ serves as a crucial check on constitutional rights. You are obviously not a scholar of Justice Brennan," Georgetown Jeff added. Scalia was one thing, but why did he drag dearly-departed Brennan into this? And had Brian actually used the words "the Great Writ"? This was definitely worse than the special two-hour Con Law class on public v. private nuisance (this crowd seemed to fall into both categories). I was speechless. Unfortunately, my silent astonishment lent support to the peanut gallery's theory that I didn't know what I was talking about.

"I don't think Sheila's comment is a reflection of her understanding of habeas at all," Matthew said. Everyone snapped to attention, as these were the first words Matthew had spoken. "I think that all she was saying is that sodomists are typically not in jail, meaning not many people actually get arrested and convicted for sodomy. As such, habeas wouldn't apply to them," Matthew explained methodically.

"That's exactly what I meant," I followed up, shooting a grateful smile at Matthew, who quickly returned to his plate-stare position. "Actually, I was reading a *New York Times* article last week which said it took Lambda years to even *find* a test case to challenge *Bowers*." This was the truth. Lambda, a nonprofit organization supporting gay/lesbian rights, had searched high and low for someone who'd been arrested for sodomy the minute *Bowers* came down. It had taken nearly a decade.

"*I* should know about test cases. After all, I did work at the *ACLU* for a summer and will definitely be back this time next year," Brian bragged. I felt sick. The first time Brian mentioned he'd worked at the ACLU, it never occurred to me that he'd actually want to return.

Most law students complete their public interest stints during the summer after their first year in law school. Thereafter, most go on to big law firms. But anything cool (i.e., non-law-firm-related) requires a clerkship, (see chapter 2), and even then, places such as the ACLU, the Federal Public Defenders Office, and the U.S. Attorney's Office still often require a couple years of litigation experience at a top firm. The long and the short of it, however, was that I'd foregone the big salary and packed it off to Pennsylvania in the hope of hopes that I'd be one of the lucky law clerks who could—and would—go straight to the ACLU. The problem was that the ACLU typically hired less than a handful of staff attorneys every year and the chances of two law clerks from the third circuit making the cut in the same year were slim to none. I'd never anticipated the intracircuit competition. Just my luck—Brian clerked for the most powerful judge on the bench. Chief Judge Fleck. The writing was on the wall. I was Flecked.

Yet again, Brian had grown tired of me, turned his back and continued to hold court as to the Supreme Court's current docket. Brian was about five foot seven. He had a wide ride and tight khaki pants. He tucked in a white oxford shirt, the collar buttoned down. He wore a dark brown braided belt and a red sweater vest. With the brown wool fedora, he looked like a drug-dealing elf. Brian was the spiritual leader of the group. Brian thought I was stupid. Ergo, everyone else did, too.

Brian's fans followed him back to the courthouse after lunch. I kept my distance, walking a half block behind everyone else. Matthew joined me.

"Hey, Matthew, thanks so much for piping up for me back there," I said, taking a deep breath, venturing to spew sacrilege. "Those people don't seem to be so much up my alley. You know?"

"They're just lawyers, that's all," he replied. "I wouldn't take it personally. And you were right. You know, about *Bowers* and habeas." Matthew shoved his hands in his pockets and pursed his lips, as if he'd said too much.

"So, um," I fumbled for a talking point, "you have a girlfriend. What's her name? Did you guys meet at Yale?"

"Ah, yeah, her name is Heidi. And we did meet at Yale," he answered, staring ahead. "She's actually clerking for a judge on the Southern District of New York." Full stop.

"Wow, great, does she like it there? I wish so badly I'd gotten a clerkship in New York."

"Ah, her judge really likes pastrami," he said awkwardly. Then, silence.

"Who wouldn't like pastrami? It's a very likable meat." Why did I always have to fill the silence?

"What I was trying to say is that the *only* thing her judge likes is pastrami. As in, the only thing he talks about is pastrami. Which is pretty weird, you know," he paused. "And I'm sure Heidi would trade places with you in a minute. She hates New York."

How could anyone hate New York? I found myself a bit cross with Matthew for dating someone who affirmatively hated New York.

"Yeah, I guess New York is tough for some people. It's expensive. Um." I searched for another negative but was coming up short.

"Well, in law school, she used to get up really early and go walking at the mall in New Haven. And there's no place really for her to do that in Manhattan."

"As in mall walking? That kind of mall? That kind of walking?" I asked, trying to suppress my shock. Was Matthew dating a senior citizen? Did we have a *Harold and Maude* sequel on our hands?

"Yeah, she likes to walk at the mall," he said, his face reddening a bit, "and, er, there was this one store she loved where she used to buy postcards for her collection. And I think she misses that, too."

I'd never been so happy to see the courthouse and was actually grateful for the security check, as I couldn't think of anything to say about postcard collections.

Entering chambers, I quickly returned to my cubicle to do some covert Internet research on the ACLU. Matthew headed for the supply closet, presumably to grab a new mechanical pencil. The judge kept taking his from his desk drawer.

"MMMAATTTTTHHEW!" Surely Matthew's mother had never intended his name to be pronounced in such a fashion.

"MMMAATTTTTHHEW!" Surely Matthew's mother heard the judge all the way in Idaho. "Get in here now!"

Matthew stumbled inside. At least six feet tall, he nevertheless looked meek next to the judge. One of the few things I knew about Matthew was that he'd grown up on a farm in Idaho where he spent his youth castrating bulls. Twenty years later, a small elderly lady was making him shudder.

"You and Sheila have been gone for over two hours!" Talk about fuzzy math. We'd left at 12:05 and it was 1:10. We'd been gone for sixty-five minutes.

"Um, Judge, actually, we left shortly after—"

"NO! NO! NO! Janet said you've both been gone since eleven-thirty!" What! Why would Janet lie? And the judge had been staring at me at 11:30. How on earth was it possible for me to have been getting stared at by her and lectured by Brian all at the same time? The ginger noodles started to stir.

"SHEEEEELLLLLLAAA!!" Shoot—I was selfishly hoping that Matthew would take the rap for the both of us. I walked into the torture chamber as Matthew headed out, nostrils flaring.

"Who do you think you are?!" Her eyes were filled with hatred. I didn't have a good answer. I used to be a well-liked, affable, relatively charming, somewhat intelligent Indian American woman. Now, I was a stupid lunch-whoring Pakistani.

"I do NOT go to lunch. I am nice enough to let you people go. But you've taken advantage of me one too many times."

Heavens to Betsy Ross! What was she talking about? We had no vacation days, weren't allowed to be sick, worked ten hours a day, couldn't speak, could barely move, and cranked out more bench memos than the Catholic Church cranked out pedophiles. All for a pittance. And *we* were taking advantage of *her* because we'd been held up for five minutes getting lectured about habeas corpus! This was outrageous. Yet she was the one outraged. My silence caused further infuriation.

"THERE WILL BE NO MORE LUNCH!!! NO MORE LUNCH!! DO YOU UNDERSTAND!!!????" Actually, I didn't. Was she outlawing the entire, age-old concept of lunch?

"Yes, Judge," I lied.

When I walked back into the clerks' cave, Matthew silently beckoned me to his cubicle.

"Sorry I left you in there like that," he whispered.

"I'd have done the same thing," I assured him. "What do you think sparked that episode? I mean, did we just deserve that?"

"I don't know, can't really answer that one," he mumbled uncomfortably. My cue to leave.

As I stood, I noticed a shimmering frame on Matthew's desk. The picture inside revealed a blond waif who managed to sport such a severe camel toe that it resembled a forklift.

"Oh, that's Heidi," Matthew explained. "That's her at her parents' house down the Jersey shore." I nodded, soaking in the cheese factor. "She, ah, she gave me this frame in case you're, you know, wondering," he quickly added. I wasn't sure if he was embarrassed by (a) the glitter, (b) the fact that he had a picture of his girlfriend in a string bikini at work (or anywhere, for that matter), or (c) the toe.

"That's nice. That's, ah, really nice. She's lovely," I muttered. Returning to my cubicle, I caught a glimpse of the judge, who pursed her lips at me, nodding her head disapprovingly.

I was in a foul mood when I got home. Out of sheer panic, before leaving work, I'd e-mailed my contact at the ACLU about the application process there. She hadn't e-mailed me back. Granted, it'd only been a few hours, but in that time I'd managed to convince myself that Brian was somehow masterminding the death of my legal career. Never mind that he had no clue that I had either worked at the ACLU or had any desire to work there in the future.

As for the day's big news, namely the Edict of Lunch, it was not only upsetting as a procedural matter (checking out the judge's tonsils for no good reason was no good) but proved substantively confusing, as well. Based on her exact words, I couldn't deduce the status of lunch: Would I ever be allowed to eat lunch again? Would the innocent people of the third circuit—including New Jersey, Delaware, Pennsylvania, and the Virgin Islands—have to abstain also? Depriving James and Kevin of lunch for a year was no way to thank them for being supportive friends. Especially Kevin, with whom I'd not yet established a long enough positive history to throw in the bad stuff.

I called Sanjay to get his take on the situation.

"Well, Sheila, um, I, can you hold on just one second . . . no, no I told you I needed those X-rays in room 602. No, I didn't say 622. Six-oh-two. OK, I'll be there in a second. Hey, um, Sheila, what were you saying?

Actually, can I just call you later?" The phone went dead before I could respond.

James was still wearing his suit when I went down to his apartment. "Hey there," he said, greeting me with neither a smile nor a frown. It was the kind of apathy that normally took a lifetime to generate. But I couldn't blame him really. It was impossible to differentiate one evening from another.

"Hi. My life sucks," I complained dispassionately, sinking (as usual) into his hand-me-down pastel couch. James had even uglier furniture than me.

"Sheila—your life sucks *right now,*" James qualified, squinting his eyes and tilting his head in an attempt to find something original to say. As if looking at me from a sharp angle might help. "And anyway, at least you don't have to dress like this," he said, pointing to his navy blue suit. "And if it makes you feel any better, I had a horrific day," he said, loosening his tie. "His scooter died—allegedly—today. I had to wheel him into court so he could hear a motion. He told one of the lawyers that he couldn't believe she'd passed the bar exam, because she was so incompetent, denied the motion, and motioned for me to retrieve him. All the while, my delicate flower coclerk just sat smiling at the judge. Anyway, I go up to the bench to get him when all of a sudden the little scooter fucking turns back on and goes fully out of control."

In spite of a concerted effort to take the situation seriously, I laughed.

"Don't laugh. He ran over my foot." James motioned to his right foot. His big toe resembled a globe with a smattering of black-and-blue continents. I placed my hand over my mouth, trying not laugh. "And then he did it again. But he didn't even realize he was doing it. So, there I was in front of all those people, literally getting run over, and I had to pretend like everything was totally normal. I managed to hit the power switch on the thing and wheeled him out of there. Limping."

"OK, you win." Getting run over by a nearly dead, power-hungry man in an out-of-control electric bike in front of a courtroom of people beats getting grounded from lunch.

My cell phone rang. It was Kevin. "Hey, Sheila. Jana and I are about twenty minutes away from Ralph's. See you in a few." Click! Drats! I'd totally forgotten about dinner with Kevin, his coclerk Jana, and James. Ever since the clerks' (un)happy hour(s), James had struck himself a fantabulous deal—he and Jana would sleep together about once a week. No strings attached. The best part about it was that Jana had started being super nice to Kevin, so as to not jeopardize the setup with James.

"Oh no. I totally spaced on tonight. I have zero personality right now and have a feeling Jana will think I'm a dud," I explained. James grabbed his wallet and keys before delivering a dose of reality.

"Sheila. Listen I hate to break this to you. I don't think today is either a particularly bad or good day for your personality. This is kind of how you've been since we've started this clerkship thing. So, get off your ass and let's go. And Jana is really nice. Trust me."

Forty minutes later, I found myself sitting at a table covered with a red-and-white-checkered cloth desperately trying to be one of the gang.

"So, Jana, I understand you went to Virginia," I said. Considering I already knew she clerked for Judge Adams, law school was next on the list.

"Yes, I did." She smiled proudly. "And I understand you work for Judge Friedman. I hear that she is one *interesting* judge," she said, with a knowing wink.

"Yes, she is *interesting*." I tried winking back, but since I'd never mastered the art, it ended up as more of an unpleasant squint. James and Kevin had been sitting mysteriously silent, each slurping an entire carafe of wine through a straw. Ralph's was the kind of place where such behavior was not noteworthy or kitschy.

"What about *you*? How do you like clerking for Adams," I asked, gently returning to what I had a feeling was Jana's favorite subject—Jana.

"Well," she said, grinning at Kevin, "Adams is, like, really the best. The woman is hysterical. Like today, for example, Kevin"—she snapped him to attention—"Kev, did you see it when she handed me that brief in that trespassing case and it was, like, huge and she just said"—and then

Jana took a time-out to chuckle, which made the rest of us feel compelled to chuckle also in spite of not knowing the punch line—"'this brief ain't so brief.'" Then, full-fledged hysteria. Tears ran down her face. Our respective spaghetti and meatballs came.

Through one particularly large bite, Jana continued: "And, like, yesterday, the judge came into me and Kev's area and it was, like, totally quiet back there, and she just said, 'Wow, you guys are quieter than Justice Thomas is on the bench'"—cackle, snort, cackle, piece of meatball went flying from Jana's mouth and landed splat on the left lens of James's glasses. To think they'd be doing it later. Kevin eeked.

James quickly blotted the ball, which smeared his lens. Jana just kept talking. I yanked what was left in the carafe from James's weary grasp.

"Yeah, so all of the clerks are like supercool. I mean, Kev for one, of course. Then there's Walt. He went to, like, NYU. As you know, I went to Virginia. I loved Virginia. I was on the *Law Review*. Were you on the *Law Review,* Sheila? I was on the *Law Review.* Walt was on *NYU Law Review.* The judge always gets, like, one guy from NYU. And Betsy, that's our last clerk. She went to Duke."

I wondered if I could choke myself if I ate a meatball whole. Stealing a glance at James, I silently implored how sex could be worth *this.*

Walking outside, Jana hailed a cab and tried to drag James along with her. Politely lying that he had an early morning conference with the judge, he managed to free himself and walked home with me and Kevin, during which time he assured us that he was done with Jana. If only he'd stuck to that plan.

About an hour after we returned to our respective apartments, James slipped back out to pay Jana a surprise booty call. Brian answered Jana's door, holding a bottle of champagne, wearing nothing more than a Mickey Mouse towel and his fedora. Unsettling to visualize. Psychologically damaging to witness.

James stayed long enough to entertain Brian's weighty question: "Hey man, how's the fuckin' *district* court treatin' you?"

Chapter Seven

There I was. Plaid skirt. Shin guards. Cleats. Mouth guard. Hockey stick. I was ready, all warmed up. The refs took position in center field. The whistle blew. I was off and running, totally in control of the ball. And then—from left field!—a small hunchbacked lady in a plaid robe carrying a massive gavel came and smacked the ball right out of my possession.

"You have to be faster, faster, faster, faster. SHEILLLAAA—FASTER!!!!" On the sidelines, my coach, my mom, and the entire commonwealth of Virginia stood staring, disappointed. We lost! It was all my fault. Little robed judge with big smile stood in the middle of the field caressing her gavel with one hand and her trophy in the other. A triumphant, toothy tyrant.

I jumped out of bed. It was 4 AM. I was panting. My sheets were soaked in sweat. The judge had managed to ruin my field hockey championship in the eleventh grade. Incredible—the woman was a time and space traveler! Her "You're not working fast enough, Sheila. You're rilly rilly slow, Sheila" was taking its toll.

A few days earlier, I had been helping David, one of our interns, with the doctrine of qualified immunity. After three years of law school and one bar exam, I still didn't understand the nuances of immunity, a particularly thorny patch of law. How was David supposed to get it after just two semesters of school? As I was flipping through his blue brief, attempting to assess the allegations, the judge came sauntering into my cubicle. The three of us. Same cubicle. Not so much air.

"*What* are you doing, Sheila?" As if it weren't totally clear. Did she think I was giving David a blow job? David had stopped breathing.

"I'm just he-hel-helping David with qualified immun—"

"NO! NO! NO! I don't. DO NOT have time for my law clerks to help my interns. Your time is *my* time and *I* certainly do not have time to talk to interns." David still hadn't taken a breath. The judge wouldn't even address him, which was rather awkward considering she'd practically shoved her face into his perfectly still stomach. "Now, tell him to go back and figure it out. That's why he is here. To learn. Not to receive handouts." With that, she spun, practically knocking one dead intern into my lap, and stomped off. The judge was right—we were there to learn, and what a rich learning environment she'd created. Halfway back to her office, she turned around.

"In case you've all forgotten, we have A LOT of work to do. We have a sitting next week. I don't have time for this fraternizing." Signature move. The look behind yell. I shoved the brief at David and gently pushed him out of my cubicle.

The judge must have forgotten that we had finished all of the work for the October sitting weeks ago and were already halfway through November. This meant every case being argued the following week had been fully researched and briefed in the form of a bench memo and all cases that didn't get oral arguments had been disposed of in nonprecedential opinions. Translation: We were over a month ahead. Nonetheless, the judge still ranted about our being behind and being slow, and I had started to buy the whole thing, hook, line, and sinker. The woman could have brainwashed Charles Manson.

Every time I shut my eyes, visions of a small woman with a large bun danced in my head. Sleep deprivation was preferable. And so I plucked my hair for about two hours before showering up and heading to chambers. I wondered if the rain gods had picked that morning to piss on me out of sheer spite. The only thing worse than insomnia is insomnia followed by a rain storm. And the only thing worse than mental abuse and loneliness is the paranoid self-absorption that follows, leading one to believe that even the weather is out to get them.

The line at Dunkin' Donuts spilled out the door. Soaked and sorry, I took my place in the back. "I'll have the large coffee with skim AND a glazed doughnut." Blank stare. "Um. A glazed and my usual coffee." I pointed to the donut.

"Yah. You nevah get do-nuh." Yes, I also had never shot up drugs but was considering joining the guys outside.

"Um, yes, you're right, I normally don't get a doughnut. Today I want a glazed." Patience was wearing thin. It was also wearing on the not-so-thin, wet UPS deliveryman behind me. Stares all around. "You know what, forget it. Just the coffee." He forgot it. I couldn't believe it. A kid twenty years younger than me put me on a diet at a doughnut shop filled with people three times my size.

Coffee in hand, I breezed by Duane ("Hey, little lady! *psst!*"—I was wearing a knee-high plaid skirt) and headed to security. I recognized the girl in front of me as one of Kevin's coclerks from a cell phone picture he'd furtively taken in chambers.

"Hey, you're one of Judge Adams's clerks, right?" I ventured to ask.

"Yeah, I'm Betsy. How did you know that? And I don't mean to sound rude, but who are you?" She eyed me curiously.

"Oh, I know Kevin, your coclerk, and my name is Sheila, Sheila Raj, and I clerk for Judge Friedman."

"PHONE IN THE BUCKET, PHONE IN THE BUCKET." The security guard forced Betsy through, but she politely waited for me at the other end.

"Wow. How's *that* going?" Betsy asked excitedly.

"It's fine, just fine," I fibbed again, "and I'm looking forward to our sitting. I have this one death penalty case that I'm really excited about."

"Ha! You're working on the Dell Nelson–Peter Nussbaum one, huh? I am, too. But since we're not supposed to be talking about cases, I should probably shut my trap." She paused. "But we should have lunch after the sitting," Betsy suggested cheerily.

"Sure, that'd be great," I said, getting off the elevator. Entering the secretaries' den, there was Eddie hovering over Janet's desk. Eddie was the chamber's janitor, and aside from a predilection for cleaning the bathroom barefoot, Eddie was by all accounts a normal sweet guy. He loved his two teenage daughters, college football, and didn't for a second seem perturbed that after a stint in the United States Army, he'd been relegated to a life of scrubbing toilets for old, mean people who treated him like he was lucky that he got to serve them. God bless America!

But even Eddie wouldn't talk to Medieval Roy, who was sedulously watering the judge's plants. While the mere existence of Roy was depressing enough to make a chicken want to cut its own head off, there was something particularly sad about him watering the judge's plants. It was inexplicably extraspecial demeaning.

"Good morning, Roy." I couldn't mask my pity. He turned skittishly, knocking over an entire stack of briefs from decades ago. Janet jumped out of her seat, nearly decapitating one of the three Pound Puppies on top of her computer and cutting off whatever Eddie was saying to her midstream.

"Roy! Roy! Can't you do anything right?!"

Roy started stuttering. The great medievalist. A few days earlier, Roy had proudly presided over a fifteenth-century feast, after which he had presumably had his way with thirteenth-century wenches from Jersey. Today, he stood over a pile of antiquated briefs, holding a pink water jug, madly batting his lashes at an angry, born-again Christian secretary. But, I couldn't blame him. Janet scared the bejesus out of me, too.

"Pick all of that up RIGHT now, Roy," Janet said. "I will not be blamed for your stupidity!" Eddie and I just stood. I felt partially responsible. It was me, after all, who had said good morning. "Now, about your daughter"— Janet casually returned to her conversation with Eddie—"I will definitely pray for her this weekend," she promised, smiling. I just stood.

"Um, good morning, Eddie. Janet," I said finally. Eddie smiled at me.

"Hitheresheilahow'reyoui'mOKhoney." That was the best part about Eddie. He anticipated your question and answered it before you could even ask. The whole string of words—incomprehensible. Janet? I'm not sure there was a best part about her.

She resumed: "You do realize that for the sitting, you'll have to get the judge together. Get her orange notebook. Xerox copies of the oral argument schedule. Give me and her an original and you people get the rest. Put her copy on her chair and the cases should go on the other chair in there." She motioned inside. I nodded, pretending like I knew exactly what she was talking about.

"Got it. Thanks, Janet."

She clenched her jaw. That was my cue to leave.

Janet hadn't warmed up a lick since my first day on the job. This was not for my lack of trying. I practically kissed her ass on a daily basis. She repaid me with assault and battery. At first, I had let it slide. After all, the judge treated Janet and Roy like crap. Friedman had once told me in passing that we—the law clerks—were never to eat lunch with them, because "they do not have JDs and will not be able to follow anything you say." In addition to being societal lowlifes, according to the judge, Janet and Roy were also responsible for anything and everything that went wrong in terms of logistics, and never once did the judge reward them with kindness. The judge didn't even say hello to them. Roy dealt with the abuse by incessantly surfing medieval Internet sites.

Janet was different.

She was strangely obsessed with pleasing the judge, like a battered wife who constantly wanted to make her violent husband proud. As for the rest of us—Janet treated us the way the judge treated her. With every passing potshot from the judge, Janet's ego dropped below sea level, leaving her a seething piranha in search of a raw piece of meat to chew on. Her personal life didn't seem to help matters. Thanks to her morning conversations with Eddie and my excellent eavesdropping skills, I was able to piece together one sad story. Janet was a devoutly religious Bible banger who spent Sundays passing around collection baskets at her church. She had moved into her parents' house in the suburbs after a dicey divorce years earlier. While her parents were long gone, her brother was still there. Brother and Janet were in their fifties and both still single. I wondered if incest was banned by the Ten Commandments.

She had two cats, which her brother hated. She enjoyed knitting sweaters for her cousins' babies and broiling pork products. She loved children but had none of her own. She didn't drink or smoke but did positively adore bright pink lipstick. And those Pound Puppies! All things considered, I couldn't blame her for being mean and nasty. I'd probably be a seething bottom-feeder too if my brother kicked my cats and wanted to feel me up.

Before I could say hello to Matthew, the elevator announced the judge's arrival. Drats! I quickly fell into my chair and turned my computer on and lickety-split—the judge was before me. So was one greasy pony. The bun was down and in its stead was a long, stringy ponytail. It was like seeing the queen in her underwear.

"I want to talk to you about the *Niltin* case. Your analysis is troubling, to say the least. With that, she turned and walked off. I, like a sick pony, followed.

"Um, do you want to talk right now?" I ventured to ask. She kept walking, without so much as a half turn.

"I am rilly busy. Not now!" She slammed her door. Troubling analysis! I'd put blood, sweat, and tears into the *Dell Nelson* bench memo. I had read and reread the briefs, trial transcript, and case law, even after office hours, to turn in what I thought was a stellar memo in a timely fashion. Maybe I wasn't cut out to be a lawyer after all.

"*Pssst!*" Matthew motioned to me. I tiptoed over.

"Hey. I can't seem to do anything right," I whispered.

"That's not true, first of all," he paused, turning greenish "but what I wanted to ask you was if you saw the judge's hair? Has she not washed it in, well, a while?"

"Yeah, it was definitely gross. Hey, would you rather wash her pony once a week for a whole year or live in a port-o-potty for a week?" I asked without thinking, accidentally unleashing my favorite game—would you rather—on a colleague who'd barely said two words to me over the course of several weeks. I'd made the same error a few years earlier with the new kid in my study group. He switched groups shortly thereafter. I'd vowed to never repeat the mistake. Matthew looked much like that kid—panic-stricken.

"Never mind. Just kidding," I squeaked out, before returning to my desk. No sooner had I sat down did Matthew come over to my part of the woods. Standing behind my cubicle, he whispered: "Sorry, the question threw me. They're both vile, but I think I'd live in the port-o-potty for a week."

At that moment, the most unusual thing happened. Matthew's phone rang and he hightailed it back to his desk to answer before the judge could hear anything. I peered in his direction and noticed that he'd turned ashen white. Out of the corner of my eye, I could see the judge heading in our direction. I jumped to head her off at the pass, but it was too late. The queen had spotted her meandering servant. She scurried over to Matthew's cubicle and hovered above him. He continued to speak into the phone.

"What! Do! You! Think! You! Are! Doing!" She seethed. I almost wet my pants. Matthew ignored her and kept listening to whomever it was talking on the other end. "I. Am. Talking. To. You. Math-You!" I could see her hands trembling through her folded arms. Get off the phone, Matthew. Save yourself, man.

"OK. What do you want me to do?" Matthew asked into the phone. That was it. The judge leaned over and yanked the phone cord out of the jack. Just like that.

"Maybe if you spent less time talking to your friends and more time working, you people wouldn't make *colossal* mistakes!" she barked. Matthew stood up, towering over the judge and coming very close to her. He was the Leaning Tower of Pisa and she an awestruck tourist. He clenched his fist. She flinched. A modern showcase showdown. And then I saw a tear glide down Matthew's face.

Clearly restraining himself—from crying and violence—Matthew calmly stated: "Judge, that was my brother. My sister-in-law has been in a terrible car accident and might die. You just cut me off from my bro—"

"I don't care who's dying. My *husband* is dying. Do you see me chitchatting all day?" I closed my eyes for a second hoping that when I opened them I would realize that I'd just imagined the whole thing. No dice.

"Fuck you, Judge," Matthew enunciated carefully, before shoving her out of his way, grabbing his duffel bag, and walking out the door. It was at that point that I did wet my pants. Peed right there in my chair. I wasn't sure what it was. The fact that Matthew's sister-in-law was on her deathbed, the fact that the judge exhibited a cruelty I'd never before witnessed from another human being, or the fact that Matthew had told the judge to fuck off. It could simply have been that I'd officially developed a bladder control problem.

Whatever the case, the judge didn't seem remotely affected by the cold hard facts—two law clerks down in less than two months. Surely that would have been a record even for her.

Instead of processing this, she marched by my cubicle, told me to see her in her office in five minutes, returned to the torture chamber, and shut the door. I had five minutes to find new underpants, a futile task given that the cafeteria didn't carry much in the way of clothing. I splashed water on my crotch and decided to tell anyone who asked that the sink had exploded on me.

As I approached the torture chamber, Janet looked positively pleased. "Did they just have a fight?" she whispered, motioning to the clerks' cave. I didn't answer. Who needed enemies with friends like Janet? Inside the torture chamber, my knees felt like they were about to give out. That, coupled with my soaked ass, made me feel like a dysfunctional mermaid. Thankfully, the judge didn't seem to notice (or smell) my wet pants. Instead, she just stood, clutching my bench memorandum.

"Seems you gave short shrift to a crucial aspect of *Nuddleton,*" she sneered. It didn't feel like the right time to remind her that the case was called *Nelson.*

"I'm sorry, Judge. I'm confused. Maybe you disagree with me as to whether or not Nelson's lawyer was ineffective but—"

"You're missing my point." It was unclear how one could miss an unmade point. "Do you even understand AEDPA?" the judge asked giddily. AEDPA (pronounced: ED-pah) was short for the Antiterrorism and Effective Death Penalty Act of 1996, a law which, according to the Supreme Court, "modified" the courts of appeals' role in reviewing state prisoner habeas corpus applications. Modified was a nice way of saying "removed" the court of appeals role altogether, a euphemism for fucked, screwed, or game over for death row inmates. Sometimes even claims of actual innocence fell short of the standards required under AEDPA for prisoners to get relief on appeal. In short, AEDPA provided a procedural hurdle to hearing the substance of death penalty cases on appeal.

"Um, I thought I understood the statute. I apologize, Judge, if I interpreted it wrong." I silently kicked myself for apologizing to a woman who moments earlier had told Matthew she could care less if his sister-in-law died. A smile erupted on the judge's small face, like lava from a formerly dormant volcano.

"I thought I understood the statute," she mimicked. "What do you think would happen if I wrote opinions based on *thinking* I understood the issues?" I quietly repented for each and every time I'd been sarcastic to my mother. "As a federal appeals court faced with a habeas petition, we are obligated to give profound deference to the Pennsylvania state court, which has already ruled that this Tip Arvents character wasn't constitutionally ineffective. Deference, Sheila. Your bench memo barely even addresses this but waxes on about how we should overturn the state's decision. It's not that I disagree with you *necessarily* about giving this man a chance to be resentenced," she said sternly, "but that I'm deeply troubled by how you brushed off a crucial aspect of how we arrive at that conclusion. It's lazy. I expect more from my law clerks."

"Judge, I-I am pretty sure that I wrote several pages on, er, on AEDPA, and I thought that I said, *on balance,* we should rule in favor of the defend—"

"Enough. I expected more from you, Sheila," she said calmly.

For some reason, her typical vitriol was easier on the nerves than her genuine disappointment in my legal reasoning. Robbing me of my backbone was one thing, but was the clerkship also making me a bad lawyer? I was sucking up what was turning out to be a hideous year for no other reason than to hone my legal skills for the ACLU. Was it actually all for naught? And had I lost my mind?—I could have sworn that I'd addressed AEDPA at length. Yikes! I'd given the *Dell Nelson* case 110 percent and it was insufficient. And if I couldn't even write a proper bench memo, it was almost certain that I'd failed the bar exam.

"I-I am sorry. Do you want me to rewrite that portion of the memo, Judge?" I offered meekly. She didn't. She just wanted to make me feel as inadequate as she felt in the face of her dying husband. It worked. I felt helpless, hopeless.

"I just want you to know that you need to THINK about every possible issue surrounding each case. You are here to think and to be thorough."

Then a near miracle happened. Her phone rang and she answered it immediately. "Hello, Mark. One second, please." She looked up long enough to deliver one final blow. "Sheila, I want your November bench memo pronto. Now get out."

Mark was the judge's son, her only child, whom she had "picked up in Namibia." He lived in Gladwyne, a nearby suburb on the Main Line, with his wife ("the White") and two small children ("the Mixed"). He never called. He never came by. She didn't seem to care. After all, who had time for kids, grandchildren, and dying husbands when she had "so much to do!"?

Early on, I learned never to inquire about Bob, Mark, or the grandkids, one of whom had been born only two months prior to my arrival. When I congratulated her on the newborn early on in the clerkship, she'd barked: "Why are you congratulating me?" It was one of her many talents, I'd come to learn—making you feeling like a grade-A moron for asking a perfectly normal question. In the beginning I hadn't caught on, so at that time I racked my mind for an answer. Didn't people congratulate others when they became parents and grandparents? Even aunts and uncles got the occasional pat on the back.

"Well, for Mark's new baby?" It was an early lesson in doubting my entire universe of knowledge.

"I had nothing to do with that," she flatly stated. Technically, I guessed she hadn't. "And I can't stand babies until they are at least two. That baby has absolutely nothing interesting to say. Nothing at all." And that was that. For the first time, I'd come face-to-face with a seventy-two-year-old woman who thought her grandchildren were dull.

Leaving the torture chamber, I considered jumping out of the window. My life was effectively over anyway. Why not just end it? I hadn't even opened the first brief for my next case, let alone started writing a word of the bench memo. She was going to flip her bun when she realized she'd have to wait at least a week for it.

The best case scenario would be getting fired. This, of course, would mean no ACLU. Then again, considering that (a) Judge Friedman just told me I had poor legal skills and (b) the Brian situation, the ACLU was probably out anyway. I'd heard back from Anika, the ACLU's director of human resources, but her e-mail had been curt (or was it?), and she'd not addressed my suggestion that we get together for coffee one weekend in New York. I'd lied and said that I was there frequently, which I wished I were. But I simply couldn't fork over the dough for the Amtrak train, and the 2.5-hour Jersey Transit–SEPTA ride proved too trying after such trying work weeks. My lie didn't seem to matter to Anika, who coldly bullet-pointed everything I'd need to include in my application.

Despite my mother's and Puja's insistence to the contrary, I knew Brian was hijinxing my chances at doing good for humankind. It even crossed my mind that perhaps he was sleeping with Anika on the side, in which case I could always hire someone to take secret pictures of him riding Jana in his fedora. I nevertheless applied, planning to wait out the rejection, which at least wouldn't come for several months. March was the earliest they'd respond to any and all applications (at least that's what Anika had said. Was she lying to me?). Considering rejection was a certainty, getting axed by the judge wouldn't make a lick of difference. But the alternative was even worse. Helga Friedman could just keep me around as a whipping post, like Roy. Spiral, spiral, spiral. Even worse, what if I was relegated to being Roy's bitch?

I was doomed. We hadn't even heard our first oral arguments for our first sitting and already I wanted to sit out. Be benched. There were five sittings after this one. Puberty had gone faster than this. Let's face it—a wet bottom was not doing much to ameliorate the situation. Trapped. Cubicle. Staring, mean, demonic judge to my left. To my right, computer, where I typed meaningless rubbish not fit for legal consumption. Around the left bend, ecstatic Janet, happy I'd been hit, petting her stuffed puppies. In front of her, persecuted Roy, somehow feeling like he'd been wronged. Behind me, Matthew's empty cubicle.

What if he never returned? What if Evan were moved to his seat, near me? While I couldn't actually see him, I had a feeling Evan was glued to his computer, creating legal genius too complex for this dunce to decipher. He was surrounded by an army of interns who hadn't spoken since the David incident. David, for one, wouldn't even return your hello in the morning. Kid would just stare down at whatever brief he was reading. Judge Friedman undoubtedly sent more business to local psychotherapists than bad marriages.

Yet even the interns had it better than the law clerks. For one, they were only in chambers two days a week. Secondly, the judge's refusal to address interns personally, considering their "mediocre" law schools, was a blessing.

"Attending Rutgers, Villanova, and Widener—they should consider themselves lucky to have the opportunity to work for a federal judge." That phrase was spewed every time the judge "hired" an unpaid intern. Friedman wanted Harvard, Yale, Columbia, NYU, Chicago, and Stanford. Penn, Duke, Virginia, and Cornell would do in a pinch. That way, when she knocked you down, there would be a substantial fall.

It had been a trying afternoon, and the last thing I felt like doing was the complex conflict of law analysis that my November case warranted. So, I slyly returned to the *Dell Nelson* case to determine where my memo had gone awry.

Tip—"you can just call me the Tipper"—Evans wasn't a bad guy, just a dreadful lawyer. It's one thing to be a crappy corporate lawyer and haphazardly draft stock purchase agreements; it's an altogether different trauma to botch someone's death penalty trial. The Tipper snoozed through the prosecution's opening statement, its cross-examination of Dell Nelson, and at one point, "awakened himself with a loud bout of flatulence, screaming 'objection.'" Indeed, a curious move, as the judge had just called for a recess. The guy even nodded off during his own direct examination of Dell, a particularly egregious act considering that he should never have placed Dell on the stand to begin with. Even the casual *Law and Order* watcher knew that criminal defendants almost never testified on their own behalf. The frequency with which Tip Evans fell asleep would lead any bystander to believe that he was getting a hot stone massage rather than trying to spare someone's life in a court of law.

The crazy part was that Dell Nelson wasn't appealing on the basis of Tip's aforementioned behavior, which occurred when the jury was considering whether or not Dell Nelson was guilty of murder. Rather, Nelson took issue with Evans's performance during the sentencing phase, namely when the jury was deciding life or death. The Tipper didn't call one witness to testify as to why Nelson's life should be spared. Not one of his sisters, nor his grandmother, all of whom clearly adored Nelson, a young guy who'd been supporting the family since he was barely out of grade school. The jury didn't hear about how Nelson often babysat for his neighbors' kids, put food on anyone's table who asked for it, and personally delivered groceries to the elderly folks in his public housing development.

The most disturbing of all was Tip Evans's treatment of Kyle Cooper, a fellow Arch Homes resident—drug-dealer—thug. Kool Kyle, as he was known in the neighborhood, should have been Nelson's ticket out of the electric chair. Thanks to the Tipper, Kyle served as the prosecution's star witness. One snippet from the trial transcript:

District Attorney: "So, Mr. Cooper, you mentioned that Dell Nelson was a big-time drug dealer, pushing speed, heroin, *crack,* preying on mere *children,* right?"

Kyle Cooper: "Ya. Ya. Man, the guy was whack. Once I even saw him peddling some shit on a little girl, she couldn't have been older than five."

District Attorney: "I have no further questions, Your Honor."

Judge Jackson: "Mr. Evans, you may approach the bench for cross-examination. Er, um, Mr. Evans? Can someone please wake up Mr. Evans."

Upon awakening, Evans was so disoriented, he simply said, "I rest my case." Resting, obviously, but where was his case? A case that could have—indeed, should have—involved questioning Kool Kyle about how he'd made repeated threats against Nelson, proclaiming their mutual neighborhood as his turf, not Dell's. How he, and not Dell Nelson, had been arrested two years earlier for selling cocaine to a group of ninth-graders. And when Kyle spent six months in the slammer, how Dell Nelson cared for Kyle's pregnant girlfriend, sending her money and food.

The jurors never heard any of this testimony, all of which would have at once discredited Kool Kyle's prior testimony and educated the jury as to Dell's good qualities. Instead, the Tipper rested his case. And the jury recommended death.

To me, "ineffective" seemed like a nice way of describing Tip Evans's services. A compliment almost. Horrific, god-awful, disgraceful would have been more accurate. The Pennsylvania Supreme Court didn't agree, finding that, while "not great," Evans's performance nonetheless fell within the "permissible range of competency" after reviewing the Tipper's explanations for not questioning Kyle Cooper and failing to call mitigation witnesses (i.e., "those sisters of his were trampy and would have made a bad impression.") The federal district court agreed. As far as I was concerned, Nelson deserved relief even under AEDPA's strict standards.

BUZZ BUZZ BUZZ. It was the judge.

"Yes, Judge," I carefully asked, shoving Nelson's trial transcript under a brief.

"Hi, Sheila, please come to my office and bring Matthew and Evan."

The weirdest part of her command was not the fact that she'd forgotten that Matthew had walked out but that she sounded nice, got all of our names right, and said please. Something smelled in Philadelphia and it wasn't my underpants. When I went to collect Evan, he was sitting perfectly still with a pocket copy of the Constitution in one hand and a *U.S. Reports*—which contained Supreme Court cases—in the other. He had a creepy smile on his face.

"Hey, Evan," I said, gingerly interrupting his mental masturbation.

"God, I *love* the takings clause. It is just amazing!" he quietly exclaimed to his computer. Jiminy crickets! Who loved the takings clause?—an utterly neutral clause that doesn't let the government take your property without "just compensation." Loving the First Amendment or the equal protection clause would be understandable. But the *takings clause*? It was like loving mops.

"Hey, Evan, I hate to rip you away from your little Constitution, but the judge wants to see us." He almost started hyperventilating with excitement.

"She—she wants to see *me?*" He pointed dramatically to himself, as if he'd just landed the lead in *Mamma Mia*. He probably would have started doing his hair and makeup had I not grabbed him and dragged him out of his seat.

We entered the torture chamber to the happiest judge I'd ever seen. Nobody mentioned Matthew. I wondered how long Evan would pretend that he hadn't heard all the commotion.

"Come around here and take a look and see," the judge said, pointing to her computer, still flashing her sparkling fake pearls. Her screen was filled with electronic people standing in front of a big glass building with the words—in big bubble red, white, and blue—"NATIONAL INDEPENDENCE CENTER, JULY 4."

"Isn't it wonderful!" she crooned.

"Yes, it's *amazing!*" Evan impulsively ass-kissed. It was unclear what the amazing part was. Computers? Yes, computers were amazing. Completely ignoring Evan, she turned to me.

"Sheila, what do *you* think?" Think? I didn't think about anything except how stupid and unhappy I was.

"Ah, it's great," I lied. That's all it took. Her curtain call.

"You see, law clerks, I'm on the board of the Independence Center. And tomorrow night we're having a big awards ceremony for all the survivors from the internment." The two of us nodded ferociously. "See this?" She clicked on something and all of a sudden we were inside Stephen Sondheim's *Pacific Overtures.* Japanese graphics flew across the screen, with a TV commercial kind of male voice narrating how America had royally screwed over the Japanese during World War II. We watched and watched and watched.

At the end of the lengthy matinee, the judge swiveled around, tears in her eyes. Barely able to speak, she murmured: "Isn't it just so moving?" Her chapped lips trembled. Pulling an *All My Children* move, Evan managed to tear up himself.

"Yes, it's really beautiful," he whimpered. Evan was the greatest jack-ass ever to have lived. It was a small wonder that some beefcake hadn't pummeled him to death in college. As for the judge, she was most defi-nitely insane. I couldn't be more sympathetic to the victims of the intern-ment, but her sheer audacity! She'd spent her day eviscerating two of her law clerks and now she was crying for Japanese victims from five decades ago? She again ignored Evan and turned to me.

"What did *you* think, Sheila?" she sniveled. While I had no clue what the Independence Center was, I did know that I was about to spontane-ously combust.

"I think it's wonderful *you* are recognizing the survivors. They deserve it." I had her at *you*.

"Very well, you all have worked so hard today. Why don't you go home," she said, as if releasing us twenty-three minutes early atoned for her sins of the day.

I was out of there lickety-split. Evan stayed behind. As I collected my belongings, I overheard him ask the judge, "Do you think I could go to the awards ceremony tomorrow?" Had he absolutely no shame? And why on earth would anyone want to spend an evening—let alone a Friday night—with the judge? It was for persons like Evan that the word *dickweed* was invented. Friedman thought so, too.

"No." Plain and simple.

As I was about to make a break for it, the judge yelled over Evan's de-feated shoulder, "Sheila, Sheila, you live in Center City, right?" She'd asked me that no less than a dozen times.

"Yes, Judge."

"I'll drive you home." It was an order. And just like that, the judge stripped me of my cherished walk home.

"I live in Center City, in Rittenhouse," Evan piped in. The judge also lived in Rittenhouse Square. She wouldn't be able to get out of that one.

"Well, get your things together, Esther. We're leaving in two minutes."

Evan rode shotgun. But the judge had no interest in talking to him. Speeding down 7th Street, she rotated 360 degrees.

"Sheila, now *where* are you from?" No, not this again.

"Judge, I grew up in Virginia," I said for what felt like the hundredth time.

"No! No! No! You're from Pakistan or something!" Deep breath. *Namaste.*

At least five people had honked at her. She didn't care. Honk. Oh no, a blond girl in tight jeans just flipped her off. Window down. Miniature lady peering out window.

"Do you even know who I am!!??? You should not make that gesture to a FEDERAL JUDGE." Crouching clerk, hidden Pakistani in the back. Giddy judge and Evan in front, cackling, excited by demeaning, then nearly killing, nice pedestrian girl. As it turned out, said pedestrian didn't give a shit if it were Judge Judy who'd nearly killed her. She gave the bird to the federal judge again.

We sped off. I was actually going to die there and then. The judge was drunk-with-power driving. Surely that was illegal. Judge suddenly had interest in her cohort. Turning to Evan, she extended her right arm to touch his chest: "You're bllaaaack." He took it as a compliment and smiled.

"Yes, Judge. I am black," he boasted. It wasn't like the dude had penned the great Dr. King Jr.'s "I have a dream" speech. Thankfully we were approaching the corner of 12th and Spruce.

"Judge, you can just drop me off here," I muttered from the back.

"No! No! No! This is where all the gays and druggies are," she exclaimed.

"This is where I live," I explained, hoping she'd realize that the two weren't mutually exclusive.

"No, no. This is a bad area. You just can't live here." She put the pedal to the metal, attempting now to move me from my apartment. The buck stopped there.

"Judge. I really live back there," I insisted. We were at the corner of Spruce and Broad, three blocks past my humble home. Maybe she really was kidnapping me and Evan was in on it, too. Torture for having done a less than stellar job on the *Nelson* memo.

"Fine. But you do realize you live amongst prostitutes and drug dealers," she announced with disgust. Evan nodded in disapproving horror. But I couldn't be bothered. She'd finally stopped and I was out of there faster than you could say Independence Center.

Walking back, I noticed my overalled friend talking to a handsome middle-aged man in a BMW sedan. He was always talking to men in cars. Come to think of it, there were always skinny guys lurking around the corner. And my neighbor upstairs always had men coming and going from his place. I'd just figured he was way more popular than me. I guess I'd never considered *why* he was more popular.

OMG! Maybe the judge was right? Was he—along with all the other loitering men on my block—selling drugs? Sex? Both? At that moment, I noticed Mr. Overalls accepting some cash from the driver before getting in on the passenger side. They sped off. Could it be that I lived in the Red Light District of Philly? No wonder my rent was so cheap. I called James, who thankfully was home.

"Hey, can you meet me outside, right now?" I asked compulsively.

"Is everything OK?"

"Just come outside, OK?"

"OK, be down in a minute." James came out moments later, in his after-hours uniform—jeans, sweatshirt, tennis shoes. "What's going on? You're home early," he commented.

"Yes. The judge drove me home. Did you know we lived in a prostitution drug circle?" I implored. James shook his head, confused. I pointed to the posse of skinny men. "Look. Those guys are always there. Random cars pull up and stop and talk to them. Sometimes they get in. And that guy who lives upstairs in our building *always* has men coming over."

"Sheila, just because they're not wearing Façonnable shirts doesn't mean they're selling drugs." James replied, smirking.

"Listen, the judge told me that corner was where prostitutes and drug dealers were." I pointed again, this time with slightly more drama.

"OK, so now Judge Friedman's the final word on coke and sex? Look Sheila, I just don't think so. This is a really beautiful, nice neighborhood," he said smugly. I was frustrated now.

"Does it not occur to you that sex and drugs could possibly be sold in nice neighborhoods? For example, Washington Square Park, Greenwich Village? I think we should ask someone."

"You want me to proposition one of those guys. No thanks. I'm still smarting from the whole Brian-Jana episode. I don't need to add getting arrested for seeking out homosexual sex to my résumé at this point." Fair enough.

"Maybe we can just ask the guy, I don't know, at the Laundromat or something?"

James didn't think so.

"Listen. I have an idea. Why don't you go to the Laundromat. Ask the nice, eighty-year-old Korean man who doesn't speak English if he knows where you can buy some crack and sex. But man-on-man sex, clarify that part. Then call me and we'll go grab a beer."

At that moment, I noticed a cop walking out of Pine Street Pizza, at the corner of 12th and Pine. I ran down the street and caught up to him before he got back into his police car.

"Excuse me, sir," I panted.

"Yeah?" He asked, irritated that I'd come between him and the foot-long sausage *stromboli* he'd shoved underneath his armpit.

"Yes, I moved down the street not long ago and my boss just told me she thought that corner," I pointed up to Spruce and batted my lashes, "was a place where prostitutes and drug dealers were." The sheer eloquence was lost on him. The cop just stared. "Is that true?" I asked. He leered.

"You must be from the country. A small town or somethin'?" Me—a farm hand?!

"If you must know, I moved here from NEW YORK CITY." I was bragging about a city I no longer lived in to a cop with a sausage up his armpit.

"Well, Ms. Big City, in that case, it should be obvious to you that's where people sell drugs and sex. Why else would all those queers be getting into those cars? Those cars are driven by Main Line faggots who screw those guys and then go home to their wives and kids." He appeared to grow enraged just thinking about it.

At least those guys didn't *beat* their wives and kids, I thought, noticing his wedding band. Good thing he carried a gun, a beating stick, and mace.

"Great, thanks." And I was off. James was standing where I left him moments earlier. "Yup. Guns, drugs, sex to the north. Scary, hateful, homophobic wife-beater cops to the south." James's mouth dropped.

"We are *such* assholes. You are such an asshole—you actually asked a cop if people were selling drugs." He shook his head. "How lame."

"Oh come on, James. Look around. It's a bunch of middle-aged men in silver Land Cruisers. How on earth could we have known that they were getting blow jobs on their way back to Little League."

While it was true that these Main Line fathers were not the most obvious felons, it was also true that we probably should have caught on—the bumper-to-bumper traffic every night at six, not a single female driver, and I should have probably figured out that the pockmarked guy in overalls was not at all homeless but instead was selling his body for sex to suburban professionals.

"Whatever, Sheila." James shrugged his shoulders. "Honestly, I don't even care. Sort of makes this whole clerkship thing that much more interesting. Edgy, almost."

Chapter Eight

⚖

A Toronto judge fell asleep in the middle of a criminal trial but woke up when a defense lawyer dropped a 2,136-page copy of the Criminal Code on the desk in front of him, a court was told yesterday. "We decided that I would drop a copy of Tremeear's Criminal Code . . . in order to wake His Honour."

—www.legalreader.com/archives/001406.html

I woke up with that weird stomach feeling. The kind where you know something dreadful is in store for you but your memory hasn't quite gotten up to speed. Five seconds later, I remembered that in a few short hours, I'd be experiencing my first sitting. I was too scared to even gasp or groan. Maybe I'd paralyzed myself in my sleep? Unfortunately, paralysis probably fit into the "you're not allowed to get sick" category and wouldn't fly as an excuse for a no-show.

B-Day—the day I'd undoubtedly pick my entire scalp bald—had arrived. To think that I had to do this with Evan, and nobody else, made it that much worse. While I'd not heard a peep from Matthew since his dramatic exit, I still prayed for his sister-in-law nightly and had my mother light a few candles for her at the Infant Jesus of Prague Church. Well, maybe not *the* church. This one had vinyl siding and was in suburban Virginia rather than the Czech Republic, but it was the pious thought that counted.

While I was at it, I should have prayed for myself and my more immediate problem. Suits appeared to be the appropriate sitting attire. The
judge's exact words were, "Don't come in here in one of those—those—
things for the sitting." And then she just pointed at me. I'd deduced she
either meant that we should shed our skin or refrain from the hideous
category of clothing we'd all taken to—the dreaded "business casual."

Considering the judge's affection for polyester pantsuits, I found her
disdain to be a bit hypocritical. Unlike the judges, we couldn't mask fashion atrocities with a big black robe. Had I ever even worn a suit? I quietly
made my zillionth empty promise to the Person upstairs and threw open
the closet doors.

On the bright side—the really bright side—there was a suit. It was neon
pink. A holdover from my news producing days in Miami. It made me
cringe that I'd found the thing so chic a few years earlier. In a federal courtroom, it would be like garlic to a vampire. Nearly strangling myself on a
hanger wading through the muddy river of five-seasons-ago clothes, I spotted the Jewel of the Nile: an old navy Ann Taylor pantsuit, circa 1990, with
the biggest shoulder pads I'd ever seen. I grabbed it hungrily, crazy with
excitement. How this veritable antique had managed to survive a decade
of spring cleaning was way beyond me, but who cared? Thankfully, bigger was better back in 1990 and it fit just fine.

On my way out, I caught a glimpse of myself in the full-length mirror
hanging on my bedroom door. What I saw would have made even Arnold
Schwarzenegger cry like a little girl. Bags under red puffy eyes. Crusty mouth.
Boxlike body. The shoulder pads made me look like an actual house. Walking gave the appearance of a mobile home. Hey, all you women, children,
and drug-addicted prostitutes, beware: "CAUTION: WIDE LOAD!"

I was too embarrassed to come face-to-face with my Dunkin' Donuts
friends and proceeded directly to the courthouse. The metal detector went
nuts when I went through. This came as no surprise. There was lots of junk
in this trunk. After the third beep, a large male guard with a bushy mustache and a uniform at least three sizes too small approached me with a

thick black instrument. He practically vacuumed Ann Taylor, and I kept beeping like a bomb, which I wished I had, for obvious reasons.

"You got a belt on under *there?*" he asked, disgust dripping from his 'stache, pointing to my stomach. Frankly, he had no right to be grossed out. He was vile. "Nope. Just the suit. No belt." He didn't believe me, and before I could stop him, he'd yanked the bottom of my jacket and shirt up, exposing my bare—and growing—stomach, rolled over wrinkled pleats. Sweet Jesus! Then he lifted them higher so that the other security guards and everyone else passing through could see my peach Victoria's Secret bra that was even older than the suit. Not to mention, my ragged underwear was sticking out of the pants. He was thoroughly grossed out now. "Go on," he muttered angrily, pushing me toward the elevators. Rolling ahead in my mobile home, I actually felt sort of bad for having given the guy a third-rate peep show.

I headed straight for my cubicle, bypassing the secretaries altogether. I couldn't deal with Medieval Roy and Janet. Just as I tried to parallel-park myself, the darnedest thing happened. "Hey, what's up?" Matthew asked nonchalantly, breezing in as if he'd never left. He sauntered into the clerks' cave, looking like a Brooks Brothers ad in a snappy gray suit and pink-and-white-striped tie.

It turned out that Allison, Matthew's sister-in-law, was going to pull through, and aside from a nasty scar on her right forearm and a lifetime aversion to cabs, she'd be fine. She'd been crossing Fifth Avenue during morning rush hour when a taxi came flying around 34th Street and pegged her. It also turned out that Matthew had yet to speak with the judge and wasn't sure whether he was still welcome in her torture chamber.

"I wouldn't worry about it," I explained. "The judge doesn't seem to have noticed you even left in the first place."

"Well, I guess that's good news," he said, getting reacquainted with his cubicle. His face suddenly reddened. "This will be taking a bit of rest," he mumbled, grabbing the glittery beach shot of Heidi and shoving it into a drawer.

Their lovers' spat was definitely none of my business, but inquiring mobile homes wanted to know.

"I take it things aren't going swimmingly with you two," I ventured.

He stared blankly, threatening to resume the sitting-up-dead position he'd mastered prior to his dramatic exit weeks earlier.

"Oh, it's been a pretty crappy few weeks. If you can believe it, Allison's accident and my confrontation with the judge weren't even the worst of it."

I shimmied myself into the narrow parking spot in front of Matthew's cubicle and gave his impeccably groomed brownish blond head one gentle pat. "So, what happened? Is everything O—"

"It's Heidi," he blurted. "She wasn't overly supportive, to put it mildly. When I got to New York, I figured that she'd meet me at the hospital, right? I mean, that's what I would have done but—"

"Um, hello? Are you guys, um, law clerks?" Matthew and I whipped around at the sound of a foreign voice.

"Hi, um, I'm Kate, I'm um, the new clerk, um." I'd totally forgotten that Laura the Lesbian's replacement was starting that day. From the looks of her, there was no way Kate would last as long as Laura. Insecurity-inspired posture. Glasses thicker than my shoulder pads. And a distracting love of the word *um*. At least she was wearing a cute suit.

"Um, is that guy, um, in the back, um, a clerk also?" She pointed to Evan's corner. It was obvious that Evan hadn't introduced himself to her, let alone provided pertinent information such as: Don't talk, don't smoke, don't get sick, and don't eat lunch.

Matthew stood up, gently grabbed Kate's and my arm and ushered us to the back. "Hey, Evan," he said brazenly, "did you meet our new coclerk, Kate?" Prior to his showdown with the judge, Matthew had barely spoken two words. Now he was taking charge, as if the showdown had broken a lifelong seal.

Pretending not to have noticed that a new clerk was in our midst and that Matthew had returned from sabbatical, Evan looked up. "Oh, hi. I'm Evan. Nice to meet you." Liar. He didn't think it was nice to meet her. He didn't think it was nice to meet anyone who couldn't do something for him. Recently, my disdain for Evan had ripened into loathing.

Evan had picked up a nasty habit: sauntering by my cubicle every day to announce status reports ("Just two days away from yet another bencher." "Just a day away from that bencher." "Turning in the bencher"). The real punishment was Evan's delivery-style, like that of an Agent Orange plane, dusting me with deathly updates without so much as a glance.

Just then, I remembered that Janet had ticked off exactly one zillion things to do for the judge in preparation of the sitting. Hot flash. "Hey, guys, don't we need to do something for the judge?" Flash. "Some xeroxing or something?" Flash. I felt the beginnings of a mustache growing in. "Matthew. Evan. I can't remember any of it. And Janet just told me the other day. Oh God!"

Evan sighed: "*I* took care of *everything* for the sitting. You guys owe me," he said smiling.

"Thanks, Evan." I forced myself to add, "In repayment, I am officially inviting you to lunch with Judge Adams's law clerks today after the sitting. Oh, and Kate and Matthew, of course the two of you are invited, too."

Since the Edict of No Lunch, I'd started bringing some form of a sandwich to work on most days and eating it in the bathroom (hereinafter "toilet lunch"). On the other days, I'd still venture out. Just like everything else she said and did, the judge only sometimes remembered the lunch ban.

"What?! Lunch with Judge Adams's clerks? How did you get that?" Evan panted with excitement.

DING!

Suddenly the judge was standing before the four of us. She produced a toothy smile and boasted a new robust bun. "Hi, Kate—so nice to have you here!" she exclaimed, with a tinge of sincerity.

"Hi, Judge Friedman," Kate replied softly, bowing her head.

Without looking at the rest of us, including the clerk who'd told her to bugger off, the judge ordered: "Now we need to get moving, people." She clapped, like we were cattle, before heading to the torture chamber. The four of us followed her like the farm animals we'd become. She abruptly stopped in front of my cubicle, causing a most unfortunate rear-ending.

"What are you people doing?" she sneered, without turning around. "I didn't mean right this second. We still have a half hour before argument starts." With that, Her Highness dragged her uneven legs into her office and shut the door.

The four of us returned to our respective homes. I felt especially bad for Kate. Unlike Matthew, Evan, and me, she hadn't sent out the truckloads of applications. She was just living her life and got picked out of the blue and at random, like jury duty except this wasn't just a few days but a year. And she couldn't say no to Judge Friedman. In her preclerking life, Kate was a staff attorney who wrote bench memos for all judges on the third circuit. She focused only on *pro se* cases, in which prisoners represented themselves rather than having the benefit of a lawyer.

Considering that Kate had worked for the entire court, including Friedman, she didn't really have the option to nix the judge's offer (i.e., *demand*) to be her law clerk. Judges were better extortionists than most convicted criminals. They were not necessarily more clever. Just above the law.

"Sheila." Matthew motioned me to his cubicle. The mobile home cruise-controlled itself over. I was hoping to get the rest of the Heidi story. "Hey, do you have your bench memos and everything else?" he whispered. Oh no! In all the excitement, I'd totally spaced on the most important thing. I quickly grabbed my *Nelson* memo and the massive appendices that went along with it. My first day of kindergarten was less nerve-racking than this, which was no small thing, since I'd barfed all over Mrs. Dalton's desk after snack time.

"SHEEEEELLLLLAAAA!" Why didn't she ever scream for anyone else? I nearly crashed into Janet speeding around the corner.

"Yes, Judge." Behind closed doors, she'd robed herself and applied lipstick. She looked like a witch trying to turn a trick.

"It's time to go. Get everyone," she ordered. And I delivered. We went into her office and collected everything Evan had prepared. I just hoped that he had done it in the correct fashion. There was no time to worry about that now. "Law clerks come with me on the judges' elevator," she announced. What a treat! Carrying stacks of paper, we followed her one floor up. Two elderly people in black robes greeted us as the elevator doors opened. Immediately, Judge Friedman started acting weird—like she liked us. She grabbed Evan and shoved him forward, nearly toppling the fragile male judge. Then again, it looked like a careless whisper could have knocked him over.

"This is Harvard. Um. Ah. E-Evan," Judge Friedman stuttered. I was next up and unceremoniously pushed into the female judge. "And this is Columbia. She-la," she enunciated carefully, before producing a grand smile and grabbing Matthew. "*This*"—she paused dramatically—"is Yale!" Then she rubbed Matthew's back.

With each stroke, more color left Matthew's face, leaving him pasty and pale. Kate stood in the corner like leftover salmon. The judge caught a glimpse of her and noted: "Oh yeah. That's Ja-Ja-Sylvia. She's from Cornell. But from forever ago." Then as an afterthought, she added: "*My* chambers are like the United Nations. I have one black," she said, pointing to Evan with a smile (which he returned), and then she touched my back, "one Pakistani," moving onto Kate, "here's my Jew," then back to Matthew, "and the White."

"That's nice, Helga," the male judge muttered.

"Law clerks—this is Judge Stevens," she said. Then, quickly spinning around to the female judge, "and this is Judge Adams." Her bun twitched and she turned green, exposing pure envy. I wanted to hug Judge Adams, tell her that I loved her.

Judge Friedman was talking like a windup doll on crystal meth, about this and that and then this and that again. We all just stood there until—thankfully—Judge Stevens whimpered: "Helga, Linda, we ought to get going."

Before proceeding through the special judge door, Friedman directed us to another, lesser passageway: "Law clerks, through there." Our United

Nations delegation passed through the secret clerk entrance to the court-room, which was packed.

"Um, Sheila, um, I'm not, um, Jewish," Kate whispered.

"I'm not Pakistani. Just play along. You are Jewish for the year." She looked puzzled. She'd learn. Judge Stevens's and Adams's clerks had already taken their positions along the side of the room. The clerk of the court directed us to place Judge Friedman's materials in front of her empty chair, which we did in no particular order. That wasn't good. In a place steeped in methodical process, our arbitrary preparations didn't bode well. But to my knowledge, none of us was a mind reader and there was no training; we weren't allowed to talk to the judge unless addressed by her, Medieval Roy had about as much information as a tongueless cat, and Anna Wintour was more approachable than Janet. We were alone.

The four of us took our seats, next to Judge Adams's clerks. I sandwiched myself between Matthew and Kevin, who grimaced at me after a careful once-over. I couldn't blame him. I was clearly the front-runner for worst-dressed in a courtroom full of pleats and polyester. There was one bald guy standing in the back who was wearing tight black slacks that were too short, revealing thick, hairy ankles, and an oversized red-and-black-striped shirt that was barely tucked in, revealing a brown braided belt. He was my only real competition. And I was pretty sure I had him beat.

"ALL RISE!" the clerk of the court announced, and we, the masses, scrambled to our feet. In walked Stevens, Friedman, and Adams, in that order. The three of them stood behind their stately black leather chairs, all in their black robes, at least a dozen feet above the rest of us. Friedman stood in the middle. She was the presider, the most senior judge on the panel. It was a miracle her ego, her bun, and my shoulder pads all fit in the same room at that point. After a few dramatic seconds during which we, the entranced audience, stared in awe at the appellate gods, they sat. Then we sat.

Judge Friedman began. "Good morning. Thank you all for joining us today," she said with a smile. I looked into a sea of worshipping lawyers. She looked down at the table before her. Suddenly, she didn't look happy anymore. She started scrambling around, obviously unable to find something. She looked over, under, right, left. And then directly at the four of us.

With one bony finger, she motioned for one of us to approach the bench. There was no way I going up there dressed like I was. Evan had gotten us into this pickle and he'd have to lead us out of it. But he just looked down, pretending not to see her. He was the only one. The way she was waving, Ernie the blind cafeteria worker probably saw her. Matthew bravely followed her silent order. We couldn't hear anything but just watched her scold him for something or another and then he left through the same door from which we had arrived.

"There seems to be a bit of technical difficulty. While each of you is probably nervous today, take comfort in the fact that you are not one of my law clerks right now." She smiled. Laughter all around. Then she turned to Evan, Kate, and me and slipped us an ominous glare. Not so funny.

After a few minutes that felt like several hours, Matthew returned with a sheet of paper and handed it to the judge, who quickly grabbed it without tipping the delivery boy. "Uh-hem. We will first hear arguments in *Nelson v. Donald Timmons, Secretary, Pennsylvania Department of Corrections.*" Great! I was first up. Nelson's shockingly young attorney approached the podium, which was situated at ground level about ten feet away from the bench.

"Good morning, my name is Olivia Northum and may it please the court. First and foremost, this case is about fairness and what the Constitution require—"

"Ms. Northum, we know what the Constitution requires. Can you please move on to why we should disagree with all the courts before us? We are, after all, supposed to defer to their judgments," Judge Friedman said pointedly, leaning forward an inch while keeping her small shoulders perpendicular to her neck. This impeccable posture, coupled with the fact that she'd nailed the lawyer's name on her first try, removed any semblance of insanity. Even her bun was at rest, lending her a regal air. Who was this woman and what had she done with Helga Friedman?

"Yes, Judge Friedman, the court of appeals is to afford deference. But deference does not mean agreeing with the courts below willy-nilly. If, as here, the state court has made a decision based on an unreasonable determination of the facts, then you are permitted, indeed, compelled, to overturn that decision," Ms. Northum replied, unflinchingly. "When a lawyer sleeps through a trial and a sentencing hearing, fails to call witnesses, fails to cross-examine witnesses, and fails to make a closing argument, it is difficult to see how one can defer to that, especially when, as here, that behavior sends someone to their death."

This was one articulate teenager. The courtroom hushed.

"Yes, fine, Ms. Northum, but it is all too tempting for defendants to second-guess counsel after he or she has lost," Judge Adams lectured, "and the district court below, in a comprehensive and incisive opinion, found that, while deficient perhaps, Tip Evans's errors did not prejudice Mr. Nelson."

"With all due respect, Judge Adams," Ms. Northum began, "I ask how prejudice isn't obvi—"

"Let's move onto the merits, I think we understand your argument," Judge Friedman interrupted, "specifically, the various mitigation witnesses, Nelson's grandmother, three sisters, friends, neighbors. It seems like there were dozens of people who loved this man and were willing to beg for a life sentence over death." Friedman tilted her head in my direction and winked. She'd taken a sentence almost verbatim from my memo and used it during argument—every law clerk's wet dream!

The teenager smiled coyly, acknowledging her friend on the bench. "That's exactly right, Judge Friedman. A host of people came forward wanting to testify on Dell Nelson's behalf, to spare his life. Tip Evans met with a handful of them, only after they contacted him first. According to Mr. Nelson's sister Izzie, he spent no more than ten minutes with each of them and then—"

"I'm glad that you bring up Izzie," Judge Adams butted in. "Isn't it true that the reason Mr. Evans excluded Izzie from testifying was based on strategy; he felt that she, that she was—"

"That she was a—and I quote—a 'tramp'?" Friedman completed Adams's sentence. Adams and Friedman locked eyes momentarily, a heavy breather during their blossoming battle. This was getting good. And hard to follow.

"Actually, what I was going to say, before you interrupted," Judge Adams said, reclaiming her territory, "was that Mr. Evans pointed to the fact that Izzie herself had filed a restraining order against her brother, Dell Nelson, a mere year earlier because he'd threatened to kill her if she didn't stop engaging in behavior he deemed unbecoming. And that if he did put her on the stand, the prosecution would decimate her on cross-examination. This was a *tactical* decision, not one born from laziness. It is not our job to question trial tactics, Judge Friedman."

Everything that followed was a blur. More slut. Less deference. Prejudice? Electric chair. Cool Kyle. Rape. Mitigation. Adequate. Fairness. The speed with which Judge Adams and Friedman fired questions almost precluded the child-prodigy attorney from speaking and transformed the courtroom into Wimbledon, the spectators dizzy from ricocheting rhetoric.

It occurred to me that oral arguments served as a forum for judges to convince one another of opinions already formed. Friedman wanted to give Dell Nelson another shot. Judge Adams didn't. The tiebreaker would be Judge Stevens, who'd not breathed a word. In fact, it wasn't clear he was breathing at all, but that didn't stop the other two from boisterously attempting to win him over.

At the end of the half-hour argument, I felt exhilarated, like riding a roller coaster for the first time, unable to remember why I'd been so afraid of Judge Friedman before. She'd actually taken my opinion to heart. Indeed, she shared my opinion. My work had not been for naught, and as a result, it was possible for a profound wrong to be righted. If Stevens came on board, Dell Nelson could be spared death. I smiled jubilantly as the next case was called.

It was one of Evan's. Evan had three of the cases, whereas Matthew and I had one each. Evan was a memo machine. The only time he'd pull himself away from his cubicle was to saunter into the judge's office to turn in yet another completed memo. His computer was like an Uzi, shooting out bench memos in rapid fire, which should have made him a shoo-in for least-hated clerk—but not so. Week after week, he'd arrive in the torture chamber, memo in hand, creepy smile on face. In fact, a few days earlier, he had proudly delivered a thick memo for the November sitting. I'd barely read the first ten pages of the defendant's brief for mine.

Per usual, Evan marched in and announced: "Judge, this case is really interesting. I just can't wait for—" But she could wait.

"Evan, I don't have time for the November sitting right now." Without looking up, she reached underneath her desk and handed him another case. The judge masked her dislike for Evan with apathy, which was lost on him. Prior to her stellar performance on the bench, it was for this, and only this, that I respected the judge just a smidgen. For some reason, she couldn't stand blatant brownnosers; at the same time, she demanded the utmost respect—the trick was finding the proper balance. This was something Evan had not picked up, as evidenced by his current behavior.

As soon as the judge called the attorney on Evan's case, he started panting like a thirsty camel. His tongue was fully distended and wagging madly. He was glued to the judge. Fixated. Obsessed. What would she say? Would she ask a question he suggested in one of his memos? Would she wink at him? She didn't. Instead, the judge fell asleep.

I couldn't blame her. She'd worn herself out during the Nelson case. Not to mention, the current lawyer wouldn't stop droning on about the statute of limitations. Judge Stevens seemed to have developed a thyroid stare. Only Judge Adams seemed to be awake and tossed a question or two at the lawyer. Judge Friedman simply tilted her head forward, exposing her bun to the crowd. It twitched a little. So much for her regal bearing. At first, I thought she was dead. So did Matthew, who nudged me and scribbled a note on his pad to that effect.

Lawyer: "And so, Your Honors, the clock should start running from the date of *discovery* of the injury rather than the *inception*."

Friedman: Tilt left. She wasn't dead. I glanced over at Evan who was still batting his lashes at the bench, so blinded by love that he didn't even notice the napping judge.

"She's going to fall. I swear it," Matthew whispered, elbowing me. The judge was almost parallel to the floor before the stack of briefs in her lap came crashing to the floor. She popped up like a jack-in-the-box and groaned into the microphone, sending a quasi-pornographic echo throughout the courtroom. Once again, a hush blanketed the crowd.

The moment she regained lucidity, Judge Friedman turned to us and glared as if her narcoleptic episode had been our fault. Back to life. Back to reality.

Medieval Roy and Janet had been jousting. Janet won. The defeated bard came tearing around the corner and smacked into Evan. Zillions of documents and one very bruised ego flew about. Roy had been reduced to tears.

"I-I-I am just so-so-so sorry."

It was true, he was a so sorry man. Evan couldn't be bothered. He had taken to emulating the judge's treatment of Roy. "Can't you do anything right, Roy?" Roy cowered.

"Roy, is everything OK?" I asked, artfully balancing the mammoth *Nelson* appendix on my hip.

"Ja-Ja-Janet is just so mean, I can't stand it," he stuttered. A speech therapist could have made a killing in that place. Evan collected his stuff and stormed off, leaving Roy midstutter and leaving the rest of us to pat his hairy back. "I was filing. You know, I can file, when she told me that I was doing it wrong. Then she called me stupid and told me that the mere sight of me made her angry." He had stopped whimpering and had regained composure. "I mean, this place is nuts," Roy said, opening his mouth wide, which was a bit of a one-two punch, since he was a close talker to begin with. Maybe it was all the Nicorette chewing gum, but we got an unsavory glimpse into a haunted house of halitosis.

"Roy, don't let her bother you so much, and look on the bright side, you've got tomorrow off, right?" Roy nodded at Matthew's question before orally assaulting us again.

"Yeah, yeah, you're right. Man oh man am I psyched for tomorrow. I'm headed down the shore to rock my harp at this awesome Markland festival. It's totally awesome. Felemid McDowell's in the house!" Roy smiled as he raised the roof.

"Roy, we have to get in there," I explained, nodding my head toward the torture chamber, grateful for the elevator that came and whisked Roy off to a happier century.

Thankfully, the judge had yet to return to chambers from the courtroom. We still had time to prepare for her meeting with the panel. After every set of oral arguments, the panel met in the office of the most senior judge. In this case, and almost always, that judge was Friedman. As far as I could tell, the woman had been on the bench since shortly after her birth. During the conference, they'd discuss the cases and decide which judge would write which opinion. Of course, nobody had bothered to explain how we were supposed to arrange the judge's materials.

Evan was standing by Matthew's cubicle when we walked in. It looked like he was hiding from something, everything. After we exchanged "What should we do's?" I decided to take control and ask Janet. After all, she'd been given a four-hour vacation from the judge, which had presumably put her in a better mood.

"Hey, Janet," I said, smiling. She didn't return the favor. Matthew, Evan, and Kate gathered behind me, using me as their collective bulletproof vest. "Can you just tell us where we should put all of this stuff?" I asked gently. This was such an easy question; it didn't even require Janet to speak. She could have just pointed. But having just kicked Roy's butt, she was apparently feeling rather macho.

"Don't you people know *anything?*" She definitely needed to fire her writers and get new ones. The judge had used that line on her last week and she'd just used a variation thereof on Roy. Mean and nasty was one thing. Mean and nasty with old, recycled material was altogether different. I refused to be bullied by such a specimen.

"Janet, listen. I don't know why you're so mad at us. But for whatever reason, can you find it within you to just point us in the direction of where we have to put this stuff for the judge's conference. She fell asleep on the bench and she's mad at herself, which means she's going to be mad at all of us. That includes you. So, just tell me. Please."

Kate whimpered. As for Janet, it seemed that I had found her price: trash-talking the judge. Not that I had *really* trash-talked the judge, but the mere mention of bench-sleeping did the trick.

"Just give them to me. I'll take care of it. And what's this about her sleeping?" Janet asked, smiling.

"She just fell asleep. Actually that case was so boring, I can't blame her," Matthew explained.

"It was *not* boring!" Evan snapped. "And I don't think she was sleeping. I think she was thinking." Before I could tell Evan *he* was boring, the judge sauntered into the secretaries' den, followed by Judges Adams and Stevens. Oh no! Her entire staff, but for the interns and Roy, who didn't count anyway, were all in the secretaries' office. She'd think we were having a tea party or something. Surely she'd go ballistic. Instead, she smiled.

"Linda, Joe—you remember Janet?" She motioned from her colleagues to her secretary. They nodded and smiled. Janet cooed. "And of course my wonderful law clerks." Smiles around once again. I wondered if Judge Friedman had been doing shots, which would explain her sleeping on the job. She buttressed my developing theory by warmly beckoning: "Law clerks, go enjoy a nice lunch. You deserve it." Definitely tequila. Tequila made people crazy. "Janet, why don't you take a long lunch. We'll be back here meeting for a while." Janet smiled like a pedophile on a playground.

"Thanks, Judge. That's really nice, Judge. Thanks." Janet curtsied.

"This morning was just so incredible. And so interesting," Evan piped in. Somewhere in Philadelphia, someone was buying Evan's and Janet's self-respect on the black market. And what was Evan referring to? It was true that the *Nelson* argument was incredible. But I had a feeling Evan didn't give a rat's bum about any cases he didn't work on. So, I surmised by "incredible" he meant the judge sleeping on the bench? Or her glaring? Was it Janet's Pound Puppy fetish or chemical imbalance? Or perhaps Roy's breath? Thankfully, none of the judges bought the crap Evan was selling. Before he could finish sucking up, Judge Friedman snatched the materials from Janet and shut the doors to the torture chamber.

The four of us headed down to the lobby to meet the others. Judge Adams's clerks—Betsy, Kevin, and Walt—were waiting for us, happily chatting among themselves. Jana wisely skipped lunch, presumably picking up on the fact that I hated her for having humiliated James. We settled on Jones, Mr. Starr's latest invention, which was modeled after the set of the *Brady Bunch*. I ordered deviled eggs and mac-and-cheese.

"Wow, you must be hungry!" Walt exclaimed. Walt had gone to Yale Law but didn't know Matthew because he'd graduated a year earlier and had worked at Thompson & Siegel, a large New York City firm, in the interim. He was five foot ten and weighed approximately 3.5 pounds. The only thing more unnerving than an anorexic woman was an anorexic man, and the only thing worse than that was an anorexic man named Walt.

Betsy had gone to Duke and emitted a casual, borderline pleasant vibe, a double anomaly considering most Dukies and law clerks seemed to be jerks by definition. Whereas Harvard churned out irritation, Duke manufactured arrogant monsters who were simultaneously not the brightest bulbs in the box. Mean + kind of dumb = intolerable. At first blush, Betsy appeared to have skirted Duke's dim fate. Not to mention, she had pretty hair.

Jana notwithstanding, Adams seemed to have chosen winners. No jerks, no egos, and no fedoras. And aside from Walt's obvious aversion to eating (or proclivity for puking), they appeared to be a well-adjusted bunch.

"Yes, I'm starving. It's been a long morning, don't you think?" I asked. Unlike with Brian and his cult of no personality, I felt like I could be honest around these three.

"Long? What was so long about it? I thought it was fascinating!" Evan exclaimed, attempting to distance himself from what he deemed sacrilege.

"Yes, Evan, I thought parts of it were fascinating, namely the arguments in *my Nelson* case. But the rest of it, not so fascinating, thereby making it *long,*" I clarified.

"Um, Evan, did you not find it slightly uncomfortable when the Judge fell asleep?" Matthew asked.

"Sheila, at least she seemed pleased with you during that death penalty case. You'd been so scared about that," Kevin offered, attempting normalcy. "That, by the way, was an amazing argument. I wonder how Stevens will come out. It was pretty clear with the other two."

"From some of his other opinions I've read in the past, it seems he's open to second chances. We'll see," I said, shrugging. "And Betsy, I know you worked on that case. Did you *actually* suggest to her that we *shouldn't* overturn the opinion below and not give this guy a fair sentencing hearing?"

"As I said before, we're really not supposed to discuss this until after the judges have decided. So, I'm pleading the Fifth, OK, Sheila?" In addition to pretty hair, Betsy could keep a secret, an unusual—and respectable— combination.

"What we *can* discuss is Friedman's sleep-sitting. Did you guys see how pissed she was when she finally woke up?" Matthew asked, popping one of my deviled eggs.

Betsy leaned in and smiled. "Totally pissed. I have to ask—is Friedman *really* crazy? I mean, Judge Adams is such a class act she'd never come out and say something nasty about anyone, especially not a colleague. Also, she's got to consider her husband's campaign but she *does* allude to not really liking Friedman," she said excitedly. I instantly loved Betsy—a gossip! So, too, was Walt.

"Yeah, I guess your judge called our judge a couple of days ago," Walt said, gasping for air, "and practically threatened her to sign on to some opinion from a previous sitting. [Gasp.] I happened to be in the office when she called and the judge just grimaced. She didn't even take her off speakerphone. Nor did she have a chance to respond. [Gasp.] Friedman just kept lecturing her about how things didn't work this way and that way and how judges are supposed to support each other and sign each other's opinions. Finally she hung up and Adams just said, 'Helga can be really difficult sometimes. I just let her talk. I can't be bothered.'" Gasp, gasp, gasp.

Evan shuddered, overtaken by agita. Having others not respect Judge Friedman somehow demeaned his clerkship. "Excuse me. But our judge is a brilliant jurist. One of the last great liberals. She stands up for the rights of the downtrodden—homosexuals, Hispanics, African America—"

"Yeah, that's why she thinks gay automatically means hookers and hash!" I blurted. Blank stares all around.

"UM! Will someone, UM, please get me up, UM, to speed," Kate demanded. I looked down, scraping my plate in search of some leftover crusty cheese. It didn't seem appropriate to tell her the truth, namely: We can't speak to anyone. Can't use the phone. We're not allowed to go online. There are blind people who try to poison you. There is a fanny-pack-wearing medievalist and a homicidal homemaker who double as secretaries. And our denture-wearing boss was plucked off the set of *Halloween 13*. Kate would have to learn for herself like the rest of us.

"Kate, we work in a strange place. You'll see," Matthew offered casually.

"So, did you know that Judge Adams is being considered for the top spot?" Betsy said, changing the subject and dropping a bomb of judicial proportions.

Blood rushed to Evan's puny head: "The Su-su-su-preeeeeme Court?!"

"Sheila, I wasn't allowed to tell anyone, which is why I haven't said anything to you," Kevin apologized.

Before I could respond, Betsy cut in, ignoring Evan, who appeared to be choking.

"This has to be on the DL," she said, her eyes bulging. "So, our secretary told us last week that the Bushies are getting paranoid, quite paranoid indeed, that this Hernandez character is getting Borked. It's clear that the Democrats are going to continue filibustering him. Which they should. He's a conservative motherfucker." Betsy paused long enough on the *fucker* part to cause Evan to turn a deep shade of purple. "But now that some moderate Republicans are on board, Pennsylvania Avenue is really freaking out. So Specter, as in Senator Specter—you know, head of the Judiciary Committee, a good friend of the Adamses'—calls last Tuesday. Seems that Specter got a call from GW himself asking about Judge Adams. *El presidente* is getting heat from his advisers to nominate someone else. Someone less controversial. Someone who doesn't fantasize about lynching abortion clinic workers. Someone who'd still kill a category. Someone still Republican. Voilà! Linda Adams. Female. Blue-collar background. She wins on gender and class. Only problem is she's not Hispanic. But what the fuck—you can't have it all."

Everyone fixated on Betsy, who clearly loved the spotlight. It occurred to me that being a clerk may be fabulous after all. We were privy to the news before it was news.

"Specter has given her his personal stamp of approval. It could be as early as next month. Now she's just waiting to get Shepard's support. He's a little wishy-washy because of her stance on abortion, but I think he'll come around." The end. She was done.

So were we.

Armageddon would follow shortly after Judge Friedman got a load of this. No doubt, this news would have profound ramifications for us. Kate didn't get it.

"I think that's just so, um, wonderful. Sending someone, um, to the Supreme Court from here would be great. I don't know the last time a justice came from the third. They always pick them, um, from the DC circuit or, um, the ninth. Not to mention the fact that I think it's great they'll fill the vacant seat with another woman," Kate cooed. She looked like one of those naive horror-flick victims moments before they're bludgeoned to death.

"Oh good God! We're finished!" I yelped. "Listen, you guys. I don't mean to sound jealous, because I *assure* you, I'm not. The last thing I'd want is for Judge Friedman to get picked for anything, especially the Supreme Court. It's just that . . . It's just that . . ." The proper words escaped me. They found Matthew.

"It's just that she hates Judge Adams more than she hates us. More than she hates Janet, her secretary. More than she hates herself, even. This is going to destroy her. As a result, this is going to destroy us." We had the captive audience now.

Betsy couldn't restrain herself. "Really? Your judge hates our judge? That's fucking awesome! Soooo high school!" she exclaimed giddily.

"It is pretty funny, you have to admit," Walt chimed in. They weren't getting it. Nobody got it, least of all Evan, who, rather than being scared, was jealous.

"I mean, what are the chances that Adams will even get picked off a short list?" Evan asked, short of breath. "I also heard that Beckmeyer from the fourth and Mendes from the first were on the short list. Then there's her abortion stance—which I wholly respect, for the record. That's going to give her trouble in Congress. And I think Shepard is going to be a huge problem."

"Well, I think it's wonderful, no matter what you all say," Kate stated clearly, head held up high. The check arrived, we paid, and I managed to slip in one final question for Betsy.

"So, do other judges know?"

"Only Fleck. He called Adams shortly after Specter did. I guess Specter had called him, being the chief judge and all. And he and Adams are super tight. He's fuckin' thrilled. This would be really good for the circuit, actually. Not to mention for us. People will think we clerked for a fucking Supreme Court justice!" For some reason, when Betsy used the word *fuck* or a derivative thereof, it was cute rather than crass. Impressive, considering she used it with the kind of frequency most people reserved for prepositions.

"Great, your happiness is our hell," I replied. The four of us then headed back to the chambers, carting a mix of pride, misery, and jealousy.

We opened the main door to Metallica.

"MATTTTTTTHEWWWWW!!!! SHEEEERRRRAAAA!!"

Good God! Was she dying? Matthew and I sped off.

"Yes, Judge!" I screamed back at her, for the first time. We looked left and right. No judge.

"MAAATTTTHHHHHEW!!!!!! SHEEEEIIIIILLLLLA!!!!"

We followed the screams and came upon the judge, standing inside her elevator, eyes hungry like a wolf's, robe being pulled east and west, arms prying doors open with mouth poised to scream again. Was that mayonnaise crusted on top of her smeared bright red lipstick? Was she stuck? I was at once worried and hopeful.

"Have you seen Judge Stevens's law clerks?" she asked, suddenly calm. We shook our heads. She pursed her lips, slid her arms inside the elevator, and off she went. DING! Thirteenth floor, going down. Matthew and I stood staring at each other. Kate and Evan peered around the corner, ensuring that the coast was clear.

"What the fuck was that?" Matthew raised his arms in the air. Betsy's use of the F-bomb was contagious.

"Well, from what I could tell she just wanted to know where law clerks, who aren't even her law clerks, were." I thought I had answered Matthew's question.

"No, I meant what was that on her mouth? Was that chicken salad?"

"Why didn't she call for me?" Evan whined and flapped his arms, exasperated. Contrary to what teachers tell you, some questions *were* stupid and didn't warrant responses. I returned to my cubicle, which proved strangely comforting amid the pandemonium.

After a few moments of staring at Camden, I turned to my computer. There was a message from James, who'd recently started playing with fire by e-mailing me from the intracourt system:

"Hey. Today was the first day of your sitting, right? I'm sure it's heinous but take pleasure in knowing that the judge just got a new engine for his scooter, came tearing around the corner about five minutes ago, honking his horn and waving madly. Then he turned to me. Came to a screeching halt and started screaming, 'Let's move those motions. Put a little potion in that motion.' Then he honked again and sped off. And to think that this guy gets laid more than I do."

As of late, I'd ignored the no e-mail policy and was about to write James when Kate approached my cubicle. "Hey, Sheila, um, I hate to bother you, but do you know what I'm supposed to do?" We weren't hearing additional cases until the next morning, so I assumed she was supposed to work on a November case.

"I guess Roy and Janet didn't give you anything this morning?" She shook her head. Now that I'd gotten Janet's number, she seemed somewhat less intimidating. I grabbed Kate's arm and dragged her into the secretaries' den.

"Janet, hey, Kate doesn't have anything to work on. Did the judge leave anything for her?" I inquired, unafraid. Instead of barking, she actually spoke.

"No. And for your information, she's gone to deal with Bob and may be gone for the rest of the afternoon." Janet was now offering up jewels of information.

"Thanks, Janet." We headed back to the clerks' cave. "I guess you can just hang out. By the way, I'm sorry today's been so weird. No way to spend your first day. I feel like we didn't get off to the best start."

She smiled and the two of us sat at the table in the middle of the room. A few feet away, Matthew couldn't have been less interested in joining us. The chicken salad thing had really done a number on him. He sat, vacantly staring and hitting the refresh button on the Boise State football page as if there'd be breaking news. I wondered if his foul mood was a result of the judge or Heidi.

"So, you were—or are—a staff attorney?" I asked. The inquisition began.

"Yep. Um, I've been here for about two years. Before that I, um, did litigation at Williams and before that I clerked on the New Jersey, um, Supreme Court." I did the math. Kate could tell.

"In case you're wondering, I'm, um, probably ten years older than you guys." She didn't look it at all but I was glad she'd offered up the information. The only thing sadder than a nearly thirty-year-old law clerk with a bladder control problem was a nearly forty-year-old law clerk with a speech impediment.

"And you live where again?" Lacking any creativity at that point, I opted for the safe geographical question.

"My husband, Tom, and our dog, Linus, and I, um, live out in Wayne." I nodded, feigning I knew (or cared) where Wayne was. To me, suburbs were suburbs and I couldn't be bothered with distinctions, especially because the chance of my ever going to any Philadelphia suburb was about as great as the judge returning from her time with Bob as Carol Brady.

"What about you? You, um, live around here, right?" Kate softly asked.

"Yeah, I live on 12th between Spruce and Pine. I like it," I replied.

She nodded. I sensed we didn't have much else to say to each other, so instead of returning to my cubicle, I did the usual. Panic manic talk. "It's fine, I mean. Apparently, there are lots of drugs there. And also hookers. But it's nice. I mean—it's totally fine. I mean, I like it. It's fine. That's what I'm trying to say." Kate looked spooked. So did Matthew, who'd been awakened from his coma by my monologue.

"Is everything OK?" He asked, swiveling around.

"I don't know. This place turns me into a total freak," I answered before returning to my desk. Kate returned to her corner in the back and Matthew to his Idaho sports page.

It was nearly six and the judge still hadn't come back. Another half hour and I was free to drop off my mobile home and dart over to Banana Republic to buy a more appropriate suit for the next day.

I wondered if the panel had come to a decision on Dell Nelson. I'd caught a glimpse of Dell in court earlier that day. He had been sitting between two guards behind the podium, so I only saw him for a split second when he stood to leave the courtroom. He was not at all as I'd expected. Actually, I wasn't sure what I'd expected, but whatever it was, it wasn't that slight, smooth-skinned man with probing eyes. He didn't seem angry, just a bit confused, which was probably how I'd feel if I'd spent my adult life on death row, fighting a sleeping lawyer. It was strange to think, however, that he was fighting not to be free of prison, but rather to remain there for decades. Talk about a will to live.

As I stood to have a heart-to-heart with myself in the bathroom, the phone rang. It had to be the judge. Nobody else ever called. Janet had gone home and Matthew was in a stupor, so I answered.

"Good afternoon, Judge Fried—"

"JAAAANNNNEEETTTT??!!!"

"Um, Judge, Janet's left for the day. It's—"

"Damn it! Nobody works around there. Who is this?"

"Ah, it's She—"

"Oh! SHEEEILLLLLAAAAA!"

I was beginning to hate my name.

"I'm in a HOLE! I'm in a HOLE!"

Huh? I put my hand over the phone and beckoned Matthew to help.

"I AM IN A HOLE. DID YOU HEAR ME???!!!!" For the billionth time in less than ten hours, we exchanged looks of pure puzzlement.

"Judge, I'm sorry. I just don't understand what you're saying," I admitted.

"ARE YOU DEAF? I was driving, now I'm in a hole on Market Street." The woman thought "How are you?" was an irrational question but thought the words "I'm in a hole on Market Street" were self-explanatory. Sensing a meltdown on my part, Matthew generously grabbed the phone.

"Judge, hello, it's Matthew."

"Thank God, someone who can do something."

"What do you need, Judge?"

"Call the marshal. I'm in a hole on Market and Seventh, right outside the building. I was driving and my car is in a hole. I need to be towed out."

"OK, we'll be there in a minute." And with that, he hung up. "She's apparently under the ground somewhere in her car. Let's just get our things and go see what she's talking about."

By the time we got outside, it was like a scene from *Law and Order*. Camera crews everywhere. Police had the place surrounded, securing the site and directing people away from a massive hole in the street. Matthew grabbed one of them who had tried to shoo us away initially.

"Excuse me, sir. Our boss is down there. She just called us." The cop looked at once confused and relieved. "Oh good, so you know whoever's down there is OK?"

"As of about ninety seconds ago, she was fine. She just wants to get out," Matthew explained.

"DAMN IT, I'M IN A HOLE!" The judge had managed to roll down her window from twenty feet under.

"That seems clear. Wow, she's got a voice on her," the cop noted, wincing.

"You have no idea," Matthew said, chuckling.

"She's also going to be arrested, your boss." The thought of the judge in handcuffs, while alluring, was absurd. "Seems that your boss didn't feel like obeying the road sign." He pointed to a quadrangular orange sign that read, DANGER: MEN AT WORK. "This manhole was surrounded by orange cones and your boss just plowed through and I guess her car went in. At least that's what a couple of witnesses said." He shook his head slowly from side to side, just like the cops did on TV. "If she's OK, then I'm sure her car is totally wrecked. And she's damn lucky all the construction workers had headed home about twenty minutes earlier. If anyone had been hurt, she'd be looking at a misdemeanor at least. Felony maybe."

The reality was sinking in much like the judge's car. Judge Friedman was in a hole on Market Street. The lady hadn't lied.

"I don't know what possessed me to return to this." Matthew shook his head.

"Well I, for one, am thrilled you did. Can you please promise not to ditch again?" I begged.

Matthew smiled: "Deal, Sheera."

It took a little more than an hour for a tow truck to come and yank the judge's red BMW out of the gaping hole. The car was unscathed, without a single scratch. The cops and remaining bystanders looked amazed. I wasn't. I knew she'd get out of it. It'd take a hell of a lot more than a twenty-foot manhole to hurt her or anything she owned. What was incredible was that the judge appeared to be furious—much like she did after awakening from her nap on the bench that morning. She surfaced from the hole, thrusting her minifist in the air like Louis Farrakhan. Matthew and I walked over to the driver's side to help her out.

"NO! NO! NO!" She swatted us like flies, practically falling out of her car in the process. She was still wearing her robe and the chicken salad—making the whole scenario unquestionably the weirdest one I'd witnessed to date.

"Are you OK, Judge?" I asked.

"Where are they? Where is the moron who did this?" she demanded angrily. I considered shoving a mirror in her disheveled face. Three cops slowly walked over. They had reason to be apprehensive. Rabies wasn't out of the question.

"Ma'am, we're going to have to talk to you." One reached for her shoulder.

"You will *not* talk to me. I want to know who's responsible. I AM A FEDERAL JUDGE!" she yelled, yanking her arm away. These guys couldn't have cared if she were *Playboy*'s Playmate of the Year. They'd just spent the past two hours redirecting traffic from Market, the main artery of Philly, during rush hour. I smiled on the inside while maintaining a stern poker face. She was aghast.

"Maybe you didn't hear me. I AM A FED-ER-AL JUDGE." The tallest and youngest-looking one stepped forward. He had a crew cut and was rather handsome in a cheesy sort of way. He was pissed. And tired.

"Ma'am, you drove into a hole that was clearly marked off-limits. I don't care who you are." He reached rather roughly for her arm. She jerked it away again. I was thrilled at the prospect of watching her take on—and take out—the young, buff cop.

"Helga? Helga?" It was Judge Fleck and he was crossing the street.

"Richard—THANK GOD!" She hugged him and shot the rookie an evil eye. Now the poor guy had two old people with massive egos to deal with. Judge Fleck leaned over and grabbed the cop's hand.

"Hello, son. What's going on?"

The cop pointed to Friedman.

"This woman. *The federal judge* decided to plow through various traffic signs and landed inside that manhole. We're all lucky nobody was down there. My brother was working in there and left just a half hour earlier. She's lucky she didn't hurt him." He was seething now.

"Well, I don't have TIME for traffic signs. I am rilly busy. Maybe you'd understand if you knew anything about JUDGES. Or knew anything about ANYTHING important." Judge Fleck took her aside, right next to me.

"Helga, you are going to be thrown in jail. Just be agreeable and I'll get you out of this. Now PLEASE just keep your mouth shut." Tall order for the short lady. He went back to the cop. She played coy and started smiling, strangely resembling my friend Anna's drunk nana from Duluth.

"Sir," Fleck had upgraded the cop from son to sir, "my friend Helga was in a hurry to get home to her husband. Her husband is really sick." Young police officer glanced at drunk nana and looked sick with disgust. I couldn't blame him. She had that effect on me, too. Fleck was undeterred. As chief judge of the third circuit, it would be mortifying for him if Friedman had to serve time. "She was in a hurry to get home and get back to him. Please let this go. She's an old woman with a sick husband." Drunk nana sobered right up.

"Tell him I'm a JUDGE," she ordered, nudging Judge Fleck. He ig-nored her. Lucky for the judge, the cop just wanted her to go away. He looked at Judge Friedman much in the way the security guard had looked at me that morning, before turning to Judge Fleck.

"Fine, I'll let it go. But please tell your old lady friend with the sick husband that if she does this again, I'll make sure she spends a little time in prison." He then stormed off.

Matthew and I approached the judge, and I gently tapped her shoul-der. "Judge? Seems like everything is under control. We'll see you tomor-row. Bye, Judge Fleck."

"WAIT. WAIT! SHEILA! I'll drive you home." No way was she driv-ing me anywhere!

"You know what, Judge, I am in a huge hurry so . . ." I fumbled, attempting to come up with an excuse. No need—the judge already had lost interest in me. The woman had created the biggest spectacle in Phila-delphia since the signing of the Constitution and what did she do? She turned to Judge Fleck to bad-mouth the police officer.

I must have unconsciously broken into a jog because Matthew was out of breath when he caught up to me several blocks from the courthouse.

"Sheila," he panted, "wait up. I just missed my train and the next one's not for over an hour. So, I thought maybe you'd want to grab a drink or something?"

"Sorry about that—I just couldn't be there another second," I apolo-gized. "I'd love to get a drink but I really need to get to Banana Republic before it closes to—well, you know," I pointed to the shoulder pads.

"Well, I for one think your suit is very, um, well, very ah—retro? But, I'd be happy to go with you, I mean, if, if that's OK by you?" He looked down sheepishly, fidgeting with his jacket button. People never ceased to amaze me—this was a guy who'd told his boss (a federal judge!) to fuck off but felt shy to ask a colleague about shopping.

"Sure, that'd be great," I said and touched his shoulder, attempting to put him at ease. "My boyfriend, Sanjay, refuses to shop with me anywhere, ever."

"Well," Matthew said, blushing, "Heidi, I think I mentioned, really likes the mall, so I'm used to it. And I didn't know you had a boyfriend. Is he a lawyer?" It started to rain and the two of us picked up the pace.

"He's a radiology resident in Virginia, so definitely not a lawyer. In fact, he finds the law, lawyers, law students—the whole bit—incredibly boring." I paused. "That's not true. The expense of medical malpractice insurance captivates from time to time." A block from the store, the sky opened up, drenching us.

"I can't say I blame him. This clerkship has kind of soured my opinion on the legal profession," Matthew said, holding the door to Banana Republic open for me. "I mean, can you believe what we just witnessed? I'm serious—can you even believe that . . . that *shit* she pulled?" he said rather loudly, shaking water from one of his sleeves.

Attempting to get out of harm's way, an appalled thirty-something woman in Burberry capris did a 360 with her Bugaboo stroller, nearly popping a wheelie. Her sixth-month-old wailed—not from Matthew's profanity—but from whiplash.

I grabbed a navy plaid suit without checking for size and maneuvered my way past the "classic chinos" to get a look in the mirror. A dressing room sounded too tiring at that point.

"Our judge is going to be on the news," Matthew continued, following me, "not for an opinion she wrote—but for driving into a *manhole. Who does that?*"

"She does that. Only she does that. If there weren't cameras to document it, I don't think anyone would even believe it," I answered, squeezing into the jacket.

Matthew gave me a strange look and leaned against a rack of slacks.

"What?!" I asked defensively, pointing at myself.

"Nothing, nothing, Sheila . . . it's just that"—he nodded toward the mirror—"it's just that this whole day is ridiculous, don't you think?"

I peered into the mirror and gasped—staring at me was a brown sausage in a plaid casing with runny hose and flattened hair. Matthew came and stood behind me, generously softening the blow. In his soaked pinstriped suit, Matthew resembled a sickly flounder with a receding hair-line. What started out as giggling quickly turned into hysterical laughter, and within moments, dozens of eyes were fixed on us.

It wasn't exactly the fifteen minutes of fame I'd envisioned as a child.

Chapter Nine

Sanjay heaved into a trash can on the corner of 22nd and Sansom. We'd escaped the Mütter Museum just in the nick of time.

"Are you all right, Sanj?" I stroked his clammy forehead. The Mütter Museum housed the country's widest collection of "human medical anomalies." I'd suggested a visit, a seemingly generous overture toward Sanjay's profession. Between the mummified Siamese twins and eighteenth-century umbilical cords, Sanjay mentioned feeling queasy. I'd chalked it up to the Cheez Whiz he'd liberally applied to his tempeh "steak" (being a devout Hindu, he didn't touch meat). Something about the jarred and jellied embryos sent him over the edge. Next thing I knew, he was bulldozing through a crowd of enthralled children.

"It's not your fault, Sheila. I should have told you about my issues. In med school, I basically died every time I had to touch a cadaver. It was awful. Why do you think I opted for radiology? I could never deal with blood, needles, tissue . . ." He shuddered, his voice trailing off.

"Sanjay, it's no big—"

"Sheila, you can't—CANNOT—tell anyone about this. Nobody likes a squeamish doctor. It is really really embarrassing, OK?" With his bulging eyes and freckles of crusty vomit on his chin, Sanjay bore a re-markable resemblance to one of the museum's exhibits.

"You can't be serious, Sanj. That's ridiculous. Why do you care? You're a great radiologist and that's what matters, right? I mean, I can't stand sitting around discussing the Supreme Court. And I'm not embarrassed to say it out loud."

"So, you'd walk into a pack of law clerks and tell them talking about recent court decisions made you sick?" He asked pointedly.

"OK. I'll shut my trap."

"Sheila, that means you can't tell your parents," he ordered. "Your mom will tell every uncle and aunty this side of Madras."

Just then, a horde of children spilled out of the museum, swinging shiny spoils of gift shop victory. One marched past Sanjay waving a bloodied hook. He retched again.

"The place sells *vaginal speculums?*" He wiped his mouth and shook his head, embarrassment transforming into disdain. In fact, Sanjay cheered up only when he hopped into his Mercedes that Sunday afternoon to head back to Reston.

It had been an unusually sedate Monday, the morning free from medieval-ism, staring, and (wrong) name-calling. I had just about polished off my toilet lunch when the silence was broken.

"Sheera! Sheera! We lost! We lost! Where is she? Where is She-She-la?"

I rinsed baba ghanoush remnants from my hands and cautiously emerged from the bathroom. To my left was the judge, who'd cornered Evan. Cow-ering in her presence, Evan—who had to be at least six feet tall—looked dwarfish. Could it be that the judge moonlighted as a human-shrinking machine? Evan strained to lift his arm, pointed in my direction, and fled.

"Where have you been?" she demanded. Wasn't it obvious? "Never mind, now. We lost." She jumped slightly. "We lost it."

"Um, Judge, I am not entirely sure what you're—"

"That case. Nelton or whatever it's called," she clenched her fists. "We lost. Stevens went along with that-that-Adams! We have a dissent to write!" I'd been wondering what the panel had decided about the fate of Dell Nelson. It had been two weeks and not a peep from the judge.

"Oh no! What happened? And how—"

"Didn't I just tell you *what happened!* I told you that we lost." She motioned me to follow her into the torture chamber. "And that we're dissenting. Adams is writing for the majority. It's death penalty—Nelson's lawyer will definitely appeal to rehear it ahn-bunk. And we'll win this thing then." I nodded compulsively, pretending to understand everything she said. "So, take your bench memo from the case and turn it into an opinion. First, get me Druttel. I'm rilly rilly counting on you, Sheba." Any more nodding and I'd need treatment for Parkinson's disease. "Now get out and get to work." She clapped.

Druttel? Ahn-bunk? Matthew beckoned me to his cubicle as I entered the clerks' cave. "What was she screaming about? Is everything OK?"

"Not really *OK,*" I whispered, kneeling. "I have to write a dissent in that death penalty case. Adams and Stevens decided to screw the guy over. Do you know what an ahn-bunk is?"

"Yeah, an en banc is when the entire court of appeals comes together to hear a case if enough judges on the court think that a panel's majority opinion is suspect and the subject matter of the case is exceptionally important," Matthew explained, leaning in.

"Martha! Marka! Matthew!" The judge blitzkrieged the room. "I do not have time for my law clerks to dillydally all day. I seem to recall that you are supposed to be writing an opinion, Sheila. Didn't I just tell you to write an opinion?"

"Um, ah," I said, standing, "yes, Judge, you did but—"

"Oh damn it. Damn it. Anyway, that's why I came here. To tell Matthew that I wanted him to work on the dissent with you. We need to move fast. The minute we file our opinions, Nelson will argue for an en banc. I've got to be ready to convince my colleagues to vote to rehear it, which

shouldn't be too hard—especially in light of the *Drexel* opinion." Aha!
Drexel was an opinion from the ninth circuit in California that I'd cited
in my original bench memo. "So, I think it makes sense to have two
law clerks on the case. Matthew, stop working on whatever it is you're
working on and get up to speed on *Nelson*. Sheila, give him the briefs,
your bench memo, and I want a draft of the dissent ASAP. Now, get to
work."

I inched toward my cubicle.

"Any conversing between the two of you will strictly involve this case."
She wobbled, steadying herself on a bookshelf.

I collected the entire *Nelson* file, which could have fit into a grocery cart,
and lugged it to Matthew's cubicle. "Happy reading," I said, trying to make
light of the situation. Matthew was frozen. I couldn't blame him really. It'd
taken me well over a month to get a grasp on the case.

"Look, just read these two briefs and my bench memo, and let's plan to
talk after that, OK?" I gave his arm a little squeeze. "It may actually be
fun to have someone to go over this stuff with."

He grabbed the pile and turned to page 1 of brief 1, eyes ballooning.
"Yeah . . . fun."

A quick Westlaw search elicited *Drexel v. California*. Although the third
circuit was not bound by decisions from other circuits (it was bound only
by the Supreme Court), appellate opinions from other parts of the country
were nonetheless persuasive. And if judges from different circuits were at
odds on the same or similar issues, the Supreme Court typically would step
in to bring legal uniformity to the country. That, of course, meant that one
court of appeals' decision would be overturned. As judges fancied themselves infallible, being overturned meant a public declaration of error and
was an inconceivable fate worse than death.

The facts of the *Drexel* case were astonishingly similar to those in the
Nelson case. It dealt with a sleeping lawyer, one who failed to provide
mitigation evidence during the trial and the sentencing. Yet, unlike Dell
Nelson, Luther Drexel received a new hearing, because the ninth circuit

found that his lawyer's "glaring omissions undermined the very essence of the Sixth Amendment, thereby resulting in nothing short of a constitutional sin. In such cases, we are compelled to right the wrong committed by the court below."

"Well? Did you find it? Is that it?" the judge screamed from behind her cluttered desk.

I clutched the opinion and approached the torture chamber. "Yes, I think I have—"

"Why is it that you always *think* you've done this or that? You have something that appears to be an opinion. Can't you just say, *I have it?*" she growled, swatting at my hands.

It was a fair point—effective litigators were resolute. "I guess you're right, Judge, I—"

"There you go again. I *am* right," she said, pounding her desk. "You don't guess anything. I! AM! RIGHT!" Effective litigators also knew when not to speak, so I silently awaited her next move, awkwardly folding and unfolding my arms. "Now, get out and shut my door." She secured her grip on the opinion. "I need some time to read this," she said, smiling coyly. "The last thing we'd want is to create a circuit split on this issue of sleeping lawyers and the like. I have a feeling I can convince my colleagues that not giving Nelson a new sentencing hearing would do just that."

"So, if there's a circuit split," I began excitedly, "then—"

"I am not one of your law professors and this is not office hours. I am rilly rilly busy and have lots of calls to make," she said, clapping.

Walking out of the torture chamber, I prayed that these phone calls would be more successful than the ones she made to Bob. Judge Helga Friedman held the fates of Dell Nelson and countless other death row inmates in her gnarled hands.

Chapter Ten

Our incoming class of first-year associates takes the Bar Exam tomorrow. There's usually one or two who fail. Pathetic. Most people here pretend it's OK, but it's all for show. You can't really expect to fail the bar exam and then be respected around the office. They're mercilessly mocked, to their faces and behind their backs. They have two months with nothing else to do but study. If they can't pass an exam on the first try, how are they going to do the cutting-edge work our clients demand? You don't get a second chance to file a motion.

Well, you can amend the motion. So you sort of do get a second chance.

Usually, failing the bar is a sign of things to come. No work ethic, lazy intellect, unprepared for life at a big firm. More suited to another line of work. Maybe another service industry. Maybe a paperboy.

—http://anonymouslawyer.blogspot.com/
2005_07_01_anonymouslawyers_archive.html

"I just know I didn't pass and that's heinous enough but when she finds out, my life will be over!"

It was early November—the season of discontent for anyone who'd taken any state's bar exam in July. It was the time when you'd discover whether you'd wasted three years and a hundred twenty thousand dollars with no chance of ever being able to pay any of it back. It determined whether you'd be at Thanksgiving dinner or in debtor's prison.

James listened as I launched into my bar angst for the zillionth time. Unfortunately for him, my plans to spend the weekend in Reston were dashed when the chief of radiology invited Sanjay's group to his McMansion for an impromptu dinner, sans guests, Saturday night. According to Sanjay, the equivalent of getting invited to the White House.

"You didn't fail. There's just no possible way you failed. If anyone failed, it's me," James said unconvincingly, taking a bite of our local diner's famous blueberry pancakes.

"What's up, you guys?" Kevin burst through the grimy door in a sweat. "Sorry I'm late," he said, scanning our cluttered table, "but glad to see that nobody waited to order." James and I shrugged.

"Anyway, the *reason* I'm late is that I have some pretty huge news." Kevin grinned nervously. He slid into the booth next to me, placing his arm around my shoulder. "Judge Adams got the nod." Full stop. James looked ill. My brain felt like an out-of-control calculator—not computing. "Both Specter and Shepard called her yesterday and she's in. She's going to be a Supreme Court justice." Kevin tried, but failed, to conceal his excitement.

Since our lunch at Jones weeks ago, there had been radio silence on the Supreme Court nomination front. The Friedman-in-manhole episode had caused President Bush to steer clear of the third circuit. While I blamed the guy for a lot of things, namely the destruction of our country, if not the world, I couldn't blame him for wanting to distance himself from anything judicial in Philadelphia.

At first, it'd just been the *Philadelphia Inquirer* and local news stations. But then it went national. The video was too good. I'd worked in television for two years, and in that time I'd never seen video like this. An old lady with spinning eyes in a crumpled black robe and bun, waving her fist in the air, spitting and screaming as she's lifted out of a mammoth hole in the street. The pictures proved more compelling than rescues, riots, or shuttle launches. A local cameraman caught the flecks of spit flying out of her mouth—audio and all: "Do you even know who I am!!!! I am a FEDERAL JUDGE. A FEDERAL JUDGE!!!"

The camera then panned to the recipient of her saliva bath. The young, handsome cop who'd just saved her life. It took exactly one afternoon for an associate producer to discover that Friedman had been appointed by Gerald Ford at a time when presidents were trying to get women and Jews on the federal bench. During her tenure, Friedman had nailed cops for racial profiling, overturned a law banning pornography on First Amendment grounds, and nine out of ten times thought company executives were sexually harassing pricks. If she weren't a tyrant who racially profiled her law clerks, she'd be worth idolizing as far as I was concerned. Rupert Murdoch owned way too many media outlets to let this one go. Having an unapologetically liberal judge appear insane and disrespectful of a uniformed officer who'd just rescued her was a crowd pleaser to the edgy underground and right-wing machine.

She'd made CNN's "news of the weird" as well as its headlines. So, too, the *New York Times, Washington Post, Los Angeles Times,* and *Chicago Tribune.* Even Tim Russert dropped her name on *Meet the Press* the Sunday after. Puja told me that she'd heard from a friend at Berkeley that some kids were planning on making stickers that read: "Fuck the Police," with a picture of Friedman, fist in the air lasered behind the words. According to the *Onion,* the cameraman who caught it all was up for a Pulitzer.

For us, the world changed. Nobody had ever publicly mocked the judge. She didn't know what to do. For the first few days, the judge exposed an emotion previously unseen: embarrassment. Janet told me that in all her years with the judge, not even when she'd accidentally locked herself in another judge's bathroom after clogging his toilet had she seen her embarrassed. But losing respect was too much. The judge came and went silently. She didn't want to be seen, closing her door while in chambers. She even refrained from yelling at anyone—including Roy—at first. This even after Roy came to work stinking of cigarettes. Even more bizarre, the judge asked me what my favorite *Indian* restaurant was, told Evan he'd written a good memo, acknowledged Kate's existence with a hello, and joked with Matthew about Boise State's season. We learned that the judge was an avid sports fan. We were ecstatic. There'd be a happy ending after all.

Then the darnedest thing happened. She suddenly became meaner, nastier, and more maniacal than pre-manhole. It was clearly a ploy to regain what she'd lost. It worked. The mocking stopped. The woman did what Richard Nixon, Newt Gingrich, and Marv Albert couldn't do. Even the great Bill Clinton couldn't do it. She stopped the presses. It was as if the incident never happened.

I must have been staring blankly for minutes, because I came to as Kevin gently shook me.

"Sheila. Sheila. Are you OK?" OK wasn't the first word that came to mind. My head felt like an overheated planet spinning off its axis. What would become of us after this news broke? Living with one leg or a half-bitten ear couldn't be that bad, could it?

"Um. Yeah. It's just that I'm shocked." I forced my neck up. "What happened?"

"Well, you know about this National Independence Center thing?" Did I ever. "Well, Friedman is on the board and she's pretty high up. And this center is a pretty big thing, I guess. Well, Condi Rice was apparently on the short list to speak at the opening. You can imagine the public image boost that'd give her. Anyway, your boss pretty much roadblocked her speaking unless the administration made some sort of public overture toward the third. Enter Adams. Nominating Adams is the perfect solution. Bush wanted her all along. She's on the third. Friedman would have to be appeased. Except—"

"Except this is her worst nightmare and they don't know that"—I finished Kevin's sentence for him—"but what could Friedman have wanted? What could the Bush administration offer to a court of appeals? They all already have life tenure. There's no chance in hell they'd ever have nominated Friedman to the Supreme Court even *before* the manhole incident."

I suddenly realized that we were in a public place and quickly surveyed the scene. Family of four. Young married couple. Famous blueberry/banana/strawberry pancakes. Want more coffee? The sheer normalcy gave the illusion that someone had hit the pause button on everyone but us.

"Kevin? Why would Friedman do that? Am I missing something here?"

"Sheila, you're not. It's not at all obvious. According to our secretary, Friedman wanted Haskell to get the nod. She has absolutely *no idea* that the only person Bush was considering from the third was Adams. I think she just assumed that Haskell would be the natural pick and—"

"Judge Haskell is her only comrade on the bench." I finished his sentence again. Now it made sense. Judge Haskell was Friedman's only true friend on the court. He was legitimately nice to her. Then again, he was nice to everyone. He'd been appointed by Clinton but was not a rabid liberal by any stretch of the imagination. A lauded moderate, with an eloquent flair. He was fifty-five, handsome, and probably didn't even have half a skeleton in his closet. The kicker—he was African American. Good-looking, perfect age, black, moderate—a perfect choice for an administration mired in right-wing controversy. Then again, there already was one black man on the Supreme Court. The Bush administration, indeed the country, wasn't ready for another.

While Friedman was unquestionably bright, she'd not considered that Judge Adams could attain the one thing she herself so badly wanted in life—a slot on the U.S. Supreme Court. Judge Friedman's hatred had made her impervious to the reality that she had, in effect, garnered the nomination for Judge Adams. Not since the hipster invasion had something been so ironic.

Heart palpitations. Dizzy. Sweating.

What if Adams got confirmed during my tenure?

Rapid pulse. Dizzier.

Death penalty.

Drop of sweat on lap.

I'm rilly rilly counting on you Sheba.

Swish.

You're too slow, Sheila.

Woosh.

You failed the bar, Sheila.

Electric chair.

I came to in my cheddar omelette. Kevin and James were saying my name on repeat. Over and over and over—for a second, I thought I was going through security at the courthouse. The restaurant definitely was no longer on pause—everyone was staring in my direction.

"OK, this is awkward," I blurted, cheese stuck to my nose.

Kevin helped me out of the booth, we tossed a twenty on the table, and exited into a sunny northeastern autumn afternoon. Somehow, the breeze felt suffocating and my company's concern ("Are you OK, Sheila?" "Can I get something for you, Sheila?") only exacerbated it. Needing air, I extricated myself from Kevin and James, wiped 7-Eleven clean of its gossip magazine collection, and crawled into bed.

I called Sanjay, whose interest was barely piqued over my fainting spell. "Sheels, that really sucks. Are you all right? Um, ah, can I actually call you back?—medical emergency." The phone went dead, signaling that it wasn't my medical emergency to which he was referring.

Exhausted, I buried myself in the world of celebrity diets and Scientology, the latter of which sounded strangely alluring.

Chapter Eleven

Betsy was standing in the elevator when I stepped in. We'd not seen each other since the sitting.

"Hey, Sheila," she said, pursing her lips smugly, "how are you?"

"Fine, fine. I, um, I'm looking forward to reading your *Nelson* opinion," I said awkwardly, steering clear of Adams's nomination, since it still hadn't been publicly announced and Kevin had sworn me to secrecy. I hadn't even spilled the beans to Matthew.

"Likewise—we all look very forward to reading what I'm sure will be a *killer* dissent—oops, no pun intended." Ding! Thirteenth floor.

"No pun taken. Bye, Betsy." I stepped off the elevator, trying to remember why I'd taken such a liking to Betsy the first time we met.

"Good morning, Janet. Roy." I strolled into the secretaries' den. Roy was watering the brittle, brown plants with what must have been his breath—something about the nicotine gum he'd taken to lately made me want to wither and die also.

Janet looked up: "Yes?"

"Um, I just said good morning, that's all."

"What's good about it?"

"Nothing, actually. It's just something I say to people when I see them in the morning."

"Just so you know." Janet fiddled with the cross around her neck. "Bob had a heart attack over the weekend. She'll be in late."

"What? She's coming in?!" My question amused Janet, who suddenly looked like a clown about to kill a kid.

"She always comes to work. Have you not learned *anything?* She even worked half a day after her brother's funeral. You think a little heart attack would keep her away!"

Roy followed me to my cubicle, tripping on a trash can along the way. "You really should check out the Markland Web site, it's awesome. Man oh man. It's so cool." He paused to blow a Nicorette bubble—pop! "And I went to the most kickin' feast on Saturday. Debauchery everywhere, man."

"Good morning, Roy. How are you?"

He cackled nervously and ran his hands through his mullet, leaving little feathers in their wake.

"Um. Um." And then he was gone. Matthew motioned me to his cubicle.

"Janet just told me that Bob had a heart attack so she'd be in late. Don't you think it's strange she's coming in at all?"

Matthew smiled at what should have been considered bad news: "She'd come in if she were dead."

"Speaking of strange, who do you think is stranger—Roy or the judge?" I whispered, pointing to the secretaries' den.

"That's tough. But I'd have to go with Roy. It's shocking that he has a wife, don't you think?" Matthew asked.

Actually, Roy's wife was shocking. Last week, I had answered the office phone after everyone had left for the day and it was her. When I offered to take a message, she barked: "That pussy better not have forgotten the cat food." Then she hung up. I didn't jot it down.

"Yes, Roy is an interesting bird. But don't you think it's annoying that he never asks us questions about us? He always just wants to talk about himself and that medieval stuff."

"He's got nothing, Sheila. If it makes him feel better talking about himself, I'm not going to rob him of that. Why do you even care?" It was a good question. Why was I upset that a medieval, pockmarked pussy-feeding "pussy" wasn't asking me questions about me?

"Wait," I said, noticing that the picture of half-naked Heidi had reappeared on Matthew's desk. "I guess this means you guys are back on? Everything's better now?"

Matthew shrugged noncommittally. "Yeah, well kind of. Yes, we are. We've worked through our issues. She apologized for her behavior when my sister-in-law was in the hospital. She's fine. She's great." He spoke rapidly, as if speed would bring truth to his words. "Yup, we're all good now."

Before I could respond to Matthew's bizarre little rant, my phone rang for the first time all year. I rushed to answer, my heart racing. Getting a call in chambers was like getting a call in the middle of the night—it couldn't be good news.

"Uh, this is Sheila Raj." Heavy breathing on the other end. "Hello? Hello?" I asked, confused. Heavy breathing.

"Listen here. This is Robert Nussbaum," he said angrily, "and my family will take this all the way to the Supreme Court if you give that murderous heathen another chance." *Robert Nussbaum? Robert Nussbaum?* "My brother was killed by that animal and—" Right! Robert Nussbaum was Peter Nussbaum's younger brother, who'd been in high school at the time of Peter's murder. Dressed to kill, toting an army of assistants, Robert Nussbaum had appeared at oral arguments weeks earlier.

"Um, excuse me. Excuse me. Mr. Nussbaum. I am not allowed to speak to you. I am hanging up now." I took a deep breath. Under no circumstances were law clerks ever to speak with anyone personally affiliated with a case. Our numbers were unlisted—how did Robert get ahold of mine? How did he know Friedman's vote in the case—the panel's opinions had not even been released within the court, let alone to the public. The judges' decisions were confidential at this point.

As I pondered how to gently break the news of Robert Nussbaum's call to the judge, an e-mail popped up. It was from Judge Adams's secretary, and it was titled: "Penn Pals Reminder." Oh no! I'd signed Matthew and myself up weeks ago for a do-gooder program that Adams had created a few years back. Law clerks and secretaries volunteered to read with inner city kids for an hour every Monday afternoon in chambers. Adams was smoking crack if she thought that one hour was going to save those kids, but I still wanted in. Any variation was welcome. So much so that I'd ventured into the torture chamber to get the judge's permission to participate. She refused to lift her head from a brief and replied: "Do whatever you feel you have to do."

Janet had warned me that the tutoring program put the judge in a foul mood and advised against it. Penn Pals was a Friedman category killer: She hated kids. She hated her law clerks doing anything that didn't involve slaving away for her. She hated Judge Adams. It was reported that last year, the cataclysmic combo drove her to tell a second-grader to "just shut up" when he read from *Mother Goose* too loudly. When the kid cried, the judge slammed the door in his tiny face. It wasn't long after that that Janet and Roy were told flat out that they were not allowed to do the program. I was an idiot. What was I thinking? I knew what I was thinking—I wanted somebody, anybody, to talk to, even if it were a six-year-old.

Before I could get up to deliver the bad news to Matthew, another e-mail popped up. It was Brian: "Sheila. Check the bar exam site and get back to me." The Web site said that New York was releasing exam results that night at midnight. Even better, they'd be posted online for the entire world to see.

I started sweating profusely, wondering if Bob needed a roommate in the ICU. My only realistic refuge was the bathroom, and Kate had been there for what felt like hours. Sweat. Wet. Cafeteria. I got up and wobbled to the second floor. The sight of Ernie in a hairnet and a "Proud to Be an American" T-shirt, trying to grab a coffee pot from the shelf but instead reaching for air was more than I could take. I sat at a table, put my head in my hands, and cried. Sniveling clerk. Loafers. Linoleum. A loud crash awakened me from my pity party. Ernie had found the coffee pot but only after accidentally punching it. The pot crashed, breaking into bits. Ernie simply started whistling and swept it up. If Ernie could get through life happily, I could survive the day.

Marching back into the clerks' cave, I stopped in Matthew's cubicle. "Is she here yet?"

"Nope."

"Anyway, I don't know if you got the e-mail but we have to start that tutoring program."

"Sheila, I cannot believe you got me into this. I don't even like children and she's going to go crazy when she comes in here from the hospital and sees a kid."

"Not much we can do about it now. And by the way, New York is releasing bar results tonight. You should check California." He looked doubly pained and quickly confirmed that, indeed, he'd be receiving his exam results that night, too.

"Shit, Sheila, talk about a bad day." He tensed his shoulders. "And I don't even know what possessed me to agree to Heidi's demands that we move to Los Angeles. I don't even like Southern California."

At that moment, Evan walked into our cave. Matthew and I looked at him, awkwardness blanketing the room. "Hey, Evan, did you hear that we get bar exam results tonight?" I asked—a silly question for someone who'd trekked to California during his Christmas break for clerk camp.

"Um. No. Oh," he muttered, before stumbling back to his cubicle.

Another e-mail from Brian awaited me. "I'm totally freaked out, Sheila. I know I failed. What am I going to do?" The sentiment was understandable, but why did Brian suddenly consider me a shoulder upon which to cry? At best, he'd been aloof since we started clerking. Yet, I still felt bad for the guy. Having a big butt and a fedora was no way to live.

It was a little after eleven and the judge still hadn't come in. Matthew and I set off to collect the kids when we heard the dreaded DING! Thirteenth floor, going down! We were stuck. The judge sauntered out of the elevator, sporting sunglasses and a brand new bun. How did she manage to get her hair done and jumpstart Bob? All in a day's work.

"Hello, Judge," we chanted in unison.

"Where are you people going!?" I had gotten Matthew into this mess, so I figured it was my duty to remind her.

"Um. Remember we're tutoring those children? Today is their first day." Not the right answer. She threw down her bags and her newly minted hair went nuts.

"NO! NO! NO!" This time, she sort of bobbed up and down. "I do NOT have time for this! You people NEVER work. NEVER!" Knees bent. Up. Down.

"O-O-K. We—we. Won't do it. We—we'll stay here." Matthew had gone from a fancy Ivy Leaguer to a common stutterer in less than four months.

"Oh shit! Do whatever you people want. I don't care!" And with that, she dragged herself into the secretaries' den. Poor Roy was a goner.

Matthew and I made a break for the elevators. "Technically she did say, 'Do whatever you want.'" I tried justifying the fact that we were bringing innocent children into the torture chamber.

"Sheila. Did you just hear me? I can't even speak anymore." Just then the doors opened into the lobby, which was filled with a sea of little children—in all colors but white—being led away by a group of uptight law clerks—in all colors but black. I spotted Kevin through the crowd.

"Hey. We're going out tonight. Bar exam results at midnight," I blurted as a miniperson tugged at Kevin's shirt. "I want to wead. Let's go wead."

"Great, see you later. By the way," Kevin said, gently guiding a cute little boy in a baseball cap over to Matthew, "this is Eric and he's your tutee." He ushered a pigtailed girl in my direction. "And this is Terry. She's all yours," he said chuckling.

"Hi, Terry." I smiled, kneeling to her level.

"This is boring. You're boring." How could she tell by just looking at me? Did I actually *look* boring? Terry thought so. She was smart. And loud.

Our pleas for no screaming fell on deaf ears. I couldn't blame her. If I screamed like her, I'd be deaf, too. She was totally out of control, pushing every button on the elevator while simultaneously jumping up and down screaming, "Boring, boring, boring." I managed to grab Terry's scrawny shoulders to deliver a little sermon.

"Terry. You cannot scream in there. Our boss is very busy and doesn't like yelling. She'll be very mad if you yell." She nodded as I spoke. We were on the same page. That is, if you counted *The Exorcist* as your book. Terry took off running the minute the door was opened. I looked left, right, up, down. She'd disappeared. I returned to my cubicle, hoping, praying that Terry was a homing pigeon who'd landed in my chair. No luck.

"You're old!" Oh my God! I nearly got whiplash from turning left so quickly. There was Terry. Three feet tall, standing an inch in front of the judge, who, incidentally, didn't look so much taller, pointing. "They said you were always mad!" That little Benedict Arnold!

"Get out! Get out!"

Terry was totally unfazed by the judge's command. Somehow, I found a bit of courage in my internal safety deposit box and headed into the torture chamber. The judge's eyes were burning. She'd been had by someone who hadn't even graduated from the first grade, let alone a top-five law school.

"Sheila. Get. Her. Out. Of. Here. NOW! We will talk about this later!"

I was so close to peeing my pants I couldn't even muster up the usual "Yes, Judge" and just nodded instead.

Mini Benedict had other plans. The moment she saw me, Terry ran and hid under the judge's desk. She wouldn't budge. It dawned on me that I must have been a serial killer in my previous life. Posthumous punishment was the only explanation.

"Terry. Please come out. Please, honey." I wobbled to the front of the judge's desk, got on my knees, and shoved my face underneath. Ugh! She had one of the judge's tennis shoes in her hands and was playing with the orthotic insert. I had to have been worse than Ted Bundy. The judge was standing right above me, breathing like a bull. Bull was about to kick victim if Terry didn't come out.

"What is *wrong* with her?!" The judge screamed, rage accumulating as evidenced by her break-dancing bun. She caught a glimpse of what the minityrant was doing. "My sneaks! My sneaks!"

Bun moonwalked.

Desperate times called for desperate measures. One. Two. Three. I shot up, maneuvered to the front of the desk, grabbed the delinquent, yanked the orthotic free of her sticky grasp, and pulled her out. In addition to being a huge brat, Terry was the biggest ingrate of all time. I'd just saved her from a fate worse than death and all she could do was scream, all the way out the door, which I shut behind us.

Terry was getting shipped to sender. "Janet, Roy—I'm going up to Judge Adams's chambers to return Terry. I'll be back in a few minutes." I headed up to the twenty-first floor. The moment we left our chambers, Terry stopped screaming.

On the elevator, she turned to me puffy-eyed: "That lady is really mean." I suddenly loved Terry but not enough to keep her. The two of us crashed what must have been the most raging party ever to have taken place at the courthouse—a joyful mess of pizza, soda, candy, and children. Terry took off to join the fun. To the left sat Kevin and Walt, reading to a few little ones. To my right were Judge Adams, another judge I couldn't quite place, and Betsy engrossed in conversation. Betsy spotted me and quickly walked over.

"What are you doing here?" she asked impatiently.

"I came to return my tutee," I replied, embarrassed. "She's kind of a nightmare." Somehow it didn't sound as good an idea now as it did moments earlier.

Betsy didn't bother to conceal her disgust. "She's a *child*. And we'll happily take her. See you," she said, leading me to the door.

When I returned to my cubicle, the judge's door was still closed. Matthew was sitting at the table between our cubicles reading to Eric, who apparently hadn't opened his mouth. Matthew got up and walked over. Eric simply sat, hands folded in his lap, staring straight ahead. They even sent the craziest *kids* to our chambers: the class mute and the class maniac.

"What *happened?*"

"Matthew, I think I may quit. For real. I can't do this. And there's no reason to do it." He grabbed me and yanked me to the back, where Evan was engrossed in yet another case. Kate was staring out the window. They didn't notice we were there.

"Sheila. You cannot quit. You think the ACLU would ever hire you if you didn't finish this thing? Never. Don't let one woman ruin your career before it's even started," he argued.

Matthew was right. Though unlikely, it was feasible for a law firm to take in a clerkship quitter. But there was no way in hell the ACLU would do it. The ACLU, after all, fought uphill legal battles on a daily basis. The people there wouldn't have much use for someone who couldn't endure one unsavory year with a sociopathic, homicidal, bipolar jurist.

"Yeah, you're right," I admitted. "I think I'm just super stressed about the bar. Listen—a group of us are going out tonight to drink our way to midnight. Want to come?"

"Sure, that'd be—"

"SHHHAYYYLA!! SHEERRAAA!"

"Yes, Judge." I tripped into the torture chamber.

"That little girl is not welcome here again. Mark's kids do not behave like that and I will not tolerate it." Terry could've been one of Mark's kids and she probably wouldn't have known the difference.

"Yes, Judge. I took Terry back to Justice Adams's chambers and they're going to deal with her." Her bun started moving again.

"She is not *Justice* Adams. She is *Judge* Adams."

Oops—I'd slipped and referred to her as the Supreme Court justice she was about to become.

"In any event, you were saying—you went up to *Judge* Adams chambers?"

"Yes, Judge." Knees wobbly. Bladder quivery.

"What was going on up there?" she demanded, running her teeny hands over a brand-new mechanical pencil.

Tip—eraser—back again.

"Um, not much. Just Judge Adams, lots of little kids, and I think one other judge. That's about it." My lip twitched as I attempted to smile, revealing one front tooth.

"*Which other judge?*"

Tip.

"Um, I recognized him as a judge but don't know his name," I answered truthfully.

Eraser and back to tip.

"You are an extension of me and don't you think it would be embarrassing if I didn't know the names of my colleagues?" The thought of being an extension was not at all appealing—what was I? Her bun? Her long leg or the shorter one?

"Um, yeah, I guess it would be embarrassing if—"

"Never mind that. Where are we with Dell Nelson?" she asked pointedly, resting the mechanical pencil on her desk.

"Well, I'm glad you asked. Um, I received a troubling call this morning . . . from Peter Nussbaum's brother." I waited for the information to sink in. The judge simply stared. "You know, Peter was the Penn student who was murdered and—"

"What?? What? Why are you telling me this now? This is the kind of information I need immediately."

"Well, Judge, you weren't here this morning and—"

"No! No! No!" She retrieved the pencil and tapped it furiously against a book. Only Helga Friedman could make a pencil ominous. I looked down, waiting for the storm to pass.

"Well? What did you say to him?" she asked after what felt like several days.

I looked up sheepishly. "He said that Dell Nelson was a heathen and I told him I couldn't talk to him—that it was against the rules. And then I hung up. Whole thing lasted less than twenty seconds," I explained, bracing for another wrist slap.

"Good, that's good, Sheila. That's exactly what you should have done," she said, sitting up straight. I'd done something right? Good even? "But how on earth did he know to call you? I know I didn't exactly hide my feelings on the case during arguments, but our decisions haven't been made public." She rubbed her forehead.

"That was my thought exactly. I just don't know—"

"Shhh," she sternly lifted one finger. I hadn't been shushed since the second grade. Just as she was about to speak, her phone rang. "Hello, Doctor," she answered, motioning me to leave.

After several hours of wading through death penalty opinions, the judge catapulted from her office, purse in one hand, behemoth sunglasses perched precariously atop her bun: "Those stupid doctors can't do *anything!*"

Before Matthew and I could respond, she'd planted herself smack in the middle of the clerks' cave, speaking to nobody and everybody all at once. "I want all of your bench memos immediately! We rilly have to move, people! We have A LOT to do! Evan! Karin! Do you hear me?" Evan and Kate hurried over. "You all—all of you. Michael. Michael? Sheera? Are you listening?" Everyone in the state of Pennsylvania was listening.

"Yes, Judge." In unison.

"You people are the slowest clerks I've *ever* had—EVER! We have so much to do and it's not getting done, thanks to you people. Now I want whatever you're working on on my desk tomorrow and you each will take new cases." And she sped off to decapitate some poor unsuspecting cardiologist. DING! Thirteenth floor, going down.

Evan started wobbling. "I . . . I . . . There's just no way. No way I can finish my memo. I *just* got the briefs two days ago. What am *I* going to do?" Matthew didn't say a word, grabbed his stuff, and motioned me to follow. Predictably Kate didn't respond and walked away, leaving me holding the bag. It was hard to believe that after four months, Evan hadn't realized that the judge forgot *almost* everything she said the moment she said it.

"Evan, forget it. Why don't you go home and get some rest. We're going to need it for the next few weeks." There. I'd done my duty. I grabbed my purse and jacket and followed Matthew, leaving Evan paralyzed in the dimly lit clerks' cave.

Chapter Twelve

Beer is proof that God loves us and wants us to be happy.

—Benjamin Franklin

"I can't. Can*not* believe she came here from Indianapolis! It's beyond creepy," James exclaimed, exasperated. Brian had ditched us for his mother, whom he'd called in an utter panic about the bar exam. She took the first flight out of Indianapolis that morning and was waiting for him at his apartment with a broccoli chicken casserole when he got home from work. Rather than being unnerved by his mother's surprise visit, Brian exhibited something quite contrary —pride. So prideful, in fact, that he'd sent me an e-mail titled "great news."

Great news was the end of poverty and achieving world peace. So, too, was winning the lottery, sleeping with Brad Pitt, and a new burrito option at Taco Bell. I could think of a dozen or so adjectives to describe a twenty-eight-year-old man coaxing his mother to catch the red-eye to hold his hand while accessing exam results. *Great* was not one of them. Throw in the casserole and it was downright deviant.

Nonetheless, I was grateful to our geeky Oedipus for providing us with a diversion. James took a long sip of his beer before asking the million-dollar question: "Do you guys think he and his mom are going to sleep in the same bed?"

"Definitely," Matthew answered with certainty.

"I bet they're spooning right now," Kevin added.

In the end, however, Brian may have been the smart one. The rest of us could have been arrested on charges of bad conversation for the ensuing hours.

"Do you think I failed?" and "I know I failed" miraculously didn't get old. Not for us, at least. But it did for the seventy-year-old man who'd had ten too many gin martinis sitting on the bar stool next to us: "Can't you talk about shumthing elsh?" Whatever he was asking, the answer was no. Anyway, why was he drinking martinis at an Irish pub?

We hopped from bar to bar, muttering the same exact words and ending up at City Tavern—"Ben Franklin drank here!" Where *didn't* old Benny F tie one on? Based on the little plaques outside of every bar in Old City, the guy—and his esteemed colleagues—spent more time boozing than drafting the Constitution. The whole thing lent credence to my theory that the Constitution framers were really just a bunch of philandering drunks who realized that drafting a "constitution" was a pretty good rap that would get them laid. Frankly, I wouldn't be surprised if Independence Hall had been a brothel. It was directly across the street from the City Tavern.

Inside was a smorgasbord of colonial fun. Butter churners. Bookbinders. Darners. You name it, they were there peddling their wares. I was certain there was a secret trapdoor, to the left of butter-churning Betty and right behind darning Dick, where sadomasochistic gimps in bonnets whipped each other for some good old-fashioned eighteenth-century fun. Wrong century, but Medieval Roy would've enjoyed it nevertheless.

We careened past the toothy pack of fiddling fifers on our way to the back, where a roaring fire roasted ill-fated wenches-cum-waitresses in thick hoop skirts. We turned down the $17.89 "Commemorative Constitutional Dinner," choosing mugs of "George Washington Woodchuck

Cider" and "James Madison Madeira" instead. Mine tasted like petrified skunk.

"I mean, really, what are the chances that any of us failed," I asked for the fiftieth time.

"You definitely passed, Sheila. I failed," James answered for the fiftieth time, motioning the waitress for another round. At this rate, we'd all be passed out before midnight.

"Jesus—we all did fine," Matthew blurted. "And I'm going outside for a little air." He stood abruptly, nearly knocking over his chair. I followed him out just as James and Kevin resumed the pass/fail intrigue.

"Hey, you OK?" I tapped Matthew on the back. He'd shoved his hands in his pockets and was rocking back and forth on his heels. Matthew's mannerisms were often louder than his words.

"Hey, sorry about that, Sheila." When he turned, I could see anguish riddling his face. "Look—this bar exam is really freaking me out. I can't fail. My parents would be devastated—they've been so proud of my having gone to Yale. Nobody in my family has ever gone to grad school. I'm the first"—he rocked—"and Heidi. God—she'd be so horrified if I failed. We studied together—and she consistently did better on those stupid practice tests." He bowed his head in premature defeat. Hulking insecurity— both advertised and internalized—seemed to be a prerequisite to the legal profession. Most cases of the internalized sort bred bogus bravado of the Brian/Evan sort. Since Matthew had consistently exhibited self-assuredness without an ounce of arrogance, I'd assumed he was the one lucky law school student who'd escaped with healthy self-esteem.

"Matthew—I'm sure you did fine. Stop worrying about disappointing everyone else. As for your family—you could always lie, tell them you passed and then just take the bar again, right?" Finally, the beginnings of a smile. "And really, that would be the worst part about failing—taking that exam again, not the humiliation." I paused. "Actually, the worst part would be having to tell Judge Friedman you had to take the exam over again."

"Ha—I hadn't even thought of her for some reason." Matthew chuckled. "Something about the woman's mayonnaise-crusted lips makes her less scary to me. Actually, I think I hate her too much to be afraid of her." Matthew shoved his hands back into his pockets.

"I have to say—I wish that hate and fear were mutually exclusive things in my book, but unfortunately the two seem to go hand in hand," I explained. "And as for Heidi, she wouldn't really be horrified as much as sad for you, right?"

Matthew pursed his lips and resumed rocking just as the clock at Independence Hall struck 11:30. It was almost midnight and we were about to turn into pumpkins.

I left Matthew to his nervous bouncing and went to retrieve James and Kevin, who were carousing with women who were twice their age and out on a self-proclaimed "girls' night out." I grabbed James from the clutches of a lady whose tight red and green twinset gave the illusion of holiday leftovers in Saran Wrap. Kevin reached for me like a life jacket. A woman with expired highlights had been gabbing to him about her son, who seemed "just like" him . . . "funny—like, you know." God bless her—she loved her boy "even still." Girls' night out seemed to inspire open-minded declarations from suburban moms right around the third cosmopolitan.

Outside, our chariot awaited us. Matthew was sitting in the back of a horse-drawn carriage with a young man in dungarees leading the way. He'd finagled a bargain rate for a ride back to James's place. Let's just say it wasn't a joy ride—drunk, packed, horse, awaiting bar exam results. Upon pulling up to the building, the horse defecated on our front stoop. We went inside.

11:56. Tick. Tick. Tick. Suddenly, I envied Brian. I wanted my mom.

11:58. Tick. Tick. Tick. Rocking.

Felt like on an airplane. With turbulence.

11:59. Tick. Tick. Tick.

Clock struck midnight. We logged on: http://www.nybarexam.org. Come on come on come on. Posting bar exam results online—at midnight no less—was cruel and unusual punishment. Especially considering that some kid named Joe actually offed himself in his basement apartment in the Bronx last year at 12:01 when he didn't find his name on the pass list. But there was no time for institutional change. Our cell phones were ringing manically. I screened out Puja, Sanjay, and my mom.

12:01 AM. The Web page still hadn't come up. That's what happens when eight billion type As try to get onto the same Web site all at once. Sweat. Heart palpitations. The only thing worse than a panic attack was a panic attack drunk on dead skunk, stinking of horse manure. Click here for Exam Results.

"Who's first?" Kevin demanded.

"Not me." There was no way I was going to be the first to fail.

James stepped up to the plate. New York divided up its scores into four departments, broken down geographically. We scoured the A–F section under the first department (New York City). No James Calloway. We assured him he was in the fourth (for anyone who took the bar in NYC but was no longer there). He didn't look remotely convinced and turned a bright orange. Sure enough—there he was. James exhaled a tornado before color returned to his face.

Kevin went next. I'd gone completely silent and still. Kevin Peterson was quickly found under the fourth.

My turn. Spinning. Sweating. Rocking.

"Are you OK, Sheila?" Matthew rubbed my back. "It'll be fine. You passed."

Ragazzo, Antonio. Raghavan, Sunil. Rahman, Abdul. Raoul, Julio. Sweat sweat sweat.

A-B-C-D-E-F-G-H-I-J.

"Oh my God! J before O. I failed. I failed! I should have been before stupid-ass Julio!" I ran into James's bathroom and splashed cold water on my face.

Kevin yelled after me: "Sheila. You're probably in the first department still. Just calm down." Easy for him to say.

Matthew put his arm around me and my cell phone wouldn't stop ringing. Claustrophobia set in.

The first department—server is busy. This was a hideous dream. Point, click. Server is busy.

Server is out to lunch. Pace, splash. Phones were ringing everywhere. Nobody was answering. Even Kevin, James, and Matthew looked worried now. Server is Dead.

FUCK!

Ring. Ring. Ring. It was my friend Rachel from law school. I hadn't talked to her since the bar. I inexplicably took the call.

"Hello?"

"CONGRATULATIONS!!!!!" she screamed. For what? Being a sweating drunk?

"Huh?"

"Congratulations. You passed!"

"What? What are you talking about, Rachel?"

"Haven't you checked the Web site?!"

"Yes, but I can't get on. Did you actually see my name somewhere?" She had, along with just about everyone else we knew at Columbia. There were two glaring omissions. Greg Jenkins and Samantha Watts from our first-year section weren't on the list. It sucked for them.

Matthew quickly found his and Heidi's names on the California site. Relieved, the four of us opened a bottle of wine, popped in some Rolling Stones, and settled in for a long, hard search of every law clerk we knew. First on the list was Brian. Pass. We surmised that he and his mom were getting busy at that very moment. James confirmed that his coclerks passed before Kevin did the same for his. It was Matthew's and my turn to find Evan. First department. No Evan Andrews. Not in the fourth, either. I wasn't fond of the guy, but I'd never wish him failure of this magnitude. Not with the judge as his boss. I said a silent prayer that he'd mistakenly been placed under the second or third—where all the kids from upstate were. Not there, either.

"Are you sure his last name is Andrews?"

"Yes. I am positive."

"What about his first name? Maybe it's, it's Sarah? Or maybe his name is really Ginger Anderson?" Nope. His name was definitely Evan Andrews. And he'd failed. The first law clerk to the Honorable Helga Friedman to have failed the bar. Potentially the first Harvard Law grad to have failed. Maybe Professor Chemerinsky taught Coping with Bar Exam Failure at the famed Clerkship Institute?

"Wow. She's really going to kill him. I feel so bad for him. I don't know what the poor kid is going to do. It's going to be heinous." I shook my head as "Gimme Shelter" played appropriately in the background. "Her husband's about to croak. And now, Evan the clerk failed the bar."

The others, including Matthew, sat speechless. What could they say?

There was nothing anyone could do to prevent what lay ahead.

Evan hid behind normalcy. "Good morning, Sheila." Smile. "How are you, Sheila?" Smile. "Good morning, Matthew." Smile. "How are you, Matthew?" George Washington was woodchucking my brain. While I probably smelled like burnt bungus, Evan smelled worse—reeked of Watergate-style cover-up. Who was he kidding? Every clerk this side of Cambodia was going to know he failed by noon, that is if they didn't know already.

Kate paid me a visit. "Hey, Sheila, is everything OK with Evan? He seems, you know . . . different."

Was I in the right place? Evan was chatting everyone up. Kate lost the stutter. What would be next? Janet would compliment Roy? Roy would brush his teeth? Maybe it was opposite day. Maybe the judge would come in and actually reward all of us with candies and sweets for being such good law clerks. And she'd give Evan an extra special treat, knowing he was hurting from his fall. Only time would tell. After sneering at me on my way to my cubicle, Janet muttered something about the judge having a doctor's appointment in New Jersey at 9 AM. She still made it to work by 9:30. I suspected it was that electric broom again.

The witch was in the house, and there wasn't a sack of treats in sight. Even worse, she didn't walk through either the clerks' cave or secretaries' den to insult anyone. Instead, she went through her secret judge door and straight into the torture chamber. This didn't bode well. Her morning insults, while unpleasant, signaled at least a mediocre mood. Silence could only mean one thing—a shit storm was on the horizon, one that would gain momentum after the clerk of the court sent out his annual pass/fail e-mail to every judge on the third circuit. Bringing dishonor to the Honorable Helga Friedman was a crime of epic proportions, and as I'd learned, Pennsylvania was trigger-happy when it came to the death penalty.

From the corner of my left eye, I could see the judge sitting, seething at her desk. What was pissing her off this super fine morning? She picked up the phone. Per usual, it was on speaker. "Give me Dr. Fermez."

"Sorry, ma'am, Dr. *Fernandez* is in surgery."

"Do you even know who I am? Do you? I am a FEDERAL JUDGE!" A twenty-foot manhole and international media blitz hadn't taught her. Like the police officer, the hospital administrator couldn't have cared less if she was a federal judge. The fact was, a federal judge should have known that if a cardiac surgeon ditched surgery for a call—any call—even one from the president of the United States—he'd be wiped out by malpractice.

"Ma'am. I'm sorry. I can't get Dr. Fernandez. As I said, he's in surgery. But what I can do is have him call you when he's finished. In the meantime, is there anything I can help you with?"

"Can you save my husband, you nurse or whatever you are? If you can't even put the right person on the phone, I have a hard time believing you can do anything! Just tell the doctor that Judge called!" And with that, the judge slammed the phone down. Suddenly, my hangover didn't seem so bad.

"Sheera!" In addition to dreading whatever it was the judge had to say to me, I feared that I looked like a prune and smelled like a brewery. No matter to the judge. She barely looked at me at all, instead focusing on the red carpet.

"I've, I've lost my bridge! My bridge!" What was she talking about. The Ben Franklin Bridge? Golden Gate? Which bridge had she lost? "Well, *do* something about it!! Find my bridge!!!" Bark bark bark. She motioned to the floor. I dropped to all fours in search of a suspension bridge underneath her desk, by her dead ficus plant, next to her stacks of briefs. Nope, no bridge there. "My bridge! My bridge! It's missing!" She was up now and running in circles around her office. Even I, who had passed the bar, couldn't begin to solve this puzzle.

"Judge, what exactly am I looking for?"

"My bridge. It holds my teeth together"—her eyes bulged and she started tapping her front teeth. "It just fell out. Just now."

I went from all fours to on the floor, my self-respect vaporized. It was one thing to be nearly thirty years old and banned from all talking, having toilet lunch be the high point of your day, and having a different name and ethnicity repeatedly thrust on you. But here I was on my hands and knees looking for my boss's dentures. This was *years* of therapy.

I found myself asking: "OK, Judge. Please describe your bridge." I was out of body, floating above a violent red sea, with an even more violent lady running circles around a poor, pathetic law clerk desperately searching for a "small, metal thingy."

"Sheera. Shayla. I know it's there *somewhere*. Find it! Find it!" I crawled east, west, north, south. Lewis and Clark weren't this thorough. "It's a small metal thingy, I said!"

"Yes, Judge, I'm looking. I just don't see it."

"You can't do anything. Where's what's-his-name?" How was it possible that I felt inadequate because I couldn't find the judge's denture Band-Aid? I didn't know the answer. I just knew that I felt like a total loser.

"Roy?"

"Yeah, whatever his name is. Tell him to come in here." Thank God for Roy. I managed to get up and drag myself out of the torture chamber.

Roy was sitting, staring at his blank computer screen. His back was perfectly straight. His mullet crisper than autumn in New England. He wasn't doing one damn thing. Then again, I couldn't find one small metal thingy. And who knew, maybe Roy would have better luck. After all, he'd been hunting people all weekend. Surely he could find a bridge.

"Yes?" Roy asked utterly petrified. So was the air that his breath violated. I wondered if you'd die if Medieval Roy gave you mouth-to-mouth resuscitation.

"The judge wants you in there." I pointed to her office. "She needs help finding her bridge." A pause. As if he hadn't heard the entire charade from the torture chamber. "It's something small and metal and holds her dentures together."

Before he could respond, I dodged the malodorous bullet and returned to my cubicle. Type type type. The Sixth Amendment to the United States Constitution provides that "In all criminal prosecutions—"

"Can't you do *anything*, Roy?!"

"The accused shall enjoy the right to a speedy and public trial, by an impartial jury of the state and—"

"Roy! Roy! Faster. Look faster." How did the woman expect us to work when she screamed like that? The best I could do was stare at Camden. The mere sight of Roy on all fours enraged her more than Dr. Fernandez's truancy.

"AAAGGHHH!"

Camden would have to wait. Matthew jumped up and hid behind our door to witness the action. I peered to my left. Large medieval man with tight khaki pants. Butt in the air. Visible tighty-whitey line due to crawling position. Judge. Big bun, standing behind him.

"Roy! Roy! Roy!" Then she kicked the bottom of his cheap loafers. He moved an inch, nose to the floor. The moan was apparently caused when Roy bumped into a table, causing one of her deceased plants to fall over. Roy had watered that plant just hours earlier. I felt for Roy.

Thank God for Bob. As it was, even Dr. Fernandez, the head of cardiology at the University of Pennsylvania Hospital, was scared of the judge and returned her call the moment he finished a triple bypass. The judge forgot about the importance of her teeth, shooed Roy away, and answered her phone.

"Yes?" she asked as if the doctor were bothering her. Dr. Fernandez was rightfully confused.

"You called me, Judge. What can I do for you?"

"So nice of you to make time for me. You know that I'm a rilly rilly busy person. I'm a federal judge."

"Listen, Judge Friedman, if there's something I can help you with, please let me know. Otherwise, I'll have to go as I've got a full list of patients today."

"Very well, Dr. Hermandez. When will Bob be ready to come home?"

"It's actually Fernandez, not Hermandez. And Judge, we've told you. He's not at all in good shape. He's very old and weak. I think it may be weeks, months maybe. I can't tell you much more than that." This was not the right answer.

"Well a lot of good you people do. To call yourselves doctors! I have a Juris Doctor, and I could probably do a lot more than you!" She put her small head in her wrinkled hands. In spite of myself, I felt sickeningly sorry for her. Bob was all she had.

From what I had heard, in addition to having been an accomplished archaeologist, he was an extraordinary person. When other judges asked about him, they seemed genuinely concerned. And judging from the one picture Friedman had of him in her office, he had honest eyes. Sometimes I'd inspect that picture after the judge went home, succumbing to my need to understand the insanity of the woman for whom I toiled. I kept thinking something in that picture would jump out at me, revealing a fellow sociopath, providing some sort of explanation for their marriage. But no, it never did. Seemed that he just loved her, which was crazy in and of itself. The paradigmatic nice guy in love with the toxic bitch. It was no wonder she didn't want him to go away. He was the only person in the world who loved her. Hell, he was the only person in the world who *liked* her. And yet, instead of being by his side, she was at work yelling at anyone and everyone she could. Anger was the only thing she knew. It was comfortable, easy, natural even.

"Janet. Janet. Shut my door. Shut it now!" The judge was on the brink of a breakdown and couldn't handle her peons witnessing anything remotely emotional.

Matthew came out from behind the door next to my cubicle. "Why doesn't she just go to the hospital?" It was a very good question, but we both knew the answer.

"Matthew, she can't deal. It's too painful for her. I feel bad for her. It just makes me so—"

"Sad. It makes you sad," Matthew interrupted. "Well, I personally don't feel sad for someone who isn't at the hospital with her dying husband." He stormed off toward the bathroom.

Matthew had recently admitted that he, too, engaged in intricate dialogues with himself in the bathroom. I'd started noticing that everyone around the chambers talked to themselves. The judge did it vocally, unabashedly. Roy whispered sweet anachronisms to himself. Janet was more of a walk-and-mutterer. Anytime she'd get up to do anything I'd hear soft slices of hate quickly escaping from her chapped frosted lips. At least Matthew and I had the good sense to take it to the toilet.

No bridge. No self-esteem. No Matthew. What I did still have was a kicking headache, the sweats, blurry vision, and rapid heartbeat. I sat back down in my cell. Was it normal to feel like this after four beers and a glass of wine? Maybe I had diabetes? I did pee very often and my mom had once mentioned that that was a big sign. Panic. Sweat. Google: "diabetes." Ugh! Frequent urination. Excessive thirst and hunger. Fatigue. Irritability. Blurry vision. I had it, I really had it. I was thirstier than a dehydrated camel, so hungry that I could eat an entire deep-fried cow with mashed potatoes on the side, so tired that I halfway envied Bob for being in a coma, and more irritable than a bloated bowel. And now I'd have to start giving myself insulin injections. Where was I going to do that? I couldn't do everything in the bathroom— talk, eat, and insulin. I needed a second opinion. WebMD.com. But before I could click enter, an e-mail from Brian popped up.

It was titled "Rock on!"

"Rock on" without irony plus an exclamation mark was in the same heinous category as "all about," and "you go, girl." This might have been it for Brian. "Congratulations to you all on the bar." Yeah, and a big congratulations to you for bedding your mom. "So, as everyone knows, Evan didn't pass the bar. I think we really need to be there for him. I say we all meet for drinks at the Vegas after work today. See you all there 😊" Roughly half the state of Pennsylvania had been cc'ed.

In all the hoopla surrounding dentures and diabetes, I'd totally forgotten about Evan. There were so many new knots in my stomach, I couldn't decipher if any of them belonged to Evan anymore. Perhaps not. And, even if I did feel bad for him, I wasn't about to join this cheer-up squad. I'd console Evan in my own way. No more sarcastic comments. No more eye rolls. At least not until the New Year. By then, I'd probably be in a diabetic coma anyway and the only eye rolling that'd be happening would be to the back of my head.

"Um. Sheila. Can I talk to you for a minute?" Standing before my cubicle was Evan himself.

"Um. Sure, Evan." We were like two kids meeting on the jungle gym for the first time.

"Mind if we go out there?" Evan nodded his head in the direction of the hallway. We proceeded past Matthew who looked up long enough to give Evan a compassionate smile.

"Sheila. This is really awkward. Um. I know we're not really friends. But I don't have any friends here and I really need some help." I summoned as much empathy as I could and nodded.

"Sure, Evan. What do you need?" Pretending not to know he failed was the best I could do.

"Well, I don't know if you know this. But"—he took a deep breath— "I failed the bar." Passable shock. Emphatic nod. "And the judge just buzzed me and said she needed to talk to me. I know this is what it's about. I'm petrified." His knees wobbled. Instinctively, I hugged him. He started sobbing.

"Listen, Evan. It's fine. First of all, you'll take the bar again and you'll pass. Don't even sweat that. As for the judge, don't cry in front of her. She'll destroy you." While not the most comforting advice, it certainly was the most sound.

"EVVVVVAAAANNNN!"

I took a deep breath, prompting Evan to do the same. Matthew stood to salute Evan as we Lamazed our way through the clerks' cave.

Then Evan disappeared into the abyss.

Matthew and I accompanied Evan to the Las Vegas Lounge that evening. The afternoon hadn't been a good one. The judge's castigation ("You're an embarrassment to yourself, to this chamber, and to the judiciary itself") seemed unnecessary, considering that Evan had punished and would continue to punish himself enough. His reaction—immersing himself in his pocket-size Constitution from cover to cover—was at once peculiar and respectable.

We walked into the bar. There were dozens. No hundreds. Thousands maybe? More people were crammed into that smoky bar than bathed in the Ganges on a sweltering August afternoon. It seemed that every law clerk in America had shown up with the express intent of making Evan feeling like a colossal jackass. Was this really the profession that I had chosen? One in which schadenfreude was veiled as concern?

"Evan, I'm *so* sorry!" "Evan. How *are* you?" "Evan, I can't even *imagine* how you must feel." I loved histrionics as much as the next drama queen, but everyone was treating Evan as though he had just been diagnosed with a fatal disease.

Matthew pushed his way in front of Evan, shielding him from the misplaced condolences. I grabbed Evan's arm and pulled him toward the bar. The last thing my body needed was a drink after the night before, but this clerkship could have made an alcoholic out of a teetotaling Mormon.

"Hold on. Hold on. Where are you *going?*" Brian said. The proud party planner had emerged displaying what must have been a bar-passage gift from his mother—a sparkling BlackBerry cradled in a plastic holster, which was pinned to his braided belt.

"We're just getting a drink," Evan responded. "We'll be back in a second."

"Hey, we should get out of here," Matthew suggested. "How about if the three of us go out solo?"

Evan squinted, aware that something was wrong with the picture but unable to pinpoint the exact problem. "No, Brian went through all this trouble. I think we should stay." Matthew shrugged his shoulders, got three beers, and for the second time that day, Evan disappeared into an abyss.

"This is so incredibly hideous," Matthew started, "I just can't understand why—"

"Well, well, well. Look who we have here." Betsy tripped her way into us tipsily. "What could be next for you guys? First you work for the craziest person on the court. Next you're on the losing side of a case. Now, one of your coclerks *fails* the bar exam. I mean, who fails the bar?"

"Nice to see you, too, Betsy," I snapped. "Actually roughly forty percent of people fail the bar. And I'm not sure how giving someone a new sentencing because they had a shitty lawyer can be construed as being on the losing side of a case."

"And—Judge Friedman is not crazy. She may be tough. But she's not crazy," Matthew added defensively in the I-can-talk-shit-about-my-family-but-you-can't vein.

"Whatever. I just wonder what could *possibly* be *next.*" Betsy winked and walked away.

"What a bitch," Matthew blurted. "And what is she talking about something happening next?" It was the Supreme Court nomination, and I'd surprisingly managed to dispel it from my mind. That is, until now. My stomach had crept into my esophagus and I needed out—immediately.

"Matthew, let's leave. I really need some air."

"Fine by me," Matthew said, scanning the room. "It looks like Evan is safely nestled between Brian and a Debbie Downer I don't recognize. I think our job is done."

We escaped the Vegas and after a seconds-long internal battle, I decided to let Matthew in on my supreme secret.

"Matthew, hey, I actually know—" His phone rang.

"Hang on a sec, Sheila. Hey, Heidi. No, no. I'm so sorry about that. All right. OK." He looked at his watch. "Uh—OK. I'll go now. Um, er, love you, too.

"Ugh! Heidi had a really"—he used his hands to make fake quotation marks—"painful day at work and is insisting that I head to New York for the night. So, I gotta catch the next train out. I'll see you tomorrow," he said, running down the street.

I called Sanjay who was in between patients and couldn't talk. Had he been this busy at the hospital while I was in law school? Maybe he had and I hadn't noticed until now—the first time in our relationship that a little moral support would have been nice. I found solace in a foot-long meatball sub. Whoever said that alcohol was the cause of and the solution to all of life's problems must never have been to Subway.

Chapter Thirteen

⚖

This court is a family, and there will be times that I will make remarks about my family members. They will not be repeated beyond the chambers door. Even if I occasionally blow off steam, remember that these judges are my colleagues and will be my friends long after you are gone from here.

—Judge Aldisert, United States Court of Appeals
for the Third Circuit

The news broke the Wednesday before Thanksgiving. It made Black Tuesday seem like a deep-tissue massage. Sanjay called, instructing me to turn on CNN (he'd generously handed me down his nine-inch TV when he got a flat screen). Wolf Blitzer was voicing over a documentary on Judge Linda Adams. Her modest beginnings in Pittsburgh. The daughter of a Sears manager and an elementary school teacher. Valedictorian of South Pittsburgh High School. Student government at Penn State. *Law Review* at Temple. Private practice. Court of appeals judge. Three lovely daughters. The creepy Kenny G background music was the backbreaking last straw, sending me into fetal position. If CNN's love song to Adams broke this camel's back, I could only imagine what was being broken at the judge's happy house—poor Bob. The phone forced me from my embryonic state. It was Sanjay again.

"Don't you think it's interesting they're not saying anything about the mayor?" he asked casually. Normally, I'd be outraged by such a comment, attributing female achievement to the husband. But in this case, it was true. Joe Adams had been Philadelphia's mayor for four years and was widely credited with the city's rebirth. As such, not since Jackie O had a first lady been as popular as Linda Adams. Weeks earlier, the mayor had been re-elected by a landslide. Everyone in our chambers pretended like the election never happened.

Foolishly, Kate had asked if she could take an extra ten minutes at lunch to vote. The judge simply stated: "I do NOT have time for my law clerks to wander around the city during working hours." I found Kate's request to be more irritating than the judge's response—she should have known better than to ask for such favors as exercising her constitutional right. The rest of us did.

As far as I was concerned, Philadelphia didn't even have a mayor. And if it did, I surmised it was probably Judge Friedman. Judge Friedman clearly agreed. She never even called Judge Adams to congratulate her. Yet another huge elephant in chambers. The place was like an invisible safari.

"Yes, I do think it's weird, Sanj. Listen—I need to get to work. I'll call you later," I muttered and hung up.

Resolving to pull myself together, I walked to the courthouse and approached security.

"Hello. I'm putting a phone in here"—I slowly placed my cell in the famous bucket—"but I have a card for it." I showed the he/she my card. Stares all around. Was I speaking Cantonese?

"Phone in the bucket! Phone in the bucket!" He/she screamed suddenly. Was this a joke? I walked through the metal detector without setting off the buzzer. "Do you have a red phone card?" He/she inquired. This exercise in futility earned the same security guard a second peep at red phone Reno in less than ten seconds. Taking control of one's life in an irrational environment wasn't easy. Logic, efficiency—those things permeated the private sector. This was the government.

Brian was standing at the elevator bank, making my already lucky day that much luckier. "Can you *believe* it about Adams?" he asked hungrily, clutching a *Philadelphia Inquirer*.

"Good morning, Brian. How was your weekend?" I asked, calmly. What I really wanted to know was whether his mom had moved in with him.

"Did you hear? Did you hear about *Adams?*" Ding! Thirteenth floor. I stepped off the elevator and headed straight for my cubicle. Adhering to my mother's motto that if you ignore it, it'll go away, I dispelled the Supreme Court from my mind and returned to Dell Nelson. No matter that the death penalty felt less menacing than a judicial nomination. Before I could turn on my computer, Janet materialized.

"So. Ah. Sheila. Hi," she said, pulling on her cross violently.

"Oh, good morning, Janet. What's up?" I smiled.

"You heard about Judge Adams, right? I mean—"

"Dude, what's going on around here," Medieval Roy said and skidded to a stop, right next to Janet. He started petting what looked like a roach on his chin. "I mean there are, like, TV people outside. What's goin' on?"

"Judge Adams just got nominated to the Supreme Court." Janet paused. "I mean—DUH!" I wondered if she'd picked up that bit of outmoded pop-culture lingo from the kids at church or the Lifetime channel.

"Judge Adams . . . the Supreme Court . . . ?" Roy gazed toward the ceiling, pretending to ponder something profound. What he meant was: Who is Judge Adams and what is the Supreme Court?

"Roy, Judge Adams, you know, a judge on this court was just asked by President Bush to be a justice on the Supreme Court—you know, in Washington DC." I stopped to allow the information to sink in.

"Hey, you like my goatee, Sheila?"

"Yeah, it looks good, Roy. Really, um, good."

While Roy's goatee wasn't exactly easy on the eyes, it was the manner in

which Janet was manhandling her necklace that was causing alarm. "Roy—
you are so stupid. You don't know—"

"Holy shit!" Matthew burst into the clerks' cave, not whispering. "Is
anyone else totally freaked out about this? Jesus—the place is swarming
with reporters." I must have just missed the media.

DING! Thirteenth floor, going down!

Everyone scurried to their respective holes like a pack of scared mice.

"Sheila, Matthew in my office. Now. And shut the door behind you,"
the judge commanded, clapping her way through the clerks' cave, greasy
ponytail in tow.

We entered the torture chamber and sat warily.

"Sheila," she murmured, her back facing us. "You're a smart lawyer."
Huh? "You graduated from a top law school." Huh? "Do you think Judge
Adams is qualified"—she turned dramatically, sunglasses still perched on
her nose—"to sit on the Supreme Court?" It was too bad Joseph Heller had
croaked—there was an amazing sequel to *Catch-22* to be had. I didn't speak,
hoping this was one of those questions that really wasn't a question. Tick.
Tock. The judge sat and folded her hands. "Well?" It turned out to be a
question after all. I didn't have a good answer.

Yes, Judge Adams was qualified—as qualified as any other person sitting on that bench. Would she have been nominated but for nepotism?
Probably not. Was she the best candidate out there? Definitely not. But
let's face it—are any of them? Clarence Thomas was a common sexual
harasser and had less to say than Matthew's mute reader. And had Tony
Scalia not become a judge, he'd probably be president of the Promise Keep-
ers. Wasn't it relative, really?

"Well, Judge," I began. "I don't know mu-mu-much about Judge
Adams to be ho-ho-honest." The judge reached for a pencil. "She seemed
to be bright based on the sitting we've had with her. I don't agree with
her-her-her take on Dell Nelson. But other opinions I've read of hers
seem sound." I shrugged my shoulders, admittedly a weak diplomatic
summation.

"Interesting. You think a *sound* opinion here and there qualifies some-one for the Supreme Court?" She smirked, pulling on her pony with one hand, cradling the pencil with the other. "What about you, Matthew? Do you agree with your colleague here—that occasional *sound* opinions qualify you for the *Supreme Court?*"

"Um. Judge, that's not really what I said," I interrupted. "What I mean—"

"Seems to me you haven't said much of anything. Did you even learn anything at Cornell?" No, in fact I hadn't, seeing as I'd never stepped foot in Ithaca in my life.

"I went to Columbia, Judge." The last thing I wanted to be mistaken for, even momentarily, was a non-top-five-law-schooler.

"Well, *none* of my colleagues can understand *how* she got nominated. Well, that's not true—it was her husband. But *we're* all very concerned about some-one like Adams on the Supreme Court." She smiled, twirling her ponytail. I wondered what dance her bun would have done at that moment—the tango? Salsa? "Don't get me wrong. We're all very happy for Linda—she's a very nice *person*. But the *Supreme Court?* I don't think so." Krumping, definitely.

"Matthew," she continued, "I understand that the two of you are just best friends with Judge Adams's clerks."

Sweat stains had crept down to Matthew's elbows. "Well, I don't know if friends—"

"No! No! No!" She pounded one fist, using the other to yank her sun-glasses free, revealing puffy eyelids. "As you people know, Judge Adams's confirmation hearings will be scheduled at some point. A bunch of us are really concerned about her ability to do the job"—she lowered her voice—"and her ethics. This whole Dell Nelson fiasco and that dead man's brother is a good example of that." The puffiness left her eyes, leav-ing them shriveled jelly beans. I wished Ronald Reagan were there to eat them. "What we discuss in here doesn't leave these doors. Then again, I trust that you people never ever speak of what happens in here with the outside world!" Before our very eyes, she appeared to turn green, as a tail crept from under her desk. "I want you two to find out everything about Judge Adams from your little play friends up there. Whom she speaks to. How her opinions get written. I have a feeling she doesn't work at all. And maybe she has some, well, less than savory people with whom she cavorts. Most important, do it in an inconspicuous way. Your friends should think *you* want to know, not me."

I was stunned. Judge Friedman was a lot of things—evil and gross came to mind—but a spy?

Matthew returned to his sitting-up-dead position and didn't stir even when the judge's phone started ringing.

"Roy! Roy! Damn it. He's good for nothing," she barked and answered the phone herself. "Oh, hello, Doctor," she said, cupping her hand over the receiver. "Get out and shut the door."

Without speaking, Matthew and I rocketed out of the courthouse, zig-zagging our way past live trucks and satellite dishes. One male reporter, a dead ringer for Tammy Faye Baker in drag, shoved a microphone in my face: "Do you know Linda Adams? Do you?!"

We collapsed into a booth at Joe's Shanghai, steam from the soup dumplings fogging up both of our eyeglasses.

"Well, this is a nightmare," Matthew said, wiping his glasses with a cloth napkin. "And what on earth is the judge talking about?"

"First of all, for the sake of full disclosure—I've known about this nomination thing for a while, but Kevin made me swear on my life not to tell anyone, so I couldn't tell you. Well, actually I was going to tell you the other night before you took off for New York. Anyway, as for what the judge is talking about. I think it's exactly what it sounded like."

"Damn! I wish I'd stuck around. Advance notice would have been nice, especially considering how annoying my night in New York was." Matthew paused to take a bite of a dumpling. "Anyway, what are we supposed to do? Spy on Judge Adams? And what does Dell Nelson and a dead man's brother have to do with any of this? Is she saying that Adams is *unethical* because she doesn't think that Dell Nelson should get a new hearing? Wrong?—yes. Unethical?—I don't think so."

Matthew had gotten up to speed on the basics of Dell Nelson's case over the past few weeks. But we'd yet to sit down and discuss the details. It had occurred to me that we couldn't even start writing the dissent until Judge Adams sent us her opinion. Dissents, after all, were written in opposition to the majority opinion.

"Well, it's maybe partially that," I said and pushed my greasy plate away. "But what I think she's really pissed about is that call I got from Peter Nussbaum's brother. And I can't blame her for that. You have to admit— it's pretty messed up that the guy (a) knew how Friedman was voting for sure on the case and (b) knew to call my line directly and actually got the number, which is unlisted."

"You know I totally forgot about that. And you're right, it is weird," Matthew said, halfway amused. "But, it almost seems normal in this case. The briefs in the Nelson case read like a trashy novel. The drugs. The money. Had there been any juicy sex scenes, Heidi would probably want to take them down the shore for beach reading."

"Speaking of—is Heidi in Fort Lauderdale for Thanksgiving?" I asked, signaling the waiter for hot tea.

"Yup. She's at her sister's place. Something about Thanksgiving in South Florida seems strange"—he paused—"but who am I to judge? I'm spending Thanksgiving by myself with a TV dinner. Hey, I have a good one." Matthew perked up. "Would you rather spend Thanksgiving with Roy and his wife or"—he paused to reflect—"give the Judge an hour-long foot massage in the torture chamber." Matthew's would-you-rathers had accelerated, both in quantity and quality, revealing an innate talent for the game.

"It'd have to be the massage," I said, wincing. "Can you imagine what Roy must eat for Thanksgiving? And what he wears? Roasted hyena with an armored thong. No thanks."

"Yeah . . . but her *feet*." Matthew shuddered. "Anyway, my vote is that we lay low and hope she just forgets about the spying game. She forgets about eighty percent of everything, so maybe we'll get lucky."

The feeding frenzy surrounding the courthouse had intensified during the forty-five minutes we'd been at lunch, leading me to believe that Linda Adams's nomination would probably fall within the 20 percent of things the judge remembered.

Shortly after returning to chambers, the judge sauntered over to my cubicle, sunglasses on, carrying three plastic bags full of briefs. "Sheba. You will be pleased to know that Eddie found my bridge this morning." She tapped on her tooth.

I found myself saying the most improbable thing. "Wow. That's great. What a lovely bridge!"

"Eddie found it under my desk. You people are clearly blind if he found it and you couldn't." As if cleaning her toilet everyday wasn't horrendous enough. Now Eddie was doing reconnaissance on her teeth. "Just don't screw up what we talked about earlier," she said with a wink. "I'm leaving now but we have lots to do. We are rilly busy."

Leaving? It wasn't even 2 PM. "Hey, Janet. What, ah, what's up with the judge?" I asked sweetly, meandering to her desk. Janet was petting a shimmering book titled *Holiday Scrapbooking*.

"Ah, oh. Yeah—she's going to Mark's house for Thanksgiving." She motioned me closer to whisper in my ear. "She's not coming back until Monday but I don't want you know who to know that." She nodded menacingly at Roy's back.

"She's taking a day off? But I thought she never did that?" I leaned forward, awkwardly cupping my hand around Janet's ear.

"This is a first," Janet whispered in a hush. "Apparently, Mark insisted that he wanted to spend what would probably be his last Thanksgiving with Bob and demanded that they stay through the weekend. So Sheila, it's your lucky day—or days, I should say." Telling secrets was fun.

My phone rang as I returned to the clerks' cave.

"Sheila Raj."

Heavy breathing—not this again. "This is Robert Nussbaum and I'll never get to spend another Thanksgiving with my brother because of that—" Click.

Cheers erupted outside. I peered below and saw a speck that must have been Linda Adams dazzling the crowd. Cheers again. My chest tightened, evidencing a scarcity of air. The room went out of focus. I don't recall any thought processes, but a daring plan had definitely been set in motion.

I turned off my computer, collected my belongings, and marched over to Matthew. "The judge won't be back until Monday. Nor will I—I'm going home to Virginia for Thanksgiving. You're welcome to join."

During the holidays, Washington DC's Union Station serves as an over-zealous understudy to the North Pole. A forest of glimmering Christmas trees. Hundreds, thousands, millions of frenzied holiday-makers decking the halls. Even the Amtrak employees seemed a smidgen merry. I breathed a sigh of relief. I was home.

"SHEILA!!! BABY!! SHEILA!! HERE!!!"

"Sheila, I think that's your mom, over there to the right?" Sure enough. In the McDonald's, which opened up into gate D like a fast-food loft, were my mother and my father, who was the quiet, slightly confused yin to her absurdly unquiet yang. My mother was standing on an orange plastic chair in a red and green silk sari, screaming at the top of her lungs. I peered around, in search of Sanjay, who was supposed to have accompanied my parents to pick us up.

She carefully hopped off the chair, grabbed Matthew and hugged him tightly. "You must be Matthew! We are just soooooo happy you decided to join us. That, that"—she lowered her voice—"bitch will rot in hell for treating you two the way she does." Volume back up. Matthew tossed to Father, who managed a handshake and monotone "Welcome."

"Sheila, my baby girl. Baby girl. Baby girl." She rocked me back and forth and I felt safe again. I wanted to move back into the womb.

"Mom, hey, where's Sanjay?"

"Oh," she released me. "He called right before we left and said he was held up at the hospital and will call you in a bit."

"Whatever," I said, grimacing.

"Sheila, he won't be a resident forever. Be patient, baby, be patient."

Matthew and I waited under the globe-sized wreath outside of the station as my parents went to retrieve the car, a green Buick only slightly smaller than the wreath. My parents kept Buick in business. Not even the other uncles and aunties drove them anymore.

Getting the car at Union Station was always a thirty- to forty-five-minute ordeal. My father would insist that the car was on level three, my mother certain it was level four. While reserved, my dad was no pushover and parking was his silent crusade. You never, ever told him how, where, or when to park. My mother used to brag that my dad had once sliced some guy's tire at Tysons Corner for having taken his parking spot. She thought it was macho and I guess for a man who's worn polyester pants and driven a Buick for forty years, going slasher every once in a while was pretty cool.

The two of them would argue —she boisterously, he in a murmur—over level three or four. This would go on for about twenty minutes, at which point either Puja or I would find the car ourselves. This was the easy part. Nine times out of ten, it'd be on level one or two.

I was pleasantly surprised this time. Just as I was going in search of them, the green ship sailed up to the curb with both parents chatting away happily. It turned out they had a new trick ("New Buick has high-tech keychain"). They would simply go from level to level, beginning on four, working their way down, hitting the trunk button on their high-tech keychain. When they heard a trunk pop open, the car was found.

My mother gave Matthew the inquisition during the drive from Union Station to my home in Reston.

"Where are you from?"

"Idaho. I'm from a small town there. How about—"

"And where did you go to college?"

"Stanfor—"

"Do you like Indian food?"

"Ah, yeah, I do. I haven't really—"

"Great. I made pork chops," she squealed. "You like pork chops, right?"

"Yeah, I love them. They—"

"Do you eat cauliflower. I made—"

"MOM. We just got here. Ease up, OK?"

My mother delivered her well-rehearsed look of hurt. "But Matthew's my friend, right, Matthew?"

"Yes, Dr. Raj, you are my friend," he replied, pleased as punch. He'd fallen for my mother's antics. This was record time for her.

"So, where were we—do you like cauliflower?"

"Yes, yes, I do." He blushed. At that point, she could have asked him how many bowel movements he had daily and he would've answered gladly. The woman would have made a genius journalist. She was truth serum in a brown bottle.

"Your sister and that new boyfriend of hers have been baking cookies," my mother said disdainfully as we pulled into the driveway.

Charlie was Puja's newest guy. Harvard undergrad ("He even wrote for the *Harvard Crimson*"). Currently freelancing (read: disgruntled writer who thinks that everything besides the *New Yorker* is beneath him because he wrote for the *Harvard Crimson*). Lived in Williamsburg with roommates he met on craigslist. Hated the gentrification of New York. I hadn't met him, but he sounded just like all of Puja's former guys, except he was thirty-five, not twenty-five, making him more sad than interesting.

Puja was smart, successful, and attractive. Yet she always dated men lacking in various departments, including looks, ambition, kindness, and solvency. If my mother hadn't cornered the market on lecturing Puja, I'd say more about it. Then again, I thought that it was precisely because of my mother that Puja handpicked the men she did. For some reason, she didn't respond well to "Puja, baby, why do you date *galeej* boys! You are *thirty* years old, find a nice *husband*." *Galeej* was Konkani, my family's South Indian language, for immeasurably gross. It was mothers like ours who kept the Charlies of the world in business.

Usually these things lasted three weeks—a month tops. But Charlie had been around for two months, and more important, had made the cut for Thanksgiving. Boyfriends never—*ever*—were welcome at Aunty Roma's Thanksgiving unless there was a ring on the finger. Otherwise, "What would everyone say?" Puja risked it for Charlie. Well, sort of. He'd be introduced as a "friend." Puja agreed only to that, eschewing our mother's request that we further lie that Charlie had been orphaned and didn't have a family of his own.

Walking into my childhood home, I felt the stress evaporate from my body. Even Charlie's trucker hat didn't spoil the feeling. We were in the middle of introductions when the phone rang. It was Sanjay.

"Hey Sheels, welcome home. Listen, I can't make dinner tonight. I've got to fill in for Mike. But, I'll see you tomorrow—right? At Aunty Roma's, OK?"

"All right," I started cautiously, walking out of the kitchen, "but I don't understand. This is the first time I've been in Reston in months. Why would you offer to fill in for someone?" Stress reentered. "Not to mention, this is so rude. You know that I really wanted you to meet Matthew. He's practically the only person who keeps me sane at work. Doesn't that mean anything to you?" It wasn't until I started speaking that I realized how frustrated I'd been with Sanjay.

"Look, Sheila. I'll meet Matthew tomorrow. You know there's nothing I can do about work. I am a *busy resident.* Look—if it'd make you feel better, I'll come after my rounds—you know, at like *five in the morning!*" he said, sounding more like an insolent child than a busy resident.

"I have no clue what's going on with you. I'll see you tomorrow," I said and slammed the phone, just like they did on soap operas. When I returned to the kitchen, everyone was seated for dinner.

Something about the masala pork chops made me laugh behind Sanjay's vegetarian back. I wanted to eat a whole curried pig out of spite. Instead, I sat silently as Charlie read from his imaginary memoir. He grew up in Darien, Connecticut, the only child of "hard-core Republicans."

He became "radicalized" his freshman year at Harvard. As predicted, he was "this close" (he spread his right thumb and index finger a centi- meter apart) to landing a piece on the Sudan in the *New Yorker* and "wouldn't consider" pitching it elsewhere. He normally hated doctors, lawyers, and bankers, but "this crowd—all of you guys" were different and "really down."

"How can you blanketly hate people just because of their profession?" Matthew asked, in between mouthfuls. "That, to me, seems more closed- minded than any hard-core Republicans I know." Charlie looked at once confused and incensed. Puja pursed her lips, delivering her prize-winning glare in Charlie's direction. It was one thing to knock bankers and law- yers, but my parents had spent their careers at the Veterans Administra- tion, foregoing wealth to care for the poor.

For once, my mother's inability to deal with open confrontation came in handy. "Well then, how about dessert." She leaped from the table, thereby ordering a cease-fire. Not long after, everyone went to bed. Puja and I bunked together in my bedroom and Matthew scored Puja's room, while Charlie got the rickety pullout couch. While not one for public fighting, my mother had mastered passive aggression, her retaliatory tactics tucked away in the trenches of seemingly banal things like sleep- ing arrangements.

By the time we pulled up to Aunty Roma's house the next day, all feel- ings of ill will had dissipated. It was Thanksgiving, after all, and the Indi- ans and a particular white man were ready to make peace.

My father maneuvered the Buick in between a dozen or so Mercedes and SUVs on the familiar cul-de-sac. We'd been coming here for Thanksgiving for as long as I could remember. Considering I barely knew my flesh-and- blood uncles and aunts, who were scattered all over the world, from Bombay to Dubai, London, and Toronto, these people were my family.

"Hey, Boss," my father said to a group of uncles, patting Uncle Kirin on the back. A slew of "Hey, Bosses" with a "Hey, Chief" or two followed. Matthew and Charlie were deposited with the bosses and chiefs.

The aunties surrounded Puja, my mother, and me—a sea of loud brown people blabbing in accented non sequiturs ("Yes, yes, yes, Sudha makes very good pakoras," "But what about that Mark Waters, he looks like bad man, I'm not woting for him," "My Shalini has found good doctor like Sanjay"). Three subjects, thirty seconds flat. What they really wanted to talk about was the presence of Matthew and Charlie, both of whom had created an unspoken stir.

The last time one of my childhood peers brought a member of the opposite sex to Thanksgiving was five years ago. Malu (twenty-six years old) had invited Rick, a beefy electrician (forty-two) from Maryland whom, we later learned, she'd met on matrimonials.com ("the meeting place for marriage-minded individuals"). Rick was one of many fetishists who cruised those Indian/Pakistani/Bangladeshi Web sites. Yet, it wasn't his lascivious lust for the brown woman that brought Rick down, it was that he was an electrician. The only thing first-generation Indians tolerate less than no marriage is marriage to a blue-collar worker. Until now, nobody had dared to bring another outsider.

I was on a mad dash for a samosa when Sanjay walked into Aunty Roma's, a pudgy, red-haired girl in tow.

"Hey, Sheels," he said, clumsily embracing me. "This is Gayle, she's a resident from Moscow." A red-haired Russian resident in Reston—who would have thought!

"I haven't ever been to Thanksgiving, so Sanj was nice enough to invite me," Gayle piped in with less of an accent than most of the people present. Strange—Sanjay always told me that, aside from his mother, I was the only person allowed to call him Sanj. "And I'm just so thrilled to finally meet you, Sheila."

"Nice to meet you, too," I said, confused by her use of the word "finally." Why hadn't Sanjay ever mentioned Gayle? I thought I knew all of his friends. "Is Gayle a common name in Russia?" I said, blurting the first innocuous thing that came to mind.

She giggled. "Oh no, no. It's short for my real name." Full stop.

"Oh, what's your real name?"

"Ludmila."

"How nice," I responded, bypassing the obvious question. "How long have you been here?"

"Twenty years."

Twenty days, twenty weeks, twenty months, even, and I'd have understood the "from Russia" introduction—but twenty years?

"Mrs. Kapur!" Ludmila said, leaping at Sanjay's mother and leaving the two of us alone.

"Look, Sheels," he started.

"Don't call me Sheels," I interrupted. "We are currently not friends and only my friends call me Sheels, *Sanj.*"

He rolled his eyes. "Whatever, Sheila. Look I'm sorry about last night. You just have to understand the life of a physician." Just as I despised when lawyers referred to themselves as attorneys, I found it equally repulsive when doctors called themselves physicians. It felt like an undeserved promotion. "It's just that—"

Matthew joined us, extending his hand. "Hey. You must be Sanjay. I'm Matthew."

"Oh, hi," Sanjay replied awkwardly. "It's nice to meet you . . . finally."

Aunty Roma shrilled—saved by the bell. It was time to eat.

The three of us passed Charlie, who was holding court with a pack of bejeweled aunties.

"At Harvard . . ." Giggles all around. He was playing the Ivy League card, a pathetic move even for Charlie. Indians, like Jews, Koreans, Lithuanians, and every other immigrant community, worshipped the Ivy. Don't get me wrong—WASPs love Harvard, Yale, and Princeton as much as their immigrant compatriots, but given how common it is for them to make it into the Ivy, it's more expected than adulated. Just then, Charlie popped a chutney-laden pakora in his small mouth, took a sip from his piña colada (all the aunties drank them), and proclaimed: "Then, my second year at Harvard, I got really into Hinduism." Charlie beamed. The aunties cooed their way to the dining room.

Puja, Charlie, Matthew, Sanjay, Ludmila, and I were at the kids' table, along with Anil, Sahil, Rupa, Ramesh, Jay (short for Jayenth), and Hema. The aunties and uncles elbowed each other for the best seat at the adult table. Uncle Bharat, Aunty Roma's husband, said an inaudible, incomprehensible prayer followed by Aunty Roma's yearly toast: "To very very good friends, family, food." Clink. Cheers.

Uncle Bharat carved Aunty Roma's famous curried turkey, stuffed with potatoes. Having grown up on the spicy bird, I found noncurried turkey repelling. Matthew appeared to be an immediate convert while Sanjay grimaced theatrically at the plates of meat. As soon as he was finished carving, Uncle Bharat sat down and fell asleep sitting up amid all the action. Nobody noticed. He did it every year.

"So, you're a radiologist—that's sounds really interesting," Matthew said to Sanjay. "I'm in awe of doctors. You guys have the hardest jobs."

"No more difficult than clerking for Judge Friedman, that's for sure," Sanjay said, grinning and toying with his plate of spinach. Puja was deep in conversation with Ludmila, and Charlie was busy surveying the scene, like a keen tourist.

"Yeah, but the cadavers . . . I just couldn't do it." Matthew shook his head. "I've always found it amazing that you guys can deal with the gore. I'm way too much of a wimp."

"Yeah, well, it's just part of the job. You know—the bodies. We just have to deal with them . . . it's no big deal," he lied, vigilantly avoiding eye contact with me. "Now, if you'll excuse me, I've got to run to the restroom." I presumed the words cadaver, gore, and bodies necessitated a receptacle.

"Wow—that's so cool. I wish Heidi and I were in different professions. It must be so interesting."

"Interesting is one way to put it," I said, smiling.

"So, do you like Charlie?" Puja whispered to me when Ludmila got up from the table. Before I could respond, Puja and I overheard the following: "So, Jay-ENTH, how do you *feel* as an Indian in the United States?" Charlie was a Helga Friedman protégé.

"It's Jay. And honestly, I don't even think about it. I was born and raised in Washington DC and now live in Chicago, where lots of Indians live." Jay stood up under the guise of wanting more food. "It's the twenty-first century, man. And you live in New York. Every other person is Indian there." Jay hit the road. Puja shook her head, annoyed. Sorry, Charlie.

The dining room was restless, as Indians aren't much for lengthy, seated meals. I took advantage of the sudden commotion to slip downstairs, the location of the secret basement bathroom. I maneuvered my way past Aunty Roma's prize-winning collection of clutter, a distinction earned from her steadfast refusal to discard anything, ever. Why throw away used wrapping paper when it can sit in your basement for decades?

I heard murmurings and peered around the corner—and gasped! Sitting Indian-style, in between a life-size Pink Panther stuffed animal and a dilapidated Sit'n Spin, were Sanjay and Ludmila.

"What the fuck!" I screamed.

Sanjay looked up, frozen with terror. "It's . . . it's not what you think!" he blurted, grease dribbling from his mouth. I didn't know what to think. In one hand, he was clutching a half-eaten turkey leg; with the other, he was pulling on the wishbone. Ludmila, his competitor, was rubbing Sanjay's knee with her free hand.

"*You're eating turkey?*" I asked, incredulous.

"Sheila, it's, it's—"

"It's bullshit!" I yelled. "You . . . you closeted meat-eating hypocrite!"

Sanjay tried to stand but got tangled in his surroundings. "Shhhh . . . Sheila, my mother will hear you. She'll kill me if she knows. Please—just please don't tell her," he implored, peering through the panther's fuzzy pink legs.

"Tell her about us, Sanj, about us!" Ludmila begged, pulling the wishbone in opposite directions by herself. It snapped and she held up the larger portion. "Look, I won," she announced victoriously.

"I don't need anyone to tell me anything," I seethed. "You know what, Sanjay—if you wanted out of the relationship, all you had to do was break up with me. But cheating on me? It's humiliating. And you certainly didn't have to make me feel bad about the meatballs."

"Sheila, Sheila, I'm sorry, it's just that my mother would have been so mad. She was dying for us to get married."

"How could such a *brave physician* be so scared of his mother?" With that, I ran back up the stairs and stormed past Charlie, who was muttering something about "hegemony" and "disenfranchisement" to Uncle Bharat.

"Mom," I whispered to her, "I can't explain it right now, but I have to leave immediately." She looked shocked. I squeezed her arm. "It's all fine. Matthew and I are going to take the Buick. Someone can give you guys a ride home, right?" I smiled, trying to assure her that nobody was about to die. Before she could insist on leaving with me, I peeled Matthew away from a plate of cutlets in the kitchen, snatched the keys from my father's jacket, and was out the door.

"What the hell is going on, Sheila?!" Matthew asked, confused.

"We'll talk about it in a second, just let me get us out of here," I answered, starting the car. Just as we were pulling away, Sanjay came running out of the house, turkey leg still in hand, motioning me to stop. Ludmila was hot on his tracks.

I flicked them the bird, which seemed appropriate considering Sanjay's newfound love for the animal, and sped off.

Matthew and I were sitting at the kitchen table, sharing a forty-ounce Colt 45 that had been hidden behind mountains of Tupperware in my parents' refrigerator.

"Sheila, I'm so so sorry this happened," Matthew said for the hundredth time, rubbing my back, "discovering that your boyfriend has been cheating on you isn't exactly what you needed right now."

"And that he's a secret meat eater," I sniveled, "let's not forget that."

"Yes, and that he's a secret meat eater," Matthew repeated after me. "Why would he be hiding that, by the way?"

"Because his parents are devoutly religious and he is one of two lame sons who listen to everything their mother tells them. Which is why he was with me, I suppose. His mom had always wanted him to marry an Indian woman, and when we started dating it was like a dream come true. Indian *and* the daughter of her best friend."

"Right. Right. I know this might not be the most appropriate question right now . . . but why did *you* like Sanjay in the first place?" Matthew grabbed the forty, taking a long sip.

"He used to be different. When we first started dating, he was unlike all the guys at Columbia. Sure of himself, but not arrogant. He'd come up to New York most weekends and we'd have a great time—eating out, taking walks, whatever. And I have to admit, being with him felt comfortable and safe. I didn't have to explain myself, my family, where I came from." I took a deep breath. "Then something changed, I guess about a year in. Maybe that's when he met Ludmila . . . excuse me, I mean *Gayle*. In fact, that's right around the time we stopped having sex."

Matthew chugged from the bottle, his face turning bright red.

"I'm sorry, Matthew—you didn't need to hear that, I guess."

"No, no, it's not that. It's . . . it's just that Heidi and I are having—or I should say, have been having similar issues for a while. I guess since the start of this clerkship." I motioned him to continue. "I mean, I know I'm partly to blame. In case you haven't noticed, I'm not exactly the most social guy in the world. I guess being with Heidi twenty-four-seven in law school was my easy out. I didn't have to make other friends. I just hung out with her and her friends. Which meant spending lots of time at the New Haven mall," he paused. "I hate malls. I guess I didn't realize how much I hated them until I

got to Philadelphia and didn't have to mall walk anymore." He gazed out
the window embarrassed, as if he'd just admitted to a murder.

"It's OK not to like malls," I said, placing my hand over Matthew's, "so
long as you like Heidi. That's the important thing."

"Well, that's just it." He looked at me directly. "I'm not even sure about
that anymore. She's not exactly supportive of me, especially now when I
actually need her."

"If nothing else," I noted, "working for the Honorable Helga Friedman
certainly does force one to reevaluate one's life."

Just then the front door opened and my parents walked in, quickly darting up the stairs. Puja and Charlie were right behind them.

"Can't you ever just shut up and be a gracious guest?!" Puja screamed.
"I cannot even look at you right now." Charlie, without a bedroom, took
refuge in the hallway bathroom.

"What happened?" Matthew and I sang in unison.

Puja grabbed a chair and our forty. "We had to leave because Charlie
picked a fight with Uncle Bharat—"

"But how can you fight with Uncle Bharat? He doesn't speak!" I
interrupted.

"Turns out, when you say—and I quote—'You don't have a nuanced
vision of the Kashmiri plight, that's what wrong with all you Indians'—
Uncle Bharat does, in fact, speak. He spoke loudly—'You are not welcome
in my home. Please leave.' The problem was you guys had taken the car,
so we, along with Mom and Dad had to wait outside until Uncle Vikram
emerged a half hour later and offered to drunk drive us home." She finished off the Colt 45. "What happened with Sanjay, by the way? As soon
as you left, he and that freaky freckled chick made a grand exit."

I sighed. "Well, he's been sleeping with freaky freckles and he eats meat."

"*Sanjay eats meat?*" Puja asked, astonished.

Chapter Fourteen

Judge Adams's majority opinion in the Dell Nelson case arrived with the pomp and circumstance previously reserved for the Second Coming of Christ. Instead of e-mailing it to Judge Friedman, as was customary, Betsy graced our chambers with a personal delivery.

The judge's secret service detail—Roy and Janet—forgot one minor detail, namely not letting strangers into the judge's office unannounced. Betsy strolled into the secretaries' den, peered into the torture chamber, and casually walked inside.

"Ahh, who—who are you?" the judge barked at her intruder.

Betsy smiled sweetly, presenting her gift with two hands. "Judge Friedman, I'm Betsy Noland, one of Judge Adams's clerks,"—the judge suddenly sat up straight and turned her frown upside down—"and here's our opinion in Nelson. I thought I'd bring it to you personally."

"Why thank you, thank you, young lady," the judge said and stood to accept the gift. "How are you? Come, come, meet my law clerks." The judge took Betsy's hand and towed her into the clerks' cave.

"Hey, Sheila"—Betsy fake smiled—"and hello, Matthew." The judge and Betsy stood side by side, holding hands.

"Oh, so you people all know each other?" The judge asked, feigning surprise. Kate and Evan were spared the spurious pleasantries. Failing the bar exam had its benefits—the judge pretended that Evan no longer existed and it wasn't clear Kate had ever existed to her.

"Oh yes, yes, we do," Betsy chirped. "Nice to see you both. And in your natural habitat." She glanced around our dingy chambers. "Well then, I must be getting back to our soon to be new justice's office. It's been a madhouse since the nomination." She winked at the judge. "We've just been bombarded by the media." Betsy pulled away, trying to liberate her hand. The judge secured her grip. "OK, then, I *really* must be going," Betsy said, yanking again and sending a ripple through the judge's bun.

Betsy used her left hand to peel the judge's fingers off of her right hand. "Bye!" Her fake smile evaporated as she jogged away.

"I rilly don't like that one," the judge announced, strangling Adams's opinion. "Roy! Roy!"

"Yes, Judge." Roy reported to duty, all but genuflecting at the judge's altar.

"Make two copies of this. Two copies, do you understand?" the judge howled. "Give one copy each to Matthew and Sheila and bring me the original." Roy squinted, confusion clouding his vision, as he reached apprehensively for the opinion.

Then she turned to us. "Read the majority opinion. You've had weeks to anticipate what it says, so I expect a draft of that dissent in a couple of days. We rilly need to get these opinions on the books so that Nelson can appeal for an en banc hearing immediately. *Oh-kay, people?*"

"OK, that shouldn't be a problem," I replied with such confidence, the judge returned to her office appeased.

The four days I'd spent at home over Thanksgiving had provided spa-like rejuvenation. Aside from the Sanjay debacle, the weekend in Reston had been divine. Puja shipped Charlie back to New York, enabling the rest of us to enjoy the weekend. We visited all the Raj family hot spots, namely the grocery store, the couch, and Tysons Corner Mall (Matthew respectfully declined this particular activity, opting to watch football instead).

All in all, I'd returned to Philadelphia refreshed. So much so that I'd even returned one of Sanjay's calls. I remained on the line long enough to hear how he hadn't meant to hurt me (then he shouldn't have been banging Ludmila), how he'd never intended to fall for Gayle (her name wasn't Gayle), how he'd felt so much pressure from his parents to marry an Indian (how novel) and wanted to be friends (not a chance).

While Sanjay's betrayal had left a sting, it'd become clear to me that we should have broken up months earlier. And in any case, who had time for relationships when dissents had to be produced ASAP?!

Matthew and I hunkered down with Adams's majority opinion, which focused solely on a court of appeals' deference to the courts below, burying the *Drexel* case in a footnote. This meant Adams had simply cited it in passing, without attempting to differentiate it from our case. We planned to use *Drexel,* the ninth circuit decision with a fact pattern similar to the *Nelson* case, as our ticket to an en banc hearing. By ignoring *Drexel,* Adams made it that much easier for us. Maybe Adams really wasn't an adequate pick for the Supreme Court.

"So my thought is that we highlight the fact that Adams has brushed over *Drexel,*" I whispered to Matthew, joining him at the table between our cubicles.

"And simply drive home that if we decide not to give Nelson a resentencing," Matthew added, "we'll create a circuit split—plain and simple."

"Exactly," I said, smiling. "It doesn't have to be long. I think in this instance, the shorter the better."

"Yeah, agreed—but even if *Drexel* didn't exist, you do realize that appeals courts can hear cases en banc in cases of exceptional importance. This, to me, seems like one of those cases. You know, Sheila, I just can't understand how someone would actually vote to not give this guy another hearing. Most of the time, I can see both sides of the issue. And honestly, I was sort of on the fence before about the death penalty. But this case has sent me far in the direction of thinking we have to get rid of it altogether. If the government can't administer death fairly, it has no business administering it at all," Matthew pronounced, impassioned.

"The best part is that some of the most vocal advocates of the death penalty are the very same people who are pro-life. Seems contradictory, no?"

"Heidi's got a terrific argument about how to reconcile the two." Matthew blushed. "If and when you two ever meet, you should ask her about it." Matthew's grievances about Heidi had been steadily growing in shape and size. Having never met the woman, I felt uncomfortable aiding and abetting the slander. And besides, why was he still dating her?

"I try not to lead with abortion when meeting people for the first time." I stood to return to my cubicle. "I vote we divide and conquer. I'll put together an outline of our dissent and then we can just split it up, OK?"

"Sounds good, Sheila," Matthew said, punching my shoulder playfully. "And you were right, you know—this whole working together thing hasn't been so bad."

Roy was standing directly in front of my cubicle, wearing a red and green knit sweater, watering what looked like potted weeds.

"Good morning, Roy."

"Hey, Sheila, I got you a Christmas present"—he lifted the pot—"it's a weeping fig. You like it?"

"I love it, Roy," I said, genuinely touched by his gesture. "Thanks so much. That was really thoughtful."

"Yeah, I love Christmas. You know, I'm the presider of this year's great medieval Christmas feast," he announced, leaning forward, petting the crocheted reindeer on his chest. How was it that the cold didn't kill Roy's breath? Instead, with each drop in degree, the smell ratcheted up one level. Any colder and Roy's mouth would be Mace. No wonder the fig was weeping.

"Hey, Roy," Matthew announced, "hey, Sheila."

"Hey, dude. I got you something, too." Roy stumbled to Matthew's cubicle, water spilling from his jug. He shoved a hand into his pocket—no easy feat considering that his pants were at least two sizes too small—and produced a small round object.

"Thanks, um, Roy," Matthew said, inspecting his Christmas gift. "It's really, ah, nice."

Roy giggled. "It's one of the napkin holders we used at last year's totally awesome Christmas feast and it's—"

DING! Thirteenth floor, going down.

The speed with which Roy tripped his way out of the clerks' cave was totally awesome.

Lately, the judge had been coming in earlier and earlier and leaving later and later. Judging from her afternoon calls, Bob's health had not been improving.

"What are you looking at, Roy?!" she barked before taking position at her desk. "Sheila! Sheila! Get in here now."

"Yes, Judge?" I stood before her in the torture chamber.

"Haven't I told you I hate seeing you people wear those thick coats inside? It makes me hot just looking at you!" She had. In fact, every day she ordered me to remove my coat, but it was colder inside than out.

"Yes, Judge. But I'm cold," I explained for the hundredth time.

"That's just ridiculous. It's not cold in here. Take it off." Technically, she was right. The torture chamber was the capital of the Bahamas, whereas the rest of chambers was a suburb of Antarctica. Like everything else, judicial jingoism controlled the thermostat.

As I'd done for weeks on end, I followed her command. Something about me in my cubicle practically naked with chattering teeth had a soothing effect on the judge. Sufficiently pacified, she wouldn't notice that I'd almost immediately put my coat back on, until the next day, at which time we'd rinse and repeat the cycle.

"Where's that dissent?" she asked, just as I'd removed my jacket and turned to leave the torture chamber.

"We, um, we have it but—"

"But nothing," she said and jumped up. "I'm going to your playroom to get it myself. I'm rilly tired of having to beg you people to do anything." Matthew and I had been working on the dissent around the clock for the past week. The judge had been otherwise engaged, yelling at most of Philadelphia's doctors about their ineptitude and negligence. It was this respite that had enabled us to write a solid first draft, one that we nonetheless were nervous about showing to her. After all, neither of us had written a legal opinion before.

Matthew was seated at the table between our cubicles, poring over the dissent, something he'd been doing incessantly since we completed the draft.

"I'll take that," the judge said, snatching it from Matthew's hand, leaving him a considerable paper cut. His jaw tightened. "I'm going to read this. In the meantime, I suggest you people start focusing on that little Adams project I assigned to you," she ordered.

Halfway back to her office, she delivered a classic look behind yell: "I don't know how you people work—it's cold in here!"

Matthew raced to the bathroom to reattach his finger to his hand, while I cautiously bundled myself up.

"Um. Sheila. Can we, um, talk for a minute?" Kate tapped me on the shoulder.

"Sure," I said, swiveling around.

"Listen, um, I've got some news. I'm, um, pregnant." Kate once told me she never wanted kids. She was almost forty, childless, and had been married for fifteen years. And then it all made sense—she actually got herself knocked up to prematurely escape the clerkship. Kate won "would you rather" and I didn't even know she had been playing.

"Uh. That's incredible. Great. Congratulations!" I gave her an awkward hug.

"The judge, um, knows," Kate continued. "She told me that she didn't approve of her clerks getting married or pregnant but said that she wasn't going to do anything about it." Kate said this as if she believed the judge could, but had decided not to, take action against her pregnancy. "I'm, um, going to tell Evan and Matthew, but can we all just not talk about it? I, um, don't want to make it, um, any more obvious than it is."

Teenagers had been trying to hide pregnancies for centuries. I wasn't sure how Kate was going to succeed where legions had failed.

If nothing else, it was an unusual Christmas morning. Never before had I spent the holiday alone and without a tree. Well, that wasn't true—I'd taken the weeping fig home the night before and placed the tiny wrapped box Matthew had given me underneath it. It was a charity gift, I presumed, considering he at least got to spend the day with Heidi at her parents' house in Trenton. Heidi seemed like the kind of girl who'd dress up as one of Santa's elves and spend the day sprinkling sugar cookies. I'd stopped trying to wrap my mind around how someone like Matthew could be with someone like Heidi—given that I'd dated a closeted meat eater for over two years.

After exchanging holiday greetings with my family, I opened the gift from Matthew. Inside were Roy's napkin ring and a note: "I figured it was big enough to squeeze your head through should the holiday take a detour south. Have a Merry Medieval Christmas, Sheila!" I laughed my way to the freezer, put a frozen pepperoni pizza in the microwave, and counted my blessing—a full day with nothing to do but stuff my face, watch romantic comedies, and read trashy magazines.

Just as I popped *Dave* into my VCR, a trauma of gargantuan proportions occurred: The crushed red pepper canister was empty. The convenience store up the street claimed it'd be open on Christmas Day, so I bundled up and made a break for it. I took advantage of the deserted streets to openly peer into a window on the corner. A young couple in flannel pajamas was opening gifts—voyeurism never went out of style. As I passed an alley on 12th Street, I noticed my favorite prostitute/drug dealer with bad skin hovering in the shadows. His guest looked up at the sound of my footsteps and made eye contact. Oh God—it was Evan! Shoving Roy's napkin holder around my neck didn't sound so bad.

Evan appeared to be hatching an exit plan as he walked over to me, eyes bloodshot. "Sheila? Um, hey. Ah. Merry Christmas?" It was one of the few times that a statement actually deserved a question mark.

"Evan. What are you doing here?"

"I-I," his teeth chattered. "Oh Sheila." And he started to cry. It was the second time in as many months that I found myself cradling Evan, strange considering we barely spoke to each other.

"Evan, listen, I live right down the street—why don't you come home with me?" He didn't attempt to resist.

This was one sorry Christmas tale. Evan's brother had been killed in a car accident six years earlier. Unable to deal with the loss, his parents divorced shortly thereafter. His father moved to Paris and Evan hadn't heard from him since. His mother, already a diabetic, had taken to drink and was drinking herself to a quick death. She'd recently been hospitalized. (The good news was that judging from Evan's mother's symptoms, I certainly didn't have diabetes).

Studying let him get away from it all—or, studying and crystal meth did. It was at Harvard Law that he'd discovered the stuff. He and his roommates at first did it only occasionally, and suddenly he couldn't get through Corporations and Evidence without it. He'd started working part-time at a local Boston law firm on the weekends to subsidize his habit. Once he'd even stolen some cash from the office. He hated himself for that and a million other things. Nevertheless, Evan had graduated at the top of his law school class, was an editor on the *Harvard Law Review,* and had landed a federal court of appeals clerkship.

He'd promised himself that he'd lay off the drugs. Philadelphia was a new start and all was going according to plan. He'd even gone out on a few furtive dates with a cute, blond district court clerk. Other clerks seemed to like him even though everyone in his own chambers—the judge included—thought he was a jerk. Then he failed the bar.

That night at the Vegas Lounge, the cute blond district court clerk ignored him at first and later told him that they "should just be friends." Brian and his minions kept saying, "You shouldn't think that you're stupid or anything." He hadn't until they said it. After all, he'd never gotten below a B on anything in his life, let alone failed a test.

The problem was, his mother had been very sick during the "bar summer" and instead of spending his afternoons studying, he'd spent them taking care of her. In the end, it didn't matter. The doctors told him they'd be surprised if she lasted through the year. Walking home from the Vegas Lounge that night, he'd remembered the judge saying that the corner of Spruce and 12th was a place for drug activity. "You know, the time she drove us home."

He decided that he deserved a little meth. After all, he'd had "a most unpleasant day." He'd immediately spotted a pack of "shady people—drug dealers for sure." Once he started he couldn't stop. He was relieved that the judge wouldn't address him, as that meant no more pressure to perform. He got through the day just so he could go home and do more drugs. The other clerks had altogether ditched him. In fact, he'd spotted Brian and the cute blonde together heavily petting each other on several occasions.

Outside, church bells rang.

"God, Sheila, all this talking has made me hungry. Maybe you can make me something to eat?" Evan propped up his feet, making himself at home on my yellow couch.

As if serving as a therapist and halfway house weren't enough, now I was spending Christmas night microwaving frozen pizzas for a drug-addicted squatter who up until a few hours earlier had merely been an irritating colleague.

Indeed, It's a Wonderful Life.

Chapter Fifteen

W e were still a couple of days away from the New Year, but the party had already started in Judge Friedman's chambers.

"It's here! It's here! Front page!" Unable to adequately express her excitement through traditional dance, the judge's bun broke into a bastardized jumping jack. "Sheba! Markhew! Did you see? Did you see?" The judge flew into the clerks' cave, waving a *Philadelphia Inquirer*. On the cover, above the fold, was the *Dell Nelson* case, with excerpts from the majority opinion as well as our dissent. With Judge Adams's nomination hearings scheduled for February, the media was watching her every move through a microscope. A death penalty case ordinarily would never have received such press.

"You both did a rilly rilly good job." The judge smiled at me and Matthew. While we were thrilled with the compliment, it was still perplexing. We'd spent a day earlier in the week, going over the opinion, line by line, word by word, with the judge in the torture chamber. When she wasn't dozing off, sitting up, clutching her mechanical pencil, she was busy criticizing every inch of the dissent, down to comma placement. I was sure she'd rewrite the whole thing behind our backs. She hadn't and now it was in the newspaper!

As soon as the judge headed for her private bathroom, paper in tow, Matthew brought up the *Inquirer*'s Web site on his computer and I read over his shoulder. Not since getting an offer to clerk had I felt so proud—entire paragraphs that Matthew and I had written appeared verbatim. Death penalty advocates and critics commented on each side, the president of the Pennsylvania chapter of the ACLU noting: "Once again, Judge Friedman has proven herself to be the rational calm amid a hateful, irrational storm of conservative jurists. We expected more from Linda Adams, but she has revealed herself to be no more than a political hostage of Republican senators." The junior senator from Texas called Linda Adams a "hero who refuses to bend our beloved Constitution to allow murderers to walk the streets and kill our children." According to Professor Neil Haltow, the constitutional law guru of the University of Pennsylvania Law School, "in finding no Sixth Amendment violation, the majority opinion has indeed, as the dissent points out, created nothing short of a circuit split, considering the striking similarity in facts between the *Nelson* and *Drexel* cases. Notwithstanding *Drexel,* ruling on sleeping lawyers falls squarely within the 'exceptional importance' category for which en banc hearings were created."

"Oh my God," Matthew whispered gleefully, "we're in the middle of a feeding frenzy."

"Yes, yes we are," I murmured, pinching myself. "I know the old lady isn't exactly a dream to work for, but you have to admit, this is exciting!"

The phone rang off the hook throughout the afternoon, Roy and Janet taking turns explaining to the press that Judge Friedman never took calls from journalists (it wasn't clear that journalists had ever called before). As for the judge, she sat staring at her name in the paper, gloating. That is, until she received a call from Dr. Fernandez.

"What! What! You rilly can't do anything?!" she screamed. I suspected that the good doctor was about one call away from euthanizing Bob. "Did you see me in the paper today?! I do things to help people. Clearly you don't." She slammed down the phone, grabbed her bag of tricks, and stormed into the clerks' cave.

"What's wrong with you?" she barked behind me. I spun around—Kate was standing directly behind my cubicle.

"Um, ah—"

"Are you sick?" In an instant the judge turned the blessing of life into an insult.

"I, um, I'm pregnant," Kate stuttered.

"No! No! No! You look weird. I don't have time for this!" the judge yelled.

Kate hobbled away, leaving me directly in the judge's view.

"Sheba, get me some answers on Judge Adams now! We should be receiving Nelson's petition for a rehearing any day now, maybe any hour. Janet! Roy!" Both appeared instantly. "Look out for the *Nelson* petition today. If I'm not here when it comes in, make copies and give them to Matthew and Sheila." With that, she stormed off to the hospital.

I spent most of the afternoon Googling "Dell Nelson" and "Friedman." The national media had picked up the story and by the time I packed up for the day, the number of search results had tripled from the morning.

As I was about to leave, Evan emerged from the back, eyes puffy. The day after Christmas, while most Americans disposed of unwanted gifts, I had spent the day at the courthouse and the evening at a Narcotics Anonymous meeting with Evan. I hoped he hadn't already fallen off the wagon.

"What's wrong?" I asked. "What's going on, Evan?"

"My mom has passed. She's gone." Evan shook his head, as though he himself didn't believe his words. "My aunt found her passed out, with an empty bottle of bourbon by her side. She wasn't breathing." He paused to process the unimaginable. "I've got to catch the next plane to Chicago and deal with her body, the funeral, her apartment." He started bawling, drawing Matthew's attention.

The two of us huddled around Evan, who bravely collected himself and headed to the airport. The minute he left, Janet's internal (and perfectly delayed) GPS led her to the clerks' cave: "Did I hear some commotion in here?" she cooed, arms cradling what looked like briefs.

"Evan's mother died. He went home," I replied angrily.

"Anyway, here are the petitions for rehearing." She sighed with exhaustion, as if she were delivering quadruplets rather than several sheets of paper. "And by the way, in case you speak to Evan, be sure to tell him that he's not getting paid for the days he misses." Didn't the Bible preach kindness?

James, Kevin, and I had nestled into our table at Friday, Saturday, Sunday, one of Philly's most celebrated restaurants. Though pricier than Ralph's, splurging on New Year's Eve was an American tradition. We were still waiting for Matthew, who'd decided to join us since Heidi was in Miami with friends. Without any vacation days, Matthew was left to fend for himself.

I took a sip of water, deciding to get business out of the way. "Kevin, look—is there *anything* you can say about Adams, *anything* at all that I can bring back to Friedman just so she knows that I actually did snoop around for her?"

"Sheila, as I told you before, the woman is squeaky clean. Do I disagree with her on this *Nelson* case the whole world is talking about? Absolutely. Does that make her a crook? Absolutely not." He gesticulated effusively, emulating an argumentative tactic picked up from oral arguments. "Speaking of—I've been meaning to mention this to you but keep forgetting. So, we all had a holiday lunch with the mayor last week, all of Adams's clerks. But Adams herself couldn't make it at the last minute because she had some photo shoot with *Philadelphia Magazine*—she's going to be on next month's cover. So, it was just me, Walt, Jana, Betsy, and the mayor—who, by the way, is quite attractive. We were about to leave the restaurant when this guy walked over, patted the mayor on the back and introduced himself to all of us as Robert Nussbaum. Anyway, when we got back to chambers, Betsy giddily told us all that that was Peter—"

"Nussbaum's creepy brother," I interrupted.

"Yeah! How did you know?" Kevin asked, shocked.

"Because he's called me twice to threaten me with 'not letting the animal who killed his brother go free' and I've received between two to ten hang-ups since oral arguments in the *Nelson* case. Did he seem to *know* the mayor?"

"Yeah, uh, yeah," Kevin said as his eyes followed an attractive waiter. "Um, ah, so what were we talking about?"

"We were talking about New Year's resolutions," James seized the opportunity to change the subject. "Where's Matthew? It's already eight-thirty—we've been here for a half hour and I want to order."

"He'll be here, don't worry," I replied, trying not to sound as irritated as I was that Matthew was late. "So Kevin, did the mayor say anything about this Robert Nussbaum guy?"

Kevin shook his head. "Nope, the mayor said nothing. He just told some golf joke, the guy's got *lots* of sports jokes. But I had a feeling you'd be interested, Sheila, you know, having worked on that case and being into gossip and all."

The truth was, I was beyond interested, but not because of gossip. I silently chided myself for not having Googled Robert Nussbaum the first time he called me. An incredible oversight considering that I'd started Googling everyone I'd ever known in my life. I'd already polished off grades K through four (Stan Miller, the bully of third grade, was serving time for child porn!).

As our waiter came by, yet again, to take orders we couldn't give without our fourth guest, my cell phone rang. It was Matthew.

"Hey, where are you?"

"Sheila, um, didn't you get my other messages?!" he screamed over what sounded like Britney Spears in the background.

"No, no, it's kind of loud in here. I guess I didn't hear the phone ring. What's the deal?" I asked, a lump creeping up my throat.

"Look—Heidi's flight got canceled to Miami because of some hurricane down there," he sighed. "So, I'm in Trenton with her and her friends."

"Chicas! We're the CHICAS!" a loud female voice corrected Matthew.

"Sorry, Sheila, I'm in Trenton with Heidi and her *chicas,*" he said, irritated. "I'm so so sorry. I'd really been looking forward to the night with you guys. Will you please apologize for me to James and Kevin."

"Sure, yeah, of course"—the lump expanded, tickling my tear ducts. "OK, I'll see you tomorrow then." I hung up and darted to the bathroom. What was the big deal? Why was I crying? No doubt, it'd been a long day, week, month, year—I was entitled to a good old-fashioned cry every now and then. But why now and not then?

Two thirty-something women burst into the bathroom, laughing, paper New Year's hats holding on for dear life on the sides of their overdone heads.

"Hey there! Are you OK?" one of the women asked, giving me the once-over, as the other there-there'd me.

"Yeah, yeah, fine thanks," I said, wiggling away. Toilet lunch could be construed as edgy, indie, alternative. Getting consoled by tipsy New Year's revelers in public restrooms was the stuff of John Hughes movies and there was a reason he'd been on the dole for decades.

"Well, Happy New Year!" the women exclaimed simultaneously. The elastic under one of their hats snapped, sending both into interminable fits of laughter.

"Happy New Year to you, too," I replied. James and Kevin stopped talking upon my return. They, too, were donning paper hats.

"What?" I asked self-consciously.

James handed me the grandest hat of all, paper tassels spilling over the top, and a glass of champagne. "Sheila, this next year is going to be awesome for you, I promise." He and Kevin raised their glasses. "No more philandering men, minus the judge, plus the ACLU."

"I'll cheers to that." I smiled, securing my hat. "So, what should we order?"

"Sheila"—Kevin put his arm around me—"he's going to come around. Everyone knows that."

"Who is he?" I squirmed away. "And who is everyone?"

"Oh come on, Sheila—Matthew, of course," James replied, pouring himself another glass. "And everyone is me and Kevin. What other opinions matter?"

Chapter Sixteen

⚖

Blizzard (n): A gale of piercingly cold wind, usually accompanied with fine and blinding snow; a furious blast.

—BrainyDictionary Web site http://www.brainydictionary
.com/words/bl/blizzard137536.html

The blizzard dumped more than two feet of snow in Philadelphia and about the same from DC up to Boston. The East Coast had shut down. President Bush had to cancel dinner with the Latvian president. Students were ecstatic. So, too, were the meteorologists who dreamed about this kind of thing. In fact, everyone was thrilled—including the Latvian leader—except for the snow plowers, EMT workers, and the Honorable Helga Friedman.

She was a furious blast.

Puja had come to visit that weekend and was stuck. Amtrak and SEPTA had shut down. So had the airport. You couldn't even walk outside, let alone drive. According to the local news, an elderly man had had a heart attack while shoveling his front steps near the Italian Market. Mayor Adams ordered the citizens of Philadelphia to stay at home. It made good sense, then, that the courthouse was closed. The clerks' office had a recorded message to that effect. Nonetheless, I called the chambers repeatedly, just in case. Puja said I was crazy.

James had come upstairs to spend the snow day with us. "Even Friedman won't make it in today," he said, adding his two cents and looking out the window.

Redial redial redial. Nobody was there. It was after nine and still nobody. Matthew had already called to tell me his train had gotten stuck about twenty minutes outside of town. When I called Evan, he stated that he was in bed and planned to stay there for the remainder of the day, as "That woman has yet to acknowledge the death of my mother. She can screw herself." It was remarkable that Evan hadn't resumed the drugs.

I didn't have Kate's number and I had exhausted my resources. In any event, there was no plausible means to get to work. James and Puja staked out prime real estate on my couch, helping themselves to hot chocolate and *Regis and Kelly*. I stood in front of them, phone in hand. Alec Baldwin was the guest. Someone told me once that he wore a girdle. I leaned in two inches from the TV and swore that I could spot a panty line on his abdomen. Redial redial redial. Nobody. Not even Medieval Roy.

Just as I was negotiating a spot on the cramped couch, the phone rang. It was Matthew.

"Sheila. Kate just picked up. She just got to the office and said the judge had called to announce that she was on her way over. Kate says the judge is *pissed* we're not there. I'm walking and—"

"You're walking on the highway?"

"Yes, I'm walking and I'll be there in a couple of hours . . ."—a screech, followed by a siren, interrupted Matthew—"unless I'm dead first. Anyway, get to work. Save yourself." Another screech and the phone went dead. How was I supposed to traverse twenty blocks?—the snow came up to my torso and I didn't have cross-country skis. Mayor Adams had just declared a state of emergency. Why couldn't I do the same?

What was Kate thinking?—she was six months pregnant and lived in the suburbs! Not to mention, had she kept herself and her unborn daughter in the safety of her home, the judge wouldn't have a basis for thinking it was even possible to get to the courthouse.

I reached for a pair of disgusting brown cords on the floor, my heart pounding in my chest, my head, my fingers. Next to them was a pair of filthy red and green socks. In a state of pulsating shock, I lifted them, wiped my armpits, and put them on my feet. I blurted incoherent nonsense to Puja and James. And then I was out.

I opened the door to my apartment building and fell down the stairs, landing splat on the sidewalk. I nearly lost a limb or two, but at least nobody witnessed the fall. Even the driver of a bus stuck on the corner had deserted for warmer pastures. Crawl. Skid. Slide. In the middle of Market Street, I nose-dived onto a sidewalk snow bank to avoid getting smooshed by a snowplow driven by a very cold-looking man willing to decimate anything and anyone in his path.

The only thing propelling me toward 6th and Market was the knowledge that I—Sheila Raj—was an essential employee to the city of Philadelphia during this crisis. Important business was going down in Friedman's chambers and I was needed. The fire department. Police. EMT. And judicial clerks. We were the backbone of the city during crises. Why was I mad? I should have been proud.

Did I mention the courthouse was closed? I had to buzz and buzz and buzz. The lone ranger let me in only after I'd explained which judge I clerked for ("Oh yeah—Friedman's clerks—you people are the only ones around here during storms"). There was no phone-in-the-bucket nonsense. No ID carding. Instead, the guy smiled wanly and waved me through. I felt sort of bad for him. Without his petty friends, the mean and nasty security guard seemed rather pathetic. He was like Puff Daddy without his entourage—big teeth with nothing to say. I was sort of bummed that the elevator was empty. For the first time, a weather conversation would have been fascinating.

I got off on the thirteenth floor. Heading toward my cubicle, I was blindsided by the judge, who took the corner like a NASCAR racer, arms outstretched. She came to a screeching halt an inch away. Arms up. Down. "WHY DID YOU THINK THE COURTHOUSE WAS CLOSED?!!!!!

WHY DID YOU EVER THINK IT WAS CLOSED???" Honesty seemed like the best policy.

"Be-be-be-cause it is?" Drats! I couldn't even say that without a question mark. She knew she'd won. And smiled.

"Well, we have A LOT of work to do. Get in here now!" I flicked an icicle from my droopy eyelash, and followed the carny to her circus, which was in full swing by now. Toothless octogenarian running like a bull from one end of the red office to the other screaming. Very pregnant suburbanite was brave matador, trying to preserve her safety while simultaneously egging on said bull. Actually, Kate was standing over Janet's desk. Horrified. Any lingering anger I had toward her was instantly gone. The bull had been screaming at her all morning because the rest of us hadn't made it to work.

Kate and I exchanged knowing glances as I walked into the torture chamber. I sat down, freezing, waiting for my order. Once seated, looking like roadkill, the judge suddenly regained composure, patted her matty bun, and smiled.

"You know, we got that rehearing, Sheba."

I'd slid my way to work, risked death and hypothermia just so the judge could tell me that Nelson's petition to have his case heard en banc had been granted? This happened a week ago, and the judge, Matthew, and I had had an extensive conversation on the matter just before the weekend.

"Ah, yeah, Judge, it's—"

"Haven't I told you people a million times not to wear your coats inside. It makes me hot!" I removed my coat, no longer enjoying the circus.

"Anyway, the en banc is scheduled for May." The judge smiled. "As Adams must sit on the case, considering she penned the majority opinion, that means that her little confirmation hearings will have to be delayed for a few months." I nodded, just as I had when the judge told me the very same thing forty-eight hours earlier. After all, Adams's hearings were originally supposed to take place a few weeks earlier, at the beginning of February. The delay had been international news. "So, that gives you more time to get the information we were talking about." Something snapped.

"Judge, I've told you that I've exhausted my avenues for information on Judge Adams. I cannot in good faith ask my friends and colleagues to fabricate bad things about Judge Adams just for your pleasure." I stopped. She was silent. I braced myself.

Her neck tightened and her matty bun quivered. "Wasn't that a powerful soliloquy, Sheila. Maybe if you reserved such passion for your work, your memos wouldn't be rilly rilly bad."

I stood up, put my coat back on, and returned to my cubicle, unwilling to acquiesce once again to the judge's penal system for failed emissaries. Matthew and I had been working tirelessly on the *Nelson* case. We'd spent the month bowing happily to the judge's every wish, which included finding, reading, and rereading pertinent death penalty cases, making copies of them, and shuttling them to various judges' chambers.

The battle lines were being drawn and Judges Adams and Friedman were negotiating alliances for their respective sides. In the end, Judge Friedman was able to convince eight of the twelve active judges on the third circuit, more than the simple majority required, to hear Nelson's case en banc.

This was no small victory for the judge, who'd become a centerpiece for the national debate on the death penalty, civil liberties advocates serving as her biggest fans. Considering the somewhat somber view these particular individuals had taken of the Bush administration's phone tapping program, I didn't think that espionage would do much to bolster Friedman's currently untarnished image.

As I stared at the gray-blue clouds hovering over Camden, the judge careened into my cubicle.

Spoken: "Did you bring lunch?" (Unspoken: You maid, you can't get lunch because you were late. In fact, I want you to clean my bathroom because Eddie didn't come today.)

Spoken: "No." (Unspoken: I didn't even get to change my underwear.) The judge suddenly transformed into a magician, producing two mangled packets of ramen from behind her back.

Correction: untarnished *public* image.

"Here"—she thrust them an inch from my eye—"take one and give the other to Kate. Bob can't eat them anymore. Too much salt." I reached for the petrified pork and chicken, doing the math. If she'd bought the packets when Bob could still eat salt, they were at least two decades old.

"Thanks, Judge," I managed to say, staring down at the microwavable witches' brew.

"You are most welcome," she smiled. I smelled tuna fish on her breath.

"You know, that Evan and that Matthew, I just can't count on them like I can you and that pregnant one." This was her peace offering.

"Thanks, Judge."

"She's rilly rilly fat," the judge said with a lowered voice, pointing to the back, before retuning to the torture chamber.

I walked to the back, like a cop delivering bad news.

"Hey, Kate. How are you?"

"I'm, um, I'm kind of tired." Kate glanced at the clock. "It's only, um, eleven-fifteen in the morning and I, um, need to take a nap." And she did. Right on her desk. I placed her ramen next to her conked-out face.

"Where's Markhew? Where is he?" the judge screamed at me from the torture chamber.

"Judge, his train stopped miles outside of Philly. He's walking here. I'm sure he'll be here as soon as he can"—I reached for the phone—"I can call him."

"No! No! No! You cannot use the phone—haven't you been here long enough to realize that?"

An e-mail popped up—it was from Puja.

"Are you OK? We're worried sick. After you left, the judge called here, screaming at me, thinking it was you. I explained to her that I was your sister and that you were on your way to work. She said that she was a federal judge and then hung up on me. Please let us know you're OK. She's even scarier than you said. XOXO, Puj."

Never before had the judge called me at home. For some reason, that was one boundary she'd respected. This was definitely unusual. I peered to my left. Act 2 was in full swing. Small judge behind big desk. Twitching. Agitated by nothing to do. Click. Speakerphone. First on her list. Judge Fleck. No answer. Judge Haskell. No answer. Judges Stevens, Greenman, and Newburg. Nothing. It was when nobody picked up at Judge Adams's chamber that she slammed down the phone, jumped up, and started hollering.

"Nobody around here works. Nobody but me. ME ME ME! And to think that *that* woman is going to be a Supreme Court justice!" I crouched. "Damn it! Shit! This is ridiculous." I tilted my head for a better view. Bun tilted to the side, hanging on for dear life.

"Shit. Damn. Damn it. Fuck. Fuck it." And my personal favorite. "Fuckshit."

At that moment, every American should have breathed a deep sigh of relief, knowing that the third branch of their government—the federal judiciary—was in good hands.

Suddenly, her bun came to a rest. She sat down, clearly pooped. Who wouldn't be after that performance? But I was mistaken. It was time for accolades not for a nap. The judge started clapping, wide-eyed. She was ecstatic. Euphoric. The courthouse was a nuclear wasteland, and we were the only survivors. Not only did she, the general, make it out alive, but she'd saved her troops. Me and comatose Kate. Just as she was about to bestow herself a Medal of Honor, her phone rang. She picked it up instantly. It was her niece Dana, whom she occasionally referred to as her "best friend."

"Aunt Judgie, what *on earth* are you doing at work?"

"Well, Dana, being a judge is not like being a housewife. I actually have a LOT of work to do." Work included muttering, pacing, slinging profanities, specifically ruining her maids' days as part of a grander scheme to ruin their lives.

"But, how did you get there? The roads aren't even plowed!"

"I drove." The judge was standing now, patting her bun.

"But what about Uncle Bob?" Bob Shmob.

"Oh, he's fine. The nurse's aide couldn't come but he's just fine by himself." The plot thickened. She'd left her fatally ill, demented husband at home all alone during a blizzard and managed to drive through two feet of snow, just to come to work to yell at her employees. Dana wasn't amused.

"You know what, Aunt Judgie, I think you've really lost it. You've never left Bob home alone, without a nurse. Why are you at work? I just heard on the news the courthouses are all closed!"

"I don't have time for this. You wouldn't understand. How could you? You don't do anything all day." Click.

Inexplicably, the sight of me was beginning to agitate her. I started to remove my coat again, hoping that might help.

"Hey, Sheila." I turned around to find Matthew standing behind me, left leg exposed, his pants ripped from ankle to thigh. Above the waist, he resembled an overaged rib eye with frostbite marbling. Matthew dropped his duffel bag to the ground, cracking a miniglacier from the zipper, and hobbled into the torture chamber.

"Hello, Judge," he managed, "I'm here. Now, if you'll excuse me." He turned to leave.

"Matthew, how nice of you to join us"—she glanced at her watch—"and it's only three-thirty in the afternoon. If we could all hold such hours."

Exhibiting superhuman self-control (or a frozen tongue), Matthew said nothing, left the torture chamber, and settled in for an afternoon of sitting up dead at his cubicle.

Shortly thereafter, Kate sauntered through the clerks' cave. Unfortunately, she'd timed her visit at the exact moment as the judge.

"All you *ever* do is walk around. And you're fat!" the judge said, jumping on the word *fat,* which caused her to resemble a strange, elderly rap artist.

"Um. Judge. I'm pregnant." Kate looked like her water was about to break.

"I cannot believe you're pregnant. I do NOT approve of my law clerks getting pregnant or married while they are here. It is only one year. And you have been bestowed the honor of working for a *federal* appeals judge. To think!" The irony was that Kate, the pregnant one, was the only person who'd risked her life—on her own volition—to get to work that morning.

"Judge. I apologize if you think me to be disrespectful." Kate suddenly stood up straight and lost the stutter. "I'm *more* than happy to return—immediately—to my job at the staff attorney's office if you see fit." Two clerks down in less than a year. That, combined with the manhole incident, Bob's illness, and Adams's nomination, was enough to send the judge to an early grave, a place where, I was convinced, she'd still manage to wreak havoc.

"Kate. Of course I don't want you to return to the staff attorney's office. I have the best law clerks in the whole world." The judge had instantly become Pollyanna, leaving Kate defenseless.

"Um. OK, Judge," Kate muttered, removing her fat self from sight.

"Sheera. She's weird," the judge said, pointing to the back as she put on her sunglasses. "Paranoid, that one. You heard the whole thing. Did I say anything that would inspire such threats on her part?" Kate threatened to live in the suburbs her whole life. She didn't threaten people.

"I don't know, Judge."

"This is my lesson. I'll never hire another staff attorney. They're not that smart. At all events, I'm off to do a little shopping. Need new sneaks. I'll be back later." She was getting new Reeboks and I hadn't had a chance to put on a bra.

Kate left about five minutes after the judge, leaving me, Matthew, and the security guard downstairs as the lone inhabitants of the courthouse.

"Do you realize that I just walked *three miles through a blizzard* to get here?" Matthew said, pulling up a chair by my cubicle. "And the bitch just leaves? What are we supposed to do all day?"

"Well, we can eat this," I suggested, handing him the ramen. Matthew didn't crack a smile.

"Between the judge and Heidi, I'm seriously considering giving up women altogether. Remind me to ask Kevin whether men are any better."

"Whoa—what happened with Heidi?" I asked, a tad buoyant.

"Ugh." Matthew shook his head. "You know how my sister flew out this past weekend from Idaho—well, Heidi was supposed to come up

on Friday night to hang out with us, mind you the first and only weekend I've asked her to come to Philadelphia rather than my traveling to
New York. Anyway, at the last second, she called and said that she wasn't
feeling well and didn't come. She must have made a miraculous recov-
ery because she ended up going to some concert that night at Webster
Hall."

"So, she didn't come up at all during the weekend? She didn't come see
your sister at all?"

"No. And I just don't know what to do—we've been together for four
years, Sheila. What am I supposed to do? I mean, can I just break up with
her because she chose a stupid boy band over my family?"

"Well, is it just the boy band?"

"No, it's not," he said, turning his head to look at me directly. "I don't
know, I've just felt differently about her since starting this clerkship."

"Well, what do you—" The phone rang.

It was the judge. "Has anyone called?"

"No, Judge, nobody has called." She hung up.

"Well, what are you going to do?" I asked, returning to Heidi.

"Oh never mind, I'll figure it out," Matthew said, scooting his chair
back a few inches. "Anyway, why don't we take advantage of today to
get to the bottom of Robbie N?" Robbie N was our pet name for Robert
Nussbaum, who'd come under our scrutiny since Kevin mentioned his
affiliation with the mayor. Google had elicited the following information: In the three years since Robert took over his father's tar company,
he'd grown the business substantially. According to one finance news
Web site, there were rumblings of an IPO on the horizon. He had a
daughter, a divorce, and a cat named Tumbler, whose coy picture came
up under Google Images. Then the trail went cold. There wasn't a shred
of evidence linking him to the mayor. Until something concrete turned
up, I couldn't tell the judge that Robert Nussbaum had publicly hugged
Judge Adams's husband. After all, Joe Adams was a beloved mayor and
I trusted that plenty of people had make-believe relationships with him.

It wasn't long ago that I'd convinced myself that I was friends with Al Gore after he gave one of his global warming lectures at Columbia.

"Yeah, I'd love nothing more than to get to the bottom of Robbie N," I answered. "I just wish there was some way to find out about who's contributed to the mayor's campaign. It's so ridiculous that it's not public, unlike federal campaigns."

"Yeah, but the judge already told the clerk of the court about the calls you got from Robert Nussbaum, so you have to presume that if they hadn't before, they'd certainly by now done background checks on that. I mean, Adams is recused from so many cases because of her husband and his campaigns," Matthew said, scratching his head.

"That's true," I agreed. "Maybe he just called our chambers solely because he witnessed Friedman during oral arguments. That's probably it."

"Oh—I meant to tell you"—Matthew popped up—"I was telling my sis about the case this weekend and we started poking around the Internet and found an insane article online about Izzie Nelson—remember Dell's sister, the one who was raped by Peter?" I nodded, mesmerized. "Anyway, about three years ago, *Time* magazine did a 'Where Are They Now' piece. You know, where they normally profile Corey Haim or Corey Feldman? This time they profiled Izzie Nelson, who is now some tough high school principal in Erie, Pennsylvania. She talked about how her brother's 'horrid lawyer' has compelled her to spend her adult life convincing kids to graduate, go to law school, and 'fix the legal system.' Oh yeah—in her free time she makes and sells T-shirts with human hair and fingernail clippings glued to them."

"What? Fingernail clippings?" I asked, fascinated.

Matthew nodded, standing to answer his cell phone. It was his sister, who'd been unable to fly back to Idaho because of the storm.

"I'm out of here. Apparently the trains just started running again," he said. He zipped up his coat and stared at me. "Do you want to come? You know, um, out to my uncle's house for the night—you can meet my sister?"

"That sounds great, but I've got my own sister in town, so I need to get home," I replied, strangely disappointed that I couldn't snowshoe out of Philadelphia with Matthew.

"Right, I forgot that Puja was in town. Please tell her hello," he said, throwing his bag over his shoulder. "But I'm not leaving you here alone. Just walk out with me, it's after five, and she's *shopping,* for Christ's sake."

The judge reappeared the moment Matthew and I were about to leave. She sauntered in, holding at least a dozen bags, completely dry. It was as if she'd spent the afternoon shopping in Beverly Hills.

"Where are you two going?" she sneered.

"Home," Matthew answered point-blank. The judge ignored Matthew, turning to me instead.

"Sheila, you'll be interested to see my new things. Come now."

"I'll see you both tomorrow." Mathew walked out the door, leaving me with front-row seats to the most unanticipated fashion show of the year. The judge shoved me into a chair in the torture chamber, which she instantly transformed into a runway of shoes. Reeboks, Nikes, Birkenstocks. Every comfortable shoe ever made she catwalked before my very eyes.

With each pair, she demanded: "What do you think?" What did *she* think? That she was Naomi Campbell modeling Manolos? She was a small lady in deeply discounted tennis shoes. And I was the loyal—and moronic—sherpa carrying her hefty ego. It wasn't until the third pair of Birkenstocks (in an impossibly hideous purple) that I decided that I'd had enough. I stood up to go as the judge pulled the second purple shoe over her clammy foot.

"Judge, I am so sorry but I've got to get home. I do love all of your shoes but—"

"No no no." Her hat trick of noes without an ounce of anger nearly knocked the wind out of me. "Sheila, please, sit, let's talk," she begged, wiping a tear from her eye. I hoped that she wanted to discuss the National Independence Center and the Japanese internment victims, the only other time I'd ever seen her shed a tear. "Everyone leaves me. Why do you have to leave me? Why?"

I sat, staring down at her purple sandals hoping this was a rhetorical question. I hoped that she would yell at me for something. Maybe tell me how stupid I was or that she was a federal judge. That would be much easier than what was quickly becoming highly uncomfortable silence.

"I mean, Sheila, my husband, Bob, I love him so much and he's going to die. I just know he's going to die soon." She sniffled. I stared so hard the purple started blending in with her feet, giving the illusion that one large varicose vein was attached to her ankle. "You know, Sheila, I feel like I can trust you. You remind me of my son, Mark." Her son, Mark, was Namibian and I was Pakistani and therefore we were one and the same. All brownies do look alike after all.

"Judge, I am so so sorry about Bob, I can only imagine what you must be going through. How this must be so hard for you." Unconsciously, I leaned forward and put my hand on top of her hand and gave it a squeeze. For a split second, we looked at each other right in the eyes and I swear I spotted a glimmer of humanity.

"Well, I don't—*do not*—have time to sit around and discuss this nonsense with you!" she barked, yanking her hand free from mine. It was suddenly clear to me that the look I saw was not humanity at all, but fear. Fear that she'd let someone in. And as soon as she let me in, I was out.

"I am rilly busy and have lots of work to do at home," she said and started scampering around her office, shoving random briefs into her shopping bags. "You go home now, Sheila."

"Um, I'm happy to wait for you, Judge. I don't want to leave you here by—"

"Go. Now!"

Most of the roads had been plowed, leaving muddied snowbanks on the sidewalks. How could the judge leave Bob at home alone in such a storm? Surely that was some sort of crime. And speaking of crime, how could Heidi continue to get away with being such a bitch to Matthew, one of the most decent men I'd ever met in my life? I wondered if the two of them would end up like the judge and Bob? If Heidi was ditching him for boy bands now, I shuddered to think what would happen when Matthew got old and senile.

I walked into an empty apartment, spotting a note from Puja on the coffee table. "James and I down at Tryst, come meet us. Hoping the day got better. XOXO, Puj."

I peeled off my dirty clothes and climbed into bed—a tryst with James Dean couldn't have coaxed me outside again.

Chapter Seventeen

Philadelphia had thawed, leaving traces of stubborn slush as the sole reminders of what had been. Stepping over one brackish puddle in Washington Square, I smiled, noting that in a matter of months, I'd be back in New York's Washington Square *Park*.

Anika from the ACLU had called a week earlier, wanting to schedule an interview "as soon as possible." Judge Friedman's newfound role as the Patron Saint of Liberty! Equality! and Justice for All! had rocketed my résumé to the top of the ACLU's pile.

Pondering my outfit for the upcoming interview, I strolled through security and off the elevator.

"Sheerra!? Sheera?!"

"Yes, Judge!" I hurried into the torture chamber.

"The nurse's aid just called"—a fleck of something decidedly heinous came flying out of her mouth, its whereabouts unknown—"and Bob is gone. He's gone! He just walked out the door!" Where was that nasty fleck? I tried to remain focused on the issue at hand—a missing Bob. But the missing blob somehow seemed more compelling.

"And he's *neh-ked!*" Okay, maybe missing, *neh-ked* Bob was more compelling. And embarrassing. The thought of a naked Bob made me blush.

"He's just so stupid!" She stood up, blue brief in her hand. "And I'm just too busy for this!" How anybody could be too busy to deal with their missing, eighty-five-year-old husband was beyond me.

"Um, Judge, maybe you should go home. You know, just in case he calls or something," I ventured. Wrong answer.

"No! No! No!" I had hoped that spring would bring a new favorite catchphrase.

"Do you even know what I do here?" Yes, in fact, I do. You intimidate, frustrate, belittle, humiliate, and gross out everyone around you. "Federal judges can't—*can-not*—just leave their chambers any old time! We have very important work to do. *I* am very important! Now get to work!"

Matthew was walking into the clerks' cave as I beelined for my cubicle.

"What is *that?!*" he asked.

I reached for my forehead. Fleck found. I wiped it off, and sure enough, it was decidedly heinous. Chicken salad.

"I'm sorry, Sheila. That is disgusting. Really *really* disgusting!"

"Thanks, Matthew, as if I willingly put canned chicken on my face," I whispered, dragging him to the back of chambers, where Kate was sleeping at her desk and Evan, having taken a lesson from the book of Matthew, was sitting up dead.

"Psst. You guys!" I said. Neither looked up. I tapped Kate on the shoulder. She lifted her head, drool streaming down her chin. Matthew slapped Evan into consciousness.

"Get this, you guys. Bob is missing. As in he finally escaped from that house. And apparently he's naked." I peered behind to ensure that the judge hadn't crept in. Her new "sneaks" were extraspecial quiet. "And she's flipped out," I added.

"Hey, Sheila. What's smeared on your forehead?" Evan asked, suddenly lucid.

"Chicken salad," I answered matter-of-factly, calmly removing the additional flecks. Pregnant Kate gagged. This was no place for a child.

"Ugghhh!" the judge said, suddenly in our company. "Erin! Erin!" She waved a bench memo at Evan. I hoped for his sake that he was back on the hard stuff. "I've had it! I've had it! Since that mother of yours died, you can't do anything right!"

"That's it! I've had it!" Evan said, plagiarizing the judge. He stood up and, for the first time all year, towered over her. "You are such a bitch!" he howled. Kate moaned. Matthew and I didn't move an inch.

"You will not talk to a federal—"

"Bitch. A federal bitch. And yes, I can—and will—talk to a federal bitch like that." The judge furrowed her brow as she silently ran through her mental Rolodex of zingers.

Evan seized the moment to do the unthinkable. In one suave move, he bent forward, reached behind the judge's head, and yanked her bun loose. A sea of pins came cascading down. Matthew and I gasped. The judge froze, like a playground bully whose jig was up.

"You know what," Evan said, squatting to see the judge at eye level and victoriously clutching one bobby pin, "maybe you should go find your missing husband rather than sit around this crappy office all day insulting everyone."

The four of us stared at her, awaiting a fury that never came. After what felt like two hours but was more like two minutes, the judge finally stirred. She patted her matted hair, hissed at Kate and marched back to the torture chamber.

The atmosphere in chambers had returned to its abnormally normal state when the first Bob sighting of the day took place. Judge Friedman received a call from her neighbor, whose teenage son had seen Bob walking into the Rittenhouse Starbucks "with nothing on but underwear and bathroom slippers. He was smiling." The son apparently was on his way to basketball practice and didn't have time to deal with it. Phone slam. No calls were made to Starbucks. No calls were made anywhere. Instead, the judge opened another brief and started reading.

The second sighting came about an hour later. The rabbi at the Friedmans' temple called to tell the judge that it was great to see Bob "out and about" at the French bistro down the street, eating cheese and drinking wine. "Was he wearing underwear? Well, I'd assume so, but he also had on pants and a sweater. He waved when I knocked on the window. Why didn't I get him out of there and take him home? Well, why would I? He looked pleased as punch." The plot thickened. Where did the guy get the threads? The judge didn't seem to care.

It was almost 5:30. Janet and Medieval Roy had split and there was no sign of the judge following them out. *Finally,* she picked up the phone.

"Tell Roderick I'm coming there now. Now! It's Judge and it's an emergency!" Roderick was her hairdresser. Her husband was missing (and potentially flashing innocent children) and the emergency was her bun? Ideology was beside the point. Senators should require judicial nominees to undergo extensive psychological testing before confirmation. Did it matter if judges were liberal or conservative if they foamed at the mouth?

The final sighting came at 6:15. It was the nurse's aid.

"Ah, Mrs. Judge, I think I've found Bob. Ah, he's at the deli on the corner of Nineteenth and Locust. He refuses to leave without you. He's not wearing much and is shivering."

I wanted to cry. The thought of a half-naked, deranged old man amid deli meats was too much to bear. Even worse was his wife's response.

"Well, tell him he'll have to wait. I'm rilly busy and have to get my hair done!" Slam.

With that, she grabbed her bevy of bags and headed to the salon.

My head was spinning. I'd never forgive myself if I didn't do something, anything. I made a break for it when Matthew got up to go to the bathroom, since I figured he'd try to stop me. It turned out he'd used the judge's absence to stealthily retrieve a new mechanical pencil, and he cut me off at the pass.

"Where are you going, Sheila?"

"I'm going, um, I'm going to get Bob." Saying it out loud paradoxically underscored the lunacy of the plan and gave me the resolve to carry it out. "So, please don't try to stop me. I know you think it's ridiculous that I even care at this point, but he's an old man and—"

"Sheila, Sheila," Matthew said, grabbing my shoulders, "I think it's amazing that you care. Crazy, yes—considering that the judge is evil incarnate but amazing that you even give a shit about her husband."

"Well, I'm sort of curious about the naked part," I joked, hoping that a little laughter would lower my escalating heart rate.

"Me, too," Matthew said and winked, "which is why I'm coming with you."

We left the courthouse, squinting north, south, east, west in search of a taxi.

"Nineteenth and Locust, please," I instructed the driver and turned to Matthew. "What if she's there? What if she actually went to the deli and not the salon and sees us? What if she—"

"Sheila," Matthew said, taking control. "Would you rather risk seeing the judge and saving Bob or not risk it and let him continue streaking the city?"

Put like that, the answer was clear. It wasn't until we stopped and Matthew let go of my right hand that I'd noticed he'd been holding it to begin with. He paid the cabbie and the two of us approached the only deli on the block. One quick casing of the joint revealed that there was definitely no judge and there definitely was going to be amazing store video.

Sandwiched between two narrow rows was a hunchbacked old (very old) man attempting to shove a tin of barbecue potato chips into his pocket. But he didn't have any pockets and was only wearing loose brown underpants (they'd been tight and white back in the seventies when he bought them, I'm sure). Behind him was a middle-aged African American woman, whom I presumed to be the nurse's aid. In front of Bob was a freaked-out teenager who'd probably never work at a deli—or anywhere—again.

"Hello," Matthew announced gingerly.

"Ah, can I help you guys?" the teenager squeaked.

"Ah, yeah, yeah, you can," I said and smiled, attempting to defuse the situation. "We're HELGA FRIEDMAN's assistants and we've come to retrieve Bob." I hoped the mention of Helga Friedman would pacify Bob. Then again, it was hard to imagine how her name could pacify anyone.

The teenager retreated behind the counter, poised to hit an emergency button as if we were about to stick up the joint. Bob looked up at us, his eyes burning with kindness. Matthew removed his own jacket and Bob flinched only slightly as it was draped over his shoulders. I reiterated my message. "Hi Bob, we're Helga's assistants. She asked that we come get you. She's waiting for you at home. She misses you very much and very much wants to see you."

"This Kris Kringle wants a little Pringle," Bob mumbled, as Matthew guided him toward the door.

The nurse's aid came around to the other side of Bob, and all together, we led him out of the deli. The teenager ran out with the can of Pringles, shoved them into my purse, and hailed us a cab, which was no easy task. We had to promise the driver that Bob wouldn't urinate or defecate in the car.

It was only three blocks to the judge's home. "We have to get out a block beforehand," Matthew explained to the nurse's aid, as I rubbed Bob's back. "The judge doesn't know—and cannot know—that we came. Under no circumstances should you tell her. Just tell her that Bob came with you freely," he instructed as we got out of the taxi.

"You think I'd tell Mrs. Judge that I didn't do this on my own?" the aid said, shaking her head. "No sirree Bob." Bob looked up at the mention of his name. He hadn't said a word since leaving the deli. As Matthew and I shut the door, he peered out the window and smiled, a small tear running down his face.

Chapter Eighteen

A white lie is a lie which is believed harmless or innocuous, or is in accordance with the conventions of the culture. A common example of a white lie is, "You look marvelous."

—Wikipedia Web site http://wikipedia.org/wiki/Lie

It came as no shock that the judge forgot having green-lighted my interview at the ACLU. While insisting that I come to work before and after the interview (bookending the day with a few minutes), she'd nevertheless been "thrilled" that one of her law clerks was considering something "meaningful" rather than the "rilly silly" law firm route. Never mind that the judge had spent well over a decade engaging in such banalities, as a partner at one of Philadelphia's white-shoe firms.

It was just after nine in the morning. I'd arrived at work fifteen minutes earlier, giving me just enough time for a bathroom chat with myself.

"Sheila, where do you think *you're* going," the judge sneered, as if I were trying to pull a fast one.

"To my ACLU interview?" I asked/stated as I entered the torture chamber.

"Hmf! You're getting too big for your britches!" she said. Well, that was definitely true. Subway apparently didn't make everyone skinny, like their commercials claimed.

"OK, well then, I'll see you afterward, Judge." I quickly backpedaled my way out and shut the door just as she prepared to fire her triple noes. Interviews were unnerving enough and her reaction wasn't exactly inspiring confidence.

"Janet, Roy, hey, I'm heading to New York for a job interview this afternoon, so I'll see you both later."

"Isn't that nice—a little trip to *New York*," Janet replied, her eyes collapsing into two slits. "Well, in case you care—Bob's doctor called a short bit ago and he's not expected to last long"—she nodded toward the torture chamber—"she's not very happy about it."

"Well, I'm sorry to hear that," I said, thinking that death sounded more peaceful than Bob's current life. Heck, it sounded more peaceful in general.

Medieval Roy swiveled around in this chair. "Kick ass, Sheila, kick ass," he said, giving me a thumbs-up.

"Thanks, Roy, I'll try."

Matthew accompanied me to the elevator.

"Sheila." He grabbed both of my shoulders, squarely looking at me. "You're going to do great. The ACLU loves Friedman right now—you're totally set."

I could hear the judge screaming a version of Matthew's name in the distance.

"To think that that woman is my ticket anywhere, let alone someplace like the ACLU, is astounding. But whatever, I'll take what I can get."

The judge's screams were closing in on us, giving me the shakes. I wasn't prepared for this interview. In fact, wobbling in my nude hose and pumps, it wasn't clear I was prepared to interact with any segment of normal society.

"Hey, I got to go. Good luck with that"—I nodded toward the torture chamber—"you know that Bob is about to bite it and she's going to be a mess when she finally tears out of here."

Calling someone else a mess at that point, even the judge, seemed a bit glass-houseish.

The interview went swimmingly. That is, if you count out-and-out lying to be a positive thing. I met with three different attorneys. First up—Lexi from Immigrants' Rights.

"So, Sheila, that's amazing. A court of appeals clerkship—and it's with *Judge Friedman.* Amazing. Tell me about it." *Amazing* wasn't the first (or last or middle) word that came to mind, but I found myself smiling and nodding.

"Yeah, it is really good. I mean, you know, it can be tough sometimes," I said. Lexi grimaced. "But really really good. Yes, *amazing.*" Lexi looked relieved. Next—Alberto in National Security.

"Hey, great to meet you, Sheila. We're so excited to have you here. And, wow! Helga Friedman. I've always had so much respect for her. I know everyone else has been blabbing about her *Dell Nelson* opinion, which is great for sure. But I've been particularly interested in her recent Patriot Act opinion—she's brilliant!" I didn't have the heart to tell him that she'd rather unpatriotically slept through oral arguments in that case and that her subpar, pregnant law clerk had written the opinion from start to finish.

"Yeah, she's brilliant for sure. And that case was really interesting. You should have been to orals—the justice department's lawyer crumbled early on . . . *amazing.*" The crevice in my bum from which I extracted that one didn't matter. What did matter was Alberto's unencumbered glee.

"Sheila, so glad you've had such a great year so far. You know—some folks get upset that we rarely hire people who haven't clerked, but you understand why that is now, don't you? One year working for a judge—especially a federal court of appeals judge—is like six years doing litigation at a law firm, as far as I'm concerned."

"Oh, I totally agree!" I nodded emphatically as Alberto walked me to Racial Justice Natasha. "The experience has been invaluable."

"Come in, please. Sorry it's such a mess. Have a seat," Natasha said, sweeping a chair clear of briefs. "So, Sheila, how are you? How's Judge Friedman?"

"I'm great thanks," I said, getting warmed up for round three. "And Judge Friedman is—"

"So incredibly amazing," Natasha finished my sentence. "I mean, I hope that working here won't be too much of a letdown after what you've just gotten to do for the judge. *I* know how devastated *I* was when *my* clerkship ended." Letdown and devastated sounded familiar.

"Yeah, you know it really has been just an extraordinary experience. Judge Friedman is basically the *best* person I've ever worked for. I've learned *so much* from her," I said.

"Wow—especially with the *Dell Nelson* case," Natasha said, admiration dripping, "everyone here is rooting for her. You know the ACLU is her biggest fan. And we're totally disgusted by that Linda Adams. I hope to God someone with half a brain will filibuster her confirmation hearings. Oh wait—does anyone in the Senate have half a brain?" She laughed at her own tired joke, signaling me to do the same. "So, can you give me the inside scoop? How's the en banc going to shake out?"

"Natasha—honestly, at this point, you know as much as I do. That there are two votes for no resentencing and one to resentence—Friedman's. The rest are anyone's guess at this point," I replied, lying. I knew for a fact that Judge Friedman had all but secured the votes of three of her colleagues. I also knew that Judge Adams had as many in her camp. Twelve judges were voting—whoever got to magic number seven first, won. A handful were on the fence and it could go in either direction. I, however, was not at liberty to divulge this information and therefore had to fib.

But who was I kidding? I'd been telling tales from the moment I arrived at the ACLU. Judging from the foam issuing from Natasha's, Lexi's, and Alberto's mouths, I knew that the truth wouldn't have gone over well. So, I lied. And got the job on the spot.

"Sheila, we at the ACLU are thrilled to extend an offer to you to be our newest staff attorney," Anika, the head of human resources, said, beaming.

As my heart did flip-flops, she added: "This is just the best job any lawyer could ever hope for!" The record stopped. I'd heard those words before.

"Well, Anika, you know what? I am so beyond honored, but I need just a few days to think this one through," I said, surprising even myself.

"Well, um, sure, take all the time you need," she replied, cautiously. "Is there anything else I can do to help you make this decision, Sheila? I sort of was under the impression that you were quite eager to come here."

"Anika, I *am* eager to work here. It's just that I have had so much on my mind recently," I fumbled, reaching for the most palatable excuse, "you know, with the *Dell Nelson* en banc and everything. I just want to give this a good think before committing. That's all."

Anika smiled and put her arm around my shoulder. "Ah yes, of course! The *Dell Nelson* case," she purred, opening the door to the building. We walked out onto a bustling street. "You know, I almost forgot to tell you. I'm glad you reminded me. Such a small world. So my sister works for that Peter Nussbaum's brother's company."

"She works at Tartac?" I asked.

"Close—*Tarmac*."

"I think the family business is Tar*tac,*" I corrected Anika.

"These names are very confusing," Anika giggled. "From what I understand, Robert Nussbaum started a spinoff company, about a year ago, that specializes in tar for airport runways. Hence the name Tar*mac*. My sister just got hired as their Web designer. It's a super-duper small company and up to now they haven't had a Web presence at all. But don't worry, she's not, like, friends with Robert Nussbaum. But small world, right?"

"Yeah, small world for sure," I responded, not quite knowing what to make of this information. "And it would be fine if she were friends with Robert. Robert hasn't done anything."

"Oh, whatever," Anika said. She shook her head, suddenly bored. "I just was tickled by the connection and wanted to let you know. So, just give me a call once you've made up your mind. We really want you here, Sheila."

"Thanks, Anika, I'll definitely call you soon."

Tarmac? Tartac? Tar-whickety-whack?

Without thinking, I hopped the 4 train to Midtown and walked into Barnes and Hellman, the law firm where I had worked as a summer associate. I found myself on the fortieth floor, asking for John Powers, the hiring partner who had extended me a permanent job offer two years earlier. John's secretary, Amy, had taken a liking to me during my summer there. Amy had gotten a bit tipsy at the Maritime Hotel during a summer event and I'd heard her call John a "hateful asshole" in the bathroom. I'd never breathed a word of it to anyone (at the firm). Amy had not forgotten the tremendous act of kindness, so she squeezed me in for five minutes with the hateful asshole.

I'd forgotten how nice Barnes's offices were, especially compared to the ACLU and Friedman's torture chamber. Big open space, lots of light, Lichtensteins adorning the walls, hardwood floors. How could such a beautiful place be bad?

"Ah, hi." John said, coming out of his office and appearing to have gained twenty pounds since I last saw him. He glanced at what looked like my résumé. "Hi, ah, Sheila? Please come in, have a seat." It was a bit disconcerting that he clearly had no clue who I was, considering I'd worked closely with him on a bond offering two years earlier. I explained to him how my clerkship was coming to a close and I was deciding between Barnes and the ACLU. While I'd not expected the red carpet treatment (in fact, I'd developed a severe aversion to red carpets over the course of the year), it was nonetheless off-putting that my former colleague didn't bother to look up as I spoke. Instead, he sat, breathing heavily, frantically thumbing away on his BlackBerry.

"Hmm, I see, yes. Ah, well I do hope you come here," he muttered, typing. "We have tons of really interesting SEC investigations right now." Weren't lawyers supposed to be convincing? Something about the way he mumbled "interesting" gave the impression that he didn't know what the word meant.

I took a good look around. Deal toys cluttered the bookshelves. "Merrill Lynch 1979" in small red, white, and blue letters on a plastic plane. "Goldman Sachs 1986" on a glass car. I squinted to read the little words on a miniglobe. Thankfully John was still glued to his BlackBerry and didn't notice my looks of disappointment. The prize was a poster of a huge ship in the middle of a raging sea. It read, "THE PERFECT DEAL," with "JPMorgan 2002" scrolled at the bottom. A knockoff from the movie poster of *The Perfect Storm*. That was it—I knew I'd drown at Barnes. I hadn't nearly died at the hands of Helga Friedman to be a nameless, faceless bitch to the BlackBerry.

"Well then, John, thanks for seeing me. I, um, will let you know what I decide." He stood, still looking down, and shook my hand.

By the time I returned to the courthouse, everyone but Matthew had left for the day.

"Well?" he asked excitedly, "how did it go?"

"Matthew—you're so nice to have stuck around for me," I replied, sitting at the table between our cubicles. "And I have a few things to report. First, I got an offer from the ACLU."

"Congratulations, Sheila!" He jumped up and bent down to hug me. "That's fantastic. So you accepted on the spot, I presume?"

"No, I actually didn't." Matthew looked confused. "But wait, I'm going to call and accept this week. After my interview there, I bizarrely trekked up to Barnes—I don't know why. Maybe just to make sure that I wasn't impetuously jumping into another horrid work situation."

"And?"

"And the hiring partner didn't even remember having hired me to begin with, didn't look up from his BlackBerry, and generally sucked. I'm definitely not cut out for a law firm."

"Not so many people are, Sheila," Matthew sighed. "Some of us have astronomical law school loans to repay, but if you don't, there's no need whatsoever to subject yourself to it."

"Yeah, I know, so I'll call the ACLU tomorrow. Speaking of—so the HR lady there told me something pretty interesting. Her sister works for Tarmac—a company owned by Robert Nussbaum."

"Don't you mean Tartac?"

"Ha! I had this same conversation with her. No, it's definitely Tarmac, a spinoff from Tartac that specializes in tar for runways. Hence, the name," I said, parroting Anika.

"And?"

"And they have no Web presence, are allegedly a tiny company, and I wonder if it's possible that Tarmac, and not Tartac, made any contributions to Mayor Adams's campaign and that's why they were so chummy that day. It's possible that the powers that be here just didn't know to do a background check on Tarmac."

"I suppose that is possible," Matthew said, rubbing his forehead. "And I hope for everyone's sake that that's the case. Apparently Judge Greenman just decided today to vote with Adams in *Nelson* and the judge is furious. It didn't help that Bob was 'acting out' again at home and she had to leave early. I honestly think if we lose the *Nelson* case, you and I might be going to the electric chair with Dell."

Chapter Nineteen

⚖

Condoleezza Rice came to the Independence Center in early May. She was honored as one of the "Women Who Have Made America." So, too, were Madeleine Albright, Hillary Clinton, Sandra Day O'Connor, Helga Friedman, Linda Adams, and a dozen or so others. Kate, Matthew, Evan, and I joined Judge Adams's law clerks at the reception honoring our respective bosses. It was a sea of middle-aged and elderly women in pantsuits with their groupies—mostly young men and women like yours truly—also dressed in pantsuits.

Judge Friedman presented Columbia Sheila and Yale Matthew to Senator Clinton. Pregnant Kate was introduced as, well, Pregnant Kate, and Evan introduced himself to the cheese plate, where the rest of us assembled once the judge cornered the senator.

"Hillary, you don't mind if I call you Hillary, now do you?"

"Of course not," our former first lady said, shaking her head. Her coiffed bob didn't budge. The judge needed to switch hairdressers.

"I'm very worried about the upcoming confirmation hearings"—the judge looked to her left and right—"that Linda, I just don't think she's going to be good for the issues that *we* care about." The judge swung her hips and tapped Senator Clinton, intimating their deep ideological connection. The senator spilled her lemonade but didn't flinch, exhibiting the same poker face the world scrutinized during a certain sex scandal.

"Judge Friedman, you know it's very rare for the Senate not to confirm nominees. And Judge Adams does share my opinion on abortion and—"

"What about the death penalty?" the judge interrupted. "Don't you care that the state's ultimate punishment come with the proper procedural safeguards?" Standing on her toes, barely reaching the senator's neck, advocating justice, it was tough to dislike the judge. It was also tough for a senator to say anything that could be perceived as soft on crime, the reason most of them shied away from addressing capital punishment.

"Well"—the senator's bob quivered a smidgen—"fairness is a—"

"*Senator.*" Judge Adams bounded over. "How are you? How's Chelsea doing up there in New York?"

Judge Friedman tapped her on the shoulder. "Linda, I was here first."

"Oh, I didn't realize there was a line," Judge Adams said with a laugh.

"It was nice talking to you both. I haven't seen Maddie in ages. Now, if you'll excuse me." The senator scurried to Madeleine Albright, betraying not even an ounce of discomfort. Maybe she was presidential material.

Judge Friedman patted her bun. Judge Adams placed her hands on her hips. I popped another square piece of mild cheddar.

"You should be ashamed of yourself, Linda," the judge whispered. "Maybe not always articulate, you've at least always been fair—fair to defendants. Is getting to the Supreme Court worth your self-respect?" Considering the Faustian bargain the judge had struck with herself, her soapbox seemed a little slippery.

"Fair? You have the audacity to call me unfair, Helga? With all due respect, the way you've treated me all these years, the way you treat everyone— your secretaries, Bob"—she swung around to reference the cheese-popping peanut gallery—"your long-suffering law clerks. I don't even know how you keep getting clerks, quite honestly." The judge glowered at us, demanding aid. I, for one, was too busy picking another bald spot with both hands. Matthew spit out a piece of Havarti. Kate rubbed her belly. Evan crossed his arms and returned the judge's stare, unwilling to provide even a look of encouragement.

"As I was saying," Adams continued, emboldened. "I don't think you are an expert on fair treatment, Helga. And if you're referring to my stance in the *Nelson* case, you're going to have to put half or more of your colleagues in that camp. I'm pretty close to the simple majority I need to win."

"I think that's the fair treatment Judge Friedman was referring to," I said. By the time I realized I'd said it out loud, everyone was staring at me. "You know—not giving a man a fair hearing before he's sent to the electric chair. I think that's what she was referring to." Judge Adams looked at me like I was a traitor, while Judge Friedman stood in silent astonishment. My coclerks held their breath. "So, why don't we wait until the en banc before declaring winners and losers. It seems that even if you win—as you put it—America has lost."

That's a wrap!

Linda Adams stormed off, seeking refuge with Betsy by the smoked salmon. Judge Friedman spun around to chase after Sandra Day O'Connor. Kate and Evan relieved their lungs and bolted for the door.

"Jesus, Sheila—*America has lost.*" Matthew laughed. "Which movie did that come from?"

"I have no clue. *A Few Good Men* maybe. But don't you agree? I think Adams seems like a lovely person, but her stance on *Nelson* is disgusting to me. And while Friedman is a nightmare personally, I respect that she's gone to bat for a man in the most hated segment of society—death row."

"It's tough for me to separate the good from the bad at this point, I guess," Matthew said, shrugging his shoulders. "Hey, I'm going to run to the bathroom, I'll be right back."

Waiting for Matthew, I took a long sip from the water fountain. Didactics were dehydrating. I felt someone breathing heavily behind me. It was the judge.

"Sheila, I will never forget what you did for me." She touched my hand. "Thank you."

Before I could respond, Matthew reappeared, the judge's face contorted, and she clapped.

"Come on, people. Back to the office. We're rilly rilly busy."

I got my period when I was twelve. Exactly three minutes later, Puja jubilantly announced to a houseful of aunties and uncles: "Sheila thinks she has butt cancer—isn't that *hilarious?!*"

The morning of the en banc was even less hilarious.

Nelson v. Pennsylvania dominated the morning news shows. Matt Lauer interviewed a former death row inmate whose innocence was gleaned from DNA evidence just a few weeks before his scheduled execution. He discussed his new book: *Off the Ledge: Faith, Healing, and Happiness.* Diane Sawyer chatted with the mother of a woman slain by a man who'd been executed a year earlier. She was pounding her fists, crying. It looked like she could use the other guy's book.

I switched it off—TV wasn't helping. Had we properly prepared the judge? What if I missed a case? That wasn't possible, right? I mean, Matthew and I had scoured Westlaw and Lexis. I'd read more cases in the past six months than I had in three years of law school combined. In fact, my life had taken on an entirely jurisprudential framework: *pizza v. pasta; Airplane v. When Harry Met Sally; Matthew v. Heidi.*

Matthew was plotting his great escape from Heidi. This had been going on for weeks and I couldn't figure out why he didn't just do it. I understood that breaking up was hard to do—the song was written for a reason. But it wasn't *that* hard.

My phone rang. It was Sanjay, whom I'd not heard from in months.

"Sheila, hey, it's Sanjay." As if I didn't have caller ID.

"Hey, Sanjay, um, is everything OK? It's really early."

"Yeah, yeah, but I just saw on CNN that your big case is being argued today, and, um, I just wanted to wish you luck . . ."

"Thanks, Sanjay." It was this kind of thoughtfulness that I'd loved about Sanjay once upon a time. "It's really nice that you called. I'd love to chat but as you can imagine, I've got to get to work."

"OK. Um, Sheila—another thing—I'm married. Gayle and I eloped to Brighton Beach over the weekend and news is spreading and I didn't want you to hear from your mom." It was this kind of horrific behavior that made me hate Sanjay now.

"Well," I said, taking a deep breath, "thanks so much for letting me know this *right before* the biggest moment of my professional life. Great timing—really. And congratulations." I hung up and splashed cold water on my face. My ex-boyfriend was married to a fake Russian and my coclerk was caught up with a camel toe. What was I doing wrong?

My doorbell rang. Standing on the other side was Matthew, holding two coffees.

"I figured you could use some company walking to work today," he said, handing me a Starbucks, "and we're going to be late." He practically dragged me down the stairs into a glorious spring morning.

"Thanks," I said. I shut the building door behind me, regaining my composure. "Hey, you look . . . um, you look really good." It was a fact. Standing in his beige linen suit, the sun highlighting the handful of freckles on his face, Matthew was turning a few heads on the street. Granted, most of them were homeless, strung-out male prostitutes, but heads were turning nevertheless.

"Likewise, Ms. Raj," he said, grinning. He led me down the street. "How are you feeling about today?"

"Barfy. I feel totally barfy. We can't lose this, Matthew. We just can't. And by the way, Sanjay is married to Ludmila. You people never cease to amaze me."

"Huh? What? Sanjay married that Gayle woman? And how am I suddenly 'you people'?"

"Never mind. Honestly, not important. We need to focus on *Nelson*."

"OK, let me know when you're ready to discuss that one," he said. "And don't worry—I have a great feeling about Dell Nelson. The guy's going to get another chance."

"I hope you're right. The thought of losing this case honestly makes me want to cry. I've never in my life wanted something so bad. It just keeps hitting me—this is real. This is not a fake constitutional law test case. This is a real, living, breathing person. Not to mention the implications the case has for hundreds of other people who've been screwed by their lawyers."

"I feel the same way, Sheila. So—if you had to do it again, would you rather have had this experience, the chance to be a part of such a monumental case and deal with crazy Friedman, *or* not have to deal with her and not have had this opportunity?"

"I would rather know if Mayor Adams took money from Robert Nussbaum's spinoff company. That's what I'd rather," I replied. "Holy shit!" We were nearing Independence Hall, which had transformed into a parking lot for live trucks, satellite dishes, and protesters.

"Wow," Matthew said, stopping. "This is even bigger than I thought. As for Nussbaum, Evan swore he'd get us the goods. So, let's just focus on getting through today, OK?"

Evan had been in contact with the clerk of the court regarding the Tarmac/ Tartac/Adams's contribution fund. The clerk felt indebted to Evan. He hadn't realized that Evan had failed the bar when he sent out the test results to every judge on the third circuit. After all, he'd started the tradition of the "annual bar e-mail" because law clerks never failed the bar and it was meant to be a congratulatory sort of thing. Shortly after the fateful e-mail, Judge Friedman had called the clerk to chew him out for "humiliating" her. He immediately contacted Evan to apologize for what he surmised would be a "hideous punishment from that Friedman character."

Though Evan felt no sense of duty to Judge Friedman, he did feel passionately about the death penalty and, therefore, he'd offered months ago to help out with the *Nelson* case in any way possible. It wasn't until Anika offered up her jewels of information that I'd found a role for him.

"You're right, we need to get through today," I said, pushing past a hulking man wearing body odor and a muscle T-shirt that read: "God Gave Second Chances." Scorning next to him was a soccer mom in an oversize windbreaker embossed with: Friedman ♡ Murderers.

On the one day that increased security would have made sense, Matthew and I were waved through by the guards after barely flashing our ID cards.

Betsy and Kevin joined us in the elevator just before the doors closed.

"Good morning, Sheila," Kevin said, uncomfortably. "And Matthew, how are you?"

"I'm fine thanks, how are—"

"I don't think it's appropriate for us to speak with the other side," Betsy snipped, imitating something she'd heard once on *Law and Order*. In real life, even lawyers on opposing sides could say, "How are you" without violating the code of ethics.

"Whatever, Betsy." I accidentally gave her a once-over, an unwitting compliment to her amazing white suit. "Kevin, I'll give you a call tonight." Matthew and I stepped off the elevator.

"What's wrong with her?" Matthew whispered as we approached the clerks' cave. "Honestly, I have to say, I've met lots of lame people in my life. But Betsy is almost unbelievable. I'm not sure who's worse, law clerks or Judge Friedman."

"So nice of you two to make it in this morning," the judge said. She was sitting at the table in the clerks' cave. She was fully robed with a rounded bun and sunglasses. "We have lots to do before arguments today," she said, folding her hands.

"Judge"—I glanced at the clock—"I thought we said we'd meet here at—"

"Tsst!" She raised a finger. "Today, I am in control." As opposed to all the other days? "I don't recall having asked you a question. Therefore, you will not speak. Please sit. Both of you." She looked down at a list. "I need to ensure I know each of these case names inside and out. So, we're going to do a little test run. *Prabakerish?*"

"It's, um," Matthew said apprehensively, "it's actually *Prabaker-an*. A sixth circuit case finding a lawyer to be ineffective when he failed to present mitigation evidence without a clear strategy."

"*Trumbel?*"

"*Trumbel* is first circuit," I flipped through my mental binder. "Finding no Sixth Amendment violation in spite of the lawyer being just shy of legal intoxication during sentencing."

"*Horn?*"

"*Horn,* that's the really great case from the fourth circuit," Matthew said, sitting up straight. "The one where the lawyer slept through portions of the guilt and sentencing phases—but less than the Tipper slept in our case—and the court found a violation."

Peterson?

Milken?

Givens?

"OK. As for *Drexel.* Please just correct any mistakes." The judge raised her sunglasses, her eyes glimmering. "*Drexel* is a ninth circuit decision, from two years ago. A unanimous panel found that the lawyer was ineffective in an almost identical fact pattern as we have in this *Drell Nuxel* case—"

"Judge, it's *Dell Nelson.* Dell. Nelson." Getting the defendant's name wrong during today's hearings would be deadly.

"Dell Nelson," she said, nodding. "An almost identical fact pattern as we have in this *Dell Nelson* case. The lawyer slept through large portions of the sentencing phase, failed to cross examine the state's witnesses, and failed to present mitigation witnesses even though many family members and friends offered to testify to spare the defendant's life. Just like we have today in Dell Nelson's case. The ninth circuit properly found a violation and gave Luther Drexel another hearing." She spoke eloquently, using one hand to make her point to her moot court—Matthew and me. It finally made sense to me that President Ford had nominated Helga Friedman to the federal bench—she'd clearly been a brilliant orator back in the day. "Are we, the judges of the third circuit, going to say that Dell Nelson deserves fewer constitutional protections than his fellow citizen, Luther Drexel in California? I think not."

The judge was on. Matthew and I were speechless.

"Well," the judge said, patting her bun. "I think I'm ready."

Evan and Kate entered the clerks' cave, all suited up.

"You two"—the judge dismissively pointed at them—"collect my briefs and appendices from my desk and meet the three of us in the courtroom." I didn't know much about pregnancy, but it didn't seem like Kate was in any position to do heavy lifting.

"Judge, I'll meet you and Matthew upstairs, I just need to run to the restroom," I lied, as Matthew escorted the Honorable Helga Friedman to her throne.

"Hey, Kate, why don't you take it easy. I'll help Evan. We'll see you in the courtroom, OK?"

"Thanks, um, Sheila," Kate said, placing her hands on her hips to support her back.

"Hey, Evan. Did the clerk say anything?" I asked, following him to the torture chamber.

"Good morning to you, too, Ms. Teacher's Pet," Evan said, smiling.

Medieval Roy was standing in the middle of the judge's office, mumbling to himself.

"Ah, good morning, Roy," I said. "What, what are you doing?"

"Sheila." He bowed. "Evan." Another bow. "Is the judge here? I came in early today to bestow upon her Gothic greetings of good luck."

"She's already left for court," I explained, wondering what the future held for Roy, "but I'll pass along your, er, your Gothic greetings."

"Now, if you'll excuse us, Roy, Sheila and I have work to do," Evan said pointedly.

Roy meekly returned to his cubicle. "As for the clerk, he's digging around still and said he should have something to me by today or tomorrow," Evan reported. "You know, as much as I hate Judge Friedman for treating me like trash, I have to say, I do hope she kicks butt today. I am so sick and tired of people shitting on poor African American men. I bet if roles had been reversed—had Dell Nelson been found slaughtered in the U. Penn dorms—we wouldn't be talking about it twenty years later."

"I agree," I said, lifting a pile of briefs and walking to the elevator. "And I think Judge Friedman knows that. The crazy part of all this —what's getting lost in the media—is that Nelson's not even asking to be freed or anything like that. All he wants is a fair hearing that will result in death once again or life in prison. It's not really asking for a lot."

We entered a packed courtroom. Midtown Manhattan during rush hour seemed less crowded. Evan and I placed the judge's materials in her chair, to the right of Chief Judge Fleck, who'd be presiding over today's hearing. Hundreds of eyes fixed on us.

I allowed myself a quick glance from the bench, like a janitor sweeping the stage at Madison Square Garden before a Rolling Stones concert. A mosh pit of law clerks, lawyers, and regular citizens. The media wasn't allowed inside the courtroom, and despite a threatening letter from Geraldo Rivera (unearthed by the Smoking Gun), most reporters seemed OK with waiting outside.

Evan walked down to our seats with Matthew and Kate. I turned to follow him when I caught Dell Nelson out of the corner of my eye. He smiled and nodded, looking meek in an oversize double-breasted suit. I returned the gesture before sitting down between Evan and Matthew.

"How are you?" Matthew asked, putting his hand on my knee. I jumped instinctively, causing him to quickly pull back.

"Fine, fine." I took a deep breath. "I just saw Dell Nelson."

"Really?" Matthew asked. "Where is he?"

"Right over there, between those beefy security guards," I said, pointing. "Oh my God, Robert Nussbaum is right behind him."

"Where?" Evan and Matthew whispered in unison.

"All rise," the clerk of the court announced. The crowd silently stood, following his solemn order. The door behind the bench opened and a stream of old people in robes paraded in one by one, taking their place behind their respective chairs, arranged—like everything else in the legal profession—according to seniority. Standing next to Chief Judge Fleck and three seats down from Judge Adams, Judge Friedman surveyed the room.

"I present the Honorable Judges of the United States Court of Appeals for the Third Circuit."

Judge Friedman nodded in our direction. I felt tearful, much like I did when the national anthem was performed before the Super Bowl.

Their Honors sat, the rest of us following suit moments later.

"Good morning. Welcome everyone," Judge Fleck began, "today is special in that we are sitting en banc, something we do in only the most extraordinary of circumstances. The case we hear today presents such a circumstance. Then again, you all know that—I trust you're here to witness history in the making and not to inspect my new haircut."

Nervous laughter erupted. Not laughing at a judge's joke was a misdemeanor in some states.

"Today, we'll hear arguments in *Nelson v. Donald Timmons, Secretary, Pennsylvania Department of Corrections.* In ordinary oral arguments, each side is allotted fifteen minutes to argue its position. Today, counsel for Mr. Nelson and for the state will each have thirty minutes to present their cases. As always, the person appealing will go first—in this case, that'll be Olivia Northum."

Olivia Northum had aged ten years since the original arguments just seven months prior, which wasn't necessarily a bad thing considering she looked barely legal before.

"Good morning and may it please the court," she began, "we are here today to breathe life back into the Sixth Amendment. An amendment decimated by Judge Adams's majority—"

"I think we all know why we're here, Ms. Northum," Judge Fleck interrupted. She'd been standing there all of five seconds—let the games begin! "And we're hearing this case from scratch; it's as though Judge Adams's majority and Judge Friedman's dissenting opinions don't exist. Please tell us something we don't know, namely why we should disturb the trial court's finding of no constitutional violation. After all, we are to afford that judgment profound deference."

"With all due respect, Chief Judge Fleck," Ms. Northum replied, without batting a lash, "that deference is only appropriate when the trial court's opinion is reasonable. Here—"

"Would you say it was reasonable for Tip Evans to keep Dell Nelson's sisters and friends away from the witness chair, away from testifying on his behalf, namely to testify what a good brother, good provider he was for the family? Is that reasonable, Ms. Northum?" Judge Friedman asked.

"Judge Friedman, I'm glad you asked that—"

"It is most certainly reasonable," Judge Adams said, leaning forward, "as a matter of strategy. Lawyers have a million reasons to do or not do things. We are not here to question their strategy."

"You're right, Judge Adams," Ms. Northum said and smiled. I sensed a future judgeship for this one. "You are not supposed to second-guess strategy—"

"But what strategy can you point to, Judge Adams?" Friedman hissed. "There isn't a shred of evidence that Tip Evans had a trial strategy."

Both Judge Adams and Olivia Northum poised themselves to respond, but Judge Haskell beat them to the punch.

"I'm glad you mention strategy," Haskell said. He looked into the distance pensively. "One thing that really struck me was this Kyle Cooper character. Can you please explain how he figures into Mr. Evans's strategy or lack thereof."

"I'm glad, Judge Haskell," Ms. Northum started, "that you bring up Kyle Cooper, or 'Cool Kyle' as he was known. He serves as an illustrative example of Mr. Evans's lack of strategy. He testified on the state's behalf against Mr. Nelson." Ms. Northum nodded ever so slightly in Dell Nelson's direction, causing every judge to look at the clean-shaven, innocuous-looking man they were about to send to the electric chair. "All Tip Evans had to do was cross-examine Kyle on a host of things—such as how he'd been arrested and jailed for drug dealing and, while he was serving time, how Mr. Nelson provided for his pregnant girlfriend—"

"Yes, but let's not get away from the basic fact that we are dealing with a man who was convicted of a gruesome murder," Judge Newburg said, waving both of his hands, "and we're not talking about a situation where a man wasn't afforded a proper trial and sentencing." Judge Newburg, a former entertainment lawyer, had been appointed by President Reagan, allegedly as a favor to a former Hollywood chum. Newburg was notoriously average. Considering the irrelevancy of his point and his misplaced gesticulation, "average" seemed generous.

"With all due respect, Judge Newburg," Ms. Northum said, looking embarrassed, "we're here to determine whether a man was, in fact, afforded a proper sentencing. That is not something presumed at this stage."

"What I think Judge Newburg was saying"—Judge Adams came to the rescue—"is that one could argue, as Tip Evans did, that he chose not to cross-examine Kyle Cooper because his testimony had been so damning; he just wanted him out of the witness chair as soon as possible."

"HE WAS SAYING MY BROTHER WAS GRUESOMELY KILLED BY THIS ANIMAL!" Robert Nussbaum screamed, grabbing Dell Nelson's ear.

Half the room, including many judges, ducked to the ground.

"My ear! He's pulling my ear!" Dell Nelson squealed, swatting at Nussbaum's hand. Even some of the folks who'd stopped, dropped, and rolled managed to crook their necks to glimpse the gruesome murderer with the voice of a preteen girl.

"Ow!" Nelson squealed again, before his ear was freed by one of his security guards. His other guard carted off Robert Nussbaum. Two courtroom police officers hovered in the back behind an American flag. So much for our bravest.

"Order! Order!" Judge Fleck yelled, returning from his hiding place under the bench. To their credit, both Judge Adams and Friedman hadn't moved from their chairs, like captains unwilling to desert their judicial ships.

"Holy shit—isn't that the guy we saw with the mayor?" Kevin asked Betsy within earshot of us.

"Shut up, Kevin," Betsy said and slapped his knee. "Just shut up."

"Did you hear Dell Nelson's voice?" Matthew asked.

"Order!"

It took another five minutes for order to be restored. A woman sitting a few feet from Dell Nelson had fainted. She came to, saying, "Nine-eleven" over and over again. The relevance of September 11 was not immediately clear to anyone.

"Oh my God, that's Izzie, Dell's sister—I recognize her from the *Time* story!" Matthew whispered as the paramedics hauled her away.

"I apologize, Ms. Northum, for the disruption," Judge Fleck said, smoothing his new haircut. Ms. Northum seemed to be the only person, aside from Adams and Friedman, who wasn't remotely phased by the drama. "And we, of course, will let you resume where you left off."

Something about the public outburst had changed the dynamic on the bench. The judges allowed Ms. Northum to complete her argument largely uninterrupted before introducing David Kang, the attorney general of Pennsylvania to argue for the state.

"Good morning and may it please the court," he started. I wondered why lawyers never changed the introduction—just for a little variety. Maybe "Greetings" or "Good day." And what did "may it please the court" mean anyway?

"We've certainly gotten an *earful* today," Mr. Kang said, giggling nervously. Nobody else did. Laughing at a lawyer's joke (if bad) during oral arguments was a felony in some states.

"Well then"—he cleared his throat—"we are here today because of judicial deference. Deference that is afforded—"

"What about *Drexel v. California*?" Judge Friedman didn't wait long to drop that one.

"Well Judge Free—Friedman"—he fumbled with some papers—"*Drexel* is a ninth circuit case and thus not binding on this court."

"I don't need a lesson in federal courts, Mr. Kang. I am a judge," Friedman retorted. It was a good thing she cleared that up for the audience. "And to make it easier for you, let's assume that *Drexel* was a third circuit case. How could you differentiate it from the case we have before us now?"

"Um, if you look at, um—"

"Oh, please, Judge Friedman," Linda Adams butted in, "for every *Drexel* there is another case from another circuit finding that the lawyer did not err. This is an issue of applying facts to the law. We are not bound by *Drexel* and therefore it is a nonissue."

Mr. Kang breathed a sigh of relief.

"Well, that's not totally true," Judge Greenman whispered, "*Drexel* is remarkably similar to the current case." Greenman's nickname (or, actually, behind-his-back name) was "Silent Ted." As he rarely spoke from the bench, nobody dared to interrupt him now. "Of course, the actual facts of the case were different. No two cases are ever exactly alike. The lawyers' behavior in both cases is almost identical. Both lawyers slept through much of the trial and sentencing. In fact, Mr. Evans slept even more than Drexel's lawyer. Both lawyers were badgered by their clients' friends and family to allow them to testify to spare their clients' lives, and they did not use them as mitigation witnesses. Both lawyers strangely allowed their clients to take the stand and basically left them there to dry. As such, for my sake and just for the sake of argument, let's use Judge Friedman's hypothetical, that *Drexel* did come from this court. What would be the outcome today if *Drexel* were a third circuit case, Mr. Kang?"

The crowd hushed. Mr. Kang looked up, down, left, right in search of the answer. Linda Adams sat silently, exhibiting Herculean restraint. Time stood still.

"The outcome would be the same," Mr. Kang whispered.

"Excuse me, Mr. Kang, we couldn't hear that," Judge Friedman said, leaning forward and cupping her ear.

"Sorry. I said that if *Drexel* had been decided by this court and not the ninth circuit, then you all would be compelled to give Mr. Nelson a resentencing."

The court went wild.

Dell Nelson clapped to himself. I could have sworn that even his security guard looked pleased.

"Order! Order!" Judge Fleck screamed for the second time in less than ten minutes. The en banc had devolved into a bad rerun of *Night Court*.

Order came and went during the remainder of Mr. Kang's deflated arguments, which were buoyed only momentarily by a few well-rehearsed questions from Judges Adams and Fleck.

"Thank you, Ms. Northum and Mr. Kang, for your arguments today," Judge Fleck announced before banging his gavel. As the judges filed out of the courtroom, chatter erupted.

"Holy shit," Matthew exclaimed, "today was worth every second of agony from this year!"

"I completely agree," I said, laughing out loud.

"Well, it doesn't really even seem like Robert Nussbaum's involvement with Mayor Adams even matters at this point, right?" Evan added. "I mean, there's no way Nelson's not getting a rehearing now."

"Don't be so sure," Betsy interrupted. "You all—none of us—has any clue what's going to happen once the judges are by themselves, without all this nonsense," she said, nodding toward the audience—in her mind, the hoi polloi, the masses, the riffraff.

Matthew and I collected the judge's belongings from the bench and delivered them to Judge Fleck's chambers, where the entire court was convening to discuss the case. We quickly placed them in front of Friedman's nameplate and managed to scurry off and out of the court-house unseen.

The indoor drama paled in comparison to what awaited us outside. Ten thousand microphones jammed into our faces as we attempted to get lunch.

Is it true that the attorney general admitted defeat? CNN.

Is it true that there was a 9/11 scare? Fox News.

Did the dead guy's brother really eat the killer's ear? Inside Edition.

Perhaps there was something to be said about letting the media inside the courtroom.

Matthew took my hand as we plowed through the mayhem. Just as we were in the clear, Joe's Shanghai in sight, I spotted a short, round balding man talking to Anderson Cooper in an alleyway.

"Matthew, I just want to get a good look at Coop, OK?" I whispered, standing a few feet behind the camera.

"So, please state your name into the camera again," the Coop said.

"My name is Tippard Evans and I served as Dell Nelson's lawyer in the Peter Nussbaum case."

Oh my God—the Tipper! The Coop was a genius—how did he find the Tipper?!

"As I said, I'm in my sixtieth day of being awake," the Tipper said, open-ing his eyes widely, "and it feels great."

"So, how, um, how did you get awake?"

"I'm in this program, called Staying Awake. It's a twelve-step thing and . . ." The Tipper spotted me. "Excuse me, miss, miss—this is an *ex-clusive* with CNN, you need to leave."

"Stop rolling," Anderson Cooper ordered the cameraman and turned to face his intruder. "Yeah, we're kind of in the middle of something, so could you please excuse us?"

I stood frozen. The Tipper. Talking to Coop? In an alleyway? A 12-step sleeping group?

"Sorry about her," Matthew said. He grabbed my arm and yanked me into Joe's Shanghai. "Sheila, are you OK?"

"I, um, I'm fine. It's just surreal, I guess. The whole thing."

"Yes, it's true. I am truly beginning to think that fact is indeed stranger than fiction." Matthew shook his head, ordered our usual soup dumplings— and then made it a double. It'd been a long morning.

Chapter Twenty

The judges tied.

According to Judge Friedman, Judge Fleck was able to convince five others that allowing the *Drexel* opinion to dictate the outcome of the case would be akin to taking orders from the ninth circuit, the judicial equivalent of getting bossed around by your twin sibling. It was bad enough having the Supreme Court tell them what to do; the chief judge of the third circuit wouldn't take such crap from anyone lesser.

I'd prematurely anticipated victory, foolishly assuming that reason might trump ego. I wasn't alone—not since O.J. Simpson had a courtroom provided such fodder for the press. MSNBC finagled a fifteen-second clip of Dell Nelson getting in the Department of Corrections car. He was timidly grabbing his ear, whispering, "Ow" as his security guard gently escorted him into the back. Every network bought the rights to the video and played it on repeat. It was tough to see how such a man could be a "murderous animal," something Robert Nussbaum kept screaming on his way out of the courthouse, flanked by police officers. This, too, was caught on tape and frequently juxtaposed with Dell Nelson's earache. Add to that the Coop's exclusive interview with the Tipper, who'd admitted to a sleeping problem, and the latest CNN poll had 62 percent of

Americans demanding a resentencing. Heck, many were demanding a retrial altogether.

As a result, Linda Adams found herself in a most precarious situation. Being tough on crime and tough on the Ear Whisperer had suddenly become mutually exclusive. But she couldn't publicly change her mind—nobody liked a wishy-washy Supreme Court nominee.

Well, that's not totally true. Judge Fricdman was positively giddy. A week after the hearings, the *New York Times* ran a picture of Dell Nelson clutching his ear. To his right was a photo of Friedman, to his left, one of Adams. The caption: "A Deadly Match Point: Friedman v. Adams."

"Good morning, law clerks," the judge said, breezing into our clerks cave holding the paper. "The *Nelson* case is looking rilly rilly good." She greeted Roy and Janet and proceeded to her office. Because the judges had tied, the past week had been spent with each judge lobbying the other to switch his or her vote. To the outside world—silence. Nothing fueled speculation like silence.

Linda Adams was apoplectic. She seemed like the murderer now. Ironically, in order to save her nomination, she needed to save Dell Nelson, something she'd so emphatically fought against over the past sixth months. Kevin said she was secretly begging two of her best friends on the court to switch their votes, votes she'd relentlessly courted prior to the en banc.

"Sheila, hey, ah, he called, the clerk called," Evan whispered to me behind my cubicle. "Grab Matthew and meet me in the back." I followed his orders.

"So, Sheila—seems you have a future, if not in the law, in investigative journalism. You were right—this Nussbaum guy has been funneling money to Mayor Adams's campaigns. Three times the amount that should have gotten Adams recused from the get-go. Anyway, Judge Fleck should be alerting the rest of the court any minute now. Adams's vote is no good."

"So the tie's been broken!" I smiled.

"We won!" Matthew hugged me. "That poor guy will get another shot."

"Sheba! Martha!" All the good press had somehow managed to increase the judge's vocal capacity. The building shook.

In the third week of June, *Justice* Linda Adams, along with her law clerks, moved to Washington. She'd been confirmed by a wide margin in the Senate.

Mayor Adams's campaign assumed full responsibility for its "negligent oversight" and "faulty donor reporting," thereby absolving Linda Adams of any appearance of wrongdoing (and killing Joe Adams's chances of running for governor one day). As it was, her belated recusal from the *Nelson* case at once silenced the press on her alleged insensitivity and started her confirmation hearings. Remarkably, Friedman's quest to derail Adams's nomination gave Dell a second chance at life and ensured Adams's life tenure on the Supreme Court. Talk about twisted fate.

Adams asked her current clerks to stay on for her first year on the Supreme Court, proving that that best things do happen to the worst people. While I was happy for Kevin, it made my skin crawl to think that Betsy would be penning the law of the land. Even worse was that Brian had scored a clerkship with Justice Breyer. The grand finale was that after completing their clerkships, Betsy and Brian would both be recruited to become managing partners at a law firm, teach at Yale, perhaps govern a Baltic state. Former Supreme Court law clerks ran the world.

It didn't help that Bob died two weeks after Justice Adams's promotion. I'd been praying (and even lit a candle) that he'd last another month, until I was safely back in New York and one of the judge's new maids was sitting in my cubicle. Funny—almost a year earlier, I'd found myself haggling on the phone with her former law clerks, the folks I'd labeled as "jerks" for not staying an extra week so that I could enjoy one measly week of vacation after the bar exam, before the clerkship. Now I understood.

Yoko Oshima from Stanford, my replacement for the upcoming year, had called a few months back asking me the same thing. I told her point-blank that I'd be out of there on the first of August. Could I stay an extra week so she could "decompress" after the bar exam? No, sorry. What about a few days so she could drive and not fly from Palo Alto to Philadelphia? Sorry, not possible. I could only imagine what she had to say about me to her friends on the West Coast.

My name would be cleared soon enough. Next year, Stanford Yoko would be pulling the same shit with the judge's next pack of chambermaids. That is, if she didn't quit first. But at least she and her coclerks wouldn't have to deal with the biggest three-ring circus of all: SHIVAH.

In the Jewish tradition, family members "sit shivah," for the seven days following death, in the home of the deceased. Basically, you were to receive visitors, mourners, etcetera. It should have come as no surprise that Friedman's shivah universe involved neither sitting nor her home but, instead, screaming in the torture chamber. She "barked shivah." As for the rest of us, we desperately wanted to join Bob. The judge had planned for a single day of mourning, one week after Bob passed away. She appointed me shivah coordinator ("Sheera, we rilly rilly have lots to do with shee-vah! Now get to it!").

My job was to order the food and flowers and contact all friends, family, and colleagues. While the judge had minimal family and friends, unless you counted Roderick, her hairdresser, Bob apparently had gazillions (or about forty). Calling them all within a few days was a little tricky as a quantitative *and* qualitative matter, considering that I was still not allowed to use the phone. But I'd found a way around this little snafu. I moved Matthew to the back, where Pregnant Kate used to sit and where he could furtively go through Bob's Rolodex.

Kate had left a week earlier, presumably to give birth. We still hadn't heard from her. I had a feeling I'd never see or speak to her again, since she managed to evade my request for her contact information. I couldn't blame her, though. I had no intention of leaving my forwarding address in chambers. Heck, I'd even considered joining the Witness Protection Program at the end of year. Maybe getting a time-share in Dick Cheney's underground bunker. But there was no time for such considerations now; Sheera had a shee-vah to plan.

Medieval Roy was in charge of the flowers. Though he'd proven himself to be a disastrous green thumb during the year, flowers still seemed a safer bet than food. I'd heard enough stories about what he and his medieval comrades ate on the weekends. It wasn't long ago, after all, that he said: "Hey, Sheila, Matt, did you guys know that for Dudley's feasts in 1575, ten oxen were eaten each day?"

Desperately wanting to be a part of the judge's personal life, Janet was overjoyed that I'd delegated the food to her. It was the least I could do. The menu so far: tongue, whitefish salad, pickled herring. I shuddered to think where the pickled fish would end up. Certainly not on Evan, who'd steadfastly refused to participate in anything funereal on the judge's behalf.

It was day three of "sitting" shivah and already this sitting had elicited more screaming than all the other sittings combined. I'd just finished appeasing Roy after a "mean florist" yelled at him when Matthew's phone rang. Since he was in the back trying to reach Uncle Henry and Cousin Mort, I answered. It was Heidi.

"Hey, you must be Sheila. I've heard so much about you." The voice was sophisticated rather than cheesy. In a minute flat, Heidi shattered my image of her in a paisley sweater-vest and hairsprayed bangs. Suddenly, I felt like a pickled fish.

"Um, ah"—jeez, though Pregnant Kate wouldn't leave her e-mail address, she seemed to have left her mild speech impediment—"um, hey Heidi. Um, I've heard lots about you, too."

"Ah, well then, is Matty around?" I stumbled to the back to retrieve "Matty," but he was nowhere to be found.

"Um, Heidi, he must have just stepped out. Can I have him call you back?"

"Sure, that'd be great, Sheila," she said, sighing loudly. "Does he seem OK to you today?"

"Yeah, he seems fine, why?" Fine was putting it mildly. I'd never seen Matthew in such a good mood. He'd arrived at work that morning with bagels and coffee for everyone, including Roy and Janet. Shortly thereafter, he'd squeezed my shoulder, announced he'd find Cousin Mort "come hell or high water," and traipsed to the back.

Heidi started sniffling. "Well," she said, "I can't believe he didn't tell you. We, we broke up last night." My head started spinning. Why hadn't Matthew told me? He'd spent days, weeks, months discussing the breakup and when it finally happened—bagels?

"Wow. Heidi, I, I don't even know what to say." I tried sounding the exact opposite of how I felt—namely, ecstatic. "I, um—"

"It's OK, Sheila. You don't have to say anything. Matty's been trying to do this for some time but I just wouldn't let him. He'd say he wasn't happy and I'd say we could work it out and on and on and then finally last night"—she was freely crying now—"he said he was in love with some-one else and that there was nothing he could do about it and there was nothing further for us to work out."

In love with someone else?

"God, Heidi, I really am so so sorry. Did he happen to mention who this someone else—"

"Who are you speaking to?" Matthew asked, confused about why his colleague was whispering into his phone.

"Um, hey, Matthew. It's Heidi," I said meekly, embarrassed that I'd been busted for attempted extraction of information from his mourning ex-girlfriend.

He took the phone slowly and I made myself scarce by checking on Roy, who immediately started rattling off his grievances about greedy greenhouse-keepers. Roy needed a blog.

"Hey, Sheila, can I speak to you?" Matthew peered around the corner, beckoning me back into the clerks' cave.

My heart was pounding so hard, I was afraid to move. Thankfully Roy opened his mouth to speak again, his breath propelling me from my seat.

"Yeah, what's up, Matthew?"

"Come with me." He took my hand and led me to the men's bathroom, locking the door behind us. "Look, Sheila, I'm sorry I didn't tell you about me and Heidi. We have a lot on our plate right now with this shivah and I just wanted to be done with it and—" He took a deep breath and started rolling on his heels. "I just wasn't sure how you felt about me and I didn't want to just assume that it was the same as me and I didn't feel prepared to deal with rejection and—"

I grabbed him by the tie and pulled him toward me. "I think we're on the same page, Matthew," I said, smiling.

When Matthew kissed me, all thoughts of whitefish salad, hydrangeas, and Cousin Mort disappeared.

Toilets weren't just for lunch anymore.

Chapter Twenty-one

⚖️

The sandwich theorem, frequently used in calculus and real analysis, states that if a real-valued function (the filling) lies everywhere between two other real-valued functions (the bread) which both converge to the same limit, then the "middle function" also converges to that limit. The ham sandwich theorem can be used to prove mathematically that a single cut can divide two pieces of bread and the filling each exactly in half.

—http://en.wikipedia.org/wiki/Sandwich

By the time the day of shivah arrived, everyone involved, including the judge, had forgotten it had anything to do with one dead Bob.

It was bad enough having to go to the torture chamber–cum–shee-vah headquarters on a Saturday. The fact that the day would be more hectic than most presidential inaugurations made it that much worse. After all, "we rilly had so much to do." Whatever that entailed, I was prepared—at least in terms of fashion. I put on a super cute black dress I'd bought at Saks when I was in New York a few weeks earlier, checking out Puja's new apartment in the West Village, where James was temporarily crashing.

James's judge had suddenly retired, after a tragic (and hush-hush) episode involving his electric scooter and a pedestrian. James had happily broken his lease in Philly and moved back to New York. Ever since the blizzard, James and Puja had been inseparable. My mother was sleeping better at night. So was I.

Over the past two months, I'd shed ten pounds and returned to my usual size. It was pretty easy actually—I'd laid off the meatballs and started jogging again. The pimples had come around with less frequency and I'd stopped picking my hair. All in all, I had started to look, if not feel, better. Having a sex life again didn't hurt either.

Matthew and I shared a cab to the courthouse from my apartment. We went through our checklist of everything necessary for the day, "tending to the judge," being the first.

A few days earlier, I'd been given the particularly grim task of accompanying the judge to a nearby department store to select an outfit. Let's just say that nobody should have to see their boss wearing nothing but their lunch, a girdle, and purple Birkenstocks. After countless black polyester pantsuits, the judge settled on one. It looked just like all the others. But I still told her it was unusually lovely, was perfect for the occasion, that Bob would be smiling down on her from above.

"Sheera"—she swatted at me from the dimly lit dressing room—"Jews don't believe in heaven!" At that point, neither did Catholic-Episcopalian-Hindu-Muslim mutts.

Once we arrived in chambers, Matthew and I dug up clipboards from the supply closet and treated ourselves to two brand-spanking-new mechanical pencils for the occasion. It sort of felt like we were doing PR for a movie premiere. Medieval Roy arrived on the red carpet. I gasped. He was wearing a tuxedo, a full tuxedo. With tails. And a top hat. His mullet was pulled back into a tight ponytail. He smiled. This movie would most likely bomb.

"Sheila, Matt"—he solemnly nodded—"the tulips have arrived." He bowed. Next up, Janet. She came wearing a brown taffeta dress with ruffles, curiously resembling a half-peeled potato.

"Janet, what's the status on the tongue?" I asked, pencil ready to check off "tongue."

"Done." Check.

"The liver?" Check.

"The borscht, the corned beef, pastrami, whitefish salad, cookies?" Check, check, check.

The phone rang. The judge, who else.

"Sheera, sheera!!!!" It was way too early for this. "Sheera, you need to get Esther. Get her. *Esther, Esther.*" Click. Thankfully, she was on speaker-phone, so I had three detectives to help me crack that one. Didn't take long. Janet had an explanation.

"Oh, Esther is Bob's sister. The judge hates her." As opposed to all the other people the judge positively adored? Where exactly were we to collect this Esther? I didn't recall her name on the list and Matthew confirmed that he hadn't contacted her. The fifteen messages Esther left on the chambers' voice mail didn't shed any light either.

The first ten were a shrill "It's ES-TER. ES-TER!" The final five were the same announcement, coupled with "Pick me up for shee-vah. Helga? Helga? You better pick me up!" Oh God. Could it be? She sounded like the judge, only scarier. Now I got it! Bob had married his sister.

"Ugh," Roy gurgled, his top hat tilting just a bit. He wasn't going to survive the day, I just knew it. I also knew we had to find Esther. Four-one-one—no Esther Friedman. White pages—not there either. We didn't know her married name. According to Janet, Bob had cut off ties with her at the behest of the judge many moons ago. So, Janet had absolutely no record of Esther. Drastic times called for drastic measures. I called the judge at home.

"Um, Judge, we—"

"Where are you people? You people are supposed to be here! It's rilly rilly embarrassing that my people aren't here. I am a judge, a federal—"

"Judge, it's only nine-ten right now. Is anyone even at your house?"

"Well, er, Sheera, the caterers are here and the flowers and—"

"Judge, we are trying to locate your sister-in-law, Est—"

"NO! NO! NO! I do not have time for this. I do not have time for her. Get over here now!" Click. She'd clearly forgotten her request from three

minutes earlier. We collectively shrugged our shoulders and hopped a
cab to the judge's.

I didn't know what I'd expected of the judge's home, but whatever it
was, it wasn't this. Stunning prewar brownstone on tree-lined Locust Street.
Window plants abounded. Bright red door, gold handle.

"PEOPLE, WHERE HAVE YOU BEEN?!" There she stood, black
pantsuit barely on, zipper undone, buttons halfway through their holes.
Most alarming was the apparent confusion of lipstick for eyeshadow. Her
perfectly rounded, fresh bun didn't do much to fix the picture. "People,
people, Sheera! This is unacceptable. You cannot come and go as you
please!" The four of us stood, staring. Factor in our costumes and it felt
like a botched trick-or-treating.

She dragged us inside. "What's that? What's that?" she asked, pointing
to Medieval Roy's head. He petted his goatee, smiling nervously.

"Yes, Judge." For once, that particular answer was totally wrong. She
furrowed her lipstick-laden eyebrows and jumped up to swat at his top hat.
Roy remained as still as a dead church mouse. Once, twice, three times a
charm. It came toppling off his greasy head. Perhaps lobotomies were common at certain medieval functions. The judge kicked the hat. She was
wearing new sneaks for the occasion. We proceeded through her immacu-
late house. It just couldn't be. Light streamed in through large french win-
dows hitting dark hardwood floors, only partially covered by lavish
Oriental rugs. Seeing the judge in such a pleasant environment was rilly
rilly rattling.

The doorbell rang. I answered it. Standing before my eyes was a rival
United Nations delegation. The Namibian, the White, and the Mixed.
An ignorant outsider would probably mistake them for your basic Ameri-
can family.

"Hi, you must be Sheila," Mark said warmly, extending a hand. The
judge had told him about me? His wife, Natalie, smiled, clearly exhausted
from the baby boy she was holding and the three-year-old girl tugging at
her dress.

"Yes, I'm Sheila and it's so nice to meet you finally. I've heard so much about all of you," I lied. He gave me a knowing smile, not buying it. "And I am so sorry about your loss," I added. He smiled again.

"Thank you. You know, my dad was very old and very sick. I think we'd all been preparing for this for a while. Anyway, I bet my mother is freaking out right now. Is she around?" Was she ever. The judge came tearing around the corner.

"Maaaaarrrrrkkk! Where have you been?! There's so much to do!" I didn't know what she was referring to. As with the other sittings, we were clearly well over a month ahead for this one. She beamed at her granddaughter, Maggie, who squirmed when the judge hugged her. As for Natalie and the baby, nothing. Babies, I remembered, weren't interesting until two. That little boy still had about eighteen months to enjoy. Mark looked around.

"Mom, it looks like everything is under control. Why don't you finish getting ready. I think we're all set," he bravely instructed.

"No! No! No!" These weren't my noes to deal with, and I fled, joining Matthew, Roy, and Janet in the kitchen.

"You know, this is the first time I've ever been here," Janet said, eyeing the room admiringly. She'd worked for the woman for more than two decades and the judge had never even had her over for a meal. Standing there in that brown dress, hungrily absorbing the walls, the tables, the chairs, Janet broke my heart. Maybe that woman, the judge, would rot in hell, as my mother had commanded on various occasions. Perhaps for no other reason than for her systematic destruction of Janet. While Janet's behavior toward all of us during the year was anything but stellar, she really seemed to love the judge, like a child loved her mother. And the judge hadn't even let Janet into her home. Not one time. Disgusting.

Roy was at the other end of the kitchen fondling the tulips. I motioned for Matthew to run interference. Another five minutes and those tulips would be dead. The doorbell started ringing. I let Mark do the honors. He, after all, was family.

I quickly placed all the sandwiches on the living room table, alongside the soft drinks and cookies. I felt a tug at my dress. It was Maggie.

"Play play play!" she screamed. These Friedmans sure were a demanding bunch.

"Maggie, why don't you go play with Matthew, you see, that boy over there," I said, pointing to Matthew, who was sitting in a chair across the room, staring at the clipboard of to-dos. He looked boring. I understood why she shook her head, unhappy with my suggestion. I took her hand and walked with her to Matthew.

"Matthew, meet Maggie. Maggie, this is Matthew. Why don't you two play together?" He grimaced. "Or you are more than welcome to man the whitefish salad sandwiches. Whichever you prefer." He reached for Maggie. "I thought as much," I said. He smiled at me. Sitting there in the maroon leather chair, in the pretty suit, playing with pigtailed Maggie, Matthew looked like a saint.

Mark led a group of elderly people into the room, making quick introductions.

"Sheila, this is Aunt Bertha, Uncle Mort, and Mrs. Worth." I smiled, reaching for their hands, attempting to register their names. The whole group pushed past me, clearly an unnecessary obstacle to the main attraction—the food. Mark laughed.

"Hey, Sheila, thanks for helping so much with the day. My mother, I know she can be difficult." Difficult? Math tests were difficult. "And she really counts on you. So thanks."

I nodded. "Sure, no problem."

He walked over to play with Maggie and Matthew. I expected a Purple Heart for one year with the judge. I wondered what kind of medal Mark would receive for a lifetime. I moseyed back to the kitchen, in search of Janet and Roy, both of whom were sitting at the table, thumbing through a Pottery Barn catalog. It was clear that they felt inferior even at the judge's husband's memorial service.

"Hey, you two, why don't you get something to eat and go mingle in there?" I asked, pointing to the living room. They both looked at me like I was a much better person than I actually was and scurried past me, leaving me solo. Not for long. Tap. Tap. Tap. I spun around. And gasped. Standing on the other side of the glass door, separating the kitchen from the back porch, was a woman who was short—really short. As in, two inches separated her from the circus. She, too, had a robust bun and bad makeup, but she had on an even more unsightly suit than the judge. She had a cane and was pounding on the door.

Esther.

I took a deep breath and opened the door.

"Where were you?! I've been waiting. I had to take *him!*" she screamed, pointing her cane at a scrawny, petrified cabdriver, waiting just outside of striking distance, by the lilies. "Pay him. Pay him!" I walked past Esther, almost tripping on her cane, and produced a twenty from my purse. He was halfway down the street before I could say thank you. I turned.

"Hi, I'm Sheila and—"

"You, you, where is everyone?!" she screamed. Maybe Bob really had married his sister. Esther was the spitting image of the judge. Or maybe I was seeing double? "YOU!" OMG—like the judge, she spit when making demands. "I can't eat wheat. No wheat! Did you hear me? Did you?"

Everyone in the neighborhood heard her, including the judge, who came speeding into the kitchen. Her bun fidgeted. I looked left. Esther's bun was also moving.

I was sandwiched between two fire-breathing octogenarians with dancing buns. What were the chances?

"Helga," Esther said. She lifted her cane, greeting the judge.

"Hello, Esther."

This monkey moved from the middle, trying to back my way out of this most undesirable situation.

No—they each grabbed an arm. Bladder quivered. They pulled.

"This is my Sheera, let go! Let go!" the judge ordered.

"She's supposed to get me lunch. No wheat, I told her." Esther wasn't giving up without a fight.

"NO! NO! NO!"

"YES! YES! YES!"

Arms pulled in different directions.

"Enough!" They let go and we all whipped around. It was Medieval Roy. He was clutching his top hat with one hand, petting his goatee with the other. I wondered if the chocolate chip cookie I'd just eaten had been laced with acid. "Um, what I meant, was, yes, Judge." He bowed and tripped his way back to the living room. Grateful, I sped after him, leaving the dueling banjos in the kitchen.

Gazing around the living room, I counted about two dozen people—half judges, half family and friends. Judges Fleck and Haskell were there with their wives. So, too, were about five others I still couldn't name. Absent was Justice Adams, who'd sent a condolence note and the most expensive fruit basket I'd ever seen. Note was on Supreme Court stationery. Note and basket had gone straight to wastebasket. No sooner had I parked myself in front of the sandwich platter did the mourning widow and sister emerge from the kitchen, arm in arm, giggling. The judge walked over to me.

"Sheila"—she smiled, revealing a chunk of liver in her bridge—"this is my dear sister-in-law, Esther. Please make sure she's comfortable." I had a feeling Esther hadn't been comfortable since the Roaring Twenties. I smiled at Esther and the judge. It was only a few more hours. I could do this.

"Sure, um, Mrs. Esther? Is that what I should call you?"

"Just Esther. I'm not missus anything. That bastard died years ago." That settled that. "Is there wheat in that? What about thaaaaat? Is there wheat in thaaaaat?" She had stashed her cane under one arm, in order to fully concentrate on the sandwiches. She went from sandwich to sandwich, asking that same question. Considering the sandwiches were quartered, you can imagine how long this exercise took. I hadn't had a chance to answer any of her questions—all the same—not just because she didn't allow me to but, more important, because I didn't have any answers.

The corned beef was on rye. The liver on pumpernickel. The pickled fish on some sort of black bread. What had wheat? What didn't? She had exhausted the platter and was staring at me: "Well? I'm hungry!" Rye? Rock, paper, pumpernickel! "Well!" she demanded, pounding her cane. Spiral, spiral. What was the worst that could happen? It was just wheat, after all.

"Hey, what's going on here?" Matthew came over, placing a hand on my shoulder. "Hi, I'm Matthew," he said, extending a hand to Esther. She smiled, batting her long fake lashes.

"I am Es-TER," she carefully enunciated. Bat bat bat.

"Hi, Esther, nice to meet you. Can I help you?" She smiled at him, then shot me the evil eye.

"That girl, she doesn't know anything. I just want to know what doesn't have wheat!" He nodded, grabbed the pickled mess, placed it on a plate, put some potato chips next to it, led Esther to the couch.

"Here, this doesn't have wheat. Enjoy." And then he returned to me. I looked at him incredulously.

"How do you know that doesn't have wheat. I mean, she can die or something, I think."

"Sheila, that doesn't sound like such a bad thing, now does it? And who is that? She looks like the judge, only slightly less gross." In a little less than a year, Matthew had gone from a God-fearing Ivy League graduate to a premeditating food poisoner. We gazed at Esther, who was licking pickled herring from her bony fingers. "OK, maybe the same amount of gross," Matthew corrected himself. I started explaining the who, what, where of Esther, when the judge jumped onto the brick platform in front of the fireplace. She clinked her plastic cup with a plastic fork crusted with mayonnaise. The crowd hushed, but for some loud potato chip chewing. The way everyone was eating, you'd have thought these people had just been bussed in from a refugee camp.

"As you all know, my husband, Bob, was a great archaeologist." And then she read from his résumé. Literally. All of his awards, publications, education, and all the while, not a word about Bob as the man, the husband, the father. "And I would like to raise a glass to Bob—Archaeologist Extraordinaire." Those who'd nodded off quickly livened up, raised their plastic cups, and clinked the air. Just before chatting resumed, Mark piped up.

"And, hi. I'm Mark. I know most of you, and for those of you who I'm meeting for the first time, I am Bob Friedman's son. And I just wanted to add that, while my dad was indeed a brilliant archaeologist, and therefore didn't have a ton of time for me, what time he did have, he was nice enough." Mark suddenly looked embarrassed and quickly sat back down.

And I thought my family was dysfunctional.

It was shortly after four and most of the guests had left. "Sheila, I think this was acceptable," the judge said, breezing by as I cleared off the last of the empty cups and plates. This was as close to a compliment as she could manage.

"Thanks, Judge," I said without thinking.

"What, why are you thanking me?" she asked, suddenly angry. Had I not learned anything? Why hadn't I stuck to "Yes, Judge"?—never deviate from that script. Before I could apologize for having said thank you, I caught a cane peering out of the bathroom. Oh no. It was Esther. I thought she'd left hours ago. She emerged. And became enraged upon seeing me.

"You! YOU! YOU!" she screamed, making a beeline. "There was wheat in that! There was wheat in thaaaaaat!" Judge Friedman came to Esther's offense.

"What? Sheera, all I asked of you was to just look after my dear sister-in-law—and you couldn't even do that? Can't you do anything?" I wasn't about to let a bit of bread take me down.

"Matthew!" I called to the other side of the room. He approached, gingerly. "As it turns out, there was wheat in that sandwich you gave to Esther here," I said, gently patting Esther on the back. Esther clearly no longer wanted to get in Matthew's pants. Esther whispered something to the judge, who nodded.

"Matthew, seems that Esther has had an accident—thanks to your incompetence with answering simple questions about *sandwiches*." The judge pointed to the bathroom. "Go clean it up."

Matthew looked like he'd been shot in the ass with a stun gun. His eyes got huge. He started stuttering. Who could blame him? For a guy who got grossed out by shirt stains, you can imagine the havoc being wreaked by this project. He stood, still staring, horror registering.

"GO!" the judge instructed, pushing him toward the bathroom.

I started gathering my belongings to return to the torture chamber, where the judge wanted to have a post-sitting-shee-vah conference. About what, Bob only knew. I was rummaging through my purse when Mark and Maggie came to say their good-byes.

"Sheila, again, thanks for everything," Mark said. Maggie jumped into my lap, as she'd done sporadically through the day. Unlike most little kids, she actually liked me for some reason.

"Bounce me bounce me bounce me," she demanded. I wanted to bounce back a vodka tonic, not a three-year-old. I nonetheless obliged. Maggie squealed with glee, getting louder and louder with each bounce. "More more more!" I obliged again. Maggie latched onto my chunky necklace, nearly beheading me. I kept bouncing. Matthew emerged from the bathroom, his face contorted in a manner evidencing permanent damage.

"Let's go," he instructed, grabbing my purse for me. Maggie wouldn't budge. I stopped bouncing. She was pissed.

"You're mean! Mean! Mean!" What was it with these Friedmans and saying everything in threes?

Suddenly I felt drenched in sweat. But I wasn't even that hot. And was that stench something Matthew brought from the bathroom?

"Oh my God, Sheila!" Matthew screamed, pointing at my cleanly shaven legs. "She pissed all over you." I hoped he was blending the literal with the figurative, but judging from the bottom half of my dress, which was soaked,

I knew that wasn't the case. There was, in fact, urine streaming down my leg, creating little puddles around my ankles. The mini-Friedman had already fled the scene of the crime and had joined Esther in the kitchen. Matthew and I held our breath before laughing uncontrollably.

"Is there wheat in this?!" Esther had propped herself against the counter and was reaching for a leftover, dried-out sandwich. "Is. There. Wheat. In. This?!"

We didn't stick around to find out.

Chapter Twenty-two

Matthew managed to grab a towel for me on our stealth exit from the judge's house. I wiped my legs, hoping that passersby would think that I'd accidentally walked into a sprinkler.

"How on earth that woman can turn such a beautiful home into a place of such abject grossness is beyond me!" Matthew exclaimed as we sped down the street.

"Matthew, that's your problem—you continue to be shocked by her." I smiled, mimicking one of his favorite lines.

"Yeah, sorry if I *am* shocked by the fact that I just served as the judge's two-hundred-year-old sister-in-law's pooper scooper. That *is* shocking."

"Yes, I suppose I, too, am shocked that over the course of the year, I peed my pants for the first time since I was three and got peed on for the first time ever by a three-year-old."

We laughed our way to a park bench in Rittenhouse Square.

It was such a perfect evening that it seemed almost impossible that we could have experienced such a traumatic day. Slight wind. The sun had set into a brilliant orange sky. The chatter of normal people milling about.

"You know who I really pity?" I asked, looking at Matthew. "Poor Roy. What do you think will become of him?" He and Janet had fought over

the last pastrami sandwich, leading Janet to call him "good-for-nothing."
Instead of retaliating—or more appropriate, walking away—he started
swaying and crying.

Matthew had removed him from the living room, taken him outside,
and listened to the horrors of his life and "that bitch," who could have been
Janet, the judge, or his abusive wife.

"I don't know, but it can't be any worse than Janet," Matthew replied.
"That woman, I understand why you feel bad for her, but she sure can be
mean, and she's going to die all alone." Speaking of dying alone—Bob's
shivah had involved (1) a résumé reading, (2) allegations of absenteeism,
and (3) a clogged toilet.

"Sheila, um, not to add any more drama to a very dramatic day, but I
just wanted you to know that I talked to the folks at Goodman," he said
nervously. Goodman was the law firm in Los Angeles where Matthew
would be starting in three weeks. "And they said they'd have no problem
letting me start in the New York office. You know, with all the litigation
out here right now, they said it might even be preferable. Spitzer really did
a number on that town."

I sat, staring at him, heart pounding, imploring him to continue.

"Um, the only reason I'm bringing this up right now is that I obviously
would have to take the New York bar in that case and the deadline to sign
up for the October test is next week and—"

I leaned forward and planted one on him. If the dude was willing to
take another bar exam for me, he was clearly committed. We made out for
what felt like seconds but must have been much longer. When we pulled
away, a half dozen Maggie clones had gathered around us and were clapping, jumping, and screaming, "Gross! Gross!" They had a lot to learn
about gross.

My cell phone started ringing. It was the judge. We'd totally forgotten
about the post-shivah conference. As far as I was concerned, the two of us
owed the judge nothing more for the day. Or forever, to be more exact.
But today wasn't the day to stand her up.

"Hey, Judge, we're on the way," I offered. Silence. Heavy breathing.

"I am taking Roy and Janet to Pagano's for dinner. You and Matthew will come." Pagano's was a sandwich shop in the food court of a mall. My legs were sticky with dried pee, and the pigeon that nearly landed on my shoulder sounded more appetizing than another sandwich. I turned to Matthew and relayed the order. He shook his head emphatically and mouthed, "No! No! No!" I smiled, taking a deep breath.

"Judge, you know what? I think we're going to pass. Why don't you, Roy, and Janet go have a nice dinner?" It was the right thing to do. After all, in a few short weeks, Matthew and I would be out of the judge's bun for good. But Roy and Janet were there for the long haul. It was about time the three of them broke bread together. Maybe something good could actually come from Bob's death.

"Er, um, OK, Sheila. ROY! ROY! JANET!" Click. OK, that didn't necessarily sound good, but it was a step in the right direction I supposed.

I sighed with relief: "Skipping a meal never sounded so good."

Matthew took my face in his hands and just smiled. I got a weird stomach feeling, but not the kind I normally had in Philly. Namely fear, loathing, indigestion. This was different. Something resembling happiness. Could it be?

"Sheila Raj, you are definitely not skipping a meal, at least not tonight. I am taking you anywhere you want to go! Hey—how about that new Stephen Starr place?" He smiled, before bending down and kissing me on the forehead.

"Matthew, let's save Stephen Starr—you know he just took over New York. How about Ralph's?"

Acknowledgments

⚖

I'd like to thank my agent, Kirsten Neuhaus, for her unwavering dedication and belief in this project from the very beginning. Most of all, thank you, Kirsten, for never screening me out in the face of what can only be described as high-level paranoia. Deep appreciation goes also to Peter McGuigan for providing critical guidance at every step.

My editor, Lauren Wein, is an expert word surgeon; she shaped the amorphous into a working novel. Thank you, Lauren, for your fresh, observant insights and for making me feel funnier than I am.

Thanks to the following people for listening (or pretending to listen) to me drone on about "the book"—patience is particularly virtuous when interminable soliloquies are involved: David Bardeen, Sarah Birdsong, Wendy Browning, Heather Cotter, John Court, Puja Dhawan, Sarah Ellison, Kane Geyer, Sahil Godiwala, Michael Greenle, Patrick Grizzard, Katharine Marshall, Mike McHenry, Jill Meilus, Ana Patel, Kevin Patterson, Suzanne Paul, Lexi Reese, Jill Royster, Erin Russell, Mike Silver, Neil Talegaonkar, Will Tims, Lisa Turvey, Karin and Dan Visnick, Anna Weber, Goldie Weixel, and Christin Wingo.

I am especially grateful to Ben Faulkner and Derrick Robinson for bringing a bit of levity to a decidedly unfunny situation; to Carey Albertine, Dana Schoenfeld, and Rachel Taylor for providing invaluable comments on an earlier draft; to Karen Newirth for her astute (and free) legal advice; and to Betsy McPherson for always agreeing with me, an often dicey venture.

The Govindans—Madhavi Achamma, Rajan, Suman, Vik, and Héléne—have been faithful cheerleaders throughout. Thank you all for your encouragement.

My parents, Sybil and Jaikar Rao, and my second mother, Mary Baj Viegas, are endless sources of love and support. Let's just say that my appreciation for the absurd came from somewhere. Thank you thank you thank you for everything.

I am deeply indebted to my sister, Nita Tooth Rao, for just about everything. Not only has she been my best friend and mentor for as long as I can remember, but she is also the most talented writer I know. This book couldn't have been written without her generous—and gentle—input.

Finally, tremendous thanks to my husband, Shiv Govindan, who sings and dances for me each and every day. Less devoted performers might shy away from this sometimes temperamental audience of one. Thank you, Beagle—you are a prince and I love you wholly.